USA

D0428041

"One of my very favorite authors."
Julia Quinn

"Indulge and be delighted!"
Stephanie Laurens

"Enoch finds the right combination
of sexy and fun for a fabulous read."
Oakland Press

"Suzanne Enoch's sparkling talent
makes each book witty, romantic,
and always an eagerly anticipated pleasure."
Christina Dodd

"A solid writer . . . with a good sense
of fun and a strong descriptive eye."
Contra Costa Times

By Suzanne Enoch

Historical Titles

Contemporary Titles

Coming Soon

SUZANNE ENOCH

Lady Rogue

AVON BOOKS

An Imprint of HarperCollinsPublishers

AVON BOOKS
An Imprint of HarperCollins*Publishers*
10 East 53rd Street
New York, New York 10022-5299

Copyright © 1997 by Suzanne Enoch
ISBN-13: 978-0-06-087524-4
ISBN-10: 0-06-087524-0
www.avonromance.com

First Avon Books paperback printing: March 1997

Avon Trademark Reg. U.S. Pat. Off. and in Other Countries, Marca Registrada, Hecho en U.S.A.
HarperCollins® is a registered trademark of HarperCollins Publishers Inc.

Printed in the U.S.A.

10 9 8 7 6 5 4 3 2 1

For Alicia Hutter Vizenor—
Thank you for being my most excellent crony
and cohort in silliness, girlfriend.
And yes, all right, you *are* a sterling boxer.

Lady Rogue

Chapter 1

"Stop gawking about, Kit. We're nearly there."
Stewart Brantley turned to give his daughter
a half-annoyed glance and resettled his drenched beaver
hat lower over his eyes as they hurried along the wet
street in the darkness.

Curious as she was to view the sights, Christine Brantley had no objection to staying close behind her father
as he hesitated and then turned north along a wide avenue lit by gas lamps and occasional flashes of lightning.
It had been a long time since she had last set foot in
London, and what landmarks she remembered were ob-
scured by the night and by the rain that had been falling
since they had left the ship at Dover. "I'm not gawking," she returned, the chatter of her teeth touching her
voice. "I'm freezing."

"I didn't want to take the hack into Mayfair," Stewart
returned. "Asking to be driven to Park Lane at this hour
would—"

"Would bring us attention we don't want," she finished. Rain stung her cheeks, and she reached up to wipe
a gloved hand across her face. "Do you truly think your
Earl of Everton will see us?"

Her father glanced back again. "He owes me a large
debt. He'll see us."

"I hope so," Kit replied, as thunder rumbled over the
rooftops of England's wealthiest nobility. "I'd hate to
think you dragged us out of Paris for nothing."

1

"I wouldn't have either of us here if I didn't have a damned good reason."

She sniffed, then grimaced, hoping she wasn't catching a cold. "I know." As much as her father detested England and the English, his being back in London pointed to just how highly he rated the importance of this journey. It was for their lives, he had said, and she hadn't doubted him.

"And you also know what you're to do here," he added.

"I do." She paused, then had to hurry to catch up when he continued on without her. "But I don't like being a spy."

"You're not being a spy, Kit," he said shortly, what was left of his limited patience apparently leeched out of his bones by the downpour. "Fouché will have my head—our heads—if the damned English stop another of his shipments. All you have to do is tell me which bastard is working against us, so I can bribe him off or outmaneuver him. That's not spying. It's . . ." He hesitated, then gave a short grin that didn't reach his green eyes. "It's good business. And no harm will come of it, except that more blunt will end up in our pockets." He looked ahead at a huge white mansion which dominated one side of the lane. "I trust that is acceptable to you?"

"Yes." She swallowed the dismay that ran through her as they stepped past the mansion's open gates and entered the short drive. The Earl of Everton's town house was massive even by London standards, the largest and most grand she'd seen since they had left the hack at Piccadilly and entered gilded Mayfair. "Of course it is."

Despite her heavy, caped greatcoat, the boy's clothing Christine wore was soaked through, and she shivered with cold and tension as she stood between the elegant, carved marble columns rising from the front portico of Cale House. If the place had been less magnificent, she would have felt easier about what lay ahead, and about the part she was to play. All she could do in the face of such grandeur was hope that everything would go as easily as her father declared it would.

He tapped the heavy brass knocker against the door. The sound echoed into the bowels of the mansion for a long moment, then died out into the rain and wind with no response.

Stewart frowned, then rapped again, louder. "I don't understand," he muttered. "Philip has always opened Cale House during the Season. He'd never be at Everton with Parliament in session."

Kit shrugged to disguise her relief. This was no petty pickpocketing or an evening's cheating at hazard that her father expected of her. "It is rather late, Pa—"

The door opened on silent, well-oiled hinges. The man standing in the entryway had donned the coat of a butler, though his baleful glare was made somewhat less impressive by the nightshirt and wool slippers he wore beneath the splendid garment. "Yes?" he demanded.

"I am here to see Lord Everton," her father returned, as if it were the most ordinary occurrence in the world for callers to come banging at the door in the middle of the night.

The butler did not appear to be impressed. "Lord Everton is to bed."

"Then wake him and inform him that Stewart Brantley is here and urgently wishes to speak with him."

"I don't believe that is sufficient rea—"

"Tell him it regards the payment of an old debt." Her father folded his gloved hands behind his back, the only outward sign that he was less than utterly calm.

The butler's eyes narrowed. "Oh." He sniffed distastefully, then motioned them into the hallway. "Wait here." Without so much as offering to take their wet things, he turned and disappeared up the stairs that curved along the wall to the right of the entryway.

A moment later the sound of muffled, angry shouting echoed upstairs, closely followed by a door slamming. The butler reappeared, and with an even deeper scowl indicated that they should follow him up to the drawing room. With most of the lights put out for the night, there was little to see but darkened space on the ground floor, despite Kit's covert efforts to look about. The place, though, had the smell of wealth, with real beeswax candles in the few lamps still lit along the hallway, and not the stench of a cheap tallow candle anywhere.

The grandfather clock on the landing boasted both a second hand and a half-circular cutout showing the current phase of the moon, and it chimed a beautifully toned quarter hour as they passed by. At the top of the stairs the scent of an expensive woman's perfume, sweet and faintly French, touched the still air.

The drawing room in which the butler deposited them bespoke tasteful wealth, as well. Gold leafing decorated the engraved cornice running along the top of the walls, and an elegant Persian rug covered the center of the floor, while small lead crystal paperweights decorated the mantel, and a Chinese vase painted with delicate blue flowers sat precisely in the center of the occasional table. Despite the impressive trinkets, Christine was happier to see the glowing embers from a nearly dead fire in the hearth, and she pulled off her gloves as she stepped forward to hold her hands out gratefully to the fading warmth.

Stewart had stopped in the middle of the room to examine the portrait above the mantel, and after a moment she looked up at it, as well. A gentleman gazed down at her, dark hair faintly edging into gray at his temples. A faint smile touched his lean face, and he was quite handsome. His eyes, though, were his most striking feature. They were penetrating, almost mesmerizing, and the shade of blue was far too deep to be authentic. The artist must have taken some liberties with his palette. "Lord Everton, I presume?" she queried, studying the face of Philip Cale, the man they'd come all this way to see.

"Yes."

The word was spoken by an unfamiliar male voice, and with a faint start Christine turned around.

The room's third occupant stood just inside the doorway, one hand still on the polished brass handle, though she hadn't heard the door open. Slowly she drew in a breath. He was a good decade younger than the figure in the portrait, lean and tall, clad in rolled-up shirtsleeves and black breeches, the open neck of his shirt and slightly tousled dark hair the only signs that he had dressed quickly. His eyes, likewise, were wide-awake and intently curious, the shade a piercing dark blue at least as penetrating as the gaze of the man in the painting. He was not at all poutingly pretty in the current French fad, but rather was astoundingly handsome, and utterly and unmistakably masculine. Unable to help herself, Kit took him in, from head to toe and back again.

"I believe there has been a misunderstanding," her father offered with a slight frown. "I need to speak with the Earl of Everton."

"I'm Everton." The eyes coolly assessed her father's wet attire. "And you are Stewart Brantley."

Her father's scowl deepened, then cleared. "Alexander Cale," he murmured, a hint of something Kit couldn't quite read in his voice. "I should have realized." He glanced up at the painting. "What happened to your father?"

"My father died nearly four years ago." The other examined his nails, then looked up again. "I can direct you to Westminster Abbey, if you'd care to consult with his remains."

"You're the Earl of Everton?" Kit broke in, willing it to be some sort of misunderstanding. An unexpected shiver ran through her as his eyes and the aggressive intelligence behind them flicked in her direction. She felt electrified, like the storm outside. This was no old man to be easily fooled. This would be trouble.

The eyes took in her wet form with a thoroughness and an intensity she was unused to, and it was with difficulty that she kept her own gaze steadily on his face—on the high cheekbones and faintly arched eyebrows, and the sensuous, cynical mouth. "I am," he said after a moment. "Also Alexander, Baron Cale, and Viscount Charing."

Her father cleared his throat, and Everton's eyes left

hers as the earl stepped farther into the room and shut the door. She took a breath, resisting the ridiculous urge to sag.

"You've grown up well," her father commented, in as close to a compliment as she'd ever heard him hand an Englishman. "I haven't set eyes on you since you were—"

"Nine, I believe," Everton supplied. For the first time, a hint of humor touched his sardonic lips. "As I recall, you informed me that I should have a sterling career as a soldier-for-hire or a pirate once my father cut me off."

"You were a rather wild youngster."

"I've not changed much." He looked at Christine again. "And who might you be, boy?"

"Kit," she answered, feeling cold and awkward in her wet attire, and wishing she could turn and run from the room before it was too late.

Lord Everton continued to gaze at her. Again she was certain he would discover her secret, though there was no real reason to believe so. The disguise she wore had become effortless years ago, and she could fool anyone with it until she chose to let them know otherwise. And she had no intention of enlightening any arrogant English lord.

Her father gestured at her. "Everton, my son."

"Mr. Brantley," the Earl of Everton acknowledged after a moment, inclining his head. His eyes remained alert, but she suspected that it was due more to their presence than a question over her gender.

"Everton," she acknowledged, meeting his gaze. He was likely a cutthroat cardplayer, she thought abruptly, for she hadn't a clue about what might lie behind those sharp azure eyes.

The earl looked at her for another moment, then stepped forward to throw more wood onto the fire. "I would assume you both to be rather chilled this evening," he commented, straightening and gesturing for her to remove her greatcoat.

She looked up at him, standing only a few feet away.

She was tall for her sex, and was very aware that he must be several inches above six feet to tower over her so . . . effectively. Uneasy at the idea of baring more of herself to his gaze, she reluctantly shrugged out of the wet garment. He took a step back to run his eyes down her wardrobe, and she couldn't help the flush that warmed her cheeks, or the shiver that ran down her spine. "You dislike my attire, Everton?" she offered with a scowl.

"French rags," he stated, turning to take her father's hat and coat and drape them over the back of one of the overstuffed chairs. He sank onto the couch, then gestured for her and her father to be seated. "Forgive my directness, Brantley, but I confess to a certain curiosity as to how you require me to pay my father's debt to you." Everton tilted his head. "Enough blunt to regain your footing in England, perhaps?"

"My lord," her father said stiffly, the annoyed look coming to his face again, "I do not require money. And I believe your father would agree that blunt would hardly be an appropriate repayment for this particular debt."

"You presume to know my father's mind. Quite impressive, for I did only rarely." Everton straightened from his relaxed slouch. "But do enlighten me."

"I saved you from drowning, my lord."

"Yes, twenty years ago. So I've been informed, though I confess to having little memory of the event."

"Surely your father told you I might be by one day and ask a favor," Stewart said, his voice and expression affronted. "I believe he took his word of honor quite seriously."

"Actually," Lord Everton said, sitting back again and stretching one arm carelessly along the back of the couch, "I rather believe he thought you were dead. It has been twenty years, after all." He gave a brief, unamused smile. "As, however, you appear to be still among the living, I will ask you once more what your request might be."

Stewart cleared his throat. "Very well," he returned. "My son is now of an age where he is expected to do his civic duty, along with other young men of his age and circumstance. With the current state of unrest in France—''

''Yes, that's right, Bonaparte has escaped Elba, hasn't he?'' the earl noted, as though the return of the monster to Europe lacked significance. To his sort, it probably did.

''Yes. And I have begun to fear that Kit will be drafted into his army. France may be our home, but I will not have him die for that madman.''

''I see,'' Everton said more quietly, looking in her direction again.

''I had therefore hoped to impose on your father, and now you, to look after him for a short time, until the situation returns to a more even keel. Through the end of the month, anyway. By then I can make other arrangements.''

''That's less than I thought you would ask, Brantley, I have to admit.''

The earl turned his gaze on his hands, his lips thoughtfully pursed. Fleetingly Kit wondered if he realized how very attractive that expression made him look. His eyes flicked over at her again, as though he was trying to read something in her face, and she quickly looked away.

''I am curious,'' Everton commented, turning back to her father. ''You are not without relations here, if memory serves. Your brother is the Duke of Furth, is he not? Why not let him wet-nurse the boy?''

Her father paled, for the first time looking truly angry. ''Never,'' he hissed.

''I don't need a wet nurse,'' Kit cut in. ''I can take care of myself. And if Everton won't aid us, then we don't need him, Father.'' They could find someone else for her to stay with in London—someone who didn't have eyes as piercing as Alexander Cale's.

''I'm afraid we do need him, Kit.'' Stewart looked at Everton. ''Do you wish me to beg you to honor your debt, my lord?''

The earl looked from one to the other of them again, then shook his head and let out a sigh. ''I suppose not.

But I don't have time to coddle the boy. I have some rather pressing duties and obligations of my own."

"I don't ask you to go out of your way for him." Stewart looked at Kit for a moment. "Anything other than keeping him here safely is, of course, unnecessary. And as I said, it will only be till the end of the month. God willing, this madness will be over by then, anyway."

The eyes turned to Kit again, though she couldn't read the expression there. "God willing," Alexander Cale repeated, then stood. "Very well. I'll show you both to rooms."

Stewart Brantley gave a relieved sigh. "Thank you, Everton."

The earl shook his head. "As you said, a debt is a debt. But this *will* make us even. My father's obligation to you is hereby settled."

It seemed as much a threat as an insult, and Stewart's jaw clenched before he nodded. "That is all I ask."

The bedchamber the earl showed Kit to was splendid. Gold and peach wall hangings framed each of the two windows, and nearly a dozen pillows were piled at the head of the soft, quilt-covered bed. It made her cot in their *appartements* in Saint-Marcel in Paris look quite shabby. After Everton left, she ran her finger along the quilt, touching the soft, cool texture with some relish. With a regretful look at the warm blankets, she sat at the dressing table to wait. Everton had given in, when she had nearly been convinced he would not. His surprise capitulation left her even less at ease than had his bald suspicion.

Half an hour later the chamber door opened, and she turned. "What now, Father?" she asked softly, as he slipped inside.

He chuckled. "That was easier than I expected."

Kit didn't agree. "He nearly turned us out."

"Nonsense."

She took a breath, reluctant to argue with him. "Do you think I can convince him to introduce me about town?"

Stewart gave a brief smile. "My dear, your powers of persuasion are unmatched. And young Alexander's contemporaries would be more likely to be involved in government trickeries than his father's, anyway. This could not have worked out better if I'd planned it."

"You did plan it, didn't you, Father?" she returned, still unsettled and unable to resist needling him out of his self-confidence. "Except for Philip Cale's being dead for four years."

He glared at her. "Don't be insolent, girl. You let me know which of these damned blue bloods is interfering with us, and we'll teach him a little lesson."

"Do you think it could be him?" Kit whispered, gesturing at the mansion surrounding them.

Her father squinted one eye, then shrugged. "From what I hear, he's always been wild and a bit ramshackle. Hardly the sort old King George, unless he was having one of his mad fits, would have chosen to help uphold the proper British way of life." He grinned. "Be glad he thinks you a boy. From what I hear, it takes women, drink, or gambling to catch Alex Cale's interest. But be careful around him, just the same, until you're certain."

She would be careful around him, anyway. "I will."

He nodded. "I'd best be off, then, in case he changes his mind after a night's sleep. You remember where to meet me if you have news?" When she nodded, Stewart leaned closer. "You can do this. I need you to do this. For both our sakes."

She took a breath, unable to resist balking one last time. "You're certain Fouché can't be put off?"

"I've told you, the greater the risk, the greater the profit. We'll get his shipment through, and we'll all be happy and wealthy."

"It would be easier if I knew what we were shipping for him."

"Best that you don't," he answered, as he had every time she'd asked.

"This is not for vegetables and blankets," she stated, to see how he would react.

He didn't. "I'll see you in a few days. Trust your father, child."

"I always have."

He started for the door, then glanced over his shoulder at her and gave her a quick grin. "Good girl."

Christine watched him leave, then sat on the edge of the fine bed and slowly shed her damp clothes. For only a fortnight, she could do this. She could meet the Earl of Everton's precious blue-blooded cronies, and find out which of them had begun interfering with their affairs of commerce, just when the Comte de Fouché had offered her father a partnership too lucrative to resist. Everton might have beautiful eyes and a devilishly handsome face, but she could fool him for a fortnight, just as she fooled everyone else. And these English would never know how Stewart Brantley had managed to slip through their fingers again. Not until it was too late, and she and her father were long gone.

Chapter 2

$\sim\!\!\!\infty\!\!\!\circlearrowleft\!\!\!\sim$

Alexander Cale was not in a good mood as he sat down to breakfast at half past eight. Debt of honor or not, Stewart Brantley might have waited for a decent hour before he came calling with his absurd demands. For the inconvenience alone, he should have declined to settle anything, handed them over some blunt, and sent them on their way. And he would have, except for the boy.

There was something about that one, something he'd sensed but hadn't quite been able to discern. It had been there, in Kit Brantley's eyes. They were dark green, he recalled quite clearly, and full of spirit. There had also been uneasiness, and unless he was mistaken, desire. Alex frowned and motioned for Wenton, the butler, to refill his teacup. The boy might be odd, but that didn't explain his own reaction in the slightest. Obviously he'd merely been tired. The interruption had been considerably ill timed, after all.

Something broke in the direction of the kitchens, and he indicated that Wenton should investigate the damage. Before the butler could comply, the breakfast room door burst open. "My lord," one of the kitchen maids panted, "there's a terrible commotion in the stables."

Wenton started out, but Alex pushed to his feet. "I'll see to it," he drawled, and followed the maid back through the kitchen, the quickest route to the stable yard. As he stepped out into the cold, damp morning, he re-

12

alized that the girl hadn't been exaggerating. From across the small yard, cheering and cursing and the sound of horses snorting and blowing were loud and unmistakable. He shoved open the double doors of the stable and stepped inside.

And paused. His houseguest, Mr. Kit Brantley, stood backed against the opposite wall with a lethal-looking pitchfork clutched in his hands, while Ben Conklin, the head groom, hung back a few feet and rubbed at a splendid welt forming across his jaw. The rest of the stable-boys and coachmen crowded in a loose half circle behind them, and they were the ones making most of the noise. "What's this?" Alex queried, and the shouting and heckling stopped.

"This bantam nearly spitted me with the pitchfork, m'lord," Conklin offered, watching the youth warily.

"You shouldn't have jumped out at me and started yelling like that," the boy growled, breathing hard.

"What, pray tell, are you doing in my stable?" Alex asked, far more amused than annoyed. Conklin rarely received the worst in a scrap, and this slightly built sprig hardly seemed the one to hand him his teeth.

"I'll send for the constabulary," Wenton offered, though Alex hadn't been aware that the butler had followed him. Wenton rarely left his stated territory, that being the mansion. The yard, by some sort of mutual agreement, was Conklin's.

"That won't be necessary," Alex replied, watching the boy's face as sudden uneasiness dampened the anger in his expression. Interesting, that. "Why don't you put your weapon down and come in for some breakfast, Mr. Brantley?" he suggested.

"I was only looking," Kit returned hostilely. He glanced down at the pitchfork, then with obvious reluctance set it aside.

Instantly Conklin jumped him.

"Damnation," Alex growled, and pushed through the jostling circle. "That's enough!" he bellowed, shoving Conklin aside, then grabbing Kit about the arms and waist and hauling him backward. The boy was surprisingly light for his height. Light, and with a very slender waist and rounded hips, which immediately began squirming in a rather familiar-feeling manner as he pulled the lad closer against him. The feel of the slim, supple body startled him.

At the same time, Kit began to struggle more violently. Almost frantically. "Let me go, you stupid lout!" he shouted.

Alex blinked and then complied, dumping him to the ground.

The damp, straw-covered figure immediately scrambled to his feet, rounding on him with fists clenched in a quite accurate classical boxing stance. "Try that again, *imbécile!*" he growled, face flushed.

Alex looked at him for a long moment, several extremely odd thoughts crossing his mind and racing toward even odder conclusions. "Hmm," he finally said, and turned on his heel. "Come inside."

"Don't order me—"

"Now!" Without glancing behind him, he crossed the yard again, went back through the kitchens, and into the breakfast room. "Wenton, have another plate brought in," he ordered, as with a baleful look Kit entered the room behind him. Before the butler could answer, Alex shut the door in his face.

"Now. Good morning, Mr. Brantley," he said, turning to face his guest again. "Care to have a seat?"

"No," Kit grumbled, backing toward the hallway door. "I should go get cleaned up."

Green eyes slid between the earl and the door, while Alex watched with intent curiosity. What he was beginning to suspect simply wasn't possible, but it was a better explanation than that he was suddenly finding young boys exceptionally attractive. "What were you doing in my stable?" he queried.

"Looking, just like I said," the boy answered defensively. "Your pair of bays is sterling. But I wasn't going to steal anything."

"Thank you, and I didn't say you were."

"Well, good. Because I wasn't."

"Is your father also not stealing from my stable? Or is he still to bed?"

"My father had to return to Paris. He has business concerns th—"

"He left you here?" Alex interrupted, frowning. If what he suspected was true, Brantley's leaving was a tremendous surprise.

"Well, yes. You did agr—"

"That was rather impolite of him, don't you think? He might have said thank you and good-bye, at least."

"That's not his way," the boy answered, shrugging. For just a moment, though, a fleeting look of what might have been loneliness crossed his features. And then Kit Brantley unthinkingly, unconsciously, raised one hand to pull a straying strand of blond hair back from his face.

That gentle, hesitant motion made everything very clear. "Sweet Lucifer," the Earl of Everton muttered, and the green eyes looked over at him. "You're a bloody female!"

If he'd doubted it at all, Kit's reaction would have settled the issue. She went white, then gave a forced laugh and raised an eyebrow. "I believe you've been drinking, Everton," she commented, her voice quavering just a little.

He strode forward, stopping directly in front of her. Without giving her time to protest, he reached out and removed the hat from her head. The band that had been holding the hair in its tail dropped to the floor, and stable straw and a short mop of curling blond hair tumbled around her face and down to her shoulders. It all made sense now. That rich, low lilt had been no schoolboy's voice; that light, supple body, no man's. And the long eyelashes, the expressive green eyes that were now looking at him in alarm, could never possibly belong to a male.

"I—"

"Don't deny it, unless you wish me to take further measures to discover the truth," Alex warned, conscious of the abrupt desire to peel this damp and dirty thing out of her wet clothes, and see exactly what lay beneath.

She lifted her chin. "Very well, Everton. I am a female."

"By God," he exclaimed, her confession not lessening in the slightest his desire to undress her. "What a neat trick. You do this often then, chit—whatever your name is?"

"It's Christine," she said. "And Stewart Brantley *is* my father. The only lie last night was my gender. And that was for good reason, I assure you."

By all rights he should have been furious at being taken for a fool. Instead, though, he found that while he was mightily annoyed, he was equally curious and intrigued. Alexander leaned back against the edge of the table and looked at her all over again. She was apparently flat-chested, but with the ratty coat, waistcoat, and breeches, it was difficult to tell much else, except that she was slender and had long legs. Exceptionally long legs.

Kit stood still, her face flushed, during his scrutiny.

"Forgive my obtuseness," he said after a moment, "but if your father wished to avoid having you drafted into Bonaparte's mad army, couldn't you have simply donned skirts?"

"I do not find it necessary to explain my life or my circumstances to you," she retorted.

"Your father gave you to me for a fortnight," he responded. "You must understand my considerable . . . curiosity at finding myself hosting a female when I had expected something else entirely." He ran his gaze down the length of her again, and smiled slowly. "This should be much more interesting."

Kit glared up at him, her jaw clenched and her eyes flashing emerald. "Go find a sheep," she snapped, grabbing her beaver hat out of his hands and jamming it on her head again. "You were to satisfy a debt of honor. Not your carnal urges. Good day, Everton."

"I don't . . ." Alex stopped in mid-retort as she strode out of the breakfast room and slammed the door shut behind her. A scattering of stable mud and drying hay drifted to the floor in her wake. Alex looked back at the door, a reluctant, admiring smile tugging at his lips, then stepped forward and pulled it open.

"You are the most absurd thing I've ever set eyes on," he said to the girl's back, already halfway out the front door. No doubt she intended on walking all the way back to Dover and then swimming on to Calais.

"I'm so pleased I've been able to amuse you," she retorted, stopping just long enough to turn and glare at him one final time. "It is why I came all this way."

"Good morning, Alexander," a soft voice cooed from the landing. With a rustle of skirts, the house's other guest stepped down to join them.

Kit paused in the doorway, looking toward the stairs, one slim hand still on the door handle. A look of swift surprise crossed her features, then vanished.

"Barbara," Everton answered, strolling to the bottom of the stairs and granting his mistress an absurdly chaste kiss on the cheek.

Her dark eyes glanced sideways at him, then turned back to regard the waif studying them from the entryway. "Taking in orphans now, are you?" she asked, reaching up to finger one of the dark curls piled in artistic profusion on her head. "Who are you, boy?"

Alex looked from one to the other, and in an instant made his decision. He wasn't ready to let this odd creature out of his sight just yet. Not until he'd learned a bit more about her. There was more to this visit of hers than just safety, or he was a complete idiot. This one wouldn't have come begging for protection. "Barbara, may I present Kit—"

"Riley," the waif supplied smoothly before he could finish, returning to the hallway to take Barbara's hand and bring it with practiced ease to her lips. "My cousin has difficulty acknowledging my Irish ancestry."

"Cousin?" Barbara said faintly, raising a carefully shaped eyebrow and gazing with some skepticism between the blond youth and the dark-haired earl.

Amazed at both the change in the chit and at her audacity, Alex took another step forward. "Kit, Lady Sinclair."

"Lady Sinclair." Kit nodded, smiling as she released the other woman's hand. "Charmed to the bone."

"Mr. Riley," Barbara noted with a faint smile of her own. "I don't recall Alex ever mentioning you."

"Well, I'm from the poor side of the family," the waif supplied, glancing at Alex with hilarity hooded in her eyes.

Barbara turned to Alex. "I didn't realize your family had a poor side."

"Just the one we don't talk about," he said absently, tilting his head to regard his newfound relation.

"And Kit is short for . . ."

"Christian," Alex supplied. The thoughts running through his head were hardly of a familial bent, but Kit had hit on a commendable explanation for her presence.

"How delightful." Lady Sinclair laughed, a light, airy chuckle. "My devil has a Christian for a cousin."

Alex frowned and belatedly returned his attention to his mistress. "Kit, for short."

Barbara stepped forward and slipped her arm around Kit's. "But why are you so . . . dirty?"

"I arrived quite late last night, and didn't want to disturb anyone," Kit answered smoothly, allowing herself to be led back toward the interior of the house.

Barbara looked over her shoulder at Alex. "Then who dragged you out of bed last night at such an . . . inconvenient moment?"

"Oh, that was me," Kit cut in again, apparently undisturbed by Barbara's implication. "I'm afraid my 'quiet' was enough to pull my cousin out of bed, and then he told me I could damned well sleep out in the stables if I couldn't arrive at a decent hour." She shrugged. "So I did."

She lied like a damned actor, Alex thought. He couldn't help but admire the skill with which she wove her tale; even Edmund Kean would have been impressed. He would make a point of remembering that he couldn't trust a word she said.

"Alex, how awful, even for you," Barbara chastised. The grandfather clock on the landing began striking nine, and she stopped. "Oh, lud, you've nearly made me forget my dressmaker's appointment. I must go." She smiled. "I am having a dinner party this evening, and I would love for you to come, Mr. Riley."

She released Kit and took Alex's arm to pull him into the entryway. "Do bring him," she cajoled. "Caroline and Lady Driscoll will think he's divine."

"We'll see," he answered gruffly, displeased with the suggestion.

Barbara pulled his face down for an openmouthed kiss, reminding him that despite her occasional snobberies, she did have her uses. With her maid following behind, burdened with her mistress's overnight necessities, Lady Sinclair allowed Wenton to help her on with her shawl and then stepped out into the drive to her waiting carriage.

When Alex made his way back to the breakfast room, the chit had already devoured half the contents of her plate and was stealing slices of ham from his. As he entered, she released the meat and sat up straight.

"Don't let me stop you," he said, motioning at her to help herself. "I don't want it now that you've had your grubby fingers all over it."

"My fingers aren't grubby," she declared, reaching out again for his plate, apparently interpreting his gesture as an invitation to eat everything that remained. "Is Lady Sinclair your mistress?"

Alex seated himself. "How old are you, anyway?" he queried, studying her as she wolfed down a biscuit lathered in honey.

"Nineteen," she replied, her mouth full. "Twenty, next month."

Apparently, in her eagerness to consume the complete contents of his kitchens, she had forgotten that she'd been halfway out his door five minutes earlier. He wasn't inclined to remind her. "You look twelve."

She nodded. "It's the disguise. Because I don't have whiskers, I look younger." She paused for a moment. "Old enough for Napoleon's army, though," she added. "How old are you?"

"Twenty-nine. Thirty in September."

"You look twenty-nine." She drained the tea in her cup and poured herself another, not glancing about first, he noted, for a servant to perform the duty for her.

"It seems as though I should be grateful you didn't devour one of my cattle this morning when you weren't stealing from my stable."

"I *am* a bit hungry," she conceded unnecessarily. "So, is she your mistress?"

"Yes." He placed one elbow on the table and leaned his chin on his palm to watch with some awe as she started on the platter of toast.

"At first I thought she might be your wife."

"Not likely. Take off your hat, chit. Unless you're some sort of jungle savage, in addition to being a female."

Kit glanced at him, hesitated, then reached up to remove it. Her blond mop was too long for the current British male fashion, and daringly short for a female, but with it tied back, she no doubt cut a dashing figure. Kit looked at the hat, shrugged, and dropped the dirty thing on the floor beside her. "Better?"

"Slightly more civilized," he returned after a moment. "If you're so intent on being a boy, why don't you cut that mess in a more appropriate fashion?" He waved his fingers at her honey-colored mane.

For the first time she looked offended. "It's not a mess," she protested, reaching up to touch her hair. "And it's all the rage in Paris." She grabbed for a peach and bit into it, not bothering to peel it, or even to slice it in two. "Why didn't you give me up?"

"Because you amuse me," he answered, watching the peach juice run down her dirty chin. She was handsome enough as a boy, and he imagined that, properly cleaned up, she could be outrageously beautiful. "Though now that you've got me related to the damned Irish, I'm not so certain it's all that funny."

"Riley is my mother's maiden name," she returned defiantly. "So I'm half damned Irish, and half insolent English."

"Damned all around then, aren't you?" Alex asked, amused again and rather charmed.

"And bloody proud of it." She looked sideways at him. "Aren't you shocked by my language?"

He laughed and she sat back, a fleeting grin lighting her face. At that sight, it took him a moment to remember what they'd been discussing. "No. As I said, you amuse me. You were less absurd earlier. Quite sober, actually."

"I was angry because you weren't going to let me stay."

"I never said that," he pointed out.

She looked straight at him, her serious gaze holding his. "I'm not a whore or a light-skirt," she stated. "My father asked you to look after me in a proper and honorable manner, in keeping with the debt your family owes mine. If you won't honor that, then I will leave."

"Direct and to the point," Alex replied slowly, impressed. "Well said." Raised in France or not, her English was excellent, and she sounded quite well educated. She was certainly intelligent, and quick as a fox, and he wondered again why in the world her father had seen the need to send her here, of all places. Not that he minded. Not in the slightest.

"So do I stay, or go?"

"You would leave, wouldn't you?" he asked quietly, studying her face.

She nodded.

He didn't hesitate either. "Then stay. I believe I can resist you for a fortnight," he said dryly, though he was less than certain it would be as easy as he made out. Perhaps she could be persuaded that there could be things much more interesting between them than a debt of honor. A fortnight was a great deal of time, after all, and if she gave in, it would hardly be his fault.

Kit paused with Alex's last slice of ham halfway to her lips. "Thank you. That does save me the trouble of extorting your good word out of you."

"Extortion?" he repeated, keenly interested. "And how would you have gone about that?"

She paused to consume the ham. "I could tell Lady Sinclair's husband that she was here with you."

Alex relaxed again, snorting at the minuscule threat. "She's married to a very understanding tombstone, my dear."

"I could tell her I'm a female. It would ruin things for you with her."

He shook his head. "Just as well for you that I gave in. Barbara knows I'm less than faithful. Apparently you'll have to wait to know me a little better before you can extort anything out of me, chit."

She gave him a quick glance, and he raised an eyebrow. For a heartbeat, there had been something almost calculating in her expression. The chit was definitely up to something, though whether it was being compromised, followed by a quick marriage, or something else entirely, he had no idea. Well, if it was a wedding she was after, she was in for a disappointment. And whatever her game was, it took two to begin it. Still, with an opponent like the one seated at his breakfast table, he looked forward to playing. And compromising her was fairly close to what he had in mind, anyway.

"If you're unfaithful, why does she see you?" Kit asked, either admirably naive or pretending to be.

Alex smiled cynically. "Because I'm rich as Croesus." He poured himself a mug of ale and took a swallow, deciding he might as well begin the first round. "But you know that, don't you?"

She tilted her head at him. "I'd never even heard of the Earl of Everton until four days ago, and I thought he was the man in the painting."

Chin still in hand, Alex tapped his fingers on his cheekbone while he studied her face. For the moment, she seemed to be telling the truth. "So your father truly abandoned you here."

She jabbed her fork in his direction. "He did not abandon me. He left me in your care, for a fortnight. He'll be back. He promised."

"Has he ever done this before?"

"Sometimes. Usually he just leaves me in our rooms

in Saint-Marcel when he has business out of the city.''
She favored Alex with a wolfish grin. "Not that I ever
stay put. It's far too dull.''

For the first time he was shocked. "You live in Saint-
Marcel?'' he repeated.

"Right now we do,'' she answered, then looked over
at the liquor decanters on the sideboard. "Do you have
any brandy?''

"Not at nine in the morning, I don't.'' He leaned
forward. "Your father is brother to the Duke of Furth.
What in God's name is he doing living in the worst part
of Paris?''

"It's not so bad,'' she protested. "Besides, I can take
care of myself. I can fool anyone into thinking I'm a
boy.''

"You didn't fool me,'' Alex reminded her, grinning
at her boast.

She scowled. "You weren't supposed to have found
out. Papa said it would make less trouble if I were a
boy.''

Alex regarded her for a moment. In one sense, her
father was correct. "It nearly didn't matter what you
were. I almost threw you two out from pure annoyance,
last night.''

"Why didn't you, then?'' she asked.

"Because you intrigued me.''

"You thought I was a boy.''

He nodded. "I did.''

She gave a nasty grin. "Do you like boys, Everton?''

Evidently Kit Brantley was not plagued with a delicate nature. Alex scowled. "No. And that was rather the
difficulty. I found myself quite relieved to discover your
true gender.''

Kit chuckled, then reached out to run one finger
around the rim of her teacup in an odd, dainty gesture
that looked studied, as though she had seen some female
do it at one time and was imitating it. "What about
now?'' she asked, looking at him from beneath long
lashes. "Are you still relieved?''

Alex pursed his lips. *Intrigued* and *extremely curious*

would have been much more accurate. "I believe so," he answered. "It's been a dull Season."

She smiled. "I will make it more interesting."

He raised his mug of ale, and she lifted her teacup in turn. "I trust you will, cousin."

The Earl of Everton set a splendid breakfast table, and even an hour after eating, Kit felt positively bloated as she wallowed in the fine brass bathtub that had been carried into her bedchamber for her. After the journey from Paris and the rain, and then wrestling with Everton's groom in the stable, she felt worse than filthy. And a hot bath, in the middle of the morning yet, with Alexander Cale and his lovely blue eyes just downstairs . . .

"Don't fall asleep in there, miss, or you'll drown," the housekeeper said sternly from behind her.

"Thank you, Mrs. Hodges," she answered, twisting to look at the plump, gray-haired woman and blinking the unexpected thought of Everton out of her mind. Dash it, she didn't have time for such nonsense. "I do think you should call me Kit, though."

Mrs. Hodges wrinkled her nose. "I could never."

"Well, calling me 'miss' could cause all kinds of confusion," she argued. Drat the woman for being so thickheaded. She hadn't wished anyone's assistance at all, but Everton had insisted on it. And considering that he already knew more about her than she had intended to reveal, she had thought it best not to argue.

"It's just so peculiar, if you don't mind my saying."

Kit sighed. "Yes. I know."

She hesitated before she stood to receive the towel the housekeeper held open for her. It was perfectly proper, of course, but she was unused to anyone seeing her naked. She had never had a personal maid, and she barely remembered her mother, for Anne Riley Brantley had died just after Kit's sixth birthday. Only a breath of time after that, her father had sold their small estate in Hampstead, and they had moved to Madrid, and then to Venice, and finally to Paris. And sometime during those travels she had become Kit Riley, either her father's son or his nephew, depending on the circumstances in which they found themselves.

Hurriedly she wrapped the soft cloth around herself, while the housekeeper stepped over to the cleaned pile of clothes a maid had brought up. "It's all right, Mrs. Hodges, I'm used to dressing myself."

The older woman picked up her cravat and examined it. "Just as well," she said, scowling. "I don't think I could, in good conscience, assist you with these things."

Kit laughed at her prudishness and motioned her out of the room. The servants had cleaned off her dirty, rain-stained clothes as best they could, but it was fairly obvious that her French rags, as Lord Everton had called them, were becoming exactly that. They felt old and stiff, and the strip of cloth she wrapped tightly across her breasts scratched her.

She sighed and tried to straighten out the drooping brim of her beaver hat. "Damnation," she muttered. Mrs. Hodges, or else Everton, had thought to provide her with a hairbrush and a strip of cloth with which to tie back her hair in its short tail, and she quickly finished what was left of her toilette.

Kit hesitated before she opened the chamber door to return downstairs. The scrutiny Everton had given her last night had been the most intense she'd ever weathered. That, though, had been nothing compared to this morning. Those eyes knew she was a female now, and they looked at her differently. He was a rakehell, her father had said, and with him knowing what he did about her, the next fortnight was going to be even more difficult than she had envisioned.

The housekeeper and Wenton, the butler, were waiting for her at the foot of the stairs as she descended. "Where's the earl?" she queried, craning her head to gaze into the room on the left.

"He's gone out, Mr. Riley," Wenton said. If the butler thought it odd that Everton had asked Mrs. Hodges to attend his cousin, he said nothing about it.

"Out?" Kit repeated, dismayed to realize that she was disappointed. But after all, if he'd asked her to go with him on his rounds, she would have been able to learn something of his acquaintances, which might have helped her task immeasurably.

"Yes, Mr. Riley. He said you were to, if I may, 'explore all you like, but don't go out, and don't, ah, steal anything.' " He gave a small nod. "Sir."

Kit sighed irritably. "Oh, very well." All things considered, it was likely a wise idea that she become acquainted with her immediate surroundings, anyway.

"Luncheon is generally served at one o'clock, if that is acceptable," the butler continued.

"Yes, that's fine, Wenton," she replied, disguising her surprise at being asked. Few meals in Saint-Marcel were planned for ahead of time, and luncheon generally consisted of scrounged bread, when it was eaten at all.

She declined a formal tour of the house, preferring to have the various rooms pointed out to her at the outset and then exploring them on her own. The butler seemed determined to lurk, but she decided to ignore him, and as she wandered from one magnificent room to another, Wenton's presence receded into a barely noticed annoyance. She'd never seen such wealth outside the walls of the Palais Royale. In fact, if the plentiful gold and silver and crystal were any indication, the Earl of Everton was not her father's traitorous noble. Alexander Cale had no need for the funds or the difficulties of a government appointment. She didn't believe rakehells were given such positions of responsibility, anyway.

Just inside the door to the morning room, she paused. It was tucked into the front eastern corner of the house, and was bright and neat, with overstuffed pillows and throw blankets carefully placed to adorn the deep couch just so. Two well-padded chairs had been set close by the windows, but just far enough away that sunlight would never touch whoever was seated in them. It felt very feminine and delicate, unlike the other rooms in the mansion—perhaps a favorite of the late countess, Everton's mother. With a self-conscious glance over her shoulder at the butler, she continued to the next door.

It was locked. "What's in here?" she asked Wenton.

"The earl's private study," he returned, taking her question as an invitation to quit lurking and step up beside her.

"Why is it locked?" As far as she had seen, other than the silver closet, it was the only room shut off from her on the first two floors.

"I could not venture to say, Mr. Riley."

The butler might suffer from a complete lack of curiosity, but then he was not the offspring of a smuggler and occasional thief. Seeing what might lie inside, though, would have to wait for a better opportunity. With a last glance at the door, she stepped around Wenton and across the hall, into the room she had saved for last.

The library was definitely masculine, and wholly the Earl of Everton's. Evidently either the earl or one of his ancestors had loved to read, for she had never seen such a collection of books as lay in the Cale House library. She suspected the collector to be the present earl, though, for some of the manuscripts looked quite recent. The room had the comforting smell of old paper, and with a faint smile Kit made her way around the shelves, running her finger slowly along the spines of the books to read their titles. Reading was an extravagance she'd had little opportunity for as she got older, and one she'd never missed as keenly as she did right then. Perhaps before the fortnight was over she would have a little time, if Everton didn't mind loaning out part of his collection.

With some servant or another in sight all day, exploring the house for anything useful remained impossible, and she wasn't interested in seeing the remainder of the bedchambers. She'd seen the drawing room, and doubted the formal dining room or the ballroom on the third floor would hold any state secrets.

After luncheon she wandered into the morning room to look out the front window. Just across wide Park Lane, the grassy avenues of Hyde Park were crowded with well-dressed gentlemen and ladies. Kit pursed her lips, then gave a slight smile. They shouldn't mind one more young lad looking about. Quickly she strode back out to the entryway, settled her hat on her head, pulled the door open, and headed across the lane.

Less than half an hour later she ferreted out a promising rat. The group of lords talking together on horseback at the edge of Rotten Row didn't even notice her as she strolled over to stand in the shade of an elm tree close by. They were discussing Napoleon and tariffs, so she turned to get a glimpse of them through the shrubbery.

"But he's hurting our own commerce, as well," a short, overweight man with a shockingly bright gold waistcoat was complaining, and Kit immediately ruled him out. Only a supporter of the tariff would be helping to enforce the blockade.

"You can't expect even a wastrel like Prinny to sell goods to a country we're at war with," a second man returned. "And three years ago, Bonaparte was confiscating every piece of British property he could get his hands on. I'll wager you weren't complaining about commerce then." He was younger than the first, with a jaunty smile and immaculately cropped brown hair, and he was mounted on a fine bay gelding. Kit took a step closer, using the trunk of the elm as shelter.

"Only that he wasn't given a cut of the gold," a third man chuckled.

"That's not amusing, Rawlings," the stout man snapped.

"Well," the jaunty one said, smiling, "I don't believe Donald's share would have amounted to much, given the lack of success of the venture."

"Indeed, my lord," Rawlings answered, "and thanks t—"

Heavy footsteps approached from behind, and Kit jumped as hot wind breathed down her collar. She whipped around to find herself looking into the left eye of a magnificent black stallion, which gazed balefully back at her. The black's rider sat looking at her with a mildly annoyed expression on his handsome face, his hands crossed at the wrists in front of him.

"Do you know what a roof is?" Alexander Cale queried.

"Of course," she retorted, noting that the Earl of Everton had long, elegant fingers. Gambler's hands, her father would say—but that didn't explain why she found them so abruptly fascinating.

"I would therefore assume you know the difference between being indoors and out of doors," he continued in the same tone.

She scowled at him, angry that she had allowed him to distract her so completely that she missed the rest of the conversation behind her. "I'm not a complete idiot, you know," she snapped.

Everton looked at her for another moment. "I did not think you were."

He kicked one foot out of its stirrup and held down a hand. With a sigh she stepped into the leather brace, swung up behind him, and wrapped an arm about his waist. His stomach beneath her hand was flat and hard, and she took a slow breath. He smelled faintly of cigar smoke and shaving soap, and she leaned forward a little to breathe him in more deeply. "I . . . was only bored," she stated shakily, dismayed at what she was doing. She straightened, concentrating on acting like the male cousin she was supposed to be.

"Obviously."

Her father had always insisted that the titled English were thin-blooded, ingrown, stupid, nasty creatures, but as the long-lashed azure eyes glanced over his shoulder at her, she thought that Alexander Cale must be an exception. There was nothing thin-blooded about his tall, lean frame, or about the way the muscles of his thighs played beneath his breeches as he brought the skittish stallion about with deceptive ease.

"Where did you go today?" she asked, to break the silence.

"Out," he responded, kneeing the stallion and heading them back to the edge of the park.

"Oh, how very exciting."

He chuckled. "Not particularly."

"Do we have to go back?" she asked, forcing a pleading smile. "Can't you introduce me to any of your friends?"

"No." They crossed the lane to Cale House. At the foot of the front steps he handed her down, then slid to the ground himself as Conklin came up to take the black.

"Are we going to Lady Sinclair's soiree, at least?" Kit followed him inside and brushed at the new wrinkles her coat seemed to have picked up.

Lord Everton stopped to look at her. "I am. You're not going anywhere else today, Miss Brantley," he informed her. "You will remain here."

Kit frowned. "But it's so dull here!" she protested. He was making her task even more difficult than she'd anticipated—both by his stubbornness and by his very annoying and distracting presence.

He gave a half smile. "It's only for a fortnight. Entertain yourself. I have a fairly good library. You can read, can't you, savage?"

She made a face at him. "Only piratical tales with swordplay and blood in them."

Lord Everton laughed, his eyes dancing. He had a rich, musical laugh, and the sound ran down her spine with an unexpected tingle. "I'll see what I can come up with for you." He headed upstairs to change.

Kit went up to her own bedchamber to clean up, for she had no intention of staying in. When Wenton later announced dinner, Kit decided she might as well eat while she attempted to figure out how she was going to attend Lady Sinclair's party. She was in the process of dissecting a roasted game hen when the door opened and the earl entered. Kit froze, a wing halfway to her lips, and simply looked at him.

She had seen men dressed in evening finery before, of course, had even attended more than one Parisian soiree in her guise as a man. As she gazed at Alexander Cale, though, it occurred to her that she had never set eyes on anyone who looked so magnificently . . . male. His coat was of the finest dark gray superfine, while the cream-colored waistcoat and gold watch fob were impeccable above black breeches that looked molded to those well-muscled thighs. With his black, wavy hair and bluer-than-sapphire eyes, he looked like some sort of English god. She swallowed.

"Here, cousin," he said amiably, apparently unaware that she was gawking at him, and flipped a book onto the table beside her.

Kit spent another moment staring at his amused expression, then reluctantly turned her attention to the book resting at her elbow. *"Robinson Crusoe,"* she read aloud.

"I don't recall if there's any swordplay, but it is fairly piratical," he noted as he leaned over the table to appropriate a steaming hot biscuit from a covered bowl.

"Thank you, Ev . . ." She stopped as his eyes flicked in Wenton's direction. "Alex," she amended, the name more comfortable on her tongue than she expected.

"Stay out of trouble, cousin," Lord Everton suggested, his eyes speaking volumes. Then he turned and was gone.

Kit looked after him for a full minute before she remembered that she was supposed to be going with him. With a frown, she bit into the game hen. Outside, thunder rumbled over the mansion, and the patter of rain sounded against the window. Of course, they barely knew one another, but it annoyed her that he had donned his fine clothes for the pleasure of Barbara Sinclair, while she had only been laughed at and abandoned. "I hope he gets drenched," she muttered, "leaving me here." She looked over her shoulder. "Wenton, does Alex have any brandy?"

"Not for you, Mr. Riley," Wenton answered. He raised an eyebrow when she scowled at him. "The earl's orders."

"Bah," Kit replied.

Chapter 3

The next day began exactly as had the previous one, except that she didn't come to blows with Ben Conklin, and she didn't see Everton at all. That seemed rather insulting. After all the care he had taken to discover her charade, and his subsequent suggestive remarks and bullying, now it seemed he couldn't even be bothered to wish her a good morning before he vanished.

"Meetings," was the only explanation she was able to pull out of Wenton, who informed her that Lord Everton had again suggested she stay in the house.

The earl's professed whereabouts sounded suspicious, especially for a rakehell, though her father had informed her that the only thing blue bloods were good for was talking, for they had more wind than brains. Rain had continued to fall throughout the night and into the morning, rendering Park Lane gray and running with water, but she'd been wet before and had no intention of remaining inside. Before she went hunting, however, there was one task at Cale House left for her to accomplish.

She informed Wenton that she would be reading in the library, then slipped across the hallway to examine the locked door of Everton's study. She checked up and down the hall for the butler or any other members of the earl's large household staff, knelt, and pulled the knife from her boot. The lock was more sturdy than she anticipated, but after a few tries she was able to wedge the door open.

The office was larger than she expected. A door off to one side stood open, and through it she viewed a billiards table and several faded, overstuffed chairs. This smaller room ran behind the staircase in the hall, and no second door opened from it back into the hallway. Fleetingly she wondered why Alex Cale would bother hiding his game room away in his own house.

Her main reason for breaking into the study, though, was not to analyze Everton, but to determine whether he had any hidden vices—such as ruining the lives and incomes of independent exporters. She gave a slight smile, hearing her father's voice in her head, as she made her way around the large mahogany desk. The physical act of smuggling, Stewart Brantley always said, only touched on their work to bring tariffed goods to the citizens of Paris. She pulled open the first of the ornate drawers.

There was nothing of interest inside, only blank parchment and sealing wax, and she went on to the next one. And raised both eyebrows. It was filled with a haphazard collection of invitations to soirees, balls, recitals, routs, dinners, picnics, luncheons, horse races, breakfasts, foxhunts, and every other sort of entertainment she could imagine. The Earl of Everton was apparently an even more sought-after guest than she had suspected.

The next drawer contained a brace of pistols, but other than taking a moment to admire their exceptional quality, Kit wasn't particularly interested in them. The long drawer across the top held a marked deck of cards, a geographical map of eastern Britain with several indecipherable markings along the coast, a handful of French coins, and a wrinkled, dirty parchment that said only "938 musket, 352 pistol." She frowned at the paper, then put it back when she could come up with nothing more sinister in its meaning than perhaps a listing of the number of game birds shot on Everton's estate last season and how they'd been dispatched. The coins, and especially the coastal map, bothered her, though. They meant she couldn't eliminate Everton as a suspect. The objects might be innocent, and he might simply own a yacht or some such thing, but she couldn't take the chance of assuming that.

Beneath the map she found a rather suggestive letter from a Countess Fenwall, and a well-leafed-through catalog of farming tools and equipment, with a letter from Everton's estate manager inserted between two of the pages. Apparently the estate's largest hay rake had bent, and needed to be replaced before the next harvest. According to her letter, Lady Fenwall promised to bend over as well, if Alex could manage to be at Fenwall while her husband was away in Yorkshire. She also promised to do several other things that Kit was rather surprised to see a lady put into writing, though she wasn't certain the spelling was correct. The letter was dated last year, and she suspected that the earl had kept the missive more because it was amusing than because he had answered the invitation.

She was taking far too long looking through his private things, but the task was fascinating. Reluctantly she put away the letters and moved on. His estate ledgers lay in the next drawer, and though it wasn't necessary to her purpose, she pulled the first book out and flipped it open. Everton's masculine scrawl filled the page, with notation after notation of income earned from his estates, of which there appeared to be at least three, and of money spent for salaries, taxes, clothes, theater tickets, furniture, a brood mare, and a hundred other items of various value. She sat back for a moment. Even from this small sampling, it was obvious that Alexander Cale hadn't been joking before. He was as rich as Croesus.

The bottom drawer was her last chance to find any further evidence, and she hesitated, realizing she didn't want to find anything that could tip the balance toward his guilt. That was absurd. It didn't matter who the spy was, so long as she found him in time to see that the next shipment went through and Fouché was appeased. With a quick breath, angry at herself, she yanked the drawer open. And stopped.

A box of chocolates, half-consumed, sat beside a bottle of port and a box of very expensive-looking cigars.

All of Everton's vices, apparently, laid out together. With a surprised, immediately smothered chuckle, Kit took one of the chocolates and shut the drawer. She munched on the candy as she checked the single book-shelf and the few papers stacked on the corner of the desk, but found nothing else remotely of interest. Apparently Everton's best-kept secret was a fondness for chocolate—or so he wanted everyone to think. Kit hadn't made up her mind about him yet. Far from it.

She exited the study, making certain the door was locked and her finger marks wiped from the shiny door handle. After hurrying across the way to the library, she immediately turned around again to make a show of ex-iting the room and shutting the door behind her. Ever-ton's abandonment would make it more difficult to gain entrance to some of the places her quarry was likely to be found, but there wasn't enough time for her to sit and wait for an opportunity. She needed to make her own luck.

Waiting about for luncheon at Cale House was out of the question, so she stepped into the breakfast room for one of the peaches left in a bowl on the sideboard. She hefted it in her hand, and then paused as she heard the front door open.

"Where is dear Alexander?" a male voice queried from the entryway.

"The earl is out," Wenton informed the three gentle-men lounging in the doorway, as Kit stepped back into the hall. All three were well dressed, obviously fellow members of the *ton*, and she straightened as one of them spied her standing there.

"You're the one," he said, looking at her with twin-kling brown eyes set beneath fashionably immaculate brown hair.

Kit's heartbeat quickened as she coolly returned his baldly curious gaze. He was the tariff supporter from Hyde Park. And he was apparently friends with a man who kept notated coastal maps and French coins in his desk. "Which one?" she asked belatedly, hoping Everton wasn't such a fool that he had told everyone in London that his houseguest was a female.

The other two turned as well, and the shorter one, a dark-haired imp with high shirt points and an achingly intricate cravat, grinned and started toward her. "You're right, Reg," he said over his shoulder.

Kit repeated the name to herself and leaned sideways against the doorframe. "Exactly which one am I supposed to be?" she repeated, unconsciously imitating the slight, affected drawl of Alexander Cale's guests.

"You know," Reg said, following the other two as they stopped before her, "the one Barbara was chattering about all night. Everton's cousin. The one who's supposed to steal Caroline's heart."

"Who is Caroline?" Kit asked, trying to keep her attention on the conversation. Staring at her quarry would get her nowhere but arrested, if she wasn't careful.

"The woman I'm going to marry." Reg grinned.

"Poor, deluded boy," the third one murmured, looking at Kit with dark, speculative eyes in a pale specter's face. The others would be easy to deceive, she decided, but she would be wary of this one.

"I say, why don't you join us at Boodle's for luncheon, and we'll let you in on the conspiracy?" Reg continued.

Kit grinned, delighted. But she had to play her part correctly, or they might suspect something. "I might, if you told me who you were."

The pale one ran a hand through short blond hair and finally offered a faint smile. "Gads, what manners. That is Reginald Hanshaw, Lord Hanshaw for long, Reg for short."

"I'm Francis Henning, Francis for any occasion," the short, dark one offered, sticking out his hand. Kit shook it, and he jabbed a finger in the direction of their third companion. "And that's Viscount Devlin. Augustus, to those who can tolerate him. He can be thoroughly unpleasant, you know."

"Only to my friends," the viscount replied with a slight nod.

"Devlin," Kit responded, taking the specter's hand. She had thought it would be cold, and was surprised to note the grip was both warm and strong. "Christian Riley, Kit for short."

"Funny, Alex never said he was related to the Irish," Reg commented with a glance at Augustus, motioning Kit to join them.

"I shouldn't," she said, feigning reluctance, and secretly ecstatic. Such a gaggle of English lords could gain her access to far more places than she could hope to enter on her own.

"Oh, do come," Lord Devlin cajoled. "We shall make Reg buy."

She smiled, rather charmed by the three of them despite herself. It seemed her father's view of the titled English was more grim than was strictly accurate. "All right."

"Heavens." Reg chuckled. "Even strangers are taking advantage of me now."

"It's so easy, don't you know," the viscount agreed, leading the way out the door.

"Mr. Riley," Wenton said, stepping forward, "I do not think the earl would approve."

"Then he should have provided me with better entertainment," Kit replied flatly.

"Hear, hear," Devlin applauded.

With a defiant look at the butler, Kit grabbed her old, stained greatcoat and stepped into the rainy streets of Mayfair.

"Where in damnation have you been?"

Kit started and nearly dropped the drenched greatcoat she was handing to Wenton. The Earl of Everton stood just inside the foyer. He was only half dressed, his shirttail untucked and his cravat smashed in one hand. In the dimness of the hallway his eyes glinted at her, piercing and dark as a demon's. No aloof, cynical noble tonight. "Out," she returned, giving the butler her hat and attempting to ignore the angry, impelling presence behind her.

"Out." He turned away. "Why don't you join me in the library for a moment, cousin?" he said over his shoulder, drawing out the last word as though it gave him some sort of authority over her.

"Go to the devil," she answered, annoyed at his presumption. She gave her damp boots a last stomp. " 'Out' was good enough for you, yesterday."

For a heartbeat he froze. Then, with surprising swiftness, he strode forward and grabbed her by the back of the collar.

"Let me go!" she demanded, startled, and kicked.

He grunted as her boot made contact with his leg, then shifted his grip and grabbed another handful of coat. Unmindful of her struggling, he dragged her into the library. She hit him, and he grabbed her wrist with fingers as strong as a vise. Kicking the door shut with one foot, he then shoved her away from him and into a chair.

She sprang to her feet again. "You lout!" she yelled, her heartbeat wild. "Don't you touch me!"

"That's twice you've gone out when I've told you not to," he snapped, rubbing at his shoulder where her fist had connected. Blast it, she had been aiming for his jaw. "You will not defy me again!"

"So you're allowed to go about with your cronies, and I have to stay here like some sort of prisoner?" she protested, shrugging her coat back into place.

"You informed me that your father wished you kept safe . . . and pure," he returned hotly, taking a long step toward her. "If you've decided to change the rules, then don't expect me to abide by them either, chit. Is that clear?"

His expression made it quite obvious what he was referring to. "The rules have not changed," she informed him stiffly.

He paused for a heartbeat. "I thought not. Pity, though." Everton turned and pulled open the door again, apparently satisfied with the outcome of the argument.

"What's that supposed to mean?" she demanded, unwilling to let him have the last word.

"Whatever pleases you, cousin."

"Well, I don't know what you expected. Father never asked you to bore me to death."

"I gave you a book," he replied less heatedly as he started up the staircase.

She tromped up behind him. "That's your idea of entertaining a guest? To give them a stupid book?"

"It's a first edition," he commented dryly.

She hadn't known that. "Then it's *old* and stupid."

Belatedly Kit realized that she had followed him straight into his bedchamber. She stopped just inside the doorway. The room was twice the size of hers, and decorated in dark wood touched with green and gold accents over the ivory-colored walls. The four-poster bed was huge, but where hers was absolutely piled with pillows, there was only one on his. It didn't have the look of a bed where one entertained a mistress, she decided.

"I didn't think you wished to embroider." He glanced back at her, cynical humor touching his gaze. "Or do I err?"

"Bah," she snarled, trying to shake out of her mind the absurd idea that being in his bedchamber was significant of something. "Robinson Crusoe had more people to talk to than me."

"Than I," he corrected, tossing his cravat to a man watching the two of them.

" 'Than I,' " she repeated, mimicking his stuffy, cultured accent. *"Vous êtes un boeuf stupide."*

"You're an English chit," he said absently, not bothering to turn away before he half unfastened his breeches and began tucking his shirt into them. "Speak English."

The gesture was meant to shock her, no doubt, and she felt her cheeks flush. What she was feeling, though, was far from scandalized. Reluctantly she tore her gaze from the fascinating sight of Everton dressing, to glance at his valet, surprised that the earl had let her secret slip. The servant, though, simply continued trying to smooth the wrinkles out of the crushed cravat.

"Vous êtes un grand boeuf stupide," she amended.

Alex looked up at her for a moment as he finished refastening his trousers, then turned to his valet. "Don't just stand there, Antoine," he admonished, "translate."

The valet stopped what he was doing. "My lord?" he queried.

"Translate," the earl repeated. "Exactly. And throw that damned scrap away and get me a new one."

"Yes, my lord." Antoine stepped over to the beautiful mahogany bureau and pulled out a crisp, snowy white cravat. "You are a . . . stupid ox, my lord," he said, clearing his throat, and returned to the earl's side.

Kit watched curiously as Everton turned away to run a comb through his wavy black hair. It was a little longer than the current fashion, curling slightly where it touched his collar, but it suited him. Her fingers twitched with an abrupt desire to tangle her fingers through it.

"Un grand *boeuf stupide,"* she repeated without heat. "Antoine?"

"A big, stupid ox, my lord."

Everton raised an eyebrow as he looked at Kit's reflection in his dressing mirror. "You barge into my house, eat my food, dirty my carpeting, abuse my favor and my friends, and *I'm* a stupid ox."

She nodded. "And a terrible host."

"My dear Miss Brantley," he said, turning to face her, "allow me to remind you once again that you are not my guest. Therefore I cannot possibly be your host."

Kit didn't recall that her father had envisioned quite this. The earl was as quick-witted as she had feared, and whether or not he was the fox she was here to hunt, she wouldn't want him in her henhouse. "Yes, I am your g—"

"You are a debt I am attempting to repay, for a promise I never made." She started to retort, but he jabbed a finger at her. "And you *will* follow the rules as I have set them out."

"Diable."

"Antoine?"

"Devil. My lord."

Lord Everton pursed his lips, then finished buttoning his splendid gray waistcoat. "Where did you go today?" he asked much more mildly than she expected.

Kit could see no reason not to answer him. "Reg, Francis, and Lord Devlin took me to Boodle's club for luncheon." And great fun though it had been, she had only discovered that both Reg and Devlin shared her own dislike for Napoleon. Reg actually seemed too whimsical to be carrying out Prince George's policies, but his friendship with Everton posed several questions. She hadn't figured Devlin out yet, so she also remained wary of him. Francis simply had a puddle for a brain, but he was quite amusing. "But Wenton already told you where I'd gone, I'll wager."

"Yes, he did."

"Then why did you ask?"

"I wanted to see if you'd lie about it."

She glanced at him suspiciously, to find his eyes still on her. "Why would you think that I would?"

He shrugged. "You seem rather adept at it."

She couldn't deny that, and considering the way she'd arrived in his care, she decided it was a perfectly natural thing for him to be suspicious about. Antoine stepped up to tie the earl's cravat, and Kit leaned sideways against the doorframe to watch. She had never seen the knot before, and rather liked it. She would have to try it. "You're going to White's," she stated.

"I am."

"Augustus invited me to come tonight as his guest, if you didn't wish to sponsor me," she informed him. Perhaps she could taunt him into taking her about London.

Everton scowled. "Augustus Devlin is not sponsoring you. And *I* am damned well not sponsoring you, at White's or anywhere else, because you are not going anywhere!" he exploded. "Is that now abundantly, unmistakably, undeniably, irrefutably clear?"

Apparently she'd pushed him too far. "You're not very nice," she grumbled, not bothering to hide her frustration. If she couldn't get out into Mayfair with a host or a guide who had connections, this entire journey would be for nothing. The Comte de Fouché would make life considerably more difficult for them than it already was, if he didn't try to kill them outright.

The earl took a deep breath and expelled it noisily. "No, I'm not," he agreed. "And whatever you might have in mind, I'm going to keep you here, safe and quiet, for the next twelve days, and then I'm going to turn you back over to Stewart Brantley so neither of you will have an excuse to pester me ever again." Antoine helped him into a blue evening coat, then handed over his white kid gloves. "Good evening, Miss Brantley."

He paused beside her in the doorway, his gaze amused but otherwise unreadable, then brushed by her shoulder and headed down the stairs to bid Wenton not to wait up for him. She grimaced. This was absolutely not going to work. Her father would be disgusted with her for letting this English lord maneuver around her so easily.

"Was there something you required, Mr. Riley?" Antoine was busily cleaning up the earl's dressing table, and he looked over at her curiously.

"No. Yes. Might I have that?" Kit queried, gesturing at the ruined cravat the valet was in the process of discarding.

"This?" he said, looking down at it. "I suppose so, Mr. Riley."

With a smile Kit stepped forward and retrieved it. Even creased and wilted, it was in better condition than her own. "My thanks." As she returned to her own bedchamber, she began untying her stained neckwear. Stay put in this drafty old mansion for twelve more days and not learn a damned thing, indeed!

"I'm telling you, Heathrow will be looking for a permanent residence in the Colonies by the end of the Season." Francis Henning jumbled the discarded cards into a pile and shook his head at the dealer. "Do be a little more kind, m'boy," he cajoled.

Alexander Cale chuckled. "You might try bribery. And even if Heathrow's completely to let, he still has the Oberlin Manor property to his name.''

"No, Alex, it's entailed. Won't do him a bloody bit of good," Reg Hanshaw said, watching as their dealer rearranged the suit of spades on the table. "It's going to be the seven this time," he muttered, placing several coins by that card.

"You've been saying that all night," Augustus Devlin noted. "But they're correct about Heathrow, Alexander. It's either the Americas or debtor's prison for our destitute marquis." He took a long swallow of port, emptying his glass, then poured himself another.

"And it's his own fault if that's where he ends up," Reg continued. "Margaret Devereaux offered to marry him."

Alex grinned, glancing at the far corner of the room where Miss Devereaux's younger brother currently sat overflowing one of White's gilded chairs. "I'd sooner face debtors' prison myself than be leg-shackled to that substantial flower of womanhood."

"English oak of womanhood, you mean," Reg corrected, chuckling.

"That's what Heathrow decided as well, apparently," Lord Devlin agreed.

"I say, Alex, why didn't you have your cousin here tonight?" Reg queried. He cursed as the dealer turned up the nine of hearts. "Seven, I said. Seven."

The earl scowled. "Because he's a great deal of trouble, and I want him out as quickly and with as little bother as possible." With that he drained his glass, then motioned Augustus to favor him with another. Christine Brantley was indeed a great deal of trouble, and other than his obvious male stupidity, he still couldn't figure out why he'd given in to the waif and allowed her to stay.

"I suppose that means you won't be spotting me any blunt to play with this evening?" a low, lilting voice came from behind him, and a slim hand was laid on his shoulder.

A shock coursed through him at the contact, and he deliberately took another swallow of port. When he

twisted his head to look up at her, Kit's green eyes were
laughing down at him, daring him to do something about
her being there. Holding her gaze, Alex reached out to
lift a stack of coins from the table and handed them up
to her. "Don't lose them," he instructed, hoping his
companions couldn't tell that the chit's arrival, and her
easy touch, had left him as unsettled as a schoolboy in
a bawdy house.

"I learned to count by playing faro," she answered,
pulling up a chair and sitting between him and Devlin.
With a swift, defiant glance at him, she reached for the
bottle of port and poured herself a glass.

"That doesn't necessarily mean you're any good at
it, does it?" Reg asked, furrowing his brow. "Seven
again, I think," he muttered, placing another few coins
by the offending card.

"Sweet heaven, Reginald, show a little imagination,"
Augustus complained with a faint smile, placing his own
bet beside the three.

"I am merely optimistic."

"Which explains why you continue to believe you
can convince Caroline to wed you." Lord Devlin ran a
farthing over and under his agile fingers, and back again.

"Of course."

"Well, I'd call it demented, m'boy."

"You want to sit out till we finish the deck, Kit?"
Francis offered. "You've no way of knowing what's
been played."

"I'm all right," the girl answered, taking a hearty
swallow of port. "What's the minimum?"

"Francis is let out till the end of the month, so it's
small change until then. One crown in," Reg explained.

Kit nodded, placing five shillings alongside the seven
of spades in company with Lord Hanshaw's coins.

"Not you, as well," Francis complained, scowling at
her choice.

"The deck's nearly finished, and he hasn't won it
yet." She shrugged, glancing at Reg. "Besides, if that's
all the blunt you're playing for, it's hardly worth it."

She spun a groat on the table, and Alex reached over

and flattened it with his palm when the sound became annoying. "Just remember that it's my blunt," he reminded her.

"Not much of it, Croesus," she replied.

Augustus laughed, sobering only a little when Alex glared at him. "Well said," he chortled, rare color touching his cheeks. A coughing fit followed, and Alex reached over to refill his companion's glass, watching as Devlin drained it.

The chit's wager was actually a wise one, considering she had no idea which cards had been turned. Alex flipped a half sovereign at the queen, for there were still two left in the deck. He regarded Kit through half-lowered lids, noting the slight flush the port had brought to her cheeks, and admitting to himself that he'd made a mistake. He'd thought Kit Brantley would be trouble, but he'd had no idea how intriguing and compelling a challenge it would be to decipher her. And he was less than surprised when the dealer turned a seven of diamonds.

"Thank God," Francis said vehemently as the dealer slid several coins toward Reg and then to Kit. "Now perhaps he'll stop whining."

"I wasn't whining," Reg protested, stacking his coins.

"I say, Alex," Francis said, leaning forward, "when are you going to spring Kit on Lady Caroline?"

Everton frowned. "I told Barbara to leave off with that."

"But she's correct, don't you think?" Augustus put in unexpectedly. "The slim, tail-haired, romantic look? Quite poetical."

"Goose-brained and damned unfashionable, I'd say," Alex muttered. Kit scowled at him venomously, and he stifled a grin.

"Even so, bring him to the Fontaine rout Thursday. I can't wait to have Caroline set eyes on him," Francis said, counting the scanty change left before him.

"I can," Reg grumbled good-naturedly.

"Who in the world is this Lady Caroline you keep

saying is going to fall in love with me?" Kit asked, raising an eyebrow.

"My cousin doesn't need to meet Lady Caroline," Alex cut in, more bothered by the conversation than he cared to let his cronies know. "He's not titled, so she won't be interested, anyway."

"I would hate to steal her from Hanshaw," the waif noted confidently, reaching out to place a crown on the queen just as Alex moved to place his wager on the same card. Their fingers brushed, her skin warm against his, even through their gloves. After a second she pulled away. With a quick glance at their companions, she licked her lips, then chuckled and looked at him. "Which queens are left?"

"Hearts and clubs," Lord Hanshaw supplied when Alex didn't answer.

"I'll make you a wager, Alex, that the next queen to come up is clubs," she said, her eyes daring him again.

Alex shook himself, trying to put the curve of her throat and the line of her jaw out of his mind. He placed a put-upon scowl on his face. "How much, cousin?"

"Ten quid," she responded promptly, giving him that fleeting grin again.

He glanced at Augustus, wondering how anyone could not see that she was a female. Hopefully none of his companions would have occasion to wrestle with her. "And where are you going to come up with ten pounds to wager?"

Wordlessly Viscount Devlin slid ten of his sovereigns over to her and finished off his port.

"Just a moment, Devlin," Francis protested. "I asked you for five quid to put on a horse last week, and you told me to go to Jericho. Now you give this boy twice that, when he didn't even ask?"

Augustus Devlin raised an eyebrow. "It's all in the family," he murmured. "Besides, I knew *you* would lose."

"And what do you want with ten quid, Kit?" Alex asked, ignoring the exchange going on beside him.

"To see London," the chit answered after a moment.

"Since you won't take me about, and I'll only be here a short time, I'll hire someone to show me."

He knew that was only said to annoy him. "All right."

He nudged the dealer under the table with the toe of his boot, then nodded. The man began turning cards one by one. Beside him Kit was calm and aloof, except for the excited light in her eyes. Six of hearts, ace of clubs, three of hearts, then there were only four cards left.

"Good thing he stopped your wagering on queens," Reg pointed out unhelpfully.

The dealer glanced up at the Earl of Everton, then turned the card. "Looks as though you'll be touring London on foot and alone," Alex said, as the queen of hearts drifted down to the table. He reached out and slid her pile of sovereigns into his, and then gathered them all in front of him. With no blunt, the chit couldn't go much of anywhere for the next fortnight, and that would make things considerably easier on him. Or so he hoped.

"You're a selfish brute," Kit said, disappointment in her eyes.

"And I'm beginning to think it's past your bedtime, boy," Alex returned, amused.

"My father sent me here to acquire some town polish, you know," she informed him, raising both eyebrows and daring him to play again.

It was more tempting than he expected. "Your father sent you here to keep you out of trouble while he's traveling," he countered smoothly. He stood, nodding at his other companions. "Let's go, brat."

Kit balked, then with an annoyed sigh finished her port, dropped the remainder of the coins he had fronted her into a pocket, and stood. "Good night, gentlemen," she said, clapping Reg Hanshaw on the shoulder and nodding at Augustus.

"Night, Kit," Augustus returned, raising his glass at her. "And if Alexander won't show you about town, I will."

"That's generous of you," Alex commented, narrowing his eyes a little. It was uncharacteristically generous, but despite his scrutiny, he could see nothing in Devlin's faded eyes but cynical, drink-dulled amusement.

"Not at all, dears."

Kit headed out, and Alex flipped a sovereign at the dealer. With a nod, the man caught it and dropped it into his waistcoat pocket.

"Cheat," Devlin murmured.

"Whenever possible." Everton followed his purported cousin outside. As soon as they were out of earshot of the crowded club, he rounded on her. "How in the devil did you get here?" he snapped, motioning for his carriage to be brought around.

"I walked," she said indignantly. "I didn't want to be accused of stealing from your stables again." She glared at him, then glanced over her shoulder at the club. "What's wrong with Devlin?"

"And our discussion of earlier this evening? Did you forget that?" he continued, gesturing her into the carriage and climbing in behind her.

"That was not a discussion. That was you telling me you couldn't be bothered to look after me." She folded her arms and sat back in the deep cushions opposite him. "Well, I didn't ask you to look after me, Everton. You don't need to treat me like a wee babe, just because I happen to be a female."

"Barely," Alex replied, amazed he had mistaken her for anything but a female even for a moment.

"And you're a poor excuse for a gentleman," she shot back.

"I'm a good enough excuse for you to be stealing my neckties," he noted, reaching forward to finger the well-tied ruffles at her throat.

She took a quick breath, then slapped his hand away. "Stop that. You'll ruin it."

He sat back, watching her pretending not to watch him. She was taller than Francis, but somehow appeared, to his enlightened gaze anyway, more fine-boned and delicate even than Barbara. And in those stained ragamuffin clothes, she looked like an escapee from a workhouse. To his surprise he wanted to kiss the waif, wanted to kiss those lips that were set in a straight, offended line and needed no paint to lend them perfection. Alex took a slow breath of his own. "Consumption," he finally said.

Her eyes, curious again, met his. "What?"

He paused for a moment, holding her gaze, before he answered. "Augustus. He's got consumption."

She fidgeted a little, then looked away again. "Oh."

"You play faro well," he offered, smiling a little and hoping he was the reason for her sudden discomfiture.

"I know."

"Your father did teach you, then?"

"He taught me everything," she said, defiant again, and lifted her chin.

"Oh, I imagine there were a few lessons he skipped," Alex said slowly, wondering whether she actually expected him to continue behaving himself. "Little things, here and there." He pursed his lips. "And not so little things."

"You've yet to shock me, Everton," she grumbled.

"I've yet to try." Curious about how she would react, he leaned forward again and reached out one hand. She followed his fingers as he drew closer. Everything about her seemed to draw him, as it had from the moment he set eyes on the waif, and he touched her knee with his palm. Her eyes snapped up to meet his. He held her gaze, slowly sliding his hand up her leg to her thigh. Her muscles tightened beneath the coarse material of her breeches, and again he was conscious of the desire to kiss those delicate, sensuous lips. Very aware of her quickened breathing and the flush of her cheeks, he leaned closer, hoping she would snap at him so he could turn a kiss into a jest. Instead she remained silent, looking at him with uncertain, wary eyes. And that was all that stopped him. Alex slipped his hand sideways up along her hip, then quickly dug into her pocket to pull out the coins she had captured, and sat back again.

"Damn you!" she snarled belatedly, reaching out to grab his hand.

He held his fist closed while she tried to peel back

his fingers, using the moment to regain his own composure. With his other hand he reached into his own pocket and pulled out a piece of paper, which he dropped into her lap. "Here," he said.

She snatched up the ten-pound note, then looked at him in ruffled suspicion. "What's this for?"

"Next time you decide to go on an adventure, take a hack. Don't go walking about London at night. Not even in Mayfair. It might be safer than Saint-Marcel, but that isn't saying much."

Kit started to speak, then changed her mind about whatever it was she had been about to say. "Worried about me?" she asked instead, looking up at him from under her long, dark lashes and smoothing the paper between her fingers.

"About the criminals, actually." He grinned, counted out the change in his hand, added more coins to it, and returned it to her. Five minutes ago it hadn't been his intention to leave her with any blunt, but returning some money to her was the only excuse he could come up with for touching her. Not that he generally needed an excuse with a woman who placed herself alone with him in a closed carriage, but these circumstances were far from typical. Their fingers brushed again, but he had to make some show of honoring his father's ill-made debt, and reluctantly pulled his hand away. "From the manner in which you continue to bash me, I imagine you can take care of yourself."

She returned his gaze evenly, though a soft blush still colored her cheeks. "You expected otherwise?"

"Not really," he said quietly. The coach pulled to a stop in the drive of Cale House, and a footman came forward to pull open the door. "So do we have an understanding now, cousin?"

Slowly she nodded, then folded the note and put it in her pocket. "Yes. But—"

He held up one hand, and motioned for her to precede him. "We'll discuss it tomorrow."

Chapter 4

❧

"**W**here is my cousin this morning?" Everton queried as he stepped into the entryway, handing Wenton his hat and gloves before motioning his companion to do the same.

"Mr. Riley is taking a bath, my lord," the butler answered, as the earl retrieved the freshly ironed morning edition of the *London Times* from the side table in the hallway.

Alex tucked the paper under his arm and raised an eyebrow. "Another one?"

"Yes, my lord."

The earl gave a slight smile. Dirty as Kit Brantley had been when she arrived, it would likely take a month of baths to wash away the layers of grime. It was a pity she didn't wish her back scrubbed. "Come along, Mr. Lewis."

"Yes, my lord," his companion replied, hefting the satchel he carried with him.

Just outside his study door, Alex stopped. A small flake of white, highly visible against the dark mahogany floor, lay close to the wall. With a glance at Mr. Lewis, he squatted and picked up the speck. It was paint, though he couldn't see a scuff on the wall where someone might have bumped into it. "Wenton," he asked, and heard the butler come up behind him. "Was someone moving furniture?"

"No, my lord."

Alex straightened, then noticed the slight mark on his doorframe at the level of the handle. "And how did my cousin spend his morning?" he queried offhandedly.

"He rose rather late, my lord, and then came downstairs for breakfast."

"And yesterday morning?"

"Reading, I believe, my lord." The butler paused. "Do you wish me to make a daily report, my lord?"

Alex shook his head and set the paint flake into the butler's gloved hand. Apparently the waif hadn't been able to resist the challenge of a locked door. He wondered what she might have been looking for, and whether she'd found anything of interest. It seemed his first hunch had been correct—she wasn't staying at Cale House for protection. Which meant that he was going to have to find out what, exactly, she was doing in London. And until he did, he would have Wenton keep the silver closet locked. With a glance at Mr. Lewis, he proceeded up the curving staircase and rapped at her bedchamber door.

"Yes?" her sleepy reply came.

"Kit," he called softly, "may I come in?"

"No!" Inside the room, water splashed wildly about, and naked skin slid against the brass tub. Alex grinned. Wet feet scrambled about the room, to the accompaniment of several muffled curses. "What do you want?" the girl's breathless voice came after a moment.

"I'd like a word with you," he responded. The mental image conjured by all the noise was very interesting indeed.

"Well, just a moment," she snapped. More rustling sounds followed, and finally the latch rattled. "Yes?" she said, yanking the door open.

Alex opened his mouth to comment on her sloth, but stopped. Kit was out of breath, her lips parted a little in a half scowl. Her hair was loose, hanging in damp, golden waves down to her shoulders, and she had neglected to tuck in her shirt. Her cheeks, flushed from the heat of the bath, were a soft rose, and Alex's breath stilled as he met her eyes. After a long moment she blinked and looked down at herself.

"Oh, blast," she grumbled, and quickly walked to the dressing table to grab a strip of cloth and tie her hair back in its customary fashion. Then she turned away, abruptly bashful, and shoved the tail of her stained shirt into her breeches. "I thought you were abandoning me again today," she said over her shoulder.

"Simply because I choose to continue my regular routine doesn't mean I've abandoned you," he countered, stepping into the room and continuing to watch as she finished dressing. He'd seen women dress and undress a hundred times, but nothing like the waif fastening her breeches before him. It was quite . . . fascinating.

"I rather thought that not going out of one's way was one of the def—" Kit turned around and stopped. She blanched, her eyes seeking Alex's and then flicking to the second figure in the doorway again. "Who are you?" she demanded.

"This is Mr. Lewis," Alex offered, wishing he'd left the man downstairs. "He is my tailor. He is also quite discreet, for it is his business to disguise the knock-knees and hunched backs of several esteemed and vain members of the peerage."

"Mr. Lewis." She nodded, her gaze still shifting uncertainly between them.

"Mr. Riley." The tailor bowed, then looked at the earl questioningly.

"Proceed," Alex said, motioning the small man forward.

"Just a moment," Kit protested, raising one hand to stop the tailor's advance. "What's going on?"

"I thought if you intended to be here for a time, you should have more than one set of clothes," Alex said offhandedly, stepping over to sit in her windowsill. She would need a chaperon, and though he was admittedly a poor choice, he had no intention of missing this.

Kit stopped and stared at him, surprise warring with the suspicion on her face. "But—"

"He knows about your . . . singular condition, cousin.

Humor me." Alex pulled the *Times* from under his arm and leaned back in the deep sill. He snapped the paper open and began reading. Or rather, pretending to read. With his elbow he pushed the window open just a little more, so he could see a reflection of the proceedings.

"I can't pay for this," Kit muttered, still looking at him.

It was the first time he'd heard anything like regret or embarrassment in her lilting voice. He lowered the paper and gave a brief smile. "My gift, then," he replied, and returned to his feigned reading.

Kit took a slow breath, blew it out, then shrugged and nodded at Mr. Lewis. The tailor pulled a measuring tape from his pocket and indicated that she should lift one arm. It was a graceful arm, her long, slender fingers curling just a little as she watched Mr. Lewis. Alex watched closely, as well, though his attention was not on the tailor. Unlike nearly every female he'd ever known, there was no artifice about her, no concern over finding the perfect pose, or turning just so to show off her slim waist to best advantage.

The measuring of her wrist and elbow followed, and Alex continued to watch, amused but increasingly mesmerized. There were unsuspected advantages to being a tailor. It would almost make it worth the disgrace of taking up a trade, to be the one circling her slender wrists with his fingers, and running his palms along her arms. As Mr. Lewis lifted Kit's short tail of hair to slide his measuring tape about her collar, the smile slowly left Alex's face. Delicate tendrils of blond hair curled at the nape of her neck, its gentle curve beckoning his caress, the touch of his lips. He shifted forward and banged the window hard with his elbow, sending her reflection swinging out over the garden.

"Don't fall out the window," Kit advised him, tilting her head to eye him as he settled himself up straighter and, with as much composure as he could muster, returned the window to its former position.

"Just reading about the Bank of London considering American investments," he muttered, lifting the paper again. "Loyalty goes behind commerce, apparently."

As she smiled at the newspaper, the measuring began again. Kit turned sideways while the tailor ran the tape down the length of her spine, and then shoulder to shoulder. Alex relaxed, and even managed a slight grin at her contortions as she sought to keep an eye on Mr. Lewis. Then the tailor motioned her to lift both arms, and stepped forward to wrap the tape about her chest.

Alex licked abruptly dry lips at the faint slither of the tape across the thin cotton of her shirt. Kit shifted uneasily and turned her head toward him again. "Might I have a new hat, as well?" she ventured, with a nonchalance that poorly hid her embarrassment.

"I suppose we can manage a visit to the haberdasher without having to swear him to secrecy," Alex agreed, shifting uncomfortably. Jaded as he considered himself to be he was dismayed to note that he was becoming rather painfully aroused. It was completely unlike him to be feeling so stirred at such a tame sight. After all, he'd seen women in far more advanced stages of undress, and in far less innocent poses. But perhaps it was the innocence of the scene that was so riveting, after all. Kit was not trying to seduce him, but merely to gain herself a new set of clothes. She obviously had no idea what the combination of her body and that damned measuring tape was doing to him—and thank God for that.

The tape slunk downward, tightening again about her waist. Another pencil-scratch of a note followed, and the tape lowered again, settling about her rounded hips. Alex exhaled, remembering the feel of those hips against him when he had first begun to suspect that Kit Riley was a female. The tape slipped a little, and with nimble fingers the tailor slid it back in place. Alex groaned silently. She was stunning, Aphrodite in breeches, and he wanted her. Badly.

Finally Mr. Lewis took a step back, cleared his throat, and knelt. "If you please," he murmured, and attached the top end of the tape to her waist. Swallowing, his hands shaking a little, Alex lowered the paper as the tailor slowly stretched the length of the cord down to

her ankle. He made another notation on his pad. As the
tailor shifted again, raising the tape toward her inseam,
Kit's cheeks colored to a deep rose. She flinched like a
wild deer, catching Alex's eyes with a pleading expression.

"Lewis!" Alex bellowed instantly, lurching to his
feet, the paper crumpled in his hand.

Startled, the little tailor jumped back and turned to
face him. "My lord?" he asked, pushing his spectacles
back onto his nose.

Alex took a breath and shook himself. It would do no
one any good if he charged the poor tailor like a bloody
wild boar. "Use the damned breeches she's got on to
measure the rest," he ordered, and motioned Kit toward
the dressing closet. "There's a robe in there," he grumbled.

She favored him with a swift, grateful smile as she
hurried into the tiny adjoining room. Alex briefly shut
his eyes and leaned back against the sill again. The
breeches flew out of the closet, and the tailor retrieved
them, measured the inseam and the cuff, then, with a
hesitant glance toward the earl, tossed them back again.
"Thank you," came the chit's muffled voice, and a few
moments later she reemerged.

Mr. Lewis made a few last notations, then put away
his tape and wet the end of his pencil with his tongue.
"All right, my lord. What would you like?"

Something he couldn't have, because of a damned
debt of honor. "I think something in gray, though I
leave the details to your discretion. Plus a new shirt and
a half dozen cravats, all for tomorrow." Feeling slightly
more composed, Alex placed his hands behind his back
and eyed Kit speculatively. "By the end of the week I
want two more suits, in blue and a dark green. No
brown. And nothing dandyish, for heaven's sake."

Kit looked over at her brown coat. "Why not
brown?" she asked defiantly.

"I'm bloody tired of seeing you in it. That's why
not," he answered. "For the evening, a black and a dark
gray, I believe. With sufficient shirts and waistcoats and

whatever else my cousin desires to accompany them.''

"Very good, my lord.''

Both of the chit's eyebrows lifted. "*Five* suits?''

Alex sighed. "I suppose this means you'll want five hats and five pairs of boots, as well?''

Kit delayed a moment before she answered. "Could I?'' she asked with a delighted laugh.

He snorted, finally giving in to his urge to chuckle. "No.''

Stewart Brantley sat at a table shoved against the back wall of a small tavern on Long Acre, just north of Covent Garden, and finished a glass of port. The innkeeper had thought him high in the instep for ordering a gentleman's drink, but he had at one time been a gentleman, after all. And at the moment he was a former gentleman who felt in the mood to celebrate.

Some damned lord might have stepped into his affairs once, but he would see to it that it did not happen again. And the fellow he had just parted company from had actually seemed eager to arrange to provide a few empty crates to a stranger in return for a quantity of blunt. A good quantity, admittedly, but not compared to what those filled crates would earn him when passed into the correct hands.

"Stewart,'' a voice called, and Brantley looked up sharply, stifling a surprised curse.

"Fouché,'' he asked in French, first looking about to make certain no patriotically rabid Englishmen were about, "what brings you to London?''

Jean-Paul Mercier looked more like a member of the French nobility than a smuggler, but in fact, he was both. His shoulder-length dark hair was pulled back into a tail at his neck in the current French fashion. The Comte de Fouché nodded pleasantly, and gracefully slid his tall, spare frame onto the bench opposite Stewart. Two other men seated themselves at another table, their presence no surprise. The comte rarely traveled alone.

"I have come to view the sights, of course,'' Fouché returned, also in French, evidently deciding that he didn't wish to risk being overheard in English, either.

"Rather peculiar time for a holiday, wouldn't you say?" Stewart commented, fiddling with the half-empty bottle before him and madly trying to figure out what in the world Fouché was doing there.

"You are not pleased to see me, I think," the comte noted, with a slight pout that made him look younger than his thirty-three years. Fouché pulled the bottle from his companion's fingers, examined the label, and poured himself a drink. "And after I went to such effort to find you."

Stewart glanced at him. "You knew I would be here."

"Yes," Fouché agreed, "but when I learned you had taken young Kit away from Paris with you, I thought perhaps you did not intend to return."

The thought had crossed his mind. "We are partners, Jean-Paul."

"Yes," Fouché agreed, "but you are also a traitor."

Although he doubted anyone in the tavern spoke French, Stewart glanced about and leaned forward. "I am no such thing."

"You provide weapons for soldiers of Napoleon," Fouché pointed out.

"I am providing them to you. What you do with them is your affair."

"Not simply mine, my friend." The soft, cultured voice had dropped into a delicate murmur, but Stewart knew better than to be fooled. Despite his refined looks, the comte was cold as Yorkshire in winter, with no compunctions about killing when the whim struck him. Brantley had seen that on more than one occasion.

He took a breath, measuring his words. "You have nothing to worry about. I am already in contact with someone willing to sell me stockpiled weapons. And Kit is on the trail of the bastard who intercepted the last shipment."

The comte leaned forward, finally interested. "You know who it is?"

"Not yet. But I will, very soon. And we won't be interfered with again."

"No, we won't. You will, of course, inform me of your news."

It was not a request. And, Stewart reflected, it would give Jean-Paul Mercier the sticky task of deciding what to do with their quarry once Kit had found him. Not that Stewart had any love for his former countrymen, but neither did he feel the need to resort to cold-blooded murder. The comte would think it sport. "Of course."

Fouché nodded and sipped his port. "Where do you have dear Kit stashed?"

"In Mayfair," Stewart answered, not wishing to be more specific.

"I do not wish to pry into your affairs, Brantley," the comte commented smoothly. "I am only concerned at your daughter being on her own in London."

It was quietly said, but Stewart Brantley sat bolt upright, whatever he'd been about to say forgotten. "My dau—"

"Do you think I am a complete fool? A very clever little game, but I've known for some time."

Stewart resisted the urge to swallow. "I have had to take certain precautions to insure Kit's safety in these times," he countered. "It was not my intention to fool anyone."

"Of course it was." Fouché gave a slow smile. "And so interesting to discover."

The look in his eyes made Stewart shift a little. "Please remember that you are referring to my child," he said.

"Your daughter is a grown woman." The smile faded. "And until you produce those weapons, you are in debt to me. For ten thousand pounds, Brantley."

"I'll not sell her to you," Stewart growled. Fouché met his gaze with cool eyes, but he refused to look away.

"Perhaps you should reconsider," the comte suggested after a moment, lifting his glass for another delicate sip. "My character is no worse than yours. Better even, perhaps. And I certainly live in more comfort."

He glanced about the dingy tavern, then shrugged, apparently reading Stewart's expression and deciding for the moment not to press the issue. "There is no hurry. We will all be in London for another few days, will we not?"

Stewart Brantley stood and dropped a few coins on the table. "I will provide you with muskets, and with the name you requested. Nothing more."

"We shall see."

Kit turned this way and that in front of her dressing mirror for ten minutes after she finished donning her new attire. The gray day suit was the most marvelous thing she had ever possessed, and she sat and stood and bent and twisted to see how very well the thing fit. The clothes had arrived just in time. After the long night she'd spent last evening tracking Lord Hanshaw from one club to another, with absolutely nothing to prove him to be other than a popular drinking companion, her brown suit was fit to be burned. Finally she couldn't contain herself any longer, and dashed down the hall to Everton's bedchamber. English spy or not, he had a splendid tailor.

"May I come in?" she queried, pounding at the door.

"Please do," came the response.

She threw the door open and pranced in to sweep an elegant bow. Alex sat shaving at his dressing table, Antoine beside him holding a towel. "What do you think?" she demanded.

"I think it's seven o'clock in the morning," the earl responded mildly, lowering his razor and turning to eye her.

"Oh, be quiet," she chastised with a grin. "It is *fantastique*. I am absolutely top of the trees!" She spun about again, laughing.

"You are magnificent," he agreed with a chuckle.

She stepped up to him and thrust her chin forward. "Feel my shirt," she ordered. "It's so soft."

Lord Everton obligingly dried his hand on Antoine's towel, and reached up to touch her collar. As he did so his fingers brushed the skin at the base of her throat, and Kit shut her eyes. After a moment it seemed that he wasn't touching the shirt at all, and his thumb ran softly along the line of her jaw. Her pulse quickened, and she held completely still so he wouldn't stop. His fingers were warm, and they made her shiver. He touched her cheek, and then the fingers jumped a little and swept back to tug at her collar, as though he were straightening it. She opened her eyes again, seeking his, but he turned away to pick up his razor again.

"It's lawn, chit," he said gruffly. "It's supposed to be soft."

Her skin seemed to tingle where he'd touched her. Taking a shaky breath, Kit watched him shave. She rarely paid any attention to her father's morning ablutions, but the movement of the sharp razor across the earl's lean face and the soft, scraping sound that accompanied it were rather mesmerizing. He tilted his head sideways, and she unconsciously imitated him as he contorted his face to stretch the skin of his upper lip. Abruptly there was a spot of red there, and he cursed and threw down the blade.

"Damnation!" he growled, turning to glare at her. "Stop hovering."

"I was not hovering. I was studying."

"Well, stop it. You don't need to learn how to shave."

"Ha, ha. I am slain by your wit." Kit humphed and turned her back, folding her arms.

"You shouldn't be in here, anyway," he continued.

"Why? I thought you didn't care about propriety." She turned to look at him balefully. "And stop being so damned cross. It's only a nick you got. I'm certain it won't even leave a scar."

His jaw twitched before he set his expression into a glare again. "I suppose you'd feel no remorse even if I'd cut off my ear."

She studied the offending body part, and the curl of his dark hair around the line of his jaw. "It would be a shame if you'd lost an ear," she admitted. "Is your wound truly so heinous?'' Kit stepped slowly forward and reached out to touch the side of his face.

Alex grabbed her wrist before she could complete the action. She started to jerk her hand free, but then looked down and met his gaze. And froze. His eyes seemed to draw her in, stopping her breath. Kit found herself wanting to taste him, to kiss his half-amused lips and his lean, soapy cheek, and the lids that were half-lowered over glinting azure.

''You're still hovering, chit,'' he grunted, shoving her back and turning away again.

She took another quick breath, then scowled. ''You sound as though you're afraid of me.''

He snorted. ''I am. I don't want your father saying I've ruined you and have to marry you, or some other nightmare happenstance.''

He might only have been teasing, but it was still a mean thing to say. *''Vous êtes une buse grande,''* she said irritably as she stalked over to sit on the windowsill, well away from him. She tentatively put her fingers on her wrist where he had touched her, to see if the skin was as warm on the outside as it felt on the inside.

''Not that damned French again. Antoine?''

''You are a big buzzard, my lord,'' the valet obligingly translated, stifling a grin as he dumped the remaining shaving soap into a bowl.

''Oh,'' the earl said, returning to his shaving. ''I suppose that means that you don't wish to accompany me to the haberdasher's this afternoon.''

With a surprised smile, Kit sprang to her feet again. Not only did that sound splendid, but she'd been looking for an excuse to get away and meet with her father, anyway. ''I'm sorry, Alex,'' she apologized. ''I was only bamming you.''

''I thought so.''

''May I get a new greatcoat, as well?'' she asked. ''With my new clothes, the old one will look horrid. And I will need some new boots, I think.''

''Good Lord. You're acting like a female, you know.''

Kit raised both eyebrows, hurt. "I am not," she protested, pouting and then slowly looking at him from beneath lowered lashes to see whether she was having any effect on him.

His eyes on her face, Alex set the razor down again, and she thought for just a heartbeat that his fingers might have been shaking. "Oh, for God's sake," he growled. "Go down and get some breakfast before you make me cut my throat."

Everton had actually intended to meet Barbara Sinclair for breakfast later in the morning, but at the last moment, following an impulse he didn't care to delve into, he scribbled out a note with his apologies and headed instead to his own breakfast room.

The servants were surprised to be dismissed from their morning's service, but with Kit currently admiring her reflection in a pair of case knives and clearly in high spirits, one of them was bound to make a slip. The fewer servants who knew the truth about his guest, the less the chance of the gossip getting out to the *ton*.

Alex smiled as she finally returned one of the knives to him and strolled over to the sideboard to begin piling breakfast on her plate. He had given women diamonds that had elicited less response than she had shown upon receiving a coat and pair of breeches, and the sparkle in her eyes was brighter than emeralds. Fleetingly he wondered when someone had last given her a gift.

"So what does this mean?" Kit asked, looking at him. She had stopped loading her plate, though there wasn't much room for anything else there, anyway. Her eyes were cool and sober, and she twirled her fork in her fingers with skilled ease. No doubt she could handle a knife, as well. Hopefully he would not have occasion to find that out firsthand.

"What does what mean?" he responded carefully, setting aside his tea and rising to select his own breakfast.

"You've bought me clothes, and now you've sent the

servants away," she replied evenly. "I was just wondering why."

Several answers came to mind, but instead Alex grinned. "You think I mean to ravish you, chit?"

She shrugged, still eyeing him warily. "Why else would you give me a gift?"

He held her gaze. "That is usually how the game is played," he admitted, beginning to realize just how wide was the gulf between Christine Brantley and every other female in Britain. Bribery and seduction was the order of the day, and there was no reason to question or comment. Unless, perhaps, one happened to be a French-raised chit in breeches. Or an earl who, for no explainable reason, didn't wish to be seen in the same suspicious light in which she apparently regarded the rest of London's inhabitants. "I, however, consider your wardrobe to be merely a defense."

"Against what?"

"Everyone knows you as my cousin," he elaborated. "And now that you've seen fit to introduce yourself to the *ton*, if I keep you locked up here, you'll likely arouse more curiosity than if I show you about a little. And I certainly can't do that with you in those rags. Very clever of you, chit."

"I was only bored." She smiled, apparently satisfied, but he raised a hand.

"I do wish you would stop making trouble for me, waif. I don't appreciate it."

Kit sat and stuffed a quarter of a peach into her mouth. "Yes, you do," she said around the fruit.

"Beg pardon?"

She hurriedly chewed and swallowed. "You do appreciate it."

He took his seat as well. "And what makes you think that?"

"Because you're supposed to be ramshackle, but you're not. Only one mistress, whom you've scarcely seen since I've been here, and you keep your own books. You're the quietest, most organized rakehell I've ever encountered."

For a moment Alex just looked at her while she waited, daring him to contradict her. Upon discovering her secret, he had thought her an absurd, antic waif, but he was beginning to believe he was merely skimming the surface of her rather complicated character. If someone had taught her to be a lady instead of an ill-mannered boy, she would be dangerous. He had the feeling he'd best not forget that, for his own well-being. Especially if she intended on routinely barging into his bedchamber and breaking into his study. And that hadn't been done to see if he kept his own books. "It's been a slow Season," he replied dryly. "And I've lately been hampered with an uninvited houseguest."

"Is that why you haven't had Lady Sinclair back over?"

"I don't believe that's any of your bloody affair, chit." Kit Brantley was exactly the reason Barbara hadn't been back over. He accepted the bowl of marmalade from her. "How many rakehells have you encountered, anyway?" he queried, spreading the jam on his toasted bread.

"Oh, several," she responded, leaning forward to eye the pair of strawberries on his plate.

"Help yourself." He sighed, and with a fleeting grin she stabbed one of them with her fork. "Continue," he encouraged, curious to hear the extent of her experience.

She paused for a moment. "There was one, in Paris, the Comte de Fouché, who used to brag about the number of conquests he made. He had very mysterious eyes."

"You found him attractive, then?" To his surprise, he found himself less than pleased at the notion that the sprite beside him would fall for a pretty fool who bedded a different female every night and then bragged about it in the morning. At least he didn't brag. Not generally.

She squinted one eye. "I don't know. I didn't trust him. It's difficult to like someone you don't trust."

The earl poured himself another cup of tea. "And do you trust me?"

It was an absurd question, and far too soon for him

to be asking it, but she chuckled, and he looked up to see her favoring him with a grin. "I'll trust you more if you buy me a greatcoat."

He laughed. "Is that the entire reason for this pleasant conversation?"

Unexpectedly she sobered again. "I do sound greedy, don't I?" she said quietly, looking down at her overloaded plate. "The last few months with Father, we . . . well, I know I said differently, but things aren't so pleasant in Paris right now."

The pale sunlight through the breakfast room window caught the high, delicate line of her cheekbone, and abruptly she looked quite feminine, and quite lovely. "So I've heard," he said, picking absently at his toasted bread and gazing at her.

She nodded and gestured at her new clothes. "I've been wearing that awful brown rag for months, and fresh fruit is nearly a franc a mouthful, it seems sometimes."

"Is that why your father sent you here?"

She shook her head. "All I know is what he told you, that I'd be safer here for the next fortnight or so."

"Even in breeches?"

Kit glanced up at him. "Especially in breeches."

"Hm," he murmured. "A pity. I would buy you a gown, if you wished it."

She narrowed her beautiful eyes, suspicious again. "You're still being quite nice. Are you certain you're not trying to seduce me?"

He chuckled, wondering how in the world he would go about such a thing if he had been free to do so. Damn all debts of honor. She was astounding. "Believe me, chit, if I were seducing you, you would know it." Everton sat back again and motioned for her to finish her breakfast. "As soon as you've completed devouring that monstrous mound, I'll take you to Colton's."

"Who's Colton?"

"My haberdasher. Who is conveniently located, I might add, directly across the avenue from a shop where they create not only driving gloves, but greatcoats and saddle pouches, as well. Though I doubt you've much need for those, unless you've decided to take up stage robbery." It had occurred to him that the best way to keep an eye on the chit was to keep her close by. If that was simply an excuse to be with her, he wasn't ready to admit it yet.

She smiled, showing no sign that his suggestion of thievery had hit close to the mark, and stood to walk over beside his chair. "Thank you, Alex."

He felt her hesitation, and then she bent down and brushed her lips against his cheek. The touch was achingly soft and delicate, and he half closed his eyes. Slowly he turned to look up at her, and before she could pull away he leaned up and touched his lips to hers. It was a feather-stroke of a kiss, and it jolted his heart. Her own eyes had shut, and surprised, she straightened and opened them to gaze at him.

He forced a careless smile, trying to make himself breathe again. "You're welcome, brat."

Chapter 5

When Kit came across a sterling multicaped black greatcoat that fit to perfection, she expected it would be a difficult, if not impossible, task to persuade Alex actually to purchase it for her. Before she could begin, though, and without even inquiring about the price, Everton simply told the shopkeeper to send him the bill, and she took it away with her.

It was the same with the haberdasher, and with the white kid gloves she wanted, simply because she'd never owned a pair so fine. Her father would applaud her taking advantage of a weak-minded peer, and that would be how she explained her new things to him—but the reality was far more complex. She was pushing Everton, waiting for him to put a condition on the purchases. There was always a condition. She knew the game, for she'd seen it over and over from the men she associated with in Paris. Posies and perfumes were to melt a girl's heart or her sensibilities, while diamonds and jewels were to win the way into her bed. Kit glanced at Alex's profile as they strolled along Bond Street. She didn't know what, exactly, coats and hats were meant to gain him. Despite the growing number of purchases, he hadn't asked for anything. He'd laughed off their quick kiss, and with the number of mistresses he'd apparently had, no doubt it meant nothing to him. She'd spent the morning trying to convince herself that neither did it mean anything to her.

She glanced up the street to see which shops remained, and froze.

Immediately Everton stopped beside her. "What is it?" he queried, his usual veneer of amused ease sliding into the alert intensity she'd sensed in him the night they met.

"Oh, nothing," she returned, forcing a chuckle. It couldn't have been Jean-Paul Mercier watching her from the corner, because the Comte de Fouché was in Paris spouting off about how splendid Napoleon's reforms were. "Is that a sweet shop?"

Alex looked toward the corner, then turned back, studying her face with eyes that could not quite hide the self-assured intelligence lurking behind them. "I am here to protect you, you know," he murmured. "You may trust me."

For a moment she wished she could. She wanted to trust someone. She wanted to trust Alexander Cale. He might even understand that she and her father were merely trying to make a living, had simply taken a step or two out of their depth, and were trying to stay alive. He might even help her find the lord she was after, if he found the idea amusing enough. And he might not. She sighed and turned away. "Protect me from what, rotted teeth?" she said, glancing at the corner again. Fouché, if he had ever been there, was gone.

Alex sighed as well. "What else could I possibly be referring to?"

The question didn't sound quite rhetorical, but she ignored it. "Where shall we go next?" she asked as they reached his phaeton.

"I have meetings," he returned, and she scowled at him, disappointed.

"Who are you, the prime minister?" she retorted. All the meetings he attended certainly sounded suspicious, but she had scoured the mansion twice now during his absences, and other than the blasted map and coins, had found nothing to suggest that he was involved with Prince George's blockade, or with any sort of government activity at all. In another sense entirely, it was almost disappointing to find him so purposeless. She could believe it of someone like Francis Henning, but Francis didn't maintain one of the finest private libraries she'd ever heard of, and Francis hadn't been in her dreams for the last few nights.

"Hardly," he replied, gesturing her up into the carriage. "I am a member of the House of Lords, however."

"I thought rakehells never performed their civic duties," she said, watching him climb gracefully up beside her.

"I make it a point to be late to all civic and social functions," he noted dryly, his glance at her amused. "The more conventional blue bloods find me quite annoying."

She wrinkled her nose. "Father says all blue bloods are worthless."

He raised an eyebrow as he clucked to the team. "You're a blue blood yourself, my dear."

"Shush," she admonished, glancing about again. "I am not."

"You're the Duke of Furth's niece. You're so blue, you're azure."

Like your eyes, she thought abruptly, then took a quick breath and looked away. "I claim no relation to that man."

She felt him look at her, but he said nothing.

"Aren't you going to ask me why?" She frowned, annoyed at his apparent disinterest, even though he already knew far too much about her.

"None of my affair," he answered, pulling out his pocket watch. He glanced down at it, then slipped the watch back inside his waistcoat and urged the team into a canter.

"Well, I'm sorry," she said indignantly, folding her arms. "I have no wish to bore you, of course."

"Are you going to call me some name in French now?" he queried, pursing his lips but still not looking at her.

She actually was considering several choice epithets, when they were hailed by a vehicle on the other side of the street.

"Alexander!"

A white, heavily powdered wig, ten years out of style, was perched perilously over a pair of blue eyes and a waving, monogrammed handkerchief. The femininely gesturing arm was attached to an elderly, formidable-looking woman of such considerable bulk that the other occupant of her barouche was invisible but for a patterned blue muslin skirt.

"Devil a bit," Alex muttered under his breath. "Good morning, Lady Cralling."

"I've told you to call me Eunice, silly boy," Lady Cralling tittered.

"Eunice, of course," Everton replied, favoring the woman with a dazzling smile.

Kit stared at him. It was simply glorious, the way he looked when he smiled like that, but this close she could see that his eyes remained cool and vaguely annoyed. The expression confirmed what she had suspected all along: that he was likely a blistering cardplayer, and the other evening he had only been amusing himself with his cronies. It seemed they could both keep secrets. She wondered again what his might be.

They would have continued on, but the hay cart in front of them lurched to a stop as an orange girl ran out into the street to offer the driver her wares. Lady Cralling likewise thumped the floor of the barouche with her walking cane, and to the annoyance of the line of vehicles behind them, her driver pulled up as well.

"Say hello, Mercia," the woman commanded.

A pale, slender young woman, perhaps a year younger than Kit, sat forward and looked across at them from beneath curling black eyelashes. "Good morning, Lord Everton," she said in a whispery, delicate voice.

"Good morning, Miss Cralling," Alex answered, tipping his hat. He elbowed Kit in the ribs, and she followed suit. "Eunice, Miss Cralling, my cousin, Christian Riley."

"Kit," Christine put in, lifting one foot up against the phaeton's frame and resting her elbow on her bent knee. "Pleased to make your acquaintance, ladies."

"Mr. Riley," the trace of a voice came again, and Kit nodded politely.

"Alexander, you are coming to the Fontaine rout tonight, are you not?" Lady Cralling asked, blinking her lashes so rapidly, Kit thought she must have something in her eye, before she realized the woman was flirting with Everton.

"I have been considering it," Alex offered reluctantly, glancing forward at the hay cart again. His long, elegant fingers twitched as they held the leather reins. He was obviously itching to send the team into a gallop and make an escape. Kit stifled the urge to laugh at him.

"And you, Mr. Riley, will you be attending?" Mercia Cralling asked with a sweet smile.

"Of course," Kit answered, grinning. Compared with her mother, Miss Cralling was the very soul of subtlety.

Alex's jaw tightened, though he otherwise made no movement. He would be angry and would say she was making an annoyance of herself again, but if she didn't take matters into her own hands, she might as well stay up in Everton's attic with his discarded furniture for the next ten days. And she had no intention of doing any such thing.

Finally the orange girl dashed back out of the street, and Everton doffed his hat at the ladies and urged his team forward. "Damn it, chit, you will stop doing that!" he exploded as soon as they were out of earshot.

"Oh," she said, batting her eyes and mimicking Mercia Cralling's soft, cultured tones, "my sincere apologies, of course, Lord Everton."

He whipped his head around to stare at her. "Good God," he said equally softly, an unsettled expression entering his eyes, "you *are* a female."

"You'd forgotten, I suppose?" she replied, lifting an eyebrow.

He gazed at her for another moment, then faced forward again. "A thorn as sharp as you is difficult to overlook, brat."

"Ah. So why do you put up with me?"

"One of my few attempts at propriety."

She glanced up at his profile. The morning breeze sent a lock of his hair straying across his eyes, and absently he lifted a hand to brush the dark strands back from his face. Kit looked away, stifling the dismaying urge to trace the curve of his ear with her fingertips. "Is Miss Cralling another mistress of yours?" she asked instead. "Were you afraid I'd steal her heart?"

His scowl deepened. "I don't bed schoolroom chits," he said, glaring at her, "chit."

"You are pledged to protect my virtue, anyway," she returned, sitting back with her arms crossed, pretending not to be flustered. Everton was damned distracting.

He snorted. "You sound as though you think me a Galahad."

"No," she replied, looking at him hopefully. "But I do think you should let me go with you to the Fontaine rout tonight."

He frowned again. "No," he said flatly.

"Blast it, Alex, why not?"

"Because I said no."

She tried to decipher whether or not he was bluffing. Defying him flat out would only get her asked to remove herself from his premises. She could go elsewhere, but now that she'd made herself his cousin, changing locales would be difficult to explain to the rest of the nobility. Besides, she wasn't ready to leave magnificent Cale House, with its fascinating occupant. "Oh, all right," she grumbled. *"Vieillard étouffant."*

The Earl of Everton cleared his throat.

"Stuffy . . . old . . . man," she translated, enunciating each word to make certain he understood.

Lord Everton nodded. "I'm still young enough that I could take you over my knee, cub." He turned the phaeton onto Park Lane.

She folded her arms. "Oh, I imagine you'd enjoy

that,'' she responded, covering her amusement at the epithet with a scowl.

He grinned wolfishly at her. "You have no idea."

As the white walls of Cale House appeared, she jumped. She'd nearly forgotten she was to meet her father. "Oh, did I remember to tell you, I'm to meet Francis Henning for a game of hazard?" she said in a rush.

He gave an irritated sigh. "I suppose you'll go, anyway. Shall I drive you?"

She was surprised he'd given in. "No. I'll take a hack."

"Be back before dark," he ordered, continuing past the mansion and stopping the carriage by a stand of coaches for hire. "And don't soak Francis, or I'll end up footing his bills for the rest of the month."

She nodded and climbed down, suddenly reluctant to leave his company. "I'll be back soon."

"You'd best be, waif. I don't wish to have to go looking for you." He clucked to the team. "And you're still not going to the Fontaine rout."

She smiled, hoping it wasn't simply his sense of duty speaking, and that he truly was concerned over her well-being. "We'll see."

The tavern her father had selected for their rendezvous was just far enough beyond the fringes of Mayfair that he was unlikely to encounter anyone who might remember Stewart Brantley. They were used to being anonymous. The odd looks she received as she stepped into the Hanging Crow Tavern on Long Acre were therefore unsettling. Only after she spied her father seated close to a back wall did she relax a little. *"Bon jour, Papa,"* she murmured, sinking onto the bench opposite him.

"You look like a damned blue blood, Kit." Stewart Brantley scowled.

"If I don't fit in, no one will speak to me," she countered stiffly. Her clothes were wonderful. And wearing them was the closest she'd felt to being the noble Everton he had said she was, since leaving England thirteen years ago.

"If you're arrested for theft, you won't fit in, either," her father pointed out. He poured her an ale and slid it across the table. "You know better than to be careless."

"I didn't steal them," she retorted, smoothing the sleeve of her coat. "Everton bought them for me."

His fingers paused for a bare moment. "Why?"

"Apparently he felt sorry for me," she answered. She had intended to tell him that the earl knew her secret, but as she looked at her father's already doubtful expression, she decided that enlightening him would only unnecessarily complicate matters. It was likely that he would drag her out of London and back to Paris, and then she wouldn't be able to assist him. There was nothing further involved in her reasoning—and it certainly had nothing to do with Alex Cale. "Said he couldn't take me about London in rags."

"I told you how persuasive you could be," he commented, and leaned forward. "Have you learned anything?"

She shook her head. "A few possibilities, but nothing for certain. Alex seems—"

"Alex?" her father repeated, raising an eyebrow.

"Yes, Alex," she answered. "He's put out that we're cousins." Again, she refrained from informing him that the lie had been her idea. It felt odd, not telling him everything, for she had always done so before. Perhaps it was the whole game of spying. She was becoming too used to twisting truths. Or perhaps, she admitted, she was becoming too intrigued with Alexander Cale. "And he's taken the idea of protecting me to heart. We should've come up with another tale."

He nodded. "I hadn't thought the scoundrel would care."

She sat back and lifted her ale. "I am wearing him down," she commented. "He's taking me to the Fontaine rout tonight."

Finally he smiled. "Splendid."

"And you promised me," she continued slowly. "Once you've settled with Fouché, you won't deal with him any longer."

"I go where the largest profit lies," he snapped. "Fouché was a risk, I admit. But if we're successful, we can go far beyond settling with him."

"If you'd tell me what you were planning, it might make my task a bit easier," she grumbled. "Unless you don't trust me." Kit looked at him sideways, but Stewart Brantley's expression didn't change.

"It's not necessary that you know. And don't question a bad cause at the expense of good money."

"I know, I know." She glanced about to make certain no one was watching them, then touched the back of his hand with her fingers. "I'll find him. Soon."

"I know you will."

"I don't care if it's going to be stupid and boring without your esteemed presence, Kit," Alex commented, "and you can stomp your feet or throw a tantrum or whatever childish thing you wish to do. I'm not changing my mind. You're not going."

Kit glared at him. She'd been after Everton for better than an hour now, since he'd returned from the afternoon session of Parliament, and she still hadn't worn him down. "You can't make me stay, and I'm not childish."

He raised an eyebrow. "Yes, I can, and yes, you are." Alex turned around, dismissing her, as Antoine availed him of his splendid gray evening coat.

"This is beyond belief!" Kit stomped her foot and harrumphed. When that failed to gain his attention, she grabbed his fine kid gloves off the dressing table and threw them on the floor. *"Vous êtes un bravache gros!"*

Alex glanced at her reflection in the mirror. "Antoine?"

"You are a big bully, my lord."

"Vous êtes un bravache arrogant!"

"You are an—"

"I understood that one."

Kit recognized the tone of his voice, and his irritated expression. She'd pushed him too far again. He turned on her, and with a curse she spun around to flee. She had barely made it into the hallway when his hand clamped down on one shoulder in a hard and unbreakable grip. Alex spun her around. "So I'm arrogant, am I?"

"Un bravache arrogant," she repeated clearly.

He wrapped both hands around her upper arms and forced her backward. She tried to stand her ground, but despite her efforts, he continued to push her until her spine came up against the wall. She could have kicked or bitten him, should have done so, but in the face of those glinting eyes she could only lift her chin defiantly.

"An arrogant . . . bully," he translated. "Care to apologize?"

In the dim lamplight, the eyes gazing down at her were almost black. His long-fingered hands were warm through the thin material of her shirt as he held her pinned, for she hadn't yet donned her own coat. *"Vous êtes un bravache, et vous avez les yeux beaux."* *You are a bully, and you have beautiful eyes.* If he'd had an inkling of French, she would have been doomed, but she couldn't help saying it, anyway.

His lips twitched. "Translate," he demanded.

"Jamais!" she responded gleefully, more relieved than she cared to admit. "Death first."

For a long moment he looked down at her, several emotions running across his lean features, then, with an exasperated snort, he released her. "You are an impossible annoyance. Go get your coat, chit. And you will behave tonight."

"Oh, thank you! Thank you, Alex!" She ran for her bedchamber. As she turned away, she failed to notice the slight smile that touched her host's lips as he returned to his own bedchamber.

"You stay close by," Everton muttered to his companion out of the side of his mouth. He smiled and stepped forward to greet Lord and Lady Fontaine, their host and hostess for the evening.

"Make me," his confederate said in the same tone, apparently having forgotten Alex's threats and warnings of the past thirty minutes.

"Harold, Elizabeth, allow me to introduce my cousin, Christian Riley," Alex offered. Kit stepped forward to shake the baron's hand and kiss the baroness's with her usual boldness. "Kit, Lord and Lady Fontaine."

"So pleased you could come, Lord Everton, Mr. Riley." Elizabeth smiled, and gestured them to join the rest of the guests in the main ballroom.

"Oh, this is wonderful," Kit breathed, gazing about the crowded room. She reached up to her collar, then glanced at him. "Is my cravat tied correctly?" she whispered.

"It's perfect," he returned, stifling the urge to wrap his arm around the chit's neck and drag her back home before she did something foolish. Or dangerous. Instead, he reached out and flicked a speck of dust from her lapel.

It had occurred to him earlier that, whatever her motivation for wanting to attend the rout, she was correct—over the last few days he had begun to behave like a stodgy, overprotective old boor. Despite that, and somewhat to his consternation considering he had no idea why she was truly in London, he was at the same time discovering that he seemed to be completely incapable of resisting any request, demand, or wish the waif might make.

"All right," he sighed, "go amuse yourself. But do be careful. Not everyone would be pleased to learn of your . . . uniqueness." Nor would everyone look kindly on him if the farce was discovered.

She leaned up toward him, and for a moment he thought she was going to kiss him, right in the middle of the Fontaine rout. And he was disappointed when instead she pulled a cigar out of the inner pocket of his coat and tucked it into her own.

"What happened to 'don't talk, don't walk, just stand in the corner, behind the draperies, and observe'?" she asked.

"I belatedly realized that as a rakehell, it is my duty to defy polite society by whatever means necessary," he answered, his eyes still on her half-smiling lips, wanting to taste them again. "Tonight, dear one, this means you."

"*Merveilleux!*" she chortled gleefully, then touched his sleeve. "That means 'marvelous.' I'll see you later."

He watched as she strolled off in the direction of the punch bowl. The fact that she knew no one in the room, and almost nothing about the blue-blooded society she found herself in, presumably had no effect on her. Apparently Kit Brantley was afraid of nothing. And though that, too, brought into question her reasons for seeking him out, he couldn't help the smile that touched his lips. She was afraid of nothing, that was, other than whether her cravat was *de trop*.

Francis and Reg intercepted her at the refreshment table, and Alex relaxed a little. They would keep her clear of anything completely unsavory, if for no other reason than to avoid facing the ire of her cousin.

"So, my devil, you haven't frightened young Christian away yet?" The sultry voice of Lady Sinclair sounded behind him.

"Barbara." He turned and reached down to take her hand. Her gown was a deep, blushing violet that didn't even bother to pretend to be demure. The daring scooped neck, with its border of filmy black lace, captured and lifted her full breasts, absolutely demanding that a gentleman's eyes be drawn to them. "No," he replied, obliging. "Kit insists that I cannot possibly be as vile as everyone says."

She gave a low chuckle. "Little does he know. Dance this waltz with me, Alex, before I expire from bore-dom."

He nodded. "Of course, my lady."

They stepped out onto the floor as a waltz began. Barbara smiled silkily up at him. "You haven't yet told me how ravishing I look this evening."

"You look ravishing," he replied obediently, returning her smile.

"Thank you," she purred. "I had the dress made with you in mind."

It seemed they'd had this same conversation before,

but the conclusion was invariably satisfying, so he was willing to play along. "Then I trust you are wearing nothing underneath?"

She gave a sultry chuckle. "You are a devil, Alex."

They would have to go to Lady Sinclair's town house for the night, for the way Kit tended to barge into his bedchamber, the chit might receive more of an education than her father had intended. Of course, if he left the girl to her own devices at Cale House for the entire night, there was no telling what mischief she might get into. He might return home and find that she'd turned the place into a faro palace to keep herself in waistcoats and cravats.

"What are you smiling at?" Barbara asked.

He blinked and looked down at her. "Beg pardon?"

"You were looking terribly amused about something."

"Oh. Apologies," he muttered.

"You should apologize. I was in the middle of telling you that Edith Denton's pet fox got out of its pen and was hunted down and killed by Viscount Harriston's hounds the other day. The poor woman was devastated."

Alex's lips quirked. "I'm certain Foxy was devastated, as well."

Barbara cuffed him on the shoulder. "Naughty man," she chided. "Harriston did offer her the tail. I believe she's going to have it put on a hat."

He smiled, glancing over at the refreshment table to see who Kit might be amusing herself with at the moment. She wasn't there, and he looked toward the orchestra in the corner. The chit wasn't there, either, and he frowned. The gaming room wouldn't open until after dinner had been served, so she couldn't be up there.

"Damnation," he muttered.

"What is it?" Barbara asked, a slight scowl creasing her porcelain features.

"My cousin. I seem to have misplaced him, and he's a devilish lot of trouble. Did you see where he might have van—"

Abruptly he saw her. There she was, not twenty feet

away, waltzing, *waltzing,* with Mercia Cralling. The chit spied him looking at her, and gave a wicked grin and a nod.

"That damned . . ." he muttered under his breath. The waif was a graceful dancer, he noted grudgingly. Better than half the gentlemen in the room.

"Mr. Riley has made a conquest, I think," Barbara purred.

"Apparently," he grumbled, his attention still on the girl.

"A shame Caroline begged off attending tonight," Lady Sinclair commented. "I've been telling her all about your cousin. She won't admit it, but I think she's quite curious to meet him."

"You don't know anything about my cousin, so how could you be gossiping about him?" Alex returned, more sharply than he intended. Damn the chit, she was making him demented.

"I know enough," Barbara supplied, her tone faintly surprised. "He is your cousin, his father sent him for you to look after while he is traveling, he's a bit rough about the edges, plays a fair game of faro, and you're quite fond of him. Besides the fact that he's exceptionally well favored."

So he hadn't been the only one to notice that about young Mr. Riley. "He's too young for you," he said.

"That's unkind." Her dark eyes cooled. "Apologize."

"Don't play games, Barbara." The waltz ended, and he turned to look for Kit again.

She sniffed. "Unless you apologize, the only game you play tonight will be solitaire."

He smiled humorlessly. "I believe that's your game for the evening. I shall simply find another player."

"Boor," she snapped. "Why can't you apologize?"

"Because I don't have to," he replied, and turned and strolled away. It was true. He didn't need to extend himself, because she had more need of his wealth than he had of her company. Especially tonight. When he turned around to find her, Kit was back laughing with Reg and

Francis and toting a spare glass of punch, presumably for Miss Cralling.

"I shall have to reexamine my family tree," a dry male voice came from behind him. "I don't recall being related to a Riley of any sort."

A glass of port appeared over his shoulder, and Alex accepted it without turning around. "Don't you remember Aunt Marabelle marrying that Irish circus performer? That"—he gestured in Kit's direction—"is the unfortunate result."

A tall, well-built man, a few years older than Alex, stepped up beside him. The dark hair was beginning to recede a little, and the light blue eyes were full of interest and curiosity as he gazed at Kit. "We don't have an Aunt Marabelle."

On Alex's other side a slim hand tucked around his arm. "I do like the circus," an amused female voice said. "Is this one an acrobat?"

"A bear baiter," Alex answered, smiling down at the petite, auburn-haired woman. "If I can get him over here, I'll introduce you."

If Alex had been alone, he was certain the chit would never have left the circle gathering around her. Seeing, though, that he had company, it only took a few gestures and a commanding glare to convince her to come away from the crowd and join him. "I'm having a splendid time, cousin," she said in her low lilt, her eyes dancing.

"No doubt," Alex replied dryly. "Kit, you remember our cousin Gerald Downing and his wife, Ivy, don't you?"

Kit actually blinked. "Why, yes. Father's spoken—"

"Mother's spoken," Alex corrected smoothly.

It didn't faze her. "No, Father's spoken of Mother's family to me, many times." Kit leaned over and put a hand on Gerald's sleeve to look at him from beneath her lowered brow. "Mother has died, you know."

"Oh, dear, poor Marabelle," Gerald exclaimed, glancing at his wife. "Did we send flowers, my love?"

"Oh, no," Ivy replied, shaking her head. "Marabelle was allergic, Gerald."

"She was dead, sweetest. I don't think she would have minded."

Kit was looking from one to the other of them, her expression wavering between amusement, caution, and complete bewilderment. "Am I being bammed?" she asked after a moment.

"Rather." Gerald reached out and shook her hand again. "Pleased to meet you, whoever you might be." He looked over at Alex. "So who is he?"

Alex glanced about to make certain no one else was near. "She," he corrected softly.

"She?" Ivy repeated at a whisper, turning to look at Kit all over again.

Kit was glaring at him, and he was certain if she'd had a pistol, she would have shot him. "I can't believe you told them!"

"Gerald is my cousin. It's not as though they didn't know something was about."

"You never told me you had cousins."

"You didn't ask."

"You bloody well should have said something, anyway."

"Are you certain he's a she?" Gerald put in mildly. "He curses rather well for a female."

"Thank you," Kit returned, her angry green eyes still on Alex.

"She's the daughter of a family friend," Alex said slowly, holding the girl's gaze. "I'm keeping her safe for a few days. No one else must know."

"Well, I'm to dance with Lydia Calloway now," Kit said after a moment, her expression easing somewhat. "Unless there's someone else to whom you wish to divulge my secrets?"

"May I claim a waltz with you later in the evening?" Ivy queried. "I should like to become better acquainted."

Kit gave her a short nod. "If you wish."

"Good God," Gerald muttered when she was gone. "And you've no designs on her?"

"Other than wanting to strangle her every few moments, none at all," Everton lied, clenching his jaw as Augustus Devlin appeared from the doorway and draped his arm over Kit's shoulder to greet her. She chuckled at something he said. He was drunk, again, and for the first time Alex found himself less than sympathetic. "I'm to keep her safe and pure. On my honor."

"How does she clean up?" Gerald continued, looking after her.

Alex shrugged. "I have no idea. I've never seen her as a female."

"Well, that's a blessing, anyway," Ivy murmured, turning away to greet another acquaintance and leaving Everton to wonder what, exactly, she might be implying.

It was past two-thirty in the morning when the coach came around to pick them up and deliver them back to Cale House. Kit sat back in the deep, cushioned seat and rolled Alex's stolen cigar between her fingers before she lifted it to sniff the deep, rich scent. "I liked Ivy," she stated.

"Yes, I'm rather fond of her myself," he returned, settling himself opposite her. "And no, she's not one of my mistresses."

"I wasn't going to ask." Kit yawned. "I am dead on my feet." She sighed, stretching her legs out beside his seat in the coach and flexing her toes inside her boots. "I don't know how those chits can stand to be in those awful pointy-toed shoes for so long. I'd rather go barefooted."

"Perhaps you shouldn't have danced so much, then," Alex suggested, his gaze on her feet beside his thigh. As the carriage passed under the gas lamps lining the street, his face was briefly illuminated and then disappeared into blackness again.

"I don't see how you possibly could have noticed how many dances I participated in, when you were so busy partnering with every female in sight," she countered. Barbara Sinclair had obviously spent most of the evening being annoyed at him before she had stalked off, but with every other woman, he had been charming and gracious. Every other woman except for her. He had badgered her incessantly, reminding her to watch herself and not be so friendly with everyone, as though she hadn't done this sort of thing since she was six. And she had two more leads now, nearly as promising as Reg Hanshaw and Everton. Both Sir Thadius Naring and Lord Lindley had recently received government appointments involving Bonaparte and France. She just didn't know what, exactly, those appointments were—yet.

"I didn't dance with Celeste Montgomery. I believe you stole her from me," he commented from the darkness.

She wished she could see his expression, for his dry voice was exceedingly difficult to decipher. "Celeste prefers younger men," she answered.

"Gads, Kit," he returned, and this time she could hear the amusement in his tone. "You fooled all of them. It was quite spectacular."

"Thank you, milord," she drawled, sniffing the cigar again.

"Do you intend to smoke that?" he asked after a moment.

She shook her head. "I just like the smell."

He chuckled at her answer, and an unexpected slow, shivering curl trailed down her spine at the low, masculine sound. Alex shifted a little in the dark, his thigh brushing her foot, and she found herself listening to the sound of his breathing. Her fingers shaking a little, she sat forward and held the cigar out to him. She felt his hesitation before he reached out and took it from her. Their fingers brushed, and the curl tightened deliciously.

"You don't want it?" he murmured, lifting the cigar himself and breathing in its scent.

His low, soft voice seemed to resonate along her breastbone, her heartbeat speeding in response. "No, but may I borrow it again sometime?"

He tucked the smoke back into his pocket and chuckled again. "Of course."

"So why aren't you with Barbara Sinclair right now?" she asked, then wished she hadn't spoken.

Unexpectedly Alex wrapped both hands about her left ankle and shifted it across his thigh. His long-fingered hands began kneading her tired calf muscles through her boots and breeches. "She says I'm a boor. I imagine it will be more than a day before she forgives me."

"Are you going to marry her?" She should be protesting against his intimate touch, but if she did, he might stop. And she did not want him to stop.

In the dark she felt more than saw him shake his head. "No."

He tugged her leg toward him, and she slid down a little in the seat. Kit shut her eyes, concentrating on the feel of his hands moving slowly along her leg, and the little shivers running from her scalp all the way down her spine. She tilted her head back, feeling the accelerated beat of her heart. "Does she know that?" she breathed, having a difficult time keeping her voice steady.

"I believe she knows my views on marriage." His hands kept up their rhythmic, circular kneading.

"Are you certain?" she pursued, to keep his thoughts elsewhere. She wanted to feel his fingers on her bare skin, his lips on hers again, and not in some kiss he could dismiss with a laugh. Her breasts tightened, scratching against the material that bound them so tightly. "You don't prefer boys after all, do you?"

He chuckled. "No." His fingers stilled. "But I did try it once," he finally murmured, so quietly she nearly didn't catch the words.

Kit took a ragged breath and pulled herself upright again. The fingers slowly released her leg, and she placed both feet firmly on the floor of the coach. "Boys?" she asked, grateful it was dark so he wouldn't see the hot flush that colored her cheeks.

"Marriage." In the fleeting lamplight, his face was turned to the window.

"You? What happened?" Christine felt the coach turn onto Park Lane, but she sat quietly, waiting for him to continue.

"She died," he continued after another pause. "We'd

only been married a few months when she caught a fever. She was quite . . . delicate, even before that, and she died just a few days later.''

"What was her name?''

"Mary. Mary Devlin Cale.''

"Devlin?'' Kit repeated slowly.

He nodded. "Augustus's younger sister.''

"That's what he meant then, when he said loaning me ten quid was all in the family.'' She'd sensed that night that there was something between the two men, but had never imagined it would be Alex's dead wife. "How long ago?''

"It's been nearly three years now.''

"I can see why you didn't want me in your home, Alex,'' Kit offered. "It must be awful, to have me there to remind—''

Alex snorted. "Good Lord, Kit, I'm not some depraved hermit. I didn't want you in the house because you're a nuisance, and because you charmed every other female in sight and irked me so much this evening that I snapped at Barbara, and now I have to sleep alone tonight. Again.'' He stood as the footman pulled open the door. "I didn't expect, however, that I'd like your company. I'm going to the horse auctions tomorrow. If you want to come, be ready by nine.''

Kit smiled a little shakily as he stepped down from the carriage and entered the house. He'd actually offered to let her spend the day with him, without her having to beg him first. Kit chuckled as she stepped to the ground and skipped in a very unmasculine fashion for the door, the tiredness in both legs forgotten. It was only after she climbed into bed that she realized what a splendid opportunity the auctions would be to follow up on her leads.

Chapter 6

"How is it that you know of Gentleman Jackson's, but you've never heard of Vauxhall Gardens?" Everton queried.

Members of the *ton* and *demi ton* thronged the horse auctions. Beside him Kit watched the collection of horse lovers, pigeons, hawks, and eccentrics with an acute interest, and Alex reflected that until he learned more of her reasons for being in London, he likely shouldn't have asked her along. The chit had been dousing him with striking imitations of Yorkshire, Northumberland, and Cornwall accents all morning, but he had the impression that she was simply amusing him while her attention was on some other task entirely.

"Well, I know how to box," she replied, climbing up onto the bottom rail of the pen, "but I've never had a garden. How long have you known Hanshaw and Devlin?"

He laughed. "We went to Cambridge together. And Vauxhall is more an amusement park than a garden, dear one. Music, fireworks, dancing, drinking, gambling, all the stuff of life."

"You must take me, then," she demanded, swinging one arm away from the fence to look at him.

Alex gazed at her steadily. "I'd like nothing better," he returned, watching her mobile expression as she gauged his words to decide whether he was engaging in some sordid innuendo.

With her feet on the rail they were almost exactly the same height, her face close in front of his. "Libertine," she charged, correctly guessing his meaning.

"Not according to you," he pointed out. Her lips were favoring him with a slight, sensuous pout, and he wondered what he would have done with her if she'd come into his life five or six years ago, when his reputation for wildness had been edged with significantly more truth. He'd been considerably less wise then, and less given to considering the consequences of his actions, both to himself and to others. But he did know one thing. He would have dissolved the conditions of the debt of honor long before now, and would have used every bit of his much-touted skills in seduction to maneuver the tantalizing Kit Brantley into his bed.

"Are they political?"

He blinked. "Are who political?"

"Reg and Devlin, of course."

She swung back to face the enclosure again, leaving him to look at her very attractive backside and to take a deep breath. This was beginning to become rather complicated. "About as political as I am," he replied absently, then gave a slight frown. "I do hope you're not thinking of bringing them into your little game," he commented, disliking the idea of her sharing her secret with anyone else. He was becoming territorial, it seemed. "They'd not be as open-minded about this as I am."

"I'm not going to tell anyone," she retorted, glancing over her shoulder at him, a disgusted expression on her face. "I leave that to you."

"Just remember that you must be careful," he pursued. "If I guessed about you, someone else could, as well."

"I *am* careful."

"No, you're clever," he corrected. That caught her attention, and she swiveled to look at him again. "Don't mistake one for the other."

"You surprise me, Everton. Was that a compliment?" she asked, green eyes twinkling.

"Not entirely," he said grudgingly. "A little one, perhaps."

"Well, then, a mild thank you, my lord," she said, granting him her fleeting grin.

It did not help his equilibrium. "Humph. So who taught you to box?"

"Father," she returned. "He's *fantastique*."

"Ah," Alex commented, amused again. "And you? How do you fare in the ring?"

"Oh, he's never actually let me try," Kit answered. From her expression, her father's unwillingness had not sat well. "I did hand the Comte de Fouché a flusher once."

"Wasn't he the French rakehell you mentioned the other night?"

She nodded. "He wasn't at all pleased, but he was being quite arrogant. Bonaparte this, and Bonaparte that. I apologized, but he gave me odd looks all evening. For a bit I thought he would call me out, but he never did."

"Perhaps he realized your true nature," Alex suggested, but she shook her head.

"I don't see how he could have. I gave him a splendid shiner."

Alex chuckled and leaned up against the fence next to her. She smelled faintly of soap, and he sidled a little closer, breathing in the clean scent of her. "So you share your father's sentiments regarding Napoleon, then?"

She nodded. "They should have strung the bastard up, instead of setting him away like a toy soldier and expecting him to gather dust."

Her words so very nearly echoed what he had expressed to a small group of friends just under a month ago that it gave him pause. The humor had left her eyes, and she was clearly serious. Or at least he thought she was. She was a good liar, and he knew her father had little love for Britain. She herself had been raised French. And with a war on, no Englishman would be caught expressing support for Bonaparte these days, anyway. "You simply exude patriotism, my dear," he drawled, eyeing with disinterest a bay gelding being led about the yard.

"If he were marching on Everton or Charing or whatever else you own, you'd take it more seriously," she retorted, resting her chin on her crossed arms and pointedly not looking at him.

By God, she was lovely. "Heavens," he gasped in mock horror, "you think Boney wants my barley crop and my pottery barns? I must plead with Prinny for assistance at once. Perhaps a squad of Royal Grenadiers will keep my sheep from being conscripted into the French army's stomach."

She blew out her breath in a snort, sucking in her cheeks to keep from laughing at him. "Fresh fruit's more to their liking than barley."

He raised an eyebrow. "You have studied the dining habits of Bonaparte's troops? How diligent of you."

Kit glanced at him, something flashing in her eyes. It brought him to immediate alertness. "It's easy to know," she returned after a very slight hesitation. "Just look to see what's most scarce on the streets of Paris."

"Of course," he said mildly, waiting for her to say something else, something that would explain why, for a moment, she had looked as though she regretted having spoken.

From the first he'd thought she might be a thief of some sort, sent by her father to rob him or the rest of the peerage. But no one from the soiree last night, or anywhere else she'd been, had so much as mentioned a missing watch fob.

She pointed her chin toward the yard. "Are you going to buy me a horse now, cousin?"

"I believe I've an adequate selection for you already," he replied dryly, aware that she was changing the subject. "Gerald's asked me to keep an eye out for a good pair for his coach."

He looked into the enclosure again. As he did, he caught sight of a young woman watching them from across the pen. She was slim and blond and very attractive, and, he noted after a startled, slightly offended moment, her admiring and speculative gaze was not on him. She was trying to catch Kit's eye. With a curse he grabbed the chit by the coattails and pulled her off the railing.

"Damnation, Alex, you gave me a splinter," she protested, staggering backward and looking completely astounded at his behavior.

Unmindful of her protest, he wrapped his fingers around her arm and yanked her toward his coach. "We're going," he snapped.

She pulled against him. "I don't want to go."

"I'm not giving you a choice." He was ready to pick her up and carry her bodily to the carriage, but apparently realizing he was serious, she stopped struggling.

"What's wrong with you?" she grumbled, looking sideways at him as he pulled her through the crowd. The disturbance garnered them a few looks, but by this time everyone had heard what a troublesome lad his cousin was, and they mostly received knowing nods and chuckles.

"Nothing at the moment," he said brusquely, waving an arm at his coachman. "And I wish to keep it that way."

"Well, stop dragging me about, then. I'm coming."

Alex hesitated, then released his tight grip on her arm. "Apologies," he grunted. She must think he'd lost his mind. "I didn't intend to maim you."

Kit lifted her hand to gaze at her finger. "It's only a prick, but I believe I shall require a new pair of gloves."

"Fair enough." He smiled briefly, relaxing as they neared the coach.

"Everton!"

Alex jumped at the sound of Reg's voice calling from the crowd, then grabbed on to Kit again when she slowed. "Come on," he hissed.

"Alex!" the voice came again, and Lord Hanshaw emerged from the spectators. "And Kit! Splendid to see you here!"

"Hanshaw," Kit acknowledged with a grin, yanking free of Alex's grip and stopping.

Alex swore under his breath. If he had any sense, he would simply make his excuses and let the next few moments unfold in his absence. He apparently had none left at all, though, for he strolled back beside Kit to shake Reg's hand.

"I nearly thought I'd missed you. Wanted you to meet someone, you know." Hanshaw gestured behind him, and the beautiful young woman stepped toward them, her maid in tow. "Kit, Lady Caroline. My lady, you know Everton, and this is his cousin, Kit Riley. The one Barbara's been pestering you about."

"Lady Caroline. Honored." Kit smiled, bending over the lady's gloved hand and brushing Caroline's knuckles with her lips. Alex waited for lightning to strike one of them dead. Instead, Caroline gave a pretty smile and retrieved her hand.

"I am pleased to finally make your acquaintance, Mr. Riley," she said in her warm voice. "Everyone's been raving about you for days."

"Well, I'm certain most of it's lies," the chit answered with a charming smile, inclining her head.

Alex stepped forward to take Caroline's hand, as well. "Oh, please," he muttered in Kit's direction. Immediately he regretted saying anything she might hear, because of course, it would only encourage her.

Kit glanced at him, daring him to intervene, and spoke again to Caroline. "I have heard some very flattering things about you, my lady," she continued, "though I see now that the arrows have all fallen quite short of their mark."

Caroline chuckled. "Your cousin is a better flatterer even than you, Lord Everton."

Kit glanced at Alex, and he could see the speculation there. She was wondering if he was courting Caroline, as well. Or something more intimate. Alex gave a smile that he hoped didn't look too pained, and inclined his head to concede defeat and hopefully end a contest before it could begin.

"You see, my lady, I told you he was a charmer," Hanshaw put in, apparently not minding that the woman he was determined to marry was enjoying another's flirtation.

"Yes, he is," Alex seconded, stepping up to take Kit's arm securely in his own. "And I offer my sincere apologies, but I'm frightfully late for an appointment. We must be going." He caught Reg's quick, curious look, but kept his face blank.

"Kit can stay here with us," his friend said unhelpfully. "We'll see he gets home."

"Oh, that's splendid," Kit agreed gleefully. "You're slap up to the echo, Hanshaw, really you are."

"Sorry, Reg," Alex put in even more firmly, not releasing his grip on Kit's arm, despite her tugging to get away from him. "But I need my cousin with me. It concerns those papers your father sent with you, don't you recall, Kit?"

Kit glanced at him sideways, obviously trying to decipher what he was trying to tell her. "Oh, dash it, Alex, all right," she grumbled, turning to follow him. At the last moment she turned back again and tilted her hat. "Good day, Lady Caroline. I do hope we shall encounter one another again."

Caroline smiled. "Perhaps we shall, Mr. Riley."

Before Alex could give in to the urge to throttle his charge, the chit had turned back and climbed into the coach. He nodded at Hanshaw and Caroline, and stepped up after her. "Just drive," he snapped at Waddle, and the coachman nodded. Alex pulled the door shut and sat as the carriage rocked forward.

Kit was chuckling. "Do you think I could steal her from Reg?" she queried, pulling off her glove to examine the hole in one soft kid finger. "She was lovely."

"Too well mannered," he replied, folding his arms and debating whether to tell the spitfire across from him exactly who Lady Caroline was.

"And her docility is the reason you looked as though you were having an attack of apoplexy, then?"

"If I were suffering from such a thing, you would be the cause of it. And it would be my own fault, because I've known all along what a damned lot of trouble you are." He sighed irritably. "And by the way, just what do you know of Lady Caroline?"

"Oh, heavens, Alex, stop being such a deuced bore. It's not as though I intend to marry her."

"I should hope not," he returned after an astounded pause—no one had ever called him a bore before. "She's Caroline Brantley. The Duke of Furth's daughter. Your cousin, cousin."

Christine's face went white. She stared at him for a moment, then put one hand over her mouth. "Stop the coach," she muttered, shutting her eyes.

Concerned, Alex sat forward and touched her knee. She was shaking. And he was a callous idiot. "Kit, I'm sor—"

"Stop the coach," she repeated, doubling over her lap. "I'm going to be sick."

"Kit . . ." He stopped his apology as she sagged further, her color alarmingly gray. "Waddle, stop! Now!" he bellowed.

The coach lurched to a halt, and he flung open the door. Kit flew out under his raised arm, and proceeded to vomit into the gutter. Alex stood where he was for a moment, then jumped down to stand beside her. They were not in the best part of London, and he glanced cautiously at the teeming avenue and the gaggle of curious spectators looking to see which peer was retching in the streets. He saw no one he was acquainted with, but with the Everton crest emblazoned on the side of the coach, he decided it would be unwise to put his arm around her or scoop her up to carry her back into the carriage, no matter what unexpected chivalrous thoughts were running through his brain. Good gossip always got out. If there was one constant in London society, it was that. So instead he sat beside her.

"Don't do that," she muttered miserably, straightening after a moment and wiping her mouth.

"Don't do what?"

"Don't sit there."

"Why not?"

"You're the Earl of Everton. You're not supposed to sit in the gutter."

He smiled, then gave a chuckle. "You are assuming, of course, that I have never had occasion to cast up my accounts in an untimely manner and in a less than private place."

She sighed and unexpectedly leaned back against his thigh, so that he wanted to reach up and curl his fingers through her blond hair. First that peck on the cheek, and now she was actually leaning on him. And he was noting each moment of trust she showed in him as though he were measuring out precious gems. One of them was behaving quite foolishly, and he didn't think it was Kit Brantley.

"Why didn't you tell me sooner who she was?" she asked accusingly.

"I was hoping to get you out of London without ever running across her. I hadn't realized you were going to become the toast of the *ton*, and that, of course, she would want to meet you."

"I remember her from when we were children. She always used to try to take my favorite doll. She was lovely, though, wasn't she?"

Kit leaned back farther, her spine against his ribs. He wondered if she could feel the beat of his heart against her back. It would have been quite easy, and natural, for him to put his arm around her shoulder, and he sternly resisted the notion. Gads, Barbara would be teasing him for being a schoolboy. "Apparently looks run in your family," he noted softly.

She sat forward, and he wondered if she considered the compliment to be stepping too far. She twisted to hit him quite soundly on the arm. "Why in damnation didn't you warn me? You knew Francis and the others have been trying to set us together since I met them."

She'd likely left a bruise. And that wouldn't be the first one she'd marked him with. He shook his head, torn between awe at the resilience of her character and genuine contrition, rare though that emotion was for him. "I'm sorry, Kit. I should have."

"Now I've flirted with her, and practically promised her a dance at the next soiree." She blanched again. "Oh, good God, what if she falls in love with me?"

Alex quickly stifled his amusement as inappropriate. "Kit, I don't think—"

She shot to her feet. "And Father will be furious."

"Your father is in Paris," he countered, somewhat surprised by the strength of her reaction. A liar and a thief, she might well be, but apparently one damned loyal to her father. "There's no reason he should find out. And Caroline will never know you were anything but a charming flirt." He stood and gestured her back to the coach. "Come, my dear, you look in fair shape. Do you feel all right?"

She nodded. "As long as I don't think about it."

"Then don't," he returned practically. "Care to join me for lunch at White's?"

She climbed into the coach and slid over to huddle in the far corner. "I don't have much of an appetite."

"Are you certain?" he cajoled, resuming his own seat. "I'll take you anywhere you like—Boodles, the Traveller's, the Society, even."

That roused a look of slight interest, but then she sat back and shut her eyes. "I think I'd just like to lie down, if you don't mind."

He nodded, pretending not to be concerned, and rapped on the door. "Waddle, home."

Whatever it was that had happened between Stewart and Martin Brantley, it was obvious that Kit took it very seriously. Fleetingly Alex wondered if their familial troubles might be the reason she'd been left to her own devices in London. He hoped that was it. Not that a family feud excluded her from participation in other, more nefarious activities, but it seemed a reasonable explanation. "If you don't mind my asking, what exactly was it that Furth did to your father?"

The green eyes opened and looked at him for a moment before they shut again. "You told me you weren't interested."

"Nonsense," he countered. "I find you endlessly fascinating."

Her breathing stilled for a moment, then she looked at him again. "Are you flirting with me?"

He shrugged nonchalantly. "I suppose I might be. Habit, you know."

"Well, stop it. I just cast up my accounts."

"Apologies," Alex murmured, realizing it was the third time today he had begged her forgiveness. "So what happened between them?"

She straightened a little. "And another thing," she continued, her voice stronger and color returning to her cheeks. "I don't appreciate being dragged about like a sack of greens."

"Quit turning the subject," he replied succinctly. "Why does your father hate Furth?" He had his own reasons for asking, besides a surprisingly intense wish to set things right for her, but nothing he could possibly discuss with Kit Brantley.

She met his gaze. Then, apparently accepting that he was genuinely interested, she sighed and shut her eyes once more. "Because of my mother. Furth hounded her from the day my father brought her home, would never give her a moment of peace, even after she begged him to do so. It finally killed her."

He examined her wan countenance and wanted to hold her, to comfort her and to kiss the lonely expression from her face. "How old were you?"

"Six."

"And do you remember your uncle?"

"Stop interrogating me, Everton, or I shall cast up my accounts again."

That reminded him that she was not any watery-eyed, weak-willed chit, but a strong-willed, beguiling, evasive one. He raised an eyebrow, but kept his silence. She had a right to be moody and depressed if she wished. Or, to pretend to be so. He was having some unexpected difficulty deciding what he wanted to believe about her, it seemed.

*   *   *

When Kit rose from her nap it was early evening, and as she had thought, Everton had gone out for the evening and hadn't bothered to inform anyone where he might have headed.

Swiftly she changed into one of her new evening suits, and left for the Traveller's. It seemed a good place not to find Alex or one of his bosom cronies, for Augustus Devlin had several times complained about the poor state of the liquor the club served. And much as she was beginning to enjoy Alexander Cale's company, she had a task to complete, and she damned well couldn't do it with him about.

She dearly hoped that her father's quarry would not be Hanshaw. Aside from Reg being Alex's friend, and a witty fellow in general, she preferred not to have to inform Stewart Brantley that the blue blood they'd been seeking was practically betrothed to Caroline Brantley. And as for Alex Cale—well, if he was involved . . . She took a breath. He couldn't be.

Alex was not at the Traveller's, but Francis Henning was, and he spied her before she could turn around and make her escape. When she was unable to dodge his company, she couldn't help but win ten quid off him at hazard. He did introduce her about the club, and the patrons, as she had suspected, were mostly minor nobles and fringe *ton* who hadn't yet or never would acquire the wherewithal to be admitted to the more exclusive haunts of the nobility.

"So what does a peer do all day, anyway?" she asked, tallying up points from the latest round.

"Oh, House of Lords on Parliament days, deciding on investments, keeping track of income from estates. Seeing, being seen, making certain everyone knows you're an Important Personage."

"What about those government appointments I keep hearing about?" she pursued. "I make it three crowns this round, Francis."

Mr. Henning sighed and nodded. "You've the devil's own luck, Kit." He sighed, then chuckled. "But then you are the devil's own cousin, eh?" Still chortling at his own brilliance, he glanced toward the door as another gentleman entered. "Thadius Naring," he informed her, jutting his chin in that worthy's direction. "You want to know about government appointments, ask him."

Kit turned to glance at the tall, thin-framed man taking a seat at an already crowded table in the center of the room. "He has one?" she asked, though she already knew something of it.

"Gads, two or three, probably. Trying to get in with Prinny. Any patriotic nonsense will do. Bought a knighthood, trying to slide into a barony. Likely do it, too." He grimaced and leaned forward. "Thing of it is, he don't need the money. Mother's side of the family's into textiles, I hear. He might leave a place for those of us who could use the income, damn him."

Kit poured her companion another glass of port. "Surely there are others besides Naring who have appointments," she suggested, trying to turn Henning's attention away from her quarry now that she had him well in her sights. When Francis looked at her, she shrugged. "As you said, it's extra income."

"If you're after an appointment of your own, you should be asking Everton," he commented, draining the glass. "I've been badgering him to put in a word for me for months, and he laughs it off. You're family, though, so you might be able to turn him to it."

Kit forced herself to take a slow breath, and swallowed a large portion of port before she sat back. "His appointment doesn't seem to amount to much, though," she noted, keeping both hands against the table so he wouldn't see them shaking. After all, it couldn't be that unusual for a peer to have an appointment. It could be any stupid duty. Counting cattle in Cumberland, or some such thing. "I doubt he has much influence."

Francis laughed. "Everton, no influence? I can name only three people who have more influence with Prinny than Alex." He raised a hand and folded his fingers over one at a time. "The Duke of Wellington, the Earl of Liverpool, and the Duke of Furth."

The last name made her flinch, and she covered it by

taking another drink. "No wonder he's so high in the instep sometimes."

"Selfish, too. Won't help me out, and last Season he and Hanshaw simply vanished for nearly a month, and no one to spot me a penny for a shoe shine."

"You mean they went somewhere together?" she queried. She was reaching the border between getting Francis drunk enough to talk, and too drunk to say anything remotely coherent. Admittedly, she had found some evidence that Alex might be involved in this mess, but it hadn't seemed all that significant. Or so she had managed to convince herself.

"Oh, I don't know," Francis whined, thumping his hand on the table. "They never tell me a bloody thing. Say I can't keep a secret." He leaned forward again, breathing a fair amount of liquor in her direction. "I think it was about some money troubles Reg's brother was having, but he wouldn't confess."

She and her father had smuggled fresh produce and various other items into France all last year, and until their current difficulty, they had been intercepted only once—during the Season—and her father had come damned close to being caught at it. She took another deep breath. Probably dozens of lords had exited London for various periods of time during the Season. It didn't necessarily mean anything. But neither could she take the chance of ignoring the possibility any longer.

"Where is Everton, anyway?" Francis queried, peering about. "Thought he was keeping an eye on you."

"He's at White's," Kit decided. "I wanted a change."

Francis was shaking his head. "No, he ain't. I was there earlier." He chuckled and drained his glass. "Making up with Barbara Sinclair, I'll wager."

That possibility hadn't even occurred to her. An image of Alex kissing and holding that woman leaped unbidden into her mind, squashing all orderly thoughts. Kit pushed to her feet and shoved the half-empty bottle into Francis's surprised hand. "I forgot," she stammered. "I'm supposed to be at the Downings tonight."

It made sense, she decided, as she hailed a hack and instructed the driver to take her back to Park Lane. Alex had wanted female companionship of the kind she'd denied him, so he had gone off to spend the evening with Barbara Sinclair. The thought left her with a queer, tight feeling in her chest.

In spite of her disarrayed thoughts, there was little further she could accomplish—at the moment, anyway. Ideally she should have been introducing herself to Sir Thadius Naring and getting him comfortably sotted, so she could ask him whether any of his government duties involved stopping smugglers along England's eastern coast. Francis would have noticed, though, and would then likely complain to one of his cronies that Kit Riley had cut him, and Alex would hear of it, and would ask all sorts of questions and look at her with those beautiful, mesmerizing eyes, and she would have to lie to him again. She'd go after Naring the next time she could slip away.

When the hack pulled into the Cale House drive, she flipped the driver a groat before she made her way inside. Neither she nor Alex had instructed anyone to wait up, so Wenton and the rest of the servants were already to bed. Late though it was, she felt too restless for sleep. She had left *Robinson Crusoe* lying on the table in the library, but the castaway's lonely solitude felt too familiar this evening. She set the book aside and walked over to peruse the bookshelves. Finally she lifted a book of poetry from its place and curled up in Alex's chair by the fire, imagining she could feel the warmth of his body lingering somewhere deep in the soft cushions.

After reading for a few moments, she stopped and turned the book around to look at the cover again. She had heard somewhere that Lord Byron wrote rather biting, sarcastic poetry, but whatever this was, it wasn't sarcastic. She opened the book again, wondering whether Alex had purchased it simply as an addition to his collection, or if he had actually read any of it. With a slight smile, she began again to read.

"Has poor Crusoe escaped the island yet?"

Kit started and nearly flung the book across the room. "Alex!" she exclaimed, flushing.

An amused smile on his face, he lounged in the doorway, lean and dark and achingly handsome. As she wondered how long he'd been there, watching her, he pulled off his gloves. "Didn't mean to startle you, chit. Saw the light. So how fares poor Robinson?"

Kit glanced at the clock on the mantel. It was nearly two in the morning. "He, ah, he's fine," she stumbled, closing the book and turning it so he couldn't see what she'd been reading. If only she'd put *Robinson Crusoe* away, instead of leaving it in plain sight. It was too late to move it now. "How is Lady Sinclair?"

"Is that where I was this evening?" he asked, as he pushed away from the doorway and stepped into the room.

"Wasn't it?" she sent back, with more boldness than she felt.

"Only if she's moved her apartments to the Society and learned to play billiards, and has taken to disguising herself as my cousin." He grinned, obviously in good humor. "Beg pardon. My *other* cousin—the tall, balding one."

He hadn't been with that woman! For a moment, that was all that mattered. Then she decided she'd missed a sterling opportunity to meet some of England's bluest bloods. "You played billiards at the Society? Without me?" she asked indignantly.

"You were asleep," he answered. "I didn't wish to wake you." He came forward and sat on the low table before her. As he did so, he scooted the book resting there out of his way, and absently picked it up to turn it in his hands. "I should have realized you would know how to play billiards."

"Of course I do," she returned, wishing he would put the blasted book aside before he realized what it was and became nosy.

"I have a table, you know, in the room off my study," he said slowly, his eyes catching hers. "Mary

. . . didn't much approve, so I moved it there to keep it out of her way."

That explained the secret game room. "How sad, that she didn't let you play."

Alex gave a short laugh. "Goose." He reached out and brushed his knuckles softly along her cheek. One finger caught a lock of her hair, and gently swept it back behind her ear as he smiled. "I daresay I might have left the blasted thing in the middle of the ballroom, if I'd wished. I was only being polite."

The caress surprised her, and it was a moment before she could muster a scowl at the insult that had preceded it. "Perhaps it was just that I didn't expect politeness from you."

The humor faded a little from his eyes. "Are you angry at me?" he asked directly, studying her face. She wondered what he saw.

"No. Apologies."

"Hm," he murmured in his deep voice. "What troubles you then, *ma chère*?" As he spoke he glanced down at his hands, and at the book still held between them.

"Nothing," she said hurriedly. "Just a bit of a headache, is all."

A slight frown creased his brow, and he turned the book over to look at the title. He glanced up at her again. "So what are you reading?"

"Are you my schoolmaster now?" she retorted, flushing.

"Not that I recall." Alex favored her with a grin. "Come, Kit, what other piratical tale have you found?"

"Just an old something to amuse myself with," she replied flippantly, then exaggerated a yawn. "I'm to bed, I think."

He leaned back a little. "I'm not going to try to take it from you. I was only curious about what might interest you."

"You are endlessly curious about me, aren't you?" she countered, then regretted challenging him. Or told herself she did, as a slight smile touched his lean, sensitive face again. She drew a soft breath at the sight. She could sit and just look at him forever, she thought.

"I am," he agreed. "Endlessly. So if you won't discuss literature, answer me something else."

His husky murmur was making it oddly difficult to concentrate. "What is your question, Everton?"

"Where did you go this evening?"

"Go?" she returned, raising an eyebrow and thinking he must have encountered that prattling Francis, after all.

"You're in your evening clothes," he pointed out, and she cursed herself for an idiot. Never tell a lie you can't stand behind, her father had always told her. It was just that Alex Cale was so damned distracting. He leaned closer, and she watched him warily. "And I detect cigar smoke in your hair," he whispered, "and port on your breath."

"I was at the Traveller's," she admitted, meeting his gaze, feeling the hold those eyes had on her. "I won a few crowns off Francis."

He nodded, and she thought he relaxed a little. "Might I?" he asked, gesturing at the book she clutched against her.

Feeling her face turn scarlet, Kit sighed and handed it over. "It's just Byron," she said carelessly.

He lifted an eyebrow. "The comedies? *Child Harolde,* perhaps?"

She shook her head again, lowering her eyes.

"Ah," he said softly. " 'By day or night, in weal or woe, That heart, no longer free, Must bear the love it cannot show, And silent, ache for thee.' "

Of course, he would have read the blasted book. For a moment she was afraid to look up, afraid to meet his eyes, but when she finally lifted her head he was perusing the book's pages, a soft, sensual smile on his lips. A lock of wavy, dark hair fell rakishly over his forehead. And for the first time in her life, Christine Brantley was conscious of wanting to be a female. Of wanting Alexander Cale to know her as a woman. "Alex?" she whispered.

Slowly he raised his head to look at her with amused eyes. "Yes, chit?" He hesitated, gazing at her, then returned the book to her abruptly clumsy fingers.

She cleared her throat and glanced at the fireplace, the window, anywhere but at him. "It's late. I should be getting to bed."

For a moment he was silent. "No more poetry this evening?" he asked quietly, and looked at her from beneath his dark lashes. "I would be happy to read you another."

Kit shook her head tightly. "I don't think that's wise," she responded, wishing she had the courage to let him continue. On occasion he read aloud from the morning paper, and she loved the sound of his voice. But to hear him read her another poem would be more than she could bear.

Alex shrugged. "Is it necessary always to be wise?" His fingers stretched out and touched her knee. "Are you afraid to be foolish for just one moment?"

Kit took a breath, wanting nothing more than to fall into his arms and feel his lips on hers again. "Yes," she said instead.

He looked into her eyes for the space of a dozen heartbeats, as if examining her face for any indication that she felt differently. Finally he nodded. "You will let me know if you change your mind, of course."

Alex stood at the same time she did, and they nearly collided. Reflexively he put out a hand to steady her, and she lifted her face again to look at him. Apparently he read her ill-hidden yearning, because something changed in his eyes, and he leaned down toward her. Not daring to breathe, her heart hammering furiously, she tilted her face up and shut her eyes. She could feel the warmth of him as his lips trailed a feather's touch away from her skin. His light breath passed slowly over her mouth and paused there, then traveled up her cheekbone, and over her eyelid, to kiss her very softly on the forehead. "Good night, Kit," he murmured, and was gone.

Kit, breathing rapidly, looked after him for a moment. When she heard his bedchamber door shut upstairs, she started. She needed to get out into the cool night and think. And she needed to get the information her father wanted. The sooner, the better.

Chapter 7

As soon as he opened his door, Stewart Brantley knew someone was in the rooms he had rented from the exceedingly uncurious Mrs. Henry Beacham just north of Covent Garden.

The sitting room was dark, the shutters still latched as he had left them earlier in the evening, but someone was in there with him. It might have been Mrs. Beacham's son, Daniel, bringing in more wood for the evening, but he couldn't imagine that stodgy boy doing so without a candle for light. It might also have been Kit, but she had no idea where he was staying.

As soon as he had the door shut, he slipped sideways and dug for the pistol in his pocket. His swift movement stirred the air, and the faint, expensive aroma of a men's cologne reached him. He knew full well who used that scent, but it wasn't until he heard the voice that he accepted who it must be.

"*Bon soir,* Stewart," the Comte de Fouché said softly from the shadows, and a lamp was lit off to the left, by the window. Guillaume and Beloche stood at opposite ends of the room like mismatched bookends, hulking and dangerous.

Stewart stopped the grab for his weapon. "I thought the custom was to wait outside someone's home for them to return," he said coolly in French, wondering how the devil they'd found him. Fouché must be having him watched. "Or better yet, leaving a calling card is considered quite fashionable, I believe."

"Old friends such as we hardly have need of calling cards," the comte returned, stepping away from the lamp. "And your home is in Paris, after all."

"In the middle of your damned war," he replied stiffly, feeling sweat curling along his temples and resisting the impulse to wipe his face.

"Tsk, tsk, Stewart," the comte admonished, watching him with dark, wary eyes. "I did not come here to debate politics. Only to find out where my muskets are. They will be needed sooner than was anticipated."

Refusing to be interested in what Napoleon might be doing to cause him to need the weapons ahead of their scheduled delivery, Stewart strolled across the room to drop into the chair before the fireplace. "I have made arrangements to remove them from where they are being stored, but I don't want to transfer them to the coast until I can be certain they won't be intercepted."

"Has Kit found our English fool yet?"

Stewart shook his head. "He, ah, she has several suspects, but if we are wrong, the complications . . ."

"I know the complications," Fouché snapped. "Just make certain she doesn't forget why she's here. She enjoys London too much, I think. You should not have given such a task to a female."

"Kit can hold her own."

A slight frown creased Fouché's brow. He sat on the edge of the couch, his dark eyes shadowed in the lamplight, a hawk on the hunt. "I hear that the cousin of the Earl of Everton is on his way to becoming the toast of London, and that this boy's name happens to be Kit. Is this how you English discover your secrets? Turn your daughters into whores?"

"Everton has no idea what she is, who she is, or why she's here. His father owed me a debt, and the son is making good on it." It wasn't entirely the truth, for Alexander Cale knew more of his personal family history than he would ever care to reveal to Jean-Paul Mercier, but it would suffice.

The comte narrowed his eyes. "I hope she realizes that a thin-blooded Englishman could never satisfy her."

Brantley heard the comte's jealousy and in the same moment decided against acknowledging it. "She is here to assist me. Nothing more."

Fouché looked at him for a moment, then gave a slight nod. "Very well. But make certain she knows that we need that name before we can proceed."

"We do have another option," Stewart said slowly. "I think I may have the crates sent north, and take them across from Suffolk rather than Do—"

"I want no more delays!" Fouché interrupted.

"And I don't want to be left with no options if Kit is unsuccessful," Brantley countered sternly. "If they are taken, you will have nothing to show Napoleon."

The comte examined his manicured fingernails. "Nothing except your head, Brantley." He straightened and strolled for the door, Guillaume and Beloche falling in behind. "I have my own eyes open. But I suggest you and Kit not fail." With that he left the room.

Stewart Brantley stood and walked over to open the shutters. He'd known when he began smuggling weapons that sacrifices would have to be made in return for the tremendous profit he would reap. Lying to Kit about the exact contents of the crates was a small worry. She would do her duty, but he didn't wish to hear her arguments. Getting either of them killed in the process of this little game, however, was not part of the bargain. And at the moment, it appeared they had stepped into waters too deep to be easily waded out of. He shrugged. At least he and Kit were good swimmers.

Alex touched his heels to the ribs of his black, Tybalt, and rocked back a little in the saddle as the animal's gait flowed into a smooth canter. His contented sigh fogged in the early morning's cool air. At this hour Hyde Park was nearly deserted, Rotten Row completely so. It was generally his favorite time of the day, coming as it did after he'd escaped from whatever late-night entanglements he'd been involved in, and before the tiresome day at Parliament began. This morning, though, something felt lacking, and it took little to realize what it was. Kit had been still to bed when he'd risen, and he'd sternly resisted the temptation to wake her so she could accompany him. He was becoming entirely too distracted by the chit's mysteries, and welcomed the opportunity to clear his head.

"Everton!"

Alex glanced up to see Thadius Naring and several of his cronies approaching on horseback, and he stifled a grimace. Bootlicks and toadies, all of them, and he couldn't imagine why Naring would ever hail him. Which was why he pulled Tybalt up and awaited their arrival.

"Good morning, Everton." Naring smiled, putting out his hand in a familiar manner.

Alex shook it, keeping his expression aloof and bored. "Naring." He nodded. He had no wish to be toad-eaten on such a splendid morning. And if he didn't return to Cale House soon, he'd miss sharing breakfast with his houseguest.

Thadius Naring's smile wavered a little. "Everton, I was just wondering if your cousin was about this morning."

"Kit?" Alex rejoined, raising an eyebrow. "Not yet. Why?"

Naring shrugged, becoming less confident in the face of the earl's coolness. "Well, it was just that he won twenty quid off me last night, and Palgrave and Traven are putting together a jaunt tonight. I wondered if he'd give me a chance to win it back."

Kit had said she'd been at the Traveller's with Francis Henning. Alex pursed his lips. "You seeking revenge over twenty quid, Naring?"

The laugh was strained, as well. "Heavens, no. It's merely that Mr. Riley's an amusing fellow, though he does ask the oddest questions."

"Well, he is a bit rough around the edges," Alex offered with a smile, alarm bells going off in his skull. What sort of odd questions was his houseguest bandying about town? "What's he after this time? Addresses to the local brothels and gaming hells?"

Apparently emboldened by the earl's query, Naring glanced at his fellows as if to boast of his conquest. "That didn't come up, no. And I certainly wouldn't pass on such information to a youngster."

"Quite high-minded of you, Naring," Alex returned, running out of patience. "So what did he ask you?"

The smile faded again. "Oh, simply about government appointments and such. I believe he had heard I have several and was curious. The boy—lad—kept me out till nearly dawn."

Alex studied Tybalt's left ear. "Dawn, you say?" That meant she'd gone out after they'd said good night. "And where was this encounter?"

"We started out at the Traveller's, and ended up at the Navy." Naring cleared his throat. "Is there some problem?"

"I'm merely having difficulty keeping track of the boy," Alex replied. "I thank you for the news." He urged Tybalt a few steps closer. "And for your sake I do recommend that you not tell him of this conversation. Kit wouldn't take kindly to being informed upon."

"Oh, of course not, Everton. Wouldn't think of it."

"Splendid," Alex continued, favoring Naring with a smile. "My cronies and I are having a bit of a jaunt at White's next week, if you'd care to join us."

"Well, yes . . . you . . . of . . . well, of course," Naring sputtered, doing a poor job of disguising his delight.

It would make for a dull evening, but it would keep him from turning the tale back to Kit. "Good day, gentlemen." Alex nodded, and kneed Tybalt back toward Park Lane.

His good humor had dimmed considerably. He had no idea why Kit Brantley would slip out in the middle of the night to ask about government appointments, but the damned chit was up to something. Something she didn't wish him to know about. Which meant that he would have to find out what it was, and the sooner the better.

* * *

"Oh, do be quiet, Kit," Augustus drawled, putting his hands over his ears in protest as they strolled down St. James Street toward Pall Mall. "You're making my head ache."

"I thought that would be the bottle of brandy you consumed last night," Hanshaw suggested.

"I was only pointing out that if you took better care of yourself, you wouldn't feel so deuced awful all the time," Kit protested, glaring at the viscount. She'd had little sleep last night, and Devlin's foul mood wasn't helping her own disposition in the slightest. Neither had Alex's being gone when she'd risen, and her own rather rash decision to skip breakfast. Staying clear of Everton, and the confusion of feelings he aroused in her, would seem to be the only way she was going to get anything accomplished.

"Why in the world would I want to pamper myself and waste away slowly, when I can amuse myself and go out in a glorious blaze?" Devlin returned mildly.

"Or a glorious haze," Lord Hanshaw countered.

"Well, I intend to live to a ripe old age," Kit declared.

The viscount chuckled, then raised a kerchief and coughed into it. "I have never understood the juxtaposition of 'ripe' and 'old,' " he commented. "I think rather that you shall live to a shriveled old age, dear boy."

"I'd be in for wealthy old age, if you'd get me a deuced royal appointment," Francis complained.

Reg snorted. "Leave off with that, will you, Francis? I keep telling you, it doesn't pay well. The way Prinny spends government funds, it's a duty, not a stipend."

Kit was grateful that Francis hadn't mentioned that they'd been discussing that very thing last evening. Hopefully he didn't remember much about the conversation at all. "What sort of duty?" she queried.

Reg gave her a jaunty smile. "A damned dull one. Not even worth discussing." He gestured across the street. "I need a new pair of Wellingtons."

"Is that Hoby's?" Kit asked, somewhat in awe. Even her father had no ill words for Hoby's footwear.

"It is. And I, for one," Augustus commented, "refuse to waste my day on boots. Do what you like, my dears. I'm getting an ale."

"I want a pair of Hoby's," Kit declared, unwilling to part from Hanshaw until she discovered what sort of government appointment he'd been given. "Hessians, I think."

Reg chuckled. "Alex will think you're aping him."

"And you'd best hope he pays for them," Francis seconded.

"I can convince him," Kit said confidently.

"No doubt," Augustus said, looking at her sideways. "Everton seems quite willing to do whatever you wish."

Kit smiled, though she wasn't entirely certain of Devlin's meaning. "It's my natural charm."

He nodded. "Then you must be the most charming individual alive," he said cryptically. With a salute, he sauntered off toward the clubs.

She glanced at Reg, who looked after Devlin for a moment, then shrugged at her and turned across the street. As Kit passed the front of a clothing shop, she glanced into the window. And stopped. Draped over a mannequin was the loveliest gown she had ever set eyes upon, sewn from a patterned rose silk. Ivory lace frothed at the sleeves and bordered the plunging neckline, and trailed down the skirt in graceful loops gathered at the waist.

"What's so enticing?" Hanshaw queried, putting an elbow on her shoulder and leaning forward to look into the window.

"I, ah, was just wondering," Kit stumbled, trying not to blush, "how it is that females can tolerate being enclosed in such intricate monstrosities."

The baron chuckled and slipped his arm around hers to turn her back toward Hoby's. "Getting them out of those things is the devil of a bother, as well."

Kit offered an unfelt smile. "I would say so." She looked over her shoulder at the dress, then sighed. She'd

lived her life in the easy company of men, with scarcely
a tremble of her heart. She'd only known Alexander
Cale for a week, and she was drooling over fine gowns
and lace like a half-wit. "I say, Reg," she said with
forced gaiety, "do you think you might get me a government appointment? Something exciting. You know,
spies or smuggling or pirates or such."

Lord Hanshaw laughed and shook his head, showing
no sign that she'd hit even remotely close to the mark.
"Alex's got far more influence over such things than I
do. Ask him."

"But is yours exciting?" she pursued.

He shook his head. "Dull as warping wood, Kit."

For the moment, she would have to be satisfied with
that. Thadius Naring was such a self-centered ass that
he couldn't possibly be the peer who'd ruffled her father's and Fouché's feathers so. Hanshaw, though, was
another tale entirely. He did have a royal appointment,
and he wouldn't talk about it, which would imply that
it was at least mildly important. Despite his connection
with Caroline, it was a good beginning, and if the middle
was as promising, she would need to look no further.
Nor did she wish to. Eliminating Everton as a suspect
would suit her quite well.

They met up with Devlin again in the afternoon, and
though his mood had become even more foul, they decided to go off to the races. When Reg won thirty quid,
that led to dinner and a game of hazard at the Army
club. By the time Kit hired a hack to take her back to
Cale House, it was well after midnight, and she had
added yet another ten pounds to her collection.

"Evening, Wenton." She grinned as the butler pulled
the door open to admit her. "Alex is out, I suppose?"

Solemnly the butler accepted her hat and gloves and
splendid new greatcoat. "Lord Everton is in his study,
and does not wish to be disturbed."

"Oh. Well, I'll just be in the library, if he needs me."

All day long she'd been thinking of that poem he'd
quoted her, and she wished to read it for herself—until

she heard two male voices coming from behind his door. With a glance back at Wenton she dragged one foot behind her, bunching up the Persian carpet on the edge, then stumbled over the mound she'd created. Letting herself lose her balance, she lurched against the study door. It was unlocked, and seemingly of its own accord the handle turned and the door fell open with her attached to it.

Kit stumbled into the study and grabbed the back of the nearest chair to catch her balance. "Apologies. I—"

Alex had been facing the fireplace, but at her entrance he whipped around to face her. His eyes were angry and distant, and they stopped her apology in her throat. A moment later he turned his back and accepted an emptied snifter of brandy from the man who stood by the window. "Thank you for your help," he said curtly.

"My pleasure, milord, as always." The visitor, sandy-haired with wind-burned cheeks and a rough-spun, dark overcoat, glanced at Kit and then leaned over to pick up a hat and gloves from the chair she still clutched. "I'll let you know what I find."

"I would appreciate it." Alex motioned his guest toward the door, and followed him into the hallway. "Don't move," he warned Kit out of the side of his mouth as he passed by. He never looked in her direction.

Kit stayed where she was. It abruptly occurred to her that she had never seen Alex angry before. And she wondered what, exactly, his visitor was supposed to find out for him. Her entrance had stopped the conversation cold, and though she was, of course, less than intimate with his personal affairs, she was certain they hadn't been discussing hay rakes.

A moment later he stepped back into the room, where she stood facing away from him. "I'm sorry," she repeated.

Behind her the door shut, and Everton brushed her shoulder as he returned to pick up the brandy he had set down. He lifted it to his lips and took a swallow, pushing the window curtains aside a little with his other hand

and glancing out into the darkness of his garden and the street beyond.

"I was heading for the library," she continued, disliking the silence, "and I tripped. I didn't mean—"

"That's rather unimaginative," he interrupted, letting the curtain slide back through his fingers. "Why don't you try another?"

She scowled and released the back of the chair. "I tripped. You're the one who left your bloody door unlocked, so don't blame me." When caught in a lie, attack. Throw the enemy off balance. Kit watched his profile, for he still wouldn't look at her, and tried to decide whether he was the enemy.

"Where were you this evening?"

"Winning five pounds off Reg at hazard," she replied shortly, deflating the figure in case he attempted to relieve her of her funds again. "Why do you let strangers share brandy with you when you won't drink it with me?"

Finally he looked at her. "He's not a stranger. And chits don't drink brandy."

Kit frowned. "I—"

He raised a hand. "Beg pardon. You're not a chit, are you? Very well. Have a seat." He gestured at the open door on the far side of the room.

With a suspicious glance at him she turned and walked into the billiards room. She already knew the layout. In addition to the table, a liquor tray sat on one side beneath the window, a folded gaming table and two worn, comfortable-looking chairs close by it. She glanced over her shoulder to see that Everton followed her, and took a seat before the mahogany gaming table.

Alex leaned over and flipped it open, his motions crisp and angry, then walked to the mantel and pulled out a deck of cards from the small chest perched there. He tossed the deck onto the table, then moved on to the liquor tray and lifted two glasses and an unopened bottle of brandy. "Your father encourages you to drink brandy, then?" he finally said, taking the seat opposite her.

"He doesn't care," Kit answered defiantly, still trying

to interpret his mood. She guessed it had little to do with her supposed clumsiness, and wondered again what the man who wasn't a stranger to Everton had been telling him. "I can drink any man under the table, anyway."

"Splendid." He deftly uncorked the bottle and poured a measure of the amber liquid into each glass. He slid hers across the table toward her, then sat back, obviously waiting for her to proceed.

It took little sense to know that she should not be drinking with him in this hidden room by themselves. "Alex," she finally said, reaching out to fiddle with the glass, "if you wish me to apologize again, I will. The dratted rug was turned up on one side, and I fell."

"How very clumsy of you," he noted.

"That's not very nice," she retorted.

"Well, I'm a bit angry. Drink."

"No."

"And why not?"

"Because I don't like you any longer, and I don't wish to drink your brandy." She stood and turned for the door.

Everton reached out and grabbed her wrist. "Sit down," he hissed.

Surprised at the contact, she jerked free and took a further step away from him. "No. If you wish to drink with someone, go find your mysterious friend."

Alex pushed to his feet, his eyes snapping with fury. "Down!"

She put her hands on her hips, not wanting him to see that he was making her uneasy. "What the deuce are you so angry about, Everton?" she demanded.

He opened his mouth, closed it again, and slowly retook his seat. "I suppose I've gotten used to having everyone around me do as I tell them. You are more . . . independent than I am used to."

At least he was speaking in complete sentences again. "Now who's being unimaginative?" she prodded, still irritated at the implication that she had been lying, whether she had been or not.

He scowled. "All right, you annoyed the bloody hell

out of me, and you being a female, I can do nothing but beat my chest and bellow at you.'' He gestured at her to resume her seat. "Please. Come drink me under the table, chit.''

There was still something remote in his eyes, but being in his company was even more inviting than the idea of finally beating him at something. Perhaps a few glasses of brandy would return him to his cynically amused self. "All right, but don't blame me for the aching head you'll have tomorrow.''

"I'll risk it.''

Kit sat again and lifted her glass. Eyeing him over the rim, she took a swallow, then another. "It's very good brandy,'' she offered with a tentative smile.

Alex returned the expression briefly and drank as well. "Brandy's actually a bit too dry for me. I prefer port, but as you are obsessed, we'll drink brandy.''

He refilled the glasses, then opened the pack of cards and began shuffling them. "Commerce?'' he asked, glancing at her.

"All right,'' she agreed. "If we play for brandy. Loser takes a drink.'' Though it was not her best game, she played fairly well, and if she could get him drunk enough, she might actually be able to obtain some information from him.

He eyed her for a moment, then nodded. "And winner gets to ask a question.''

Apparently he was seeking information, as well. "What sort of question?''

"Any sort at all. We've been together for a week, and know little of one another. Whatever comes to mind.''

It felt like a trap, but it could close on him just as well as on her. "Agreed.''

He dealt them three cards apiece, and set the deck at his elbow while he examined his hand. She did the same, and then looked up at his questioning expression. "One,'' she said, discarding the diamond and hoping for a flush of spades.

Alex slid the card over to her and took one himself. "Well, chit?''

She sighed. "Queen point."

"Pair of threes," he said, displaying them for her.
"Drink up."

Kit took a swallow. The liquid burned as it traveled
down her throat. "And your question?"

"Why did you go out again last night after we said
good night?"

For a moment her heart stopped. Swiftly she set an
affronted look on her face. "How did you know that?"
she demanded.

"It's my turn to ask a question," he reminded her.

"I'd . . . spied Thadius Naring drinking earlier, and
thought he'd be an easy mark," she said slowly, watching his expression to see if she'd given away more than
she should have.

"You might have told me," he said after a moment.
"We could have fleeced a few coins out of him together."

"Seeing you at the Traveller's would have had him
pissing in his breeches. And I need the coin. You
don't."

He nodded. "True enough." Alex slid the deck over
to her for the deal.

This time she ended up with a flush to his pair of
sevens. She gestured at his glass, and he took a long
swallow, as though taunting her. "How did you know I
went out again?" she asked.

"I ran across Naring this morning. He wanted a
chance to recoup his losses."

Alex won the next hand, and looked at her for a heartbeat after she took the obligatory drink. "How long have
you spoken French?"

At least these first questions seemed to be ones she
could answer without too much difficulty. Perhaps it was
simple curiosity that motivated him, after all. "I'm not
certain. For a time after we left England I didn't understand a word of it, and then I did."

He won the next round as well, and she would have
thought he was cheating, except that she had dealt the

hand. "Have you always lived in Saint-Marcel?" he asked as she drank.

If this kept up, she wouldn't be in a condition to ask him anything if the opportunity ever arose. "No. After Madrid and Venice we lived in Saint-Germain for a while, but we've lived in Saint-Marcel on and off for five years or so."

Finally she came up with three nines, and refilled his glass to the brim before he drank. "Let me see," she mused, while he watched her. She would have called his expression wary, but it was too aloof for that. But she knew that he had secrets, too. Everyone did. The trick was to uncover what she needed to know without him guessing what she was seeking. "Where does all your money come from, Croesus?"

He raised an eyebrow. "What kind of question is that?"

"Ah ah," she admonished, wagging a finger at him. "It's my turn."

Alex sat back. "Well, do you wish to see an estate ledger, or may I just give you a general breakdown of income?"

"A general summary will do."

He gave a slight smile and shook his head. "The majority comes from investments. I am a shareholder in several textile, mining, and shipping companies. The rest comes from government appointments, tenant rent, and from my brickwork, and crop, wool, and stock sales at Everton, Charing, Hoaroak Abbey, Castle Gandailey, and Corredor Timederia. And a little wagering, for amusement."

Well, he'd said it, but he'd managed to smuggle it in the middle of a breath-stealing mound of wealth. To focus on his appointments above the rest would be far too obvious. "My," she offered, rather stunned to actually hear it all laid out before her, and he chuckled.

"You asked," he said dryly.

In the next hour she learned that despite his reputation as a rake, he took his duties as a member of the House of Lords very seriously, and that he had sold off his shares in a French textile company when the board had voted to support Bonaparte's ascendancy. She'd tried to nudge her questions in the direction of his politics and his particular duties, and he'd just as skillfully misread her meanings and given answers that had little to do with what she truly wanted to know. At least, she imagined that his misdirection was on purpose. For his part, he'd won the majority of hands, and Kit was forced to acknowledge that he was better at cards than she. Of course, as the loser, she was consuming far more liquor, which wasn't helping her game in the least.

It seemed only wise, then, when she lost a hand and Alex rose to throw another log on the dying fire, that she turn her wrist as she lifted the glass. Deftly, the swallow that was supposed to go down her throat slid wetly down her sleeve instead. She hated the idea of ruining her shirt, and quite possibly her lovely blue coat, but she hated the idea of losing to Everton, and losing her wits, even more.

"All right, chit," he said with a half smile as he retook his seat, "how many times have you visited England since the age of six?"

His questions had been like that all evening, queries that could be interpreted as either idle curiosity, or a wish to discover something deeper. She wondered whether he had guessed anything about her true purpose for being in London, and why he would have reason to suspect her. "Oh, I don't know," she offered, grimacing as though trying to remember. "Three or four times. We never stayed very long."

For the next half hour she succeeded in distracting him enough to dump nearly a full glass down her sleeve, though it didn't make answering his increasingly complicated questions any easier. "What time is it?" Alex asked, stretching sleepily and glancing over at the mantel.

"Nearly three," she answered quickly, grinning. "Your deal." Slyly she tilted her glass into her sleeve again.

"I lodge a protest. That was not my ques—" Everton

lurched across the table, grabbed her arm, and yanked her over the cards toward him. Hearts and diamonds went flying as he pushed her sleeve up to reveal the brandy-soaked elbow of her shirt. "You little fraud!"

"Let me go!" she protested, flushing and trying to pull backward. She had forgotten how strong he was, for her flailing about had little effect. Instead, he hauled her around the side of the table and stood her upright.

"Strip," he ordered.

She just stared at him. "What?" she queried, her heart thudding unevenly.

He smiled lazily. "Take off that damned coat. We're going to finish this game, and I paid too much for this bottle for you to be dumping it down your sleeves."

"Oh, all right," she grumbled, and shrugged out of the coat. It was with some difficulty that she kept her balance. She looked over at Alex, to find his gaze was directed somewhat lower than her face. "Everton," she muttered, blushing.

"Hm?" he said absently, raising his eyes to hers again. "How did you learn to tie your cravat like that?"

"Antoine taught me," she returned. "He says it's the very latest thing, only you won't wear it."

"It looks foppish."

"It does not," she protested, looking down at her chest. "I'm the pink of the *ton*."

"By God, you are, chit," he said admiringly, the cynical, slightly drunken twinkle in his eyes mocking her good-humoredly. He stepped over to the liquor table and procured a second bottle, for they had nearly consumed the first one.

"You must remove your coat as well, *monsieur le châtelain*," she demanded as he returned.

Alex glared at her as he removed his own gray coat. "And what does that mean?"

"I only called you the lord of the manor. Not very insulting at all, really." His sleeves were unsoiled, so he'd been drinking every glass she'd set in front of him. Even so, the advantage remained his, for he outweighed her by better than five stone.

She stood there for a moment, looking at him in his shirtsleeves, fighting the abrupt, scandalous desire to unbutton his waistcoat and pull his shirt free, to run her hands over his bare chest. The curl in her stomach tightened deliciously, and spun downward.

Alex resumed his chair, and leaned forward to grasp one end of her cravat and pull her back down opposite him. Her splendid knot came undone. "Stop that," she said belatedly. The protest seemed weak, so she reached out and tugged his cravat loose, as well.

Before she could retrieve her hand, he grasped the ends of her fingers. Alex examined her palm for a moment, running his fingers featherlight across her skin, then turned her hand over to brush his lips slowly along her knuckles. His breath was soft and warm, nearly as soft as the touch of his mouth on her fingers. In her guise as a man she'd never had her fingers kissed before—but this was no polite greeting, anyway. Her eyes met his, and he yanked her half over the table again and closed his mouth over hers.

Christine shut her eyes and kissed him back, kissed his lips which were soft and firm at the same time. She had expected a kiss, even his kiss, to be mauling and sloppy, like those she'd seen in Parisian taverns since she was fifteen. But there was nothing mauling and sloppy about Alexander Cale at all, or about the shuddering pulse in her veins, or the sudden electric heat coursing along every nerve in her body. When he let her go she sat slowly back down in her chair again, for a moment still unable to breathe. Her cravat, caught in his long fingers, slid loose from around her neck. Azure eyes spent a long time looking at her, then blinked and glanced down. "We seem to be missing half the deck," he muttered.

Her body trembling, Kit slipped sideways out of her seat and gathered up the scattered cards. When she sat again, he was slowly winding her cravat around his fingers and watching her from half-closed eyes. "Don't you wish to concede?" she suggested instead, her voice unsteady.

"Why?" he said softly. "Did you have something else in mind?"

"You are under a debt of honor, Everton," she stated, as though the words were some sort of shield. Byron's poetry ran through her mind, soft and sensuous, making her want to give in to what she'd been imagining from the first moment she'd set eyes on him.

"And you have sweet lips," he murmured.

"You're drunk," she said, even less steadily.

"*In vino veritas.*" He grinned lazily. "That's Latin, chit."

"I know what it is." Kit stacked the cards. "It's my deal."

Distracted as she was, she didn't stand a chance, and of course, he won the hand. He studied her face, then reached out one hand to tug the ruffles of her sleeve up to her elbow. As his fingers brushed her skin, she shivered again.

"Don't you trust me?" she asked.

"No. And no more cheating," he repeated huskily, watching closely as she set the glass to her lips and drank. "All right. When did you last wear a dress?"

She hadn't expected the question, and glanced down before she faced him again. If he was trying to unsettle her, it was working better than she cared to admit. "I was six. Nearly fourteen years ago."

Surprisingly, she bested him the next hand with a flush of hearts. "Who was the first woman you kissed?" she asked, deciding turnabout was fair play. And she wanted to know.

He chuckled. "My mother," he answered, and slid the deck over in front of her.

"That's not what I meant."

"It's what you asked."

"Coward."

"Beg pardon?" he returned, raising an eyebrow.

"You heard me."

"What an aggravating female you are," he said, then smiled again. "Lucy Leviton. My tutor's daughter."

"How old were you?"

She didn't expect him to reply, for he'd been quite adamant about only giving one answer away at a time. Alex pursed his lips. "Fifteen." He tilted his head to eye her sideways. "Do I get a free question, as well?"

Kit shrugged, half-afraid to meet his gaze in case he should kiss her again, and wanting nothing more than to feel his mouth on hers. They were both too drunk to be having any sort of conversation. "I suppose."

He stood and walked around behind her chair. "Do you consider kissing to be dishonorable?"

His tall presence behind her seemed to radiate heat. Questions about her past and her father, she had answers ready for. Questions about her heart and her feelings were far more difficult. And dangerous. "Dishonorable? No, I wouldn't call a kiss exactly—"

He leaned down over her shoulder, tilting her head back with his fingers on her cheek and touching his lips to hers again. "Good," he murmured, straightening and coming to stand before her. "Then I couldn't possibly be dishonoring any debt with a mere touch of the lips." Everton pulled her to her feet. "The rules seemed a bit strict, anyway." Slowly and softly he lowered his mouth to hers.

Somewhere this evening had completely slipped out of her control, if it had ever been there. His lips tasted of brandy. Kit shut her eyes, trying to shut him out, but the warmth and strength and nearness of him seemed to engulf her. She found herself seeking his mouth, running her hands along his arms and down his ribs to his waist, pulling herself harder against him, yearning for more, and knowing that she'd stepped far beyond the bounds of where she should be. "Alex," she finally murmured.

"Shh," he replied, running his hands down the small of her back and kissing her again. "Be foolish for once."

No one would know, she thought for a wild moment as she clung to him, drinking in his nearness. Everyone thought she was a man. If she were to begin an affair with Alex, no one would know. Kit tried to take a breath, reaching for her lost senses, and then turned her head away and shoved at him. "Everton, stop it."

Slowly his hands slid away from her shoulders, and she finally looked up at him. His expression was unreadable, his eyes focused on her mouth. "All right," he said after a moment, clearing his throat. "If you insist. Back to the questions, then. Am I the first man you've kissed?"

"My father is," she returned flippantly, turning back to take her seat.

He caught her by the arm, keeping her on her feet. "And your father hates the English."

It wasn't a question, but she sensed that he wanted a response. Lying would serve little purpose, and it took a great deal of effort to keep any tale straight. At the moment she couldn't even keep her eyes from trailing longingly down his body. She let them shut again, feeling weariness trailing over her, despite the fact that falling asleep in Alex Cale's presence was the last thing she wanted to do. "Yes, he does."

"And do you?"

"It's my turn to ask a question," she countered, pulling free of his arm and stumbling backward into her chair. The deuced thing was entirely too soft and comfortable. "Why did you kiss me?"

"Because I wanted to," he replied, folding his arms.

"And you always do whatever you want to?"

Slowly he shook his head. "No, not always."

"Why not?"

He gave a slight, lopsided grin and, before she could protest, leaned forward to place his hands on the arms of her chair. "Stupidity," he murmured, kissing her once more with the softness of a sigh.

It truly could be him, she realized, as he straightened and dropped into the chair opposite her again. He could be the one her father was seeking. And if his politics were anything like his card-playing and his seductions, he would be a dangerous opponent. But then again, perhaps she was just tired. And perhaps she just needed to put her head down for a moment, because she wasn't thinking clearly at all. She wondered if she could convince Alex to kiss her when they were both sober, because he seemed rather good at it. But now, just for a moment, she needed to shut her eyes, to escape from the azure gaze watching her from across the table.

Alex sat back in his chair and watched her, watched the soft flutter of her eyelids and the slow, steady lift and fall of her shoulders as she breathed. So much for his angry, calculated interrogation. If his friend and former Bow Street detective James Samuels hadn't come by with news he would have given good blunt not to hear, there was no telling what he would have been doing right now with Christine Brantley. He sighed. He knew damned well what he would have been doing. And there was a certain portion of his anatomy that was uncomfortably reminding him that it was something that he still wished to be doing, whatever he had learned about her.

He'd known for months that someone was working to steal British armaments and transport them to France, just as he had suspected that Bonaparte would not sit and quietly rot on Elba. What he had never expected to hear, and what Samuels had sworn on his honor not to pass on yet to his compatriots, was that the shipment of muskets they had intercepted on its way to Calais two months ago had been arranged for and purchased by one Stewart Brantley. And that, in accompaniment with the information he had received earlier, that a thousand more muskets had just vanished, was news he simply had not been prepared for.

At the moment he would be within his rights to have Kit Brantley arrested and tried for treason. "Are you a spy, chit?" he murmured.

A slight smile crept across her face, and he felt one touch his own lips in response. What a conundrum she was. An enigma, a puzzle, a mystery, a riddle, and a very great problem. And a very intriguing one. She was becoming more tangled into his life than he had ever expected, than he had ever meant to allow.

With another sigh he stood and crossed around the

small table to her side. Very carefully, aware that he was
less than graceful, he leaned over and slid one arm under
her knees, and the other behind her shoulders. In boots
she lacked only a few inches on him, but she was far
lighter than he expected as he lifted her into his arms.
Her head sagged against his shoulder, her breath warm
against his cheek.

He managed to pull open the door and stepped out
into the hallway. Wenton had apparently given up on
them and gone to bed, and all the lamps but the ones
lighting the hallway and stairs had been extinguished.
The door of her bedchamber was open and the bed
turned down, and he carried her inside and gently laid
her down. Both sleeves of her shirt were hopelessly
stained; he would have to purchase her another.

He opened the top button of her waistcoat, then pulled
off her boots and lifted the sheets to her shoulders. She
sighed again and turned on her side, curling up with her
hand resting beside her cheek on the pillow. Whether
she was a spy for Napoleon or not, until he knew more
about her motives, he couldn't turn her in. And he
wouldn't turn her out. For a few more days he could
keep her from learning whatever it was she had come to
London for. He would track down the muskets, and
while she would learn nothing of his own activities, he
could easily keep an eye on hers. When her father came
for her she would have nothing to report, and once they
were gone he would turn the recovered weapons over to
Prince George and make his own report.

Only secondarily did it occur to him that he was willing to withhold information from, and lie to, his compatriots until he discovered the truth about her—even
knowing that at least one of them was going to be exceedingly angry at him for it. The strength of his desire
to see that no harm came to her was surprising, but he
wasn't yet ready to question whatever tendencies toward
chivalry seemed to be surfacing in him.

Very slowly he leaned over and brushed his lips
lightly over her forehead. With a sigh he straightened,
and stepped over to blow out the candle by her bedside.
For a few more days, he could resist her.

Chapter 8

Kit awoke to find that half her clothes had been removed or unbuttoned and, even worse, that she had apparently fallen asleep just when things were beginning to become interesting.

With her fingers she traced the outline of her lips. They had both been far too drunk last night. Otherwise, whatever she might secretly wish, whatever thoughts had been burning at her for the past few days, she would never have let him near her. Nor should she have.

She sighed, surprised at how miserable she felt. And the sensation had nothing to do with her blistering headache. But whatever unbidden thoughts crossed through her mind, there was more to consider than the Earl of Everton and what she might feel toward him. From this point on, until she discovered otherwise, she was going to have to assume that Alex was the one she had been sent to find. There were too many fragments that didn't quite fit together until *royal agent* was added into the equation.

She had been careless. Nearly unforgivably so. "Damnation," she muttered, sitting upright and rubbing at her throbbing skull. He'd won their wager, carried her upstairs, and left her sleeping like a babe. No doubt she'd even managed to snore or drool for his amusement.

After she made use of the chamber pot, she pulled off her ruined shirt and yanked a clean one on over her head.

That accomplished, she ran a comb through her disheveled hair and retied it in its short tail, then stomped out her door and over to Alex's. She was not a child he could tease and trick into a confession. Nor was she some pea-headed female to be seduced for amusement and then set aside, untouched. And if he laughed at her, well, she would hand him a flusher he wouldn't soon forget.

When she pushed open the door to his bedchamber, though, Alex was not laughing at her. In fact, he was sound asleep, sprawled across the bed in much the same state of disarray she had been in earlier.

It made her pause, seeing him so . . . vulnerable. Kit licked dry lips and glanced about for Antoine or one of the other servants, but none was in view. Silently she closed the door behind her and stepped into the room. Alex lay on his back, one leg bent and crossed under the other, and both arms outflung as though he had simply tumbled backward onto the bed and fallen asleep that way. His gray and black waistcoat lay tossed on the floor, beside his boots and his rumpled shirt. That was apparently as far as he had gotten in undressing, for he was still clothed in his breeches and stockings.

She leaned her cheek against the cool, polished wood of the post at the foot of the bed. A lock of his wavy black hair had fallen over one eye, and his lips were slightly parted. A light tangle of curling dark hair dusted his chest, and followed the line of his well-muscled abdomen to disappear into his breeches.

"How can I hate you?" she whispered.

That small sound was enough. The dark lashes fluttered and opened. Alex blinked, then sat bolt upright as he spied her. "Sweet Lucifer," he hissed, then clutched at his head and fell back onto the bed again. "Oh, good God," he continued, digging his fists into his temples.

A fine pair of spies they were. Despite the pounding of her own skull, and the fluttering along her nerves at the mere sight of him, Kit managed a chuckle. "Serves you right."

He opened one eye. "You nearly scared me witless, lurking there like the grim reaper."

Everton certainly didn't sound as though he suspected her of anything. Perhaps he had been more drunk than she realized, and didn't remember anything that had happened. "I was not lurking," she protested.

Gingerly he sat upright again. "Skulking, then."

"I came in here to shout at you, but you were asleep, and I thought it would be unkind."

"Shout at me about what?" he queried, sliding to the edge of the bed and gripping the post she leaned against as he stood. His fingers brushed over hers, and she quickly pulled them free. He glanced at her, a hesitation in his gaze that made her realize he did remember everything about last night. Everything. And that he was trying to decide in which direction to steer, as well.

"You undressed me," she stated, though she wanted to shout that she knew he was a damned British spy and she didn't want him to be one, because kissing him had been the most enjoyable thing she could ever recall experiencing.

"If I'd undressed you, you would have been naked. I loosened your clothing so you wouldn't strangle," Alex retorted. He made his way over to the curtains and tugged them open. "Good God," he repeated, squinting and turning away. "Sunlight."

She looked at him, lean and shirtless and handsome, as he stepped across the room to pull on his dressing robe. Even hungover and cranky, he moved gracefully, comfortable in his own skin. And she was standing gawking at him, when she should be trying to decide how to obtain proof that he was indeed who she suspected, and whether he had any clue about when her father planned to smuggle out the next shipment.

Alex stopped before his chamber pot. "Go have someone get us some coffee," he ordered over his shoulder.

She scowled at the order, but stalked out into the hallway. An upstairs maid was placing a vase of roses on the table there, and Kit requested the coffee as she had been instructed.

"Alex?" she asked, scratching at his door.

"Come in, brat," he returned after a moment.

When she entered the room again and shut the door behind her, she saw the earl had seated himself at his dressing table and was engaged with lathering shaving soap over the stubble of beard that covered his chin and cheeks. He glanced at her in the mirror, then lifted the razor. "Did you, ah, sleep well?"

At least it was an innocent question. She didn't feel ready for anything more complicated than that. And neither did he, apparently. "Yes. Did you?"

"Yes." His jaw twitched. "Thank you." He cleared his throat, glanced at her again, and began shaving.

The silence felt awkward, but cast her mind about though she did, she could come up with no topic of conversation that didn't feel suspicious. And yet, there weren't many days left before she was to leave, and she needed more proof than her own emotion-twisted, pathetic hunches. "I suppose you have more meetings today?" she ventured, watching the blade slide along the tanned skin of his face.

The razor paused, the eyes in the mirror speculative. "No meetings today."

"Oh." He lifted his head to scrape beneath his chin, while she watched, fascinated. "Why not?"

"Why do you care?" he retorted sharply.

"I was just attempting to determine how to amuse myself today."

"Ah. Well, I am going to purchase a hay rake." He pursed his lips as though weighing his next words. "You're welcome to accompany me."

"Oh," she repeated. His cheek where the razor had passed looked so smooth, her fingers twitched with the effort of not reaching out to stroke it. "I actually thought I might go with Hanshaw and Francis. There's some sort of boat race on the Thames or something."

"You spend a damned lot of time with my friends, chit," he snapped.

Kit put her hands on her hips. "Stop being such a lout," she suggested, "and I might go with you, instead. But you're never nice to me, and you're always dragging me about, so I don't see why you're surprised if I don't—"

He yanked her arm, pulling her off balance, then twisted her slender body sideways so she fell backward onto his lap. "Shut up."

"You big, stupid—"

His kiss was hard and rough, and ran like lightning through every inch of her body. His hands at both sides of her face kept her imprisoned against his mouth, and she reached up to cup his jaw, cool and warm at the same time, and still damp from the shaving soap. He slid one hand down around her waist, his mouth hungry on hers. She shivered at the feel of his lean body cradling hers, at the desperate craving to be close to him.

Out in the hall, a feminine voice called, "I can find my own way, thank you very much!"

With an oath, Alex broke the kiss. Swiftly he shoved Kit off his lap and stood her upright, as the door rattled and burst open. Barbara Sinclair, out of breath, her skirts twisted in one hand, shoved into the room. Wenton entered behind her, his expression even more dour than usual.

"Apologies, my lord. She insisted on—"

Alex raised a hand. "That will be all, Wenton."

"Yes, my lord." The butler nodded and pulled the door shut behind him.

"You need something, do you, Barbara?" Everton suggested, crossing his legs at the ankles, and Kit was amazed at his composure. She was having difficulty just steadying her breath.

Barbara Sinclair stepped over to the bed, noting its rumpled appearance. She ran a hand along the quilted coverlet and then turned back to face the earl. "At first I thought you were merely occupied with showing your cousin about," she began, "but then it occurred to me that you would never bestir yourself to be any kind of proper host. Something else must be occupying your time."

The black eyes turned to view Kit, and the abrupt speculation there left her uneasy. As Alex had warned her, if he had discovered her secret, someone else might as well. Barbara strolled up and raised one finger toward her face. Though her instinct was to slap the woman's hand aside, a man would not, and so Kit stood still. Lady Sinclair's finger brushed her chin, and came away with a thin froth of shaving soap.

Though for a moment her breath caught, Kit looked down at the soap and scowled. "Damnation, Alex, I told you to quit flinging that blade about when you talk," she complained, and made a show of examining the rest of her person for splotches of soap.

"I would, if you would cease being so opinionated regarding matters about which you obviously know nothing," he shot back with excellent timing, and tossed the towel at her.

He meant to keep her secret, then, even from Lady Sinclair. Kit was unable to keep from glancing swiftly in his direction, but his vaguely annoyed gaze was on his mistress.

Kit wiped at her face while Barbara glided up to Alex with a rustle of taffeta skirts. "It's not that I've begun to care for you," she murmured, turning her head sideways to regard the earl with an expression that made Kit wish to do some damage to her perfectly coifed raven hair.

Everton pushed to his feet. "Good," he returned. "I told you never to do so."

Barbara stepped aside to take the towel out of Kit's hands, and then returned to Alex. "Yes. It's only that Viscount Mandilly has been absolutely hounding me, and he's such a bore." Slowly she wiped the remaining shaving soap from Alex's face. "When you're about, you merely give him that contemptuous look of yours, and he slinks away."

"Well, that's sterling of you, cousin," Kit interrupted.

Damn Barbara Sinclair, anyway, for barging into the middle of everything.

Barbara glanced over her shoulder at Kit, her expression cryptic, then turned back and leaned up to whisper something into Alex's ear.

The earl stiffened, his swift glance at Kit unreadable. "Indeed," he murmured, his gaze returning for a moment to his mistress. "Kit, do leave us alone for a moment, won't you, my boy?" he suggested, not looking at her again.

That was simply too much. "I am the guest here," she stated angrily. "Simply because she decides to be an idi—"

Everton strode over and grabbed her by the arm. "That's enough," he said flatly, and jerked her forward. "Go get some breakfast." He opened the door and shoved her out into the hallway.

Kit stood looking at the door as it slammed in her face, all the delirious, desirous thoughts that had been spinning through her mind crashing to the carpet. She was nothing to him, after all. Simply a distraction until his mistress could arrive and offer him up what Kit would not. Could not. She wiped at her eyes, unexpected tears running down her face.

If she had needed any more proof that she was being a fool, Alex Cale had just provided her with it. With a sniff, she turned for the stairs and her hat and gloves. She certainly had better things to do than hang about while Everton and Barbara Sinclair humped all over one another. Now that she had a suspect, she merely needed to ask a few careful questions to be certain she was correct. And then it would be time to tell her father. However odd and foolish Everton might think her, she had still outmaneuvered him. She had still won.

"All right, Barbara," Alex said, leaning back against the bedpost and folding his arms across his chest. "Would you care to elaborate?"

"As I said, I've been checking into your family history," his mistress commented, strolling to the window and gazing with feigned interest at the roof of his carriage house. "You had no Aunt Marabelle. Therefore, you have no cousin Christian Riley."

A dozen swift responses coursed through his mind, and were just as swiftly rejected. Barbara would never have confronted him unless she was certain of her facts. "And?" he responded, deciding the wisest course would be to determine exactly how much his mistress did know about his houseguest. He raised an eyebrow and looked at her expectantly.

"And," Barbara repeated, turning to face him again, "so who is she?"

He'd known all along, he told himself, that Christine Brantley was trouble. Worse than trouble. She was a virgin, dressed like a boy, swore like a sailor, cheated at games of chance, and was likely working in the service of Bonaparte or one of his followers. And she was easily the most beguiling woman he'd ever encountered. "No one you need concern yourself with," he returned slowly, making the words a warning.

"But I am concerned," Lady Sinclair countered, not taking the hint. "I value your wealth, and your . . . companionship. I don't wish to lose them to some skinny-legged whore in breeches."

Alex regarded his mistress for a moment. He'd known Barbara could be arrogant, but it was an unpleasant side of her character she generally reserved for social climbers and inept servants. With him she was for the most part pliable and pleasant, but as she had said, she needed him for something. It had now become a question of how far she was willing to go to keep hold of what she wanted.

"Don't look at me that way, Alex," she continued when he said nothing. "You would do the same if someone stepped between you and something you wanted, and you know it."

"Yes, I would," he replied. And Barbara had just stepped between himself and Christine Brantley. "My guest will not be in London long," he said carefully, giving her as little information as he could. "Any arrangements between us are temporary. And so I suggest you tread carefully. I do not take kindly to cheap theatrics and threats."

Barbara looked at him from beneath her dark lashes. "So you want her kept a secret, do you?" she murmured, and took a step closer. She began to take another, but the chill in his gaze stopped her advance. "Very well, my lord. I can keep a secret, as well. If to do so is worth my while."

"Blackmail now? Harry would be so dismayed," Alex chided, inwardly seething. If the secret had been his own, he wouldn't have stood for any of this. The secret, however, was not his. Kit would be hurt and angry, and whatever sort of criminal she might be, he would not have Barbara Sinclair bandying her tale about for some petty revenge.

"My late husband had little head for business," she replied. "Hence my desire to keep company with you."

"What do you want, then?"

She was surprised he'd capitulated; he could see it in her eyes. "Well. Only your . . . continued interest, for now, Alex," she murmured, though she still came no closer. Less confident than she wanted him to believe, then. "Later perhaps we can discuss an additional arrangement."

He nodded. "I shall agree, for now," he answered coolly. "But I suggest for your sake that you not make a misstep, Barbara. I won't allow you more than one."

The last was said to keep her cautious, and to keep her silent. And it would work, so long as he kept his end of her little bargain. With a nod at him, she stepped from the room and quietly shut the door behind her. Alex strode to the window, threw it open, and breathed deeply of the cool May air. With but a handful of days left before Kit's departure, he'd begun taking risks with her, and with himself, that he should not. Even so, he had not anticipated being found out.

He slammed his fist against the sill. After last night, the game he and Kit had embarked on had become much more complicated. This morning the whole table had been flipped on its end. And for once in his life, he had no idea what to do, and little time to figure it out. "Damnation," he muttered. If only he hadn't become so involved in the chit's machinations and schemes, and if only he hadn't kissed her. If only he could do something, anything, other than think about kissing her again, about the graceful curve of her throat, about what her breasts looked like under her bedamned waistcoat, about peeling those tantalizing breeches down over her luscious hips and running his hands over her bare skin, about what it would be like to be inside her, to have her limbs entwined around his.

A scratch came at his door. "My lord?"

Alex jumped. "Antoine. Come in." He took a steadying breath and turned around. "Impeccable timing, as always. You've managed to miss most of the debacle."

The valet nodded. "Thank you, my lord."

"Hm." Alex shrugged out of his dressing gown and breeches as Antoine fetched him a clean wardrobe. "Did you happen to notice whether my cousin destroyed any furniture or irreplaceable works of art on the way to the breakfast room?" He couldn't tell her about Barbara's little scheme, he realized. It would have Kit angry and suspicious of him all over again, and he'd have no time to regain her trust if he wished to stop her game and keep her from harm at the same time.

"I may be mistaken, my lord, but I believe Mr. Riley has departed."

Alex turned so quickly, he pulled the cravat out of his valet's hands. "What?"

"I saw him in the front hallway with Wenton, my lord. I assumed he, your cousin, that is, was heading out for the day."

"Blast." Alex quickly and carelessly knotted the tie around his neck as he strode out into the upstairs hallway. "Wenton!" he bellowed, leaning over the railing.

"My lord?" The butler came into sight below.

"Where did Kit go?"

"My lord, Mr. Riley required that if you asked his

whereabouts, I was to inform you that . . .'' The butler trailed off.

"Out with it, man," Alex demanded impatiently, taking the stairs at a pace that made his head pound all over again.

"Very good, my lord. I was to inform you that you and that . . . suckling-pig mistress of yours could fly to Jericho for all he cared, because he was going to Covent Garden, my lord."

Alex's first impulse was to go charging out into the street and retrieve the chit before she got herself into trouble. His second reaction was to wonder whether she had slunk out to deliver intelligence to one of several Bonaparte spies he knew to be lurking in the area of Charing Cross and Covent Garden, and if he had by accident let something slip last night. He hadn't exactly been at his sharpest. But he hadn't exactly wanted to be. Finally, he decided she was willfully driving him mad, and that his head ached far too much for him to do anything until he had poured some coffee down his gullet.

The butler was eyeing him expectantly, so he nodded and turned for the breakfast room. "Very well. Send Drake in when he arrives. And inform me at once if my cousin should return, or if you should hear of anything calamitous which you believe he may have been the cause of."

"Yes, my lord."

He could convince himself he needed Kit's trust in order to win the game, but deciding just which game the two of them were now playing was a more difficult task entirely.

Chapter 9

Kit wandered among the rows of fruit and vege-
table stalls of the Covent Garden market and
peeled a peach. She had actually started out along Bond
Street looking for Hanshaw or Thadius Naring, but when
Viscount Devlin had ridden by, looking so intent on
something that he hadn't even noticed her, despite her
salutation, she had decided on the spur of the moment
to follow him. It was better than returning to Cale
House, better than thinking about what was going on
there in her absence.

Devlin was several stalls in front of her now, flirting
with a woman who boasted a cheap, low-cut gown, ample breasts, and rouged lips. She didn't recall that he
dallied with light-skirts, but then he didn't seem to be
making any effort to exert himself. Unless Kit was in
error, Augustus was distracted about something, a far cry
from his single-minded intensity all the way to Covent
Garden.

Devlin half turned in her direction, and Kit smoothly
stepped behind a cart and out of his line of sight. She
counted slowly to ten, then moved out of cover to stroll
over to a bread-maker's stall. When she glanced back
down the way, the viscount was gone. The woman,
though, remained. With a frustrated frown, Kit approached the viscount's would-be companion.

"You happen to see a friend of mine just a moment
ago?" she queried.

"I'm your friend," the woman replied saucily, in an accent a fishmonger would envy, and reached out to finger a button of Kit's waistcoat.

"And might this be your friend, as well?" Kit returned, holding a groat up in her fingers.

The woman took it from her, examined it, and then placed it somewhere on her person. "What's your friend look like?" she asked.

"Tall, pale, and light-haired, coughs sometimes." A female would have described him as handsome, and Kit was dismayed that for a moment she had nearly said it. Alex had her thinking like a chit, and it would get her into trouble.

"Oh, him." The woman scowled. "Aye. He didn't have no time for me, but went off with some other fine gentleman, down that way." She pointed behind her.

Kit glanced down the alley she had indicated. Curious as the incident had her, she was not fool enough to go wandering down a deserted way by herself. She thanked the woman and handed her another groat, then strolled half a block away, took up a good spot against one wall, and settled in to wait.

The Earl of Everton was becoming annoyed. At half past one he had finished meeting with his man of business. By five in the afternoon he had purchased two hay rakes and written out instructions to his estate agent at Everton, informing him that barley prices were increasing on the London market, and that he wished to change over twenty acres of oat fields in favor of the other crop. At six, tired of waiting about, he went out to an early dinner at Boodle's.

Reg and Francis had headed off to Barbara's for dinner, but he begged off, still more inclined to strangle his mistress than to dance attendance on her, and arranged instead to meet them at the Worthington ball later. He returned to Cale House to change, only to learn from Wenton that Mr. Riley had not yet returned.

"Damnation," he muttered, slapping his gloves against his thigh. Covent Garden in the dark was less than savory—if she was there at all, and not in some tavern telling a Frenchman all the secrets of the English blockade. He dearly hoped she had instead gone off to one of his clubs, and was charging expensive bottles of liquor to his account and cheating some worthy out of his inheritance for a laugh. That, he wouldn't mind.

He waited about, kicking his heels and swearing, until nearly eleven. "Wenton," he finally said, heading back downstairs, "I'm off to the Worthingtons'." Antoine trailed down the stairs behind him, smoothing out any remaining wrinkles in the earl's evening attire.

"Very good, my lord."

"If my cousin should return, let him know where I am. If he decides to attend, inform him that I strongly suggest he dress soberly. Worthington's a stuffy old *buse.*"

"Buzzard, my lord," Antoine translated, handing over Alex's pocket watch.

"*S'attendes à mon cousin, s'il vous plaît,*" the earl instructed his valet, feeling more comfortable with someone who knew Kit Riley's true gender looking out for her, as well.

"*Certainement,* my lord," Antoine agreed.

"*Merci,* Antoine." Damn the chit for going off alone, when he'd told her not to. If she hadn't returned by the end of the evening, he was going to have to go looking for her. At the moment, he refused to consider whether his concern was over letting a spy loose in London, or letting an obstinate young lady, of whom he was becoming absurdly fond, wander the streets alone.

Wenton held out his greatcoat. "My lord?" he prompted after a moment.

"Hm? Oh, yes. Well, I'm off," Alex said unnecessarily, realizing he was stalling. He shrugged into the overcoat and stepped out into the darkness.

He arrived at the rout late, actually a blessing considering how dull the evening looked to be. Lady Caroline and the Duchess of Furth arrived shortly after he did, and Caroline pointedly asked after the health of his cousin. At least Martin Brantley rarely spent the Season in London, for if Kit had cast up her accounts at the sight of the daughter, he could only imagine what her reaction would be if placed face-to-face with Furth himself. And he, too, hoped the duke remained in Wiltshire, for his life was as complicated as he ever wished it to become, without adding that into the mix. He turned to greet Hanshaw as he approached.

"Alex." The baron nodded, handing over a glass of brandy. "Any news?"

He shook his head. "I've sent Hunt to Dover, and James north. They'll let me know in a few days. I can't think a thousand muskets could be that easy to hide."

"Even so, I do believe it's got our glorious leader agitated."

Alex scowled. The last thing he needed was to bestir his sometime mentor over this mess. Apparently the complications were just beginning. "You wrote him?"

Reg lifted an eyebrow. "You didn't?"

"I find it more pleasant to convey the message that we have recovered crates of weapons, than that we are searching for them," Alex replied coolly.

The baron grimaced. "Quite right. I have little wish to anger him at the moment, anyway."

"Neither do I," Alex returned feelingly. Francis Henning approached from the stairs, and he flicked his eyes at Reg, warning him, then grinned. "That's quite a bauble you've acquired," he noted, pulling Francis's arm up to eye the ring he had jammed on one finger. "Whomever did you steal it from?"

Francis laughed. "I won it from Lindley. Said he got it straight off the boat from India."

"What were they using it for, ballast?" Reg asked, leaning over to examine the deep red stone.

"It's priceless, I'm certain," Francis replied indignantly.

"It's glass, I'll wager," Hanshaw countered.

Francis scowled and waggled his finger again in Alex's direction. "What is it, then, Everton?"

Alex gave a brief grin. "Sorry, Francis." He glanced toward the door, then clenched his jaw as Barbara Sin-

clair entered and was announced. Best to get it over
with, before Kit made her own appearance and left him
with adversaries on both sides. "If you'll excuse me,
gentlemen," he said, and strolled over to greet his mistress.

"Everton." She smiled, and swept a graceful curtsy.
Her eyes, though, were wary, as though she expected
him to cut her.

There was nothing he would rather do, and Alex had
to remind himself that this was for Kit's sake. He could
be pleasant to Lady Sinclair until this game ended, one
way or another. "Barbara." He nodded, taking her fingers. "May I have this waltz?"

"Of course," she said graciously. They stepped out
onto the floor and into the dance. "I don't see your
cousin," she commented after a moment. "I'd hoped
that he would be here this evening."

"Don't push me, Barbara," Alex murmured with a
smile. "You have a reputation to think of, as well."

"And so we dance," Lady Sinclair whispered.

"And so we dance," he agreed.

When Kit returned to Cale House at half past eight
the next morning, Wenton informed her that his lordship
had returned home only a short while earlier, and was
currently in the breakfast room.

"Does he want to see me?" she asked wearily, handing over her outer garments and wishing for the soft bed
upstairs.

"He did not say, Mr. Riley."

"Oh." She wasn't certain whether she wanted to see
him, either. He'd slammed a door in her face yesterday
morning, and then apparently spent the night with his
mistress. And evidently all of his close acquaintances
were tied into smuggling and government appointments
and Napoleon. Why Augustus Devlin, the one dying of
consumption, had been left to meet with several suspi-
cious-looking individuals in a Covent Garden alley until
sometime well after midnight, she didn't know. It didn't
seem very intelligent of them, and if Alexander Cale was

anything, it wasn't stupid. Even odder was the way Devlin had returned home, slipping through his garden gate and in by the servants' entrance, as if he didn't want his own staff to know what time he had arrived back at Devlin House. Of course, she might have done the same thing on her return to Cale House, if she hadn't fallen asleep behind his brick wall waiting to see if he would exit again.

She started toward the stairs, then stopped beside the breakfast room door. There were six days left. If she allowed Alex to suspect that she knew what he was up to, there was no telling what might happen. Neither, though, was she ready to forgive him for his exceeding rudeness. With an aggravated sigh, she pushed open the door.

Everton was seated at his customary place beneath the garden window. He glanced up over the edge of the morning paper and raised his cup of tea to his lips.

"Good morning," he said, and resumed reading.

"Good morning," she returned shortly, and dropped into the seat at the opposite end of the table, hoping he would notice the cut. A footman poured her a cup of tea, while another brought her a plate laden with fruit and toast. As soon as they were finished, Everton motioned with one hand, and they left the room.

"For purposes of etiquette," his mild voice came from behind the paper a moment later, "that is generally considered to be the chair of the lady of the house."

"So she can be as far from her husband as possible, no doubt," she grumbled. He might have apologized for yesterday, instead of pretending that nothing had ever happened. "Stupid English custom."

There was a short delay while the earl's teacup vanished behind the paper and then reappeared. "Well, as we're apparently being blunt today, might I ask where the devil you've been since yesterday morning?"

"None of your bloody affair," she answered the newspaper.

There was another brief pause, during which Kit's heart pounded inside her chest, and then the paper lowered and folded in half. "Indeed," Alexander murmured, leaning forward in his chair. "Have you seen this, then?"

He slid the paper over to her. The headline shouted, "Napoleon Rallies Followers," and was accompanied by an artist's rendering of Bonaparte speaking to his council in Paris. She glanced up at Everton.

He studied her, no doubt assessing the reason for the tired lines around her eyes and her wilted cravat. Alex didn't look as though he had slept much, either, but at least she could guess where he had been. Pride, though, wouldn't let her mention it. If all she was to him was a debt of honor and a foolish chit, naive about seduction and easy to tease, then so be it. As long as she was aware of that, it wouldn't happen again.

She slid the paper back to him, but he didn't look at it. "I'm not surprised," she stated. "I didn't think he would be off to Russia again."

"Nor am I surprised," he agreed. "I was wondering, though, what further plans your father had."

Kit started, and attempted to cover it by reaching for the bowl of fruit set halfway between them. "My father?"

"Yes," Alex answered. "I was to watch you for a fortnight, and then he was to make other plans for your safety. The Duke of Wellington is headed toward the north of France. Paris does not appear to be growing more safe, nor the army less likely to conscript a likely lad such as yourself."

Kit shrugged. If his concern was still her safety and his debt of honor, perhaps he didn't know the truth about her reasons for being in London. If that was the case, it was foolish to make him angry at her. She glanced down for a moment, no longer certain whether she was making excuses to help her father, or because she couldn't get Alex out of her mind for one moment—even when she was almost certain he was working directly against her father, even when she should be hating him. "I'm certain he'll think of something."

"Yes, he's quite resourceful."

"How do you know that?" she queried, suspicious again.

"The proof stands, or rather sits, before me," he answered. "Not many fathers would think of dressing their daughters as sons to keep them in safety." He stood and moved over to the seat next to her. "Now, with that in mind, let me ask you again. Where were you last night?" Slowly he reached out and touched the fingers gripping her teacup. "And if you don't answer me, in order to ensure your safety until your father comes for you, I will be forced to lock you in your room."

The voice was soft, the eyes steel. He meant it. She jerked her hand away. "You bully," she spat. "You could never keep me here."

"I could."

She glared at him, and saw that he was as suspicious of her as she was of him. And they had just reached an impasse. "I'll tell you where I was," she said slowly, taking a controlling breath to keep her voice from shaking, "if you tell me where you were."

Everton searched her gaze for another moment, then nodded. "I went to the Worthington ball, then accompanied Barbara Sinclair home." She opened her mouth, but he shook his head at her. "We played piquet until three in the morning, after which I stopped back here and then went looking for you. So don't tell me you were at one of my clubs, please."

"You played piquet?" she repeated, for that seemed far more significant than the fact that her whole tale was slowly beginning to fray.

"We played piquet," he affirmed. "And I let her win. Which was quite difficult, because she's a careless player. Unlike yourself."

"And that's all," she pressed skeptically.

"Yes."

"A rakehell of your reputation?" she asked flippantly, wanting with all her heart to believe him. "Why?"

He looked down for a moment, then caught her gaze again. His sensuous lips pursed ruefully. "Because Barbara Sinclair is a poor substitute."

Kit narrowed her eyes, her heart beating quite fast. "A poor substitute for what?"

"For you, my dear."

She swallowed, then took a deep breath. "You are under a debt of—"

"Yes, I'm quite aware of that, thank you very much." His voice was pained and exasperated, and his fingers sought hers again. "Which has nothing to do with my . . . feelings toward your person."

" 'Feelings'?" she repeated, exceedingly curious.

He snorted, his lips quirking in a half smile as he slowly shook his head. "Shall I detail them for you?"

"Please do." She very much wished to hear what he would say, and besides, he seemed to have quite forgotten his demand to know how she had spent the night.

Alex looked sideways at her. "Let me put it this way, so as not to shock your delicate sensibilities, chit. I believe it to be your choice of attire."

"You like my clothes?" She raised an eyebrow.

"I hate them."

"Well, excuse me, Everton, but you're the one who—"

"Now, now," he interrupted, raising a hand to fend her off. "Let me finish. Even the most modest of women's clothing is designed to . . . reveal the form beneath," he explained in a bemused tone. "This, I believe, is done for purposes of sale and marketing. You, however, have seen fit to remain determinedly concealed beneath lawn shirts and waistcoats and cravats and evening coats and breeches. The only flesh I've seen of you is above your neck and below your wrists." He looked at her, his eyes amused again. "And it's deuced frustrating, chit."

He desired her. Alexander Cale, the Earl of Everton, desired her, a smuggler's daughter. Making a mighty effort to gather her puddling wits up from the floor, Kit returned his gaze. "Scoundrel," she muttered.

What he had said, unsettling though it had been, provided her with a possible answer to a very sticky question. It had occurred to her sometime last night. She had been so concerned with finding proof that he was the quarry her father was after that she hadn't considered what was to be done with him once she did know for certain. Alex, she recognized, could not and would not be bribed to leave them be. Short of killing him—and the mere thought of that had left her frantic with distress—she had been unable to come up with another solution. Until now.

If he wouldn't be bribed, and she wouldn't allow him to be hurt, then perhaps she could distract him. Immediately the idea was distasteful to her, for she'd lost enough of her heart to Alexander Cale to wish not to hurt him. But it was infinitely better than seeing him dead. She wasn't certain, though, that she could pretend to be as captivated with him as he seemed to be with her, and not forget what her true purpose was.

"Kit," Alex said, and she started. His chin was resting in one palm, his elbow on the table, his intrigued and speculative gaze on her face.

"Hm?" she returned, blinking back to the present.

"Twopence for your thoughts," he murmured.

"I, ah, I was just thinking that I doubt Father had your particular . . . reaction in mind when he dressed me in breeches," she offered.

"So cool, you are," he muttered. "I'd hoped for a slightly more flattering response."

"I don't know what you want me to say," Kit replied stiffly.

"An honest answer would be refreshing," Everton commented, unmoving.

"Does it matter whether I tell you how I feel about you?" she countered, unable to keep the slight, desperate edge from her voice. "It wouldn't change anything."

"It would matter," he said quietly.

She couldn't meet his searching gaze. "I find you very annoying, then," she shot, and stood.

Moving with startling swiftness for a man of his height and strength, Alex beat her to the door and leaned back against it, blocking her escape. His hand strayed down to his coat pocket, and her eyes followed it.

Slowly, he lifted a key and dangled it before her face. "Forgetting something, aren't you?"

"You weren't serious!" she protested, alarmed and angry, and oddly exhilarated.

"Deadly serious," he murmured.

"Lourdaud! Âne! Bravache!"

"I believe you've used at least one of those on me before," he commented mildly, though his eyes bespoke a different emotion entirely. "Best for you if you keep in mind that I have a fairly good memory."

"As do I."

"Good. Then I don't need to repeat the question."

"I hate you."

"Not quite what I was looking for, but at least it's honest."

She wasn't so certain it was, even under these circumstances, but it gave her a moment to think up a lie for her whereabouts of the evening, as he knew she hadn't been at White's. "I went to Covent Garden, hired a hack to take me to Dover and thought about purchasing a place on a ship to Calais, changed my mind, stomped about Dover for a time, and took a hack back to London again." She folded her arms and prayed she had sounded angry enough that he believed her.

He lowered the key, something swift and almost vulnerable running across his lean features. "Why did you change your mind?"

"I don't know. I wish I hadn't, now."

For a long moment Everton looked down at her. "Well, this leaves me with something of a dilemma," he finally said.

"And what might that be, pray tell?"

"You've told me what I wished to know, but I can't very well have you running back to Paris in the middle of a war and nearly a week short of the fortnight. Your father would be rather annoyed, and I would have failed in honoring my own patriarch's debt."

Damnation. She'd meant only to rattle him, not to box herself into a corner. Or rather, into her room for the next week. "I wouldn't consider locking me away to be the least bit honorable, either,'' she told him.

"Yes, well, we'll decide that later,'' he said, and pocketed the key. "For now, why don't you finish eating, and we'll go to Gerald and Ivy's?''

"I don't want to go to—''

"Don't make me repeat myself, Kit,'' he said darkly, and she realized she had hurt him. "I need to go, and therefore so do you. If you'd been a female out all night, you'd be ruined.''

With that he stepped out into the hallway and shut the door behind him.

"I am a female.'' she muttered.

Chapter 10

"**W**ho are you disemboweling?"

Alex finished his shot and stood the billiards cue on end, before he looked across the table at his cousin. "Beg pardon?" he returned, though he had heard the comment quite clearly.

Gerald Downing gestured at the number three ball, still rolling about the table in a rather haphazard fashion. "As I recall from your gloating victory speeches on innumerable past occasions, the secret to winning at billiards is a cool head and a snifter of—"

"Brandy," Alex finished with a half-amused scowl. "You're full of pale platitudes this morning, aren't you?"

"You've provided me with most of them. I do hang on your every word, you know."

"Oh, stuff it and get me a brandy, Gerald."

He shrugged and strolled over to the liquor tray to do as he was bid, while Alex studied the disaster he'd made of the table. At the sound of female laughter emanating from the morning room across the hallway, he scowled again and looked in that direction. The damned chit was making a wreck of him, and she likely knew it perfectly well. A door shut, and the attractive music vanished behind it.

"It's our lot in life, you know." Gerald sighed, approaching to hand over the brandy.

"What's our lot?" Alex lifted the snifter and took a healthy swallow. It didn't help.

"Being laughed at and never having a clue about what we've done that's so damned amusing," his cousin replied, stepping around to plan his shot.

Alex's frown returned. He had a very good idea what Kit Brantley found so amusing. On the ride over to the Downings she'd scarcely looked in his direction, the stiff line of her spine letting him know precisely how angry she was at being ordered about. He had been angry as well, mostly at himself for letting her get to him again. It had shaken him, when she'd said she'd gone all the way to Dover, and had nearly taken herself back to France. Her response was not the one he was used to receiving when he expressed interest in a woman. Until she'd said she hated him, he would have been much more amenable to throwing her onto the breakfast table, ripping her clothes off, and licking every inch of the body she'd been keeping concealed from him for the past eleven days. And he was still thinking about it, thinking about her.

Gerald sank two balls before he missed, and Alex stepped up to the table again. His cousin had actually left him a fair shot, and a chance to take back the entire game. He raised an eyebrow. "Perhaps you should have poured yourself a brandy while you were at it," he commented, leaning his stick across the table.

"How much longer will dear Kit be staying with you?"

"Six days," Alex muttered, choosing his angle of attack.

"And how are you holding up?"

Alex glanced up at his cousin and shifted his stance a little. "Splendidly."

"No tangled bedsheets yet?"

"Shut up, Gerald."

Gerald chuckled. "Given the appalling lack of restraint and manners you have heretofore exhibited, I am quite proud of you, m'boy."

Alex made his shot, and watched, unsurprised, as the

nine ball dropped into the corner pocket, the cue ball following close behind. "Gerald," he said succinctly as he straightened, "I possess an exceptional degree of restraint, for which you should be exceedingly grateful."

Gerald eyed him. "Why don't you simply go to Barbara or one of the other half a hundred women who would be more than willing to service the Earl of Everton?"

Because I want Christine Brantley. "What makes you think I haven't been?"

"You're drawn tighter than a bowstring, Alex."

"I do have other—"

His cousin raised his cue and pointed it at Alex's chest. "Don't even attempt to blame it on Bonny Bonaparte," he stated, then sighed, leaning over the table. "At least you've only six more days to worry over her virtue."

Alex turned to look at his cousin, for the first time realizing what six days meant. She would be gone. She would leave for Dover, and not change her mind and return. He'd never see her again. "Yes, thank goodness," he muttered, looking toward the doorway again.

"No, I'm glad you told me"—Ivy smiled—"and I truly don't think there's anything wrong with you."

"But I was standing there, gawking, *gawking,* at a dress. Hanshaw must have thought I was demented."

"However you were raised, Kit, you're still a female," Alex's cousin said patiently, as though the whole twisted mess was perfectly clear to her. "And one who has perhaps begun to think of herself as a female for the first time?"

"Oh, I suppose so," Kit said irritably. She'd spent the morning spinning lies for Alex, and then found herself telling more to explain her dour mood, when Ivy trapped her into having a coze. Everything was becoming so complicated. And the easiest thing to do was blame everything on Alex Cale. If he hadn't been so handsome and witty and interesting, she wouldn't have minded all the terrible things she was doing. She'd never even thought of them as terrible until she met him.

"Are you and Alex ... getting along?" Ivy asked, looking at her from over the rim of her teacup.

"What do you mean by that?" Kit asked sharply.

"Just that you were having quite an argument the night we met you. Gerald tried to wager me that the two of you would have Cale House burned to the ground within the week."

"Well, Everton's a very irritating man," she pointed out.

"Yes, he can be." Ivy sat back and looked at her for a moment. "You know, I have an idea." She sipped at her tea. "You're not quite my size, but if you'd like to try a gown on, I think we can manage to find one for you."

That stopped Kit. "I ... no, I don't have time for that," she stammered. "Really, I ... I mean thank you, but ..." She paused. Once she returned to Paris with her father, she would never be able to do such a thing. The risk was far too great. "Do you think I might?"

Mrs. Downing laughed. "If you have time, yes, I don't see why not." The bell rang for luncheon, and she stood. "Tomorrow, perhaps?"

"Tomorrow?" She truly had no time for this. She needed to make certain that delaying or distracting Alex would enable her father to transport the goods he'd acquired across the Channel. If Reg or Augustus was actively involved, and not just supporting Everton, she would have to find a different way to slow them down. "All right."

Gerald and Everton were already in the dining room when they arrived, and with a quick look between Kit and Alex, Ivy dismissed the servants. The earl's expression was still cool as the two men stood at their entrance, but Kit decided it was his own fault. He was the one ordering her about as if she were one of his footmen.

Ivy seated herself, and Alex immediately followed suit. After a moment he looked up at Gerald, still standing and glaring at him, and then over at Kit. She clutched the back of her chair and clenched her jaw.

She'd hurt his feelings, and now he was pretending he didn't remember that he'd kissed her, that he'd told her he desired her, that she was even a woman.

He sighed and pushed to his feet again. "Pardon me, my lady. I hadn't realized you were being a female today, after all."

Kit's first instinct was to curse him in French, her second was to ask him when he'd acquired the ability to read minds, and her third was to burst into tears and flee the room rather than continue lying and fighting with him. Instead, she gave a forced smile and dropped into her chair. "One can never tell, I suppose."

His gaze lingered on her face for a moment, but she refused to look at him as she passed the platter of roast chicken to Ivy.

"Alex," Ivy said with a smile, "I was wondering if I might borrow Kit tomorrow, if you've no objection."

Everton looked at his cousin-in-law, then at Kit again. She glared at him. "I won't ruin your stupid debt," she whispered.

He pursed his lips and sighed. "I have absolutely no control over Kit's actions, so I suggest you ask her."

"I'd love to, Ivy," she put in, attempting to shorten the conversation, and thereby the entire meal, by as much as possible.

Alex lifted his fork, but paused with it midway to his mouth. "Why, just out of curiosity?"

"I merely find her company more tolerable than yours, *cochon*," Kit replied hotly.

The earl raised an eyebrow, while Gerald choked on a mouthful of bread. "Excuse me, Kit, but are you completely certain you're a female? I can't recall a single chit who's called Alex a pig *before* he's broken with them."

That was simply too much. Kit shoved to her feet and slammed her fork back down on the table. "Yes! I am a female!" With an exasperated, infuriated snarl she stomped from the room.

She was out on the drive, wiping tears from her face

so she could step out into the street without being gawked at, when Alex caught up to her.

"Not fleeing again, are you?" he queried, falling into place beside her.

"I'm sorry I called you a pig. I didn't know Gerald spoke French," she grumbled, hoping tears wouldn't ruin her coat sleeve.

"Only in regard to fine wine and farmyard animals," Alex commented. "Do stop for a moment, won't you? Hessian boots were not made for running to Marathon."

With a scowl, she tromped to a halt and turned to face him. Silently he held a white rose out to her. Her heart gave a flop, her anger and frustration melting into something else entirely, as she reached out and took it from him. "Thank you."

"I wanted to apologize," he said, licking his lips and glancing aside for a moment.

"For what?"

"For telling you that I'm lusting after you. It would seem to be my own problem, and I will simply have to struggle with it."

Kit looked at him skeptically. As far as distracting him, if she simply fell upon him, he would be suspicious. Subtlety where Alex Cale was concerned, though, was not one of her strong suits. "And will you be successful, do you think?" she ventured.

He gave a short grin. "I really don't know. It's a test of my character I've never had to engage in before." He put his arm out, inviting her to return to the Downings' house.

This confusion of hearts was a new experience for her, as well. "No, I really don't wish to right now," she grumbled.

"Well, come on, then, chit," he said with an unexpected smile, "and I'll teach you to drive the phaeton and let you terrorize the pedestrians in Hyde Park. That will perk you up, don't you think?"

"Yes, it might," she admitted. With a last wipe at her eyes, Kit took a breath and followed him back to his carriage. He climbed up, then held a hand down to her.

She clasped it and let him help her into the seat. He delayed a moment before he released his grip, but she didn't dare look up at his face for fear that she would kiss him in front of the Downings' groom. As they started off, he reached into his coat pocket and pulled out an apple, which he wordlessly handed to her.

She accepted it with a grin and bit into it. A juicy chunk came loose with a crunch. "Thank you, Alex."

"Well, actually it was to give to the horses, but you're welcome," he answered dryly, then gave her his dazzling, breath-stealing smile and chuckled.

Abruptly everything was all right again. She had days to think of something, after all. "I can share," she offered, finally relaxing again, and with a laugh took another bite.

As with everything else Alex had witnessed her attempting, Kit Brantley took to driving a phaeton as though she'd been born to it. "Ease up a little on Benvolio," he instructed, sitting back and crossing his arms to watch her profile. "You've got Mercutio doing all the work."

"I've got it," she acknowledged, glancing at him with the faint grin she'd been wearing for the past half hour, since he'd turned the ribbons over to her. "Can I set them into a gallop?"

"I'd advise against it," he answered smoothly.

"Just thought I'd ask."

"At least you did so *before* you sent us careening into oblivion."

In the mottled, leaf-obscured sunlight of Hyde Park, her green eyes sparkled as she laughed. After her disappearance of yesterday and her subsequent tale, he remained uncertain whether he was being played for a fool, but it was obvious even to a thick-skulled male such as himself that something was dreadfully upsetting her, though he hadn't a clue what it might be. Still, as he had lately discovered, the chit's low spirits immediately caused him to forget his own troubles, and his duties, in a quest to cheer her up.

"Everton! Kit!"

Alex turned his head to see a phaeton approaching them, and felt his own team jump as Kit also recognized the carriage's occupants. "Steady, chit," he murmured, nodding as Hanshaw, with Lady Caroline, pulled alongside them. "Stop the carriage," he continued out of the side of his mouth.

"Alex . . ." Kit's voice was tight, and he glanced at her, concerned that she was about to cast up her accounts again. Her face was pale, her eyes looking beyond him at the other carriage.

Sensing she was near panic, he reached out one hand to grasp her wrist. She jumped, her eyes darting to his face as he took the reins out of her shaking fingers. "She won't bite," he whispered in her ear, "and I certainly wouldn't let her maim you."

"I say, what are you two conspiring about?" Reg complained, leaning around Caroline to eye them.

"My cousin is attempting to destroy my cattle," Alex offered, "and is generally ignoring my advice about the fine art of two-in-hand."

Kit settled back to lean against his arm, as though seeking the comfort of touching him. He had no idea how to figure her out. One moment she was distant and hostile, and the next, vulnerable and trusting. He could spend a lifetime discovering her, he thought—and was immediately dismayed by the thought. He had no plans to give his heart away ever again. And she was a damned spy, for God's sake.

"My mother never informed me how insufferable the other side of the family was." Kit grinned at Alex, who had a difficult time not gaping at her. The chit had more backbone than some soldiers.

Caroline laughed. "I have often wondered, if each side of a family claims the other is intolerable, which one is actually correct, or whether we should all be locked up somewhere."

Kit gave a reluctant, almost shy smile, an expression Alex found to be among the most enchanting he had ever seen. "Finding an impartial observer would seem to be deuced difficult," she offered after a moment.

"Kit, Alex says you're only here another few days," Reg broke in. "What say we round up Devlin and Francis to give you a proper send-off at the Society night after next?"

She nodded happily. "That's sterling, Hanshaw."

"You've been here such a short time," Caroline protested. "Lord Everton, you're not sending him away, are you?"

"Heavens, no," Alex returned, glancing again at the chit and feeling something painful tighten in his chest. "His father's returning for him."

"Can't you convince your father to let you remain through the end of the Season?" Caroline asked.

"He . . . no, I, ah, he has some business back in Ireland, and I'll need to assist him with it," Kit offered.

Alex wondered if she would be pleased to be leaving. She hadn't spoken much of her father, and he couldn't believe she could possibly be looking forward to returning to Saint-Marcel—unless that had been a lie, as well, so he wouldn't be able to track them later. They took their leave of Reg and Lady Caroline, and he caught Kit turning to look after them. "That wasn't so terrible, was it?" he ventured, clucking to the team.

She sat back and sighed. "I suppose not. Perhaps she doesn't see much of her father, and doesn't resemble him."

Actually, the resemblance was rather striking. "You like her, you mean."

Kit shrugged. "I could, I think. If she wasn't who she was, and if I"—she glanced down at her blue day suit— "weren't what I am."

"So when you're fifty, say, do you still intend to be Kit Riley, boy adventurer?" the earl queried as he guided the team out of Hyde Park.

"I don't know," she answered after a moment, facing away from him. "I haven't really thought that far ahead."

"You'll be twenty soon, my dear. Perhaps you should begin."

She sighed, keeping her gaze on the horses. "Perhaps."

"You still planning on visiting Ivy?" Alex asked the next morning, taking a last swallow of tea and rising from the breakfast table.

Kit looked up at him. "Unless you have something else in mind," she said after a moment, giving him another expression he had no idea how to read. He'd never had that problem before, he reflected. Telling what Mary was thinking had always been effortless, and deciphering the thoughts and wishes of his various mistresses hadn't been exactly taxing. Of course, he'd never been as curious about a woman as he was about this one, either.

He shook his head. "More meetings."

"Oh, blast it, Alex! You're not a rakehell at all, are you?"

Alex gave a shout of laughter. "You sound completely disappointed." He chortled, leaning back against the wall.

Her expression did make him think for a moment that she wished he were a rakehell. She wiped the corner of her mouth with her napkin in a dainty gesture, but he could practically see the gears turning in her head, and waited patiently for her next lie.

Instead, she tilted her head at him. "Are they important, these meetings? Might you skip one?"

He shook his head. "No. Important or not, with the slight problem of Bonaparte's escape from Elba, meetings do seem to be in order, wouldn't you say?"

"An army would be more in order," she returned, rising as well.

That, coming from a Bonaparte sympathizer, was a surprise. "You wish me to lead an army to France?" he asked, studying her expression for anything that might give her true sentiments away.

"No," she said hurriedly. "That would never do."

"Why not?" he murmured, pushing away from the wall as she stopped in front of him.

She swallowed, a soft blush coloring her cheeks.

"Wellington can lead the army," she said, and turned her back again.

Slowly he reached out and touched her arm, turning her around. "And what would you have me do?" he queried quietly. Her light green eyes met his, and his fingers twitched on her sleeve. He wanted to pull her closer, to touch her, to hold her.

She swallowed, then gave him a grin that didn't touch her eyes. "You may lead your meetings." She sighed theatrically. "Though I have no idea how the wives of peers can stand to sit about all day while their husbands attend meetings. It would drive me mad."

He chuckled. "Most wives, I believe, gain their revenge by going about Bond Street and spending all of their husband's income."

"Well, I only have fifteen quid, so I suppose I must remain bored."

Fifteen quid, and a lifetime of poverty in Saint-Marcel. With a forced smile Alex motioned her to accompany him to his study. He leaned over the desk and pulled a piece of parchment from a drawer, scrawled a quick note on the page, and handed it to her. "There you go."

She looked down at it, and her eyes widened. "You're giving me your note of credit?"

He nodded and smiled, wondering whether he was about to be sent to debtors' prison, or worse, for his generosity to the chit. "Avail yourself of whatever you'd like to take back to Paris with you."

"But . . ." she stammered, looking up at him again, "but I could ruin you with this."

"You already have, my dear," he said softly, and touched her cheek with his palm. "I shall have to trust you." And while she was shopping, hopefully she wouldn't be revealing any state secrets. Some strategist had once written that distraction could be as formidable a weapon as a direct attack, and it certainly seemed less painful.

Kit studied his face for a long moment. Finally she

grinned. "Thank you, Alex." She folded the note and stuffed it into her inner coat pocket.

He raised a finger at her. "I *would* advise against estates or large vehicles," he warned her, half-seriously, "and livestock."

She laughed. "If you'd given this to me last week, you could have spent every minute in meetings plotting against Napoleon. That's much safer for you, anyway."

"Safer than what, Kit?"

A muscle in her jaw twitched. "Leading armies and such nonsense," she said flippantly, and he knew that was not what she had meant. She lowered her gaze and turned away. "I'll be spending your wealth on Bond Street if you need me, Croesus."

Alex drew a ragged breath as she stepped outside. She truly didn't sound as though she supported Bonaparte, but neither did she sound like the daughter of a man who was smuggling weapons for that very cause. For a moment he nearly gave in to the impulse that had been tugging at him all morning, to follow her out the door, damn all matters of state. He simply wanted to spend the day with her.

Reluctantly he headed upstairs for his gloves. With only a few days before she returned to France, he should be arranging to stay as far from her as possible. And he truly did have things to do, especially with muskets heading north somewhere along the coast, and Bonaparte beginning a march toward Belgium.

Kit and Ivy started at one end of Bond Street. Shopping for a gown with Mrs. Downing was very nearly as much fun as buying hats and gloves with Alex. Of course, a married lady shopping in the company of a younger man, even her cousin, was enough to elicit odd looks and even a few muttered comments, but Ivy didn't seem to mind. And Kit was so intrigued with the clothes and fabrics and accessories that she barely noticed.

"Mr. Riley?"

Kit looked up quickly from the row of hair ribbons she was picking through. Mercia Cralling stood on the far side of the table, looking at her curiously. "Miss Cralling." She smiled, reaching out to take the girl's hand. "Pleased to see you again."

"But what are you doing here?" Mercia whispered, blushing and glancing about the small shop.

"Oh, Ivy's been kind enough to assist me in bringing some things back home for my mother," she answered offhandedly, casually leaning sideways to see how Miss Cralling's hair was held up in the back.

"But I thought your mother was dead," Mercia answered, a slight scowl crossing her pale, perfect features.

"Oh, yes, she is," Kit returned smoothly, cursing herself. Alex would be furious if he discovered she was being so careless. She shook herself—her *father* would be furious. "My father remarried. This is for my step-mother, of course."

"That's so kind of you." Mercia smiled, putting her hand out to rest it on Kit's.

Kit bit her tongue to keep from laughing and smoothly pulled her hand free. Mercia Cralling would be in for something of a surprise if this flirtation went on any longer. "Well, she's a good sort, really," she responded, turning her head to look for Ivy, who was patiently trying to explain to the shopkeeper that her aunt-in-law, Kit's mother, was actually rather tall for a female, and quite fashionable for someone of her age.

"Kit, do you think Aunt . . ."

"Celia," Kit supplied.

"Celia would prefer a blue muslin, or a green and peach one?" Ivy asked, indicating the two gowns the shopkeeper was holding.

"The green and peach, I think," she said, eyeing the creations and shivering at the thought of actually wearing a gown.

Ivy nodded at the shopkeeper. "If you please."

Kit cleared her throat and strode up to the counter. "And these as well," she stated, placing a pair of bone clips beside the dress and a pair of stockings Ivy had procured. Shoes were proving to be more difficult, as she couldn't very well slip off her Hessian boots to try on a pair. Finally they had settled on a pair of green, or rather, true verdant, slippers at a shop down the street, in hopes that even if they were too small, they would stretch enough to be passable.

"That is for your mother, Mr. Riley?" Lady Cralling tittered, stepping up to the counter and reaching past Kit to finger the material of the gown.

"Yes, my lady," Kit answered, her fingers twitching with the effort of not slapping the woman's hand away.

"Far too bold, I say. Undignified, as well. I'd never be caught in such a rag. I hardly think the earl would approve." With a twitch of her brocade skirt, the woman waddled away.

Kit looked down at the dress again. "Mother will like it excessively," she countered stoutly, handing Alex's note over to the shopkeeper.

As had happened at the last three shops where they had made a purchase, the attendant immediately asked if there was anything else the young master wished to take home to his dear mother. "Thank you, that will be all," Ivy returned, and instructed the woman to box up their purchases.

Kit lifted them and followed her mentor out the door and onto the street, aiming silent curses at Eunice Cralling's substantial backside. Another blow to her confidence was not what she needed.

"Lady Cralling," Ivy said, apparently reading her mind "is hardly the one to criticize fashion. Don't listen to her, my dear. It might not be the very pink, but it will do for one afternoon."

"Oh, I don't mind," Kit returned firmly, handing the packages to the coachman as they reached the Downing carriage. "I do wonder, though, what Alex will say when he begins receiving bills from all the women's shops on Bond Street."

Ivy flipped her hand. "You'll be gone before he gets them. Besides, he told you to indulge yourself." She turned to eye Kit critically. "Now. I believe we've taken care of all the unmentionables, and the stockings. I can't think of anything else. Can you?"

"I really wouldn't know, Ivy," she admitted, already somewhat overwhelmed by her lack of knowledge in regard to women's fashion. It was much easier to shop as a man, for then she always knew what was *à la mode*.

"Well, then," her companion said with an expectant grin, "let's get you back home and see what happens."

The Comte de Fouché slipped back around the corner as the Downing coach rolled down the street toward Berkeley Square. It seemed that Stewart Brantley had overestimated his daughter's commitment to the cause, after all. The girl was supposed to be spying for them, not going about buying fripperies while Napoleon Bonaparte risked his life for the betterment of France. And Kit was spending coin as though she had the contents of the Bank of England at her disposal. No doubt the Earl of Everton was paying well for the services he received. The comte sneered as the carriage vanished around a corner, and motioned for his two companions to join him as he headed back in the direction of Covent Garden.

"Come, *mes amis*," he muttered, "we have someone to meet." It was just as well that he hadn't left everything to the Brantleys. And he would teach the daughter some manners, and some proper respect for a French nobleman, before this was finished.

"Well, what do you think?" Ivy asked, as she fastened the last button of the muslin gown and stepped back.

Kit swallowed, opened her eyes, and lifted her head to look into Ivy's full-length mirror. Huge eyes black-ringed with face paint looked back at her. She saw arms bare from the elbows down, a gown that was a little too big and kept slipping off her left shoulder, a neck untouched by sunlight, a face that had seen perhaps a little too much sun, and a mop of blond hair held up on the sides by clips and hanging unevenly around her face. And worst of all, breasts that seemed huge, completely out of proportion with the rest of her anatomy. "I am ridiculous," she whispered, turning away, her eyes filling with tears.

"Oh, my dear," Ivy soothed with a slight chuckle, taking her by the arm and turning her around again, "you are lovely. Don't look at yourself as Kit Riley. You are Christine."

Kit took a deep, despairing breath, and looked again. Nothing had changed. She backed away a few steps from the mirror, awkward and tripping in the thin slippers that covered her feet. Smoothing the muslin and squinting a little so she couldn't distinguish her own features, she stared hard at the odd creature before her. If she pretended it was someone else she was looking at, perhaps the chit in the mirror wasn't so ugly and ungainly as she knew her to be. Perhaps the arms and the neck were the elusive porcelain men so admired, and perhaps her figure wasn't quite so hideous as she had thought at first sight. "The dress is too big," she grumbled, turning sideways and looking at herself in profile.

"Yes, it is," Ivy agreed, stepping up and tugging it down a little in the back. "But we didn't have time to have one made for you. And I'm afraid my maid is more adept than I at doing hair, but, Kit, believe me, there is nothing lacking about you. Nothing at all."

"I feel practically naked," Kit continued, turning her back and trying to look over her shoulder at her reflection.

"That's the idea," her companion said dryly. "Do you wish me to—"

A scratch came at the door, and both women started.

"Yes?" Ivy called.

"My lady," her maid's voice came, "the Earl of Everton is here, looking for Mr. Riley."

"Oh, no!" Kit squawked. She kicked off the slippers, and hoisted up her long skirt to tug at her stockings.

"Kit, whatever are you doing?"

"Help me, Ivy!" she pleaded desperately, reaching around her back to pluck at the complicated row of buttons.

"I thought you wanted Alex to see you as a female,"

her companion commented, her expression amused as she stepped forward to lend her assistance.

"Oh, no, no, no. He'll only laugh, and then he'll be angry that I spent all of his blunt on female items." Most of all, she didn't want him to laugh at her. He could be amused at her as a boy, but she wouldn't be able to stand it if he called her silly and absurd while she was wearing a gown.

"It was hardly all of his blunt, my dear." Ivy started on the row of buttons.

This time the sound at the door was a loud, assured knock. "Ivy," the earl called, "is my cousin ravishing you?"

"You'll have to wait a moment, Alex!" Ivy returned. "Do go back downstairs before Gerald returns, and has to decide who to call out to defend my honor."

"I'll be right down, Everton!" Kit hissed, frantically shrugging out of the gown as the last fastening opened.

There was a pause. "No worries. I'm not in any hurry. But whatever are you two doing in there?"

"Nothing!" she snapped, yanking on her breeches. "Go back downstairs!"

"I am, I am." He chuckled, and after a moment his footsteps retreated toward the staircase.

"Damnation," Kit grumbled, snatching up her wrap and tying it tightly across her breasts. The only excuse she'd been able to make to herself for spending time playing dress-up was that with the House in session, following Alex or Augustus or Reg about would have been pointless. And it was still a very poor excuse. She was a complete half-wit, donning dresses when she should be assisting her father.

"How can you stand that, Kit?" Ivy asked, gesturing at the snug band. "It would drive me mad."

Lately it had been driving her mad, as well. "I'm used to it, I suppose," she said, pulling her shirt on over her head and swiftly tucking it in.

At the last moment she remembered the face paint, and frantically wiped it away with a cloth. Regretfully she looked down at the heap of discarded gown.

Ivy must have read her expression. "Take it with you," she suggested. "If you can't take a moment to wear it at Alex's, perhaps in Paris, when no one else is about."

Impulsively Kit hugged the smaller woman. "Thank you, Ivy. It was fun today."

Ivy chuckled. "Yes, it was."

Kit dumped everything into a satchel and fastened it shut. When she made her way downstairs, Alex was in the game room idly rolling billiard balls across the table with his fingers. She paused in the doorway for a moment to watch him, wishing that she had possessed the courage to step out of Ivy's room in her gown and ask him what he thought of it.

"I'm ready," she said, and he straightened and turned around.

"What did you purchase today?" he asked, dropping the last ball back onto the table and strolling toward her.

"Nothing really." She sighed, hoping with all her might that she would be gone before he received the bills. "Just something to carry my things in back to Paris. Not much else I could purchase in Mayfair would do me well in Saint-Marcel."

His smile faded, and he nodded. "Quite right, and rather foolish of me. My apologies."

"It was a very nice gesture," she stated.

His smile returned as he lazily laid his arm across her shoulder, his fingers dangling carelessly over her chest. "Quite the gentleman you are, my boy," he drawled. "Shall we be off?"

Kit was surprised he didn't feel the bolt of lightning that ran down her spine at his casual touch. With difficulty she stifled the urge to lean into his half embrace, and instead turned to lead the way out into the hallway. Ivy stood at the foot of the stairs, a slight smile on her face. "Alex, may I speak to you a moment? I need your assistance with Gerald's birthday gift."

"Of course," he said, motioning Kit to wait for him. "What is it?" he murmured as he reached Ivy's side. "Gerald's birthday is in February."

His cousin-in-law took him by the arm and led him farther down the hall. With a glance back at where Kit stood lounging in the entryway, she looked up at him. "Can you truly let her go back to Paris?" she asked quietly.

Alex looked down at her, an abrupt ache of trepidation and keen yearning in his chest. "Her father is returning for her," he whispered. "There is little I can do."

"If her father sent her here to keep her safe, how can he take her back to Paris in the middle of a war? And don't tell me that she made it through Napoleon's last rampage all right. She was a child then, Alex, who probably thought it all a great romp. She's a grown woman now. Something terrible might happen to her."

"I know that," he snapped, flicking his eyes in Kit's direction as she glanced curiously at him. Something equally terrible might happen to her here, if she stayed long enough for him to gather proof against her father, and perhaps even against her. He would have to see her arrested. And he was no longer certain that he could do such a thing. "How much longer do you think she can go about without someone realizing what she is? Do you think that would be better for her? For everyone to think the Earl of Everton's latest light-skirt has been playing games with them all Season?"

Unexpected tears came to Ivy's eyes. "It will break my heart to see her go."

Alex took a deep breath. "I am not unsympathetic to your sentiments," he murmured, and while she looked up at him, surprised, he turned back to collect his charge.

"Finished gossiping?" the chit queried, pushing herself upright.

"I believe so," he replied. Noticing something, he put a hand on her shoulder. "Just a moment," he said, turning her to face him.

"What is it?" she asked, a soft blush touching her cheeks.

He took her chin in his fingers and gently turned her head sideways. If the butler hadn't been standing there holding the door for them, he would have kissed her.

Instead he reached out and touched the corner of her eye with the side of his thumb. Her eyes closed, and his breath caught. "What's this?" he asked after a moment, indicating the dark smudge on his finger.

Her flush deepened. "Ivy was . . . trying out a new eye paint, and asked me to assist her," she offered.

"Kit, you must be careful," he admonished, releasing her.

"I know that," she grumbled, turning away to head past Fender, the butler.

"It is a good color on you, though," Alex added with a slight smile, wiping it away on his breeches and wishing he'd seen her in it properly.

She whipped back around, grinning. "Do you think so?"

"Indeed, brat. Come on."

Chapter 11

Five days remained. It was the first thought in her mind when Kit awoke. A pair of robins squabbled noisily outside her window, the sound echoed by a pair of rag and bone men in the street below. She lay there, listening to the sounds of the house, already well awake, around her.

Five days remained, and she didn't know what to do. Only in a dire emergency was she supposed to try to contact Stewart Brantley at anywhere other than the tavern before he came to retrieve her. And her father would hardly consider the dilemmas of her heart to be life-threatening. But still, with three peers involved, if even one of them couldn't be bribed or threatened to leave off, her information would have gained him nothing. He would find another way, of course; he always did. But somewhere deep inside was the fear that his solution would be something she wouldn't like—or worse, something she wouldn't be able to allow.

"Cousin?" a soft voice spoke through her door, and she started and sat upright.

"Yes?" she returned, angry that his voice had set her heart fluttering like a bird's wings.

"May I come in?"

With a quick look around her, Kit pulled the sheets up to her neck. "All right."

The handle turned, and Alex stuck his head in through

the door. "Apologies." He smiled. "I didn't mean to wake you." He started to back out again.

"Wait," she called, afraid he'd leave for more of his blasted meetings and she'd lose track of him and his cronies again. "I was awake. Just being lazy."

He nodded and came into the room, taking a moment to shut the door behind him. Her eyes followed him as he strolled over to the window and pushed the curtains open, then wandered over to her dressing table. His long fingers lifted her hair band, then set it aside to uncover the wrap she used beneath her shirt. He raised it up, examining it curiously, while she began to fume.

"I don't recall this being part of a gentleman's wardrobe," he stated, fingering the cloth and holding it up before his own blue and cream striped waistcoat as though trying to find a match.

"It's not. And put it down, if you please."

Instead he draped it over his hand, taking it back to the window with him. "It seems to me I've never seen a woman wearing anything like this, either," he continued, glancing at her sideways, his eyes amused.

"You know very well what it's for, or you wouldn't be pestering me about it. Put it down at once, sir," she demanded, torn between wishing to snatch it out of his hands, and reluctance to leave the scant protection the sheets afforded her.

"Ah, so now you address me with respect," he commented, lifting a sardonic eyebrow. "Tell me what it's for, and I shall return it to you."

Kit clenched her jaw. Things were difficult enough without him tormenting her. "Do not tease," she ordered, color touching her cheeks.

"I do not tease," he protested, stepping forward and actually seating himself on the end of her bed. "Mere days ago you were dazzling me with 'deuced' this and 'bloody' that. Don't tell me you've become fainthearted. I merely wish to hear you explain to me what this apparatus is for."

It was obvious that he had no intention of leaving off the topic until he was satisfied. "Very well." She scowled, taking a breath and wondering if this was another of his ways of seduction, or if he was merely amusing himself this morning. "I use it to conceal my female form so that I may more easily pass as a boy."

He grinned and briefly lowered his eyes. "Well done. This is to say you do have breasts, after all?"

She kicked him from under the sheltering blankets. "You said you weren't teasing," she snapped.

"I am merely curious." He reached over to hand her the wrap, and she snatched it out of his hand while he chuckled.

"And I am curious," she retorted, "to know whether you consider throwing my undergarments about to be preserving my purity, Everton."

"I believe you're concerned enough for the both of us."

"Are you calling me prudish?" she asked incredulously, deeply offended.

He smiled. "God strike me dead if I ever thought such a thing." Unexpectedly he stood to wander again about the room, obviously distracted about something.

"What is it?" she queried, her curiosity overcoming her aggravation.

"Hm?" He turned to face her. "Oh. Well, I have two questions to ask you." Surprisingly, he returned to sit beside her on the bed, even closer than before. Absently he fiddled with the corner of the sheet, the gentle tug pulling across her legs.

"I'm listening," she murmured, her heart hammering all over again as she studied his profile.

He turned, his gaze catching and holding hers with startling seriousness. "Do you wish to return to Paris?"

For a moment she simply looked at him. "Beg pardon?" she finally asked.

"If you could do anything, anything you chose, would you wish to return to Paris? To Saint-Marcel? To Bonaparte's blasted, nonending revolution?"

"Where else would I go?" she countered, shrugging. The sheet began to drop, and his eyes followed it downward. She was wearing a nightshirt, but his lazy, inquisitive gaze made her feel as though she were completely naked. Kit shivered a little and pulled the covering up again.

"You could stay here," he said slowly, glancing toward the window. "In England."

"As a boy? You're the one who keeps warning me I'll be found out."

"Well," he said after a moment, dropping his gaze to look at his restless, long-fingered hands, "I was actually thinking that you might like Everton."

It was a tempting trap. Forget her father, forget the smuggling, and forget dirty Saint-Marcel, and be with Alexander Cale. "As your mistress?" That was what he wanted, she sensed—or at least he thought he did. It would last a while, until he grew tired of her or she was found out and he decided he didn't want the scandal.

"Of course not," he snapped with too much force, and rubbed his fist along his thigh. "There's no price you must pay."

"But you would wish it," she suggested quietly.

He looked at her. "Yes, I would."

The question she had dreamed last night, he didn't ask. She couldn't have answered it, anyway. She was sunk too deep into her father's bog for that. "Alex," she said slowly, trying to keep her voice steady, "I don't need anyone's protection. I don't need anyone to look after me. And I won't be kept locked away somewhere." She forced a smile. "And I certainly don't wish to be a burden, or an annoyance, which you keep reminding me that I am." Kit took a breath, truly regretting what she must say next. There were so many lies, when she only wanted to tell him the truth. "My father is in Paris. He is my family. I will stay with him."

"You have family here," he offered.

"I do not," she returned stiffly, an image of lovely Caroline crossing her thoughts.

"Stubborn chit," he muttered.

"So what is your second question?" she prompted, trying to change the subject.

"Not nearly as exciting. I only wished to ask what you'd like to do today."

She eyed him curiously. "You're giving me a choice?"

Alex shrugged. "You have yet to visit some of the more famous landmarks, I believe. A private tour of Buckingham Palace, perhaps? Or Parliament? Then there's the Tower, or the—"

"And where will you be while I'm off sightseeing?" she interrupted, looking away and fleetingly wondering what her father would think of her, so near to shedding tears at being ignored by someone whose clear duty was to destroy them.

Unexpectedly he touched the wavy blond hair brushing her cheek, and gently curled the ends around his fingers. Kit froze and shut her eyes, her scalp tingling all the way down her spine. She stayed completely still, fearing even to breathe lest he stop playing with her hair. Her breasts tightened beneath the flimsy nightshirt.

"With you, if you want the company."

Kit's heart flip-flopped. "What about your meetings?"

"Hang the meetings." His fingers gave her hair a tug and then released her. When she looked at him he was grinning that dazzling smile of his, azure eyes lighting. "I've been behaving far too respectably. I'm attempting to make up for it in one fell swoop. So what's it to be?"

"A picnic," Kit answered promptly, then blushed when he raised an eyebrow.

"A picnic where?" he asked slowly.

"In the country."

"Give me a moment, chit. You have baffled me." He gave her a look of mock suspicion, which might have been real. "You have all of London to explore, and you wish a picnic, out of town?"

"Yes."

"But why?"

Because I want you to myself. "I haven't been on a picnic since I was five," she answered. "If you wish to do something else, I will, of course—"

He raised a hand. "A picnic it is." Alex stood, the bed rocking slightly as his weight lifted from it. "Do you wish me to invite Ivy and Ger—"

"No," she interrupted sharply. She wanted no one else there. No more lies to spin, and no one for him to look at but her.

He gazed at her. "Just us, then." He nodded, not questioning her further. "I've one brief errand to run, and I'll have Wenton see to preparing things."

"Do you want company?" she asked, telling herself she'd asked because she was supposed to be keeping an eye on him.

Alex shook his head. "I'll be back in a shake. Get dressed, and don't forget . . . that." He gestured at her wrap. "Unless you want to."

"Blackguard," she muttered, and he laughed and exited the room.

Given the opportunity to go anywhere in London, Alex would have thought a spy would opt for a tour of Parliament, or one of the other government buildings. At least a good look at some strategic point or other would have been expected. Never would he have anticipated that a French spy would want to go on a country picnic, and certainly not alone with one of the few people who knew her secret.

He rode to Reg's under a lowering sky, only to find that the baron had gone out riding with Lady Caroline. It was likely just as well that Hanshaw was not available, for there was a great deal Alex wasn't yet ready to tell his partner. Intercepting the second load of weapons would buy him a little time and provide a distraction, but until he heard from one of his men in the field, it would be foolish to make a move. He left his calling card with Reg's butler, and returned to Cale House to prepare luncheon and fetch Kit.

"No, Wenton, the Madeira," he instructed as the butler entered the breakfast room to load a bottle of wine into the picnic basket he'd had Mrs. Hodges dig out of the cupboard. The butler turned on his heel and exited again.

"My lord?" a timid female voice came, and he turned to view one of the kitchen maids hovering nervously in the doorway.

"Yes?"

"My lord, Mrs. Hodges says the peach pies for luncheon are set out to cool, but that Brundle put too much wood in the oven, and the apple tarts are burned." She curtsied.

"Blast," Alex grumbled, for he had noted several days ago that his houseguest was fond of apple tarts.

"My lord," the girl continued hurriedly, her face paling, "Mrs. Hodges said I might go down to the bakery to inquire for tarts, if the pies won't do."

Wenton stepped back into the room and took a moment to eye the girl hostilely, obviously feeling she'd overstepped her bounds in coming into the main part of the house. "My lord?" he queried, presenting him with a bottle.

"Yes, that's the one." Alex nodded, and the butler deftly wrapped it in a cloth and deposited it into the basket. "And no," he continued, turning back to the girl, "peach pies will be fine. Wenton, take the basket down to Mrs. Hodges, will you?"

"Of course, my lord," the butler said, lifting the wicker and, with a cluck of his tongue, sending the girl out of the room before him. After a moment Alex heard his chastising voice, and the girl's sharp-voiced answer. He smiled.

When the servants had departed, Everton dropped into his customary chair at the table and blew out a noisy breath. He was practically frothing at the mouth over the contents of a damned picnic basket. All for duty and country indeed. That was why he'd decided this picnic was going to be the most magnificent alfresco luncheon since the heyday of Rome.

A long, low rumble sounded outside, and he turned toward the window. Lightning flashed over the stable, and as he watched, a gray cloud swept across the rooftops and crested Cale House with a heavy patter of rain-drops. "Damnation," he grumbled, his good humor dashing into the ground along with the rainwater.

Kit's low, lilting laugh drifted down the stairs, followed by the self-assured padding of her booted feet on the steps. "The all-powerful Earl of Everton will grant me any wish for the day," she announced regally, laughing and swinging into the room to view him sitting like a dour gargoyle in his chair. "Except that he didn't count on it raining."

Alex gave a reluctant grin. "All those books in the library, and I didn't think to consult the almanac," he said. "I'm sorry."

"It's not your fault," she replied, sobering a little as her green eyes studied his face.

He returned her gaze, wondering how long he would be able to continue his charade of ignorance and still look into those lovely eyes. "My other offers for the day still stand."

Kit glanced toward the window and gave a small sigh. It was fairly obvious that despite her jesting, she had truly wished a picnic. Alex frowned. It was bad enough that he was fretting over a picnic like a half-wit with his purportedly male cousin in front of the servants, but now he was worried that he had somehow ruined a spy's day in London.

Wenton reappeared with the basket, and took a moment to glance dubiously at the window before he placed the heavy thing on the sideboard. Alex started to motion him to take it away, then stopped. "Wenton," he said, gazing at his houseguest and feeling a smile tugging at his lips again, "bring that to the library, and get us some help."

"Help, my lord?" the butler asked, obediently lifting the basket again.

"We're going to move some furniture."

Kit waited until the butler had left the room before she ran her finger along the edge of the table and looked up at Alex sideways. "A picnic with your cousin in the library?'' she drawled in a fine imitation of him. ''Quite irregular.''

''And?''

''And so I thought you wanted to avoid rumors and that I was already too much trouble, anyway.''

She was right, and the servants had likely guessed a great deal more than he cared to inform them. They'd already proven themselves a discreet lot, however, for shortly after Mary's death, he'd had several spectacularly disastrous affairs which had for the most part escaped the ears and sight of the *ton*.

''The omnipotent Earl of Everton will do his best to satisfy your wish,'' he said dryly, trying to make light of the fact that he knew damned well he had other things to be doing, and that being alone anywhere in private with Christine Brantley was unwise.

He followed her into the hallway, and instructed Wenton and the footmen who had gathered at his summons to move his mahogany desk, the overstuffed chairs, and the occasional table to the far end of the room.

''Wouldn't it simply be easier to move the couch in the morning room? We could picnic in there just as easily,'' Kit suggested from beside him.

''No. Not the morning room,'' he said flatly, turning his back so she wouldn't see that her remark had agitated him.

''Oh.'' She took a step closer. ''I'm sorry,'' she murmured, her low lilt at his shoulder making him pause. ''It reminds you of Mary?''

He stiffened again, then took a breath. By now he should have known that Kit would not let up on something that had caught her attention, until she had an answer that satisfied her. ''It reminds me of perfection,'' he answered, stepping into the library. ''Wait here.''

Kit stood looking after him for a moment. In the short time she had known him, Alex had spoken of his late wife very seldom and only reluctantly. She glanced over her shoulder at the morning room. The earl certainly hadn't left her with the impression that he continued to deeply mourn his wife, but from his conversations with both her and Barbara Sinclair, neither did he seem anxious to lose his heart again. And though with him it was difficult to be certain, his voice for a moment had sounded almost contemptuous. Odd, that.

"Kit, m'boy," Alex's voice drawled several minutes later from the library as the footmen trooped out again, "do come in."

She smiled at the summons. Ten days ago she had never expected to be invited for a picnic in the Earl of Everton's library; even less would she have expected to feel pleased about the notion. Her smile faded. After she betrayed him to her father, she doubted she would be left with any pleasant memories of London at all.

She stepped into the library, and stopped. Alex sat cross-legged on the blanket that had been opened out in the middle of the floor, the wicker picnic basket beside him. The painting on the far wall, a beautiful white country manor she had assumed to be Everton, had been removed and sat on the floor facing the blanket. The other side of their picnic spot was flanked by one of the paintings from the formal dining room, a pastoral with a lake and deer and a flowering meadow.

"Welcome to the country." His eyes dancing, he lifted a bottle of Madeira in her direction.

Christine couldn't speak. She couldn't breathe. She couldn't do anything but stand and stare at the Earl of Everton sitting on the floor of his library, just for her. Her heart hammered, trying to burst through her ribs. That was what it felt like, then, a rush of lightning through every nerve and muscle. Quickly she turned her back as though looking for something, hoping that Alex wouldn't see it in her eyes, hoping he wouldn't see that she was in love with him.

"Is something wrong?" his voice came after a moment.

With a deep breath she turned around and flashed him a grin. "I was merely trying to imagine you doing this sort of thing with Barbara Sinclair," she replied, plunking herself down on the blanket beside him.

"I wouldn't," he noted mildly, handing two glasses over for her to hold while he poured. "She would hardly appreciate it."

"Why not?" Kit queried, furtively studying his profile. Everything had been an impossible muddle before. That, though, was nothing compared to this. Her father would be furious.

"I don't believe she would find it dignified," he commented, drawing out the last word and sniffing at the end.

Kit laughed. "So she is always 'dignified'?" she returned, imitating his pronunciation.

He pursed his lips and glanced sideways at her. "Almost always."

This was becoming interesting. "When is she undignified, then?"

His amused eyes holding hers, Alex took one of the glasses back. "You may look something like a boy, chit, but I happen to have it on very good authority that you are a virgin who wishes her purity maintained. I am not going to relate any sordid sexual tales to you."

Kit made a face at him. "You'd rather enact them with me, I suppose?"

He smiled, something very enticing touching his eyes for a moment. "So bold, you are. One would almost think you were trying to seduce me."

It gave her an idea, a sort of last chance. Remembering how Mercia Cralling had flirted with her, Kit lowered her head to look up at Alex from beneath her lashes. And she had no idea whether she was acting to help her father or to help herself. But she had begun to doubt very seriously whether she could follow through on any plans to help Stewart Brantley that would in some way hurt Everton. Distracting him from his duties seemed to be the only option left her. Her fingers shaking a little despite her efforts to keep them steady, she reached out to brush them along his collar. "What if I were?"

His eyes had followed her hand, but slowly he lifted his head to gaze at her. "Hypothetically speaking, of course," he murmured, the change in his eyes pointing out that she had just stepped into a game in which he had far more experience than she, "what would this seduction entail?"

It would have been easier if he'd simply fallen upon her. Now, though, she was expected to answer in kind. Thinking as quickly as her muddled thoughts would allow her, Kit leaned closer. "Perhaps a trip to Everton, just the two of us?" Just for a few days, until her father's shipment was in Calais and Alex would be safe from him. She would be lost, of course, but then she already was.

He tilted his head a little and then took a slow sip of Madeira. "And for this journey would you wear lace instead of lawn, and pearls rather than pocket watches?"

Christine swallowed. "If you wished it."

For a long moment Alex looked at her, then slowly he shook his head. "You give in too easily, chit. What is it you want?"

She scowled, then covered it up by batting her lashes at him. "You've simply worn down all my resistance," she breathed.

Alex threw back his head and laughed. "Oh, good God."

That hurt. "I don't think it's amusing that you find me laughable, Everton," she snapped, the part of her that said the conversation was just a game, flattened by the part of her that wanted him to take her seriously as a female.

He blinked and sat back, his smile fading. "I hardly find you laughable, Kit."

"You're always teasing."

"No, I'm not," he protested.

"Always, always, always," she countered. "And I'm sorry if you think the way I look is so stupid. There's nothing I can do about it!" she shouted, climbing to her feet. She still held one glass of Madeira, and angrily looked about for a place to set it down.

Alex stood as well, and she shoved the glass at his chest. Reflexively he grabbed it, and she turned and strode for the door. Behind her she heard both glasses hit the carpet, and then came to an abrupt halt as Alex's hand clamped down on her shoulder. He spun her around and shoved her back against the wall.

"I was not teasing," he said, his eyes glinting, and bent his head to close his mouth over hers.

After a stunned moment Kit leaned up into him. His hard, strong body pressed her into the wall as a tingling rush of arousal ran through her. Alex's arms came around her waist, pulling her closer against him. This was what she had always imagined. All the times she had seen couples embracing and had wished to someday, somehow, place herself there, this was what she had imagined it would be like—the breathless, time-stopping sensation of being on fire. He lifted his head to look down at her, but before she could protest his absence, he captured her lips again in a deep, hard kiss.

His mouth teased at hers, and when she parted her lips in response, he ran his tongue slowly along her teeth. The gesture felt shockingly intimate, as did his hands as they stroked down to her hips. Her own hands lifted to run across his muscular chest and shoulders. She took a shallow, ragged breath when his mouth released hers again. "Alex," she whispered.

He didn't answer, but gently pulled her short tail of hair and tilted her head back. His lips, his mouth, caressed the sensitive hollow of her throat, so that she gasped. One thigh shifted to press up between her legs, rubbing slowly at the sensitive, throbbing place through her breeches. A growing swelling pressed against her abdomen, achingly hard. She held desperately to him, aware of nothing but his warmth enfolding her. If not for his body against hers, she thought she must fall to the floor in a boneless heap.

Thunder boomed so close that the window rattled with the force of it. Alex lifted his head and looked down at her, a dazed, disjointed look in his beautiful eyes. "My God," he murmured, drawing a ragged breath. "My God."

Farther away thunder rumbled again, and he blinked and took a step back. Another step followed the first, and her hand reluctantly slid from his chest. "What is it?" she asked, her voice and body trembling.

"I . . . apologize," he muttered.

"But, Alex, I want—"

"And I want you." He gave a grim smile. "But too much rests on it. Too many others might pay for my . . . weakness." Slowly he reached out and touched her lower lip with fingers that shook a little. "I'm sorry."

With that he turned and was gone, shutting the door softly behind him. A tear ran down Christine's cheek as she turned back to their ruined picnic, the spilled glasses of burgundy wine staining into the blanket and the carpet beneath. He knew, then. At least part of it. He knew. Her heart felt like it was rending in two, and she closed her eyes for a moment to steady herself. There was more at stake than her stupid, shattered dreams of a life and a love she could never hope to have. Even with nothing else between them, she was a smuggler's daughter, and he was the Earl of Everton.

One thing had become clear, though. She needed to find her father, after all.

Martin, Lord Brantley, Viscount Trawbry, Marquis of Fens, and Duke of Furth, disliked London.

It was not that he resented the amusements of the Season, or that he discounted the importance of Parliament or the rules of law. Far from it. Rather, and very simply, London was two days' distance from Furth. That left him with a round trip of four days, at the least. And four days away from Furth, as far as Martin Brantley was concerned, was four days too many.

Circumstances, however, one opportune and one not nearly so, had dictated that he make the journey. And so it was with an annoyed, impatient sigh that he stepped down from his crested, mud-spattered coach and climbed the granite steps of his town house on Grosvenor Square in the heart of Mayfair, while his butler bowed in the entryway.

"Your Grace," Royce greeted, straightening in time

to catch the hat and greatcoat tossed in his direction, "welcome to London."

The duke pulled off a glove and dropped it into his hat, his eyes and his attention directed toward the interior of the house. "Spare me, Royce. Where is the duchess?"

"In the drawing room, Your Grace."

"And Caroline?"

"Lady Caroline is out to luncheon, Your Grace."

Martin Brantley returned his eyes to the butler's solemn, efficient personage. "With whom?" he asked succinctly, playing the role of irritated, affronted parent with the ease eighteen years of practice afforded him.

"I believe it was Miss Cralling, Miss Montgomery, and Lady Feona, Your Grace."

The lowered brow resumed its normal position. "Very well."

"As it pleases you, Your Grace."

"It does not, Royce." The duke removed his second glove and deposited it with the first. Ignoring the downstairs servants who had begun popping their heads out of various doorways to verify for themselves that the master of the house was indeed in residence, he turned for the stairs. The drawing room door was open, and he stepped inside to view his wife embroidering, her back to the door.

Silently he reached into his pocket, and curled his fingers around the four-line missive that had provided him with the opportunity, or rather the necessity, of making the journey to London. Wordlessly he dropped the letter into the duchess's lap.

"I am here, madame," he stated.

The Duchess of Furth started, then stood and hurried around the chair to clasp his hands. "Thank the dear Lord you've come," she said, leaning forward to kiss him on one cheek.

He returned the gesture, then stepped back and gestured at the missive, which had fallen to the floor beside the duchess's embroidery. "Explain," he commanded.

"It is even worse than I feared," she said, taking her

seat again and fanning at her face with one hand.

"Do dispense with the theatrics," he suggested. The duke stepped around and bent over to retrieve the folded piece of parchment. It crinkled a little as he opened it. " 'The worst has happened,' " he read, though he'd had ample time to memorize both that message and the one in his other pocket on the ride to London. " 'I fear our Caroline has fallen for a complete commoner. Come at once, before it is too late. Yours, Constance.' " He looked at his wife. "Who is this complete commoner?"

"Half the eligible misses in London are ready to swoon at his feet," his wife complained, knotting her hands in her lap. "He is admittedly charming, from what I hear, but completely unacceptable."

"Who is he?" Furth repeated, lowering his brow. His wife was given to exaggeration and hysterics, but it was possible Caroline could go against everything they had planned for her, in favor of some romantic flight.

"The Earl of Everton's cousin."

The duke paused. "That bloodline hardly makes him a commoner." Everton *would* be involved in this, damn his unpredictable hide.

"He is untitled. And an Irishman."

"I see," Furth uttered, his countenance stern. "And what is this untitled Irishman's name?"

"Christian Riley. They call him Kit."

"Well," the duke said after a moment, turning for the door. "I'll have my bags brought up. It seems I've something to take care of before I return to Furth."

Kit didn't go into the Hanging Crow tavern to speak to her father.

She started to, slipped out of Cale House after Everton rode off somewhere, hired a hack, and then walked up the last few streets through the driving rain to Long Acre. Half a block from the tavern she noticed the figure lounging in the doorway, and with a cold start ducked into the bakery at the corner.

Apparently her feeling of being followed over the past few days had been correct. Beloche, one of the Comte de Fouché's henchmen, leaned against the rough stone-work of the tavern and surveyed the passing crowd of pedestrians. Kit took a seat near the window and ordered coffee and a hot pastry. If Beloche was about, then Fou-ché would be, as well. And that made no sense.

Napoleon was in Paris, gathering an army to stand against the British. Jean-Paul Mercier, one of the few French nobles who had supported Bonaparte's first grand revolution and lived to tell the tale, would not be in London away from his esteemed master. Not without a very good reason. And compared to regaining Europe, smuggling anything seemed less than important. Yet apparently Fouché *was* in London, with her father. Kit frowned. It had been the comte spying on her before, after all. Which would imply that all was not well between Jean-Paul and Stewart Brantley.

She watched for nearly an hour, but when no one else came or went, she slipped out of the bakery and up the street the way she had come. She needed to speak to Stewart Brantley, because of what Alex apparently had been able to discover, though she had no idea precisely how much he knew. But she knew the rules. They were to meet only when there was no one else about. Kit wiped the rain from her face and hunched her shoulders into her splendid caped greatcoat. Whatever Alex knew, he hadn't directly accused her of anything. And with Fouché between her and her father, and five days remaining, she would have to make do as best she could. If she could. If she could face Everton and smile, and pretend that she didn't know what he had been speaking of, and that she was not desperately in love with him.

Chapter 12

"The library carpet is ruined, my lord." Wenton stepped into the earl's office with a tray of tea and biscuits.

"Well, throw it out, then," Alex snapped, without looking up from his rather lengthy correspondence to Everton Manor. His agent hardly needed such detailed instruction, for the man had been looking after Everton for decades. But he'd had little else to do this afternoon but wonder how he could have been such a fool as to let Kit out of his sight again.

"Yes, my lord."

Alex shut his eyes for a moment as the butler deposited his tray on the desk and left the room. Closing his eyes didn't banish the damned chit from his thoughts, though, and with a curse he opened them again and dashed his signature across the bottom of the missive. He had kissed women before, blast it, women with experience to match his own. He had bedded innumerable women in highly imaginative ways and places, and enjoyed having the freedom to do so. Which explained not at all why there had been no one since he had discovered that Kit Riley was a blasted female.

He told himself that it was only because he wasn't supposed to touch her, that it was dangerous to lose himself in thoughts of her, that she was able to drive him to distraction. It was only frustration at not being able to act either in having her or in stopping her from whatever her damned plot with her father was. "Blast," he muttered, running his fingers through his hair.

Before Reg had invited them to Kit's farewell salute at the Society for the evening, he'd had something else to do, though he couldn't remember what it was. With an irritated sigh, he dug through his pile of correspondence until he found the engraved invitation to Lady Crasten's very exclusive dinner soiree. The more daring, libidinous members of the *ton* could be counted on to attend, and to make the evening generally quite . . . engaging. That was where he had first bedded Barbara Sinclair, in fact, two years ago.

Alex sat back, scowling at the card. This afternoon, the thought of the whole lewd thing disgusted him. He tore the invitation in half and tossed it into the wastebasket beside the desk. The clock chimed four; Kit had been missing for better than three hours. And since he'd let it slip that he suspected her, no doubt she'd fled. She was killing him. She was driving him mad, and he couldn't let it continue. With a curse aimed more at himself than at her, he yanked a piece of parchment out of his desk and slammed it down onto the smooth mahogany. In the same motion, he pulled the pen from its well and scrawled a salutation across the top of the page. And stopped.

For a long moment he sat with pen poised above paper, ready to make his report and confess that he knew who the smuggler was, and that immediate steps needed to be taken. Instead he took a long, shuddering breath, and set the pen back where it belonged. She was involved. He knew she was involved. But until she confessed to it, he couldn't condemn her.

The front door opened. "Afternoon, Wenton," came jauntily from the entryway, and Alex crumpled the letter and threw it into the wastebasket.

"Kit!" he roared, refusing to rush out into the hallway to see her, to let her know how relieved he was that she'd returned.

After a moment she pushed the door open and stepped into his study. Her hair was wet, straying ends hanging in straggles around her face. The rest of her was none too dry, either. "You bellowed, Everton?" she queried coolly, leaning against the doorjamb as though nothing had happened between them. Only the green eyes determinedly avoiding his told a different story.

He wanted to brush the wet locks back from her forehead and kiss her soft, sweet lips. "We're to meet Reg and the others tonight," he said, as cool as she was, and burning inside. "Don't forget."

"I haven't," she answered. Kit looked toward the door and back again. "I'd best go change before I catch pneumonia."

He nodded. "And put your hair back. You look . . . quite feminine with it down like that." Slowly he stood and strolled over to her side.

"Do I?" She reached up to touch her hair, then stopped herself. Her shoulders heaved as she took a breath. "Alex," she ventured, "may I ask you a question?"

"Anything," he murmured, leaning against the edge of the door and studying her lovely face.

Kit's gaze touched his, saying something he wished he could read, then slid away again. "Do you have a portrait of your mother anywhere?"

Of all the questions she might have asked, he hadn't expected that one. "I do. In the ballroom. Would you like to see it?"

She nodded. "I would."

He gestured her toward the stairs, followed her up the two flights, and then down the hallway to the two doors on the east side of the mansion. They were both unlocked, and he lifted a lamp from the hall table and entered the room before her. There had been only one gathering in the room since his mother's death, shortly after his marriage. The servants had kept the floor well cleaned, and the chandeliers covered to protect them from dust. On the wall opposite the door two life-sized portraits hung side by side, each covered with a heavy sheet. Silently he stepped forward and freed them from their shrouds, then moved back and lifted the lamp to illuminate them for her.

Kit took the light from his fingers and stepped closer. "She was beautiful," she breathed after a moment. "How old was she when this was done?"

"About your age. And Father was about mine. They were commissioned a year after their marriage, by my grandmother. As a gift." Their voices echoed a little in the huge, empty room, and the covered chandeliers chimed faintly in response.

"You have her look," Kit observed, tilting her head to view the tall, dark-haired woman with the laughing gray eyes who shared the empty room with her smiling husband. "What was she like?"

Alex looked away from the portrait and smiled as he gazed at the damp, blond waif before him. "Well, other than the fact that she didn't wear breeches or curse very often, she was a great deal like you."

"I don't believe you," Kit protested, glancing over her shoulder at him with a shy, intrigued smile. His favorite smile.

"No, truly. She had a startling wit. Most men were terrified of her."

"Men aren't terrified of me," she said to the painting.

"Because they think you're one of them. Being made to look like complete fools is acceptable if it comes from one of your own. If you donned petticoats, throwing devastating set-downs about like dandelions would be greatly frowned upon. You would be expected to simper and faint and say 'lud' quite a bit more frequently than you do."

Grinning, she turned to face him. "I've never even said 'lud,' I don't think."

"My point, exactly."

Her smile faded as they stood looking at one another, the lamplight yellow and flickering between them. In the uncertain light his parents seemed to be looking down at them and laughing. Whether it was in approval, or in amusement at the hole the two of them had managed to put themselves in, he didn't know. The frustrated craving for her burned at him still, whatever duty and conscience told him he shouldn't be doing. She seemed to see it in his eyes, for she moved first, swallowing and looking back toward the doorway.

"I must go change," she muttered, and glanced over her shoulder again. "Do you wish me to help you cover them again?"

He shook his head. "The servants can do it. I, ah, don't like to leave them behind like that." Alex smiled slightly, embarrassed at the sentiment. He believed, though, that she would understand. "Can't shake the feeling they don't like being left here in the dark to miss everything that's going on."

Kit looked up at Victoria Cale, the Countess of Everton. "I think you're right," she agreed softly. She turned back to him. "And I'm sorry about this morning."

He took a breath. "Not your fault, chit." He'd been thinking about it all day, about how he could turn what he'd said into something more innocent-sounding than what had nearly amounted to a direct accusation. "I'm still having a bit of difficulty remembering that I'm Galahad rather than Don Juan."

The lie was flimsy as a kite in a windstorm, and from her expression she didn't believe for a moment that it was his sense of chivalry that had stopped him. She had come back to Cale House, though, which made him believe that she hadn't yet gotten whatever it was she had come for. He was therefore unsurprised when she grinned and nodded. "And I keep forgetting that I'm Christian and not Christine."

Alex should have left it at that, but as she handed back the lamp and walked past him, close enough to touch, he was unable to remain silent. "It's not a matter of forgetting, but of fooling," he said quietly to her back. "And you shan't fool me again, Christine. I'll never mistake you for anything but what you are."

She stopped, and her shoulders stiffened. Slowly she turned around. "And what is that, *monsieur*?"

"Beautiful."

He shouldn't have said it, for he was close enough as it was, to grabbing her and making love to her on the ballroom floor, but her fleeting, self-conscious smile as she turned and left the room made the risk worth it. Alex took a deep breath and lifted the lamp again. "Lovely, isn't she?" His parents still laughed, and he thought that perhaps they had enjoyed meeting her. "Good night," he whispered, and blew out the light.

Augustus Devlin was already drunk by the time Kit Brantley and Alexander Cale reached the Society at the height of the evening. Reg Hanshaw was there before them also, and the quick glance the baron sent Alex was almost one of warning. That made sense, though, Kit decided, for if she were involved in a secret government assignment, she wouldn't care to have any of her cohorts sotted, either.

"Good evening, my dears." She nodded, sinking into the chair beside Augustus and hoping to have the opportunity to take advantage of his inebriated state. Another confrontation like the one with Alex that morning, and she would be finished in London, like it or not. There was little time left. "Where's Francis?"

"Visiting his grandmother," Reg replied. "He sends his apologies at missing your send-off."

"Is she ill?" Kit asked, accepting the snifter of brandy Alex handed her. She met his gaze for a moment over the glass, and he gave a slight grin, eyes dancing, before he looked away. She couldn't figure out why he'd lied earlier and made it possible for both of them to continue as they had, but then, fleetingly in his eyes, she had seen something that unsettled her even more than his kisses. She took a long, hard swallow of brandy to disguise the reason for the blush that touched her cheeks.

Augustus drained his own glass, far more easily and efficiently than she ever could. "She's been on her last legs for five years now, with all the grandchildren stumbling over one another to be named her favorite. Francis goes to see her and begs a few quid whenever he's to let. She'll drag him about town and make him look foolish, then open her fist one finger at a time."

"That sounds dreary," Kit commented. It also sounded very like her father's description of her uncle, the Duke of Furth.

Devlin glanced at her. "I've told him not to give her the satisfaction, but whatever does one do without blunt?"

"Not much," Kit agreed. Out of the corner of her eye she couldn't help but notice that Everton kept looking at her. She was going to have to kick him if he didn't stop it. Male cousins simply did not gaze at one another like that, and while Devlin was drunk and might not notice, Reg was sober enough.

"Speaking of blunt," Hanshaw put in, "dinner is on my bill tonight, *mes amis*."

Alex finally shifted his attention to Reg. "What's the occasion?" he queried.

"Lady Caroline's agreed to venture out on a picnic with our intrepid hero," Augustus offered, his fingers twiddling with his glass.

"I actually believe her purpose for agreeing was to give her more opportunity to question me about you, Kit." Reg chuckled. "However, I'll take any attention from her as a good sign."

It was Kit's turn to scowl. "I don't know why you keep insisting she's smitten with me," she protested. "I've barely spoken five sentences to her."

"It's very simple," Augustus put in, leaning back in his chair. "Reg has thrown his entire being into pleasing Caroline. She knows every nuance of his thought and character. You, however, are a mystery, to be explored, solved, and resolved."

When Kit looked over at him rather sharply, she couldn't decipher whether Devlin meant anything more than the obvious by his comment. She glanced at Alex, to find that he, too, was eyeing the viscount, and the cold distrust on his face stopped her for a moment. It was a possessive, angry look, the look of someone who had a secret he didn't want to share. With anyone. A small thrill ran down her spine.

"I'm hardly a mystery." She chuckled, and the azure gaze flicked for a bare moment in her direction before returning to the viscount. "I've merely been attempting to avoid stepping on Reg's toes."

"Ah, how gallant, dear boy," Augustus congratulated. "Would that we all possessed such powers of restraint. You could learn a lesson from your cousin, Everton."

"Speaking of lessons," Reg put in, just a little too quickly, "I thought you were teaching Barbara one, Alex. Why so friendly the other evening?"

"Oh, you know me," Everton returned absently, his gaze remaining on Devlin, "never one to burn bridges." He leaned forward, his elbows on the table. "Is something bothering you, Augustus?" he murmured, and Kit couldn't mistake the anger in his tone.

"Me, my boy? Nothing at all." Devlin slowly refilled his glass, the amber liquid swirling toward the curved brim. "It's odd, though," he said, speaking to the brandy, "how different Reg's courtship is from yours. He must actually woo, and not merely the female, but the entire family."

"Augustus," Reg murmured, looking with some anxiety in Alex's direction.

Kit, though, was becoming more interested in the conversation. Lately the details of Alex's brief marriage had been occupying more of her thoughts than they should. She glanced at Devlin, to find his gray eyes on her, apparently reading her curiosity.

"Don't know the story, lad? Allow me, then. Reg must work for his lady, but not our Alexander," the viscount continued. "Already had me, and he was the future Earl of almighty Everton, don't you know. Alexander Lawrence Bennett Cale, who could have had any, *any* female he wanted, chose *my* sister." Devlin gave a drunken rattle of a laugh. "And she, by God, hated him."

"That's enough, Augustus," Alex warned. His expression was set and unreadable, his eyes gazing at the darkness outside the window. And he was furious. It was in every line of his taut, muscular frame.

"Oh, please, Everton. Reg and I know, and Christian is family, after all." The viscount's eyes took her in again. "They were married for six months, and every moment of it was hell. Ask him if it's not so."

"Sweet Jesus, Augustus," Reg muttered, and stood. He faced Alex. "I don't know what set him off, but he's been like this all evening. I'll see him home."

Devlin shrugged his arm free of the baron's grip, and chuckled again. "I believe he made her . . . uneasy, you know. They had so little to do with one another that she had the fever for three days before he even knew about it. Then you waited, what, another day, was it, before you sent for a doctor?"

"She insisted that I not." Alex's eyes were cold and remote, and Kit found herself on her feet.

"Come, cousin," she said, avoiding Augustus's faint smile. "He's too drunk to realize that in insulting you, he also insults Mary."

"Do I?" the viscount asked, tilting back his glass to finish it. "That was not my intention. Oh, dear me, no."

With the grating of wood against wood, Alex shoved his chair back and stood. "If you weren't already dead, Augustus," he snarled, "I'd call you out. As it is, you're not worth the lead." Everton spun on his heel and strode for the door.

Kit turned after him.

"Christian!" Augustus called after her.

She paused. The viscount would talk to her, she sensed, looking for a friend when he'd driven one away. And drunk as he was, it wouldn't even be that difficult to get information out of him. She took a breath, glancing toward the doorway and Everton and the night beyond. "I have nothing to say to you, Devlin," she returned, and left.

Alex was seated in the phaeton, his gaze fixed on Mercutio's ears, when she emerged from the club. As she climbed up beside him, he glanced at her. "Damned unpleasant way to end the evening, I'd say," he growled, and snapped the reins to start off the team.

"Tomorrow he won't even remember he said anything," she offered, watching his expression carefully.

"Oh, he'll remember it, all right," the earl returned. "Damned muckworm has a memory nearly as good as yours." He drew a slow breath. "Thing of it is, he was right."

"It's none of my affair," she said quietly, though she keenly wanted to know what had transpired between him and his late wife. Just as keenly she wished to see the look of frustrated anger and pain leave his lean, sensitive face.

Despite the late hour and the chill in the air, an orange girl stood at the street corner, and Alex pulled up the phaeton and motioned to her. She rushed out into the street at his summons, and Alex gave her a florin in exchange for two oranges. Wordlessly he handed one of them over to Kit. Her eyes on his face, she pulled out her boot knife and slowly peeled it as Alex set the horses in motion again.

"My father had just died, you know," he said after a moment, his eyes and apparently his attention on the evening traffic around them. "He and my mother wanted grandchildren to spoil, had teased me about it since I can remember. But after she died, he never mentioned it again." Alex glanced at her, but quickly returned his gaze to the street. "When he died, it started me thinking that I was all there was to the Cale line, and that I was failing miserably in passing on the birthright of the earls before me. I became . . . obsessed with the absurd notion that I needed to get an heir. Immediately."

"And you fell in love with Mary Devlin," Kit supplied quietly, fiddling with the orange in her hands, and bothered by the absurd notion that she was jealous of a dead woman for being the one to catch Alex's heart.

"I'd known Augustus since Cambridge. He, of course, introduced me to his sister when she came out. Mary was graceful, quiet-spoken, elegant, and completely proper." He sighed. "Exactly what a young idiot looks for when trying to find a woman to bear him children.''

"But you said she was perfect," Kit commented, studying his profile.

"Oh, she was. I was the one found lacking."

"You?" she returned, raising an eyebrow. "But you're . . ." She trailed off. *Magnificent,* she wanted to say, but didn't dare.

He grimaced. "As I said, she didn't much care for faro or billiards or brandy, and was of the school which held that women who read or had any sort of political interests were bluestockings, which left us little common ground. And my . . . passions left her somewhat appalled, I believe. Letting me touch her was her wifely duty, so long as the sole purpose was to beget children. It was never anything more to her, and believe me, I did my damndest to make it pleasant."

For a long moment Kit looked at him, unable to imagine how Mary Cale could possibly have turned away from him. "Lud," she finally said.

His eyes flicked in her direction, and he gave a short laugh. "Apologies, chit," he murmured. "It's your own fault, for listening."

"She was wrong, Alex," Kit said firmly. And Mary had also been a fool, though she decided against voicing that opinion.

"So say you. All I know is that within weeks, our marriage, if it could even be called such, had deteriorated to the point that I only saw her when we were supposed to appear somewhere together. She spent her days in the morning room with her tittering, waspish friends. Her bedchamber wasn't even on the same floor as mine. That's why she was feverish for three days before I even knew she was ill." He looked down at his hands, clenching the ribbons so tightly, his knuckles stood out. "I didn't wish her dead, but I would be lying if I didn't say that part of me was relieved. I can't imagine a lifetime of that misery. It wasn't even that she was content to ignore me, you know. Augustus was right. She loved being the Countess of Everton, but she flat out hated me." He gave a brief, humorless smile. "At least I can tell my ancestors I've done my part, and they can go to hell if they expect me to go through it again."

That last part bothered her more than the rest. It wasn't that she imagined any sort of future with him, for of course, that was ridiculous. But Alex had left nothing for himself. Nothing but wasted time with Barbara Sinclair, or whichever woman caught his fancy for a night. "That's very sad," she murmured, wanting to move closer beside him, put her arm around his waist, and tuck her head against his shoulder. "But I don't think every marriage is like that."

He looked over at her. "Ah. You think I should give it another try?"

There was no mistaking the sarcasm in his tone, but neither could she ignore the fleeting loneliness that touched his eyes. "Your parents had a good marriage, yes?"

He pursed his lips, then nodded reluctantly. "Yes. Which makes mine doubly a failure, wouldn't you say?"

Kit shook her head. "You're missing the point."

Again he gave a short laugh, the sound brittle. "Well, I beg your pardon, but I believe that's enough marital advice from a virgin chit dressed like a boy and wielding a knife."

"I was only trying to help, *cochon*," she snapped, and slammed the knife back into her boot.

"Where did you get that damned thing, anyway?"

"I've had it for years. And go duel with Devlin," she suggested. "Not me. I've been very pleasant this evening."

His jaw clenched, then he took a breath and rolled his shoulders to relax the tension there. "Do tell," he returned in a more even tone. "I appreciate your pointing that out. I wouldn't want to miss it by mistake."

"I'm going to go see Ivy in the morning," Kit announced, mostly to see if he would let her go. And she needed to check once more to see if her father was at the Hanging Crow. At any rate, being around Alex was far too distracting, when she still had to decide what to do about him and Reg and Augustus.

Surprisingly, he didn't argue, but only nodded. After a moment he glanced around and turned the phaeton north. "We seem to have run out before eating again," he noted. "Hungry?"

"Always."

He laughed. "Boodles?"

"If you're buying," she suggested, absurdly relieved that his somber mood seemed to have lifted.

"I'm always buying, chit."

Chapter 13

Stewart Brantley was not at the Hanging Crow when Kit strolled in.

She had waited outside the establishment for an hour in the pale sunlight, making certain that Fouché and his men were absent, before she entered. As she took a quick turn about the large, dim tavern and then exited again, she was aware of being somewhat relieved. She'd done her duty by trying to contact her father, and at the same time, his absence gave her time to come up with her own plan of how to deal with her English lord and his cronies, before he could decide on something less pleasant. The idea of killing a peer over an intercepted cargo was both absurd and dangerous, but Stewart had seemed so serious about the entire game. It hadn't bothered her before, but over the last few days, the consequences of her task in London had begun to concern her more than she was prepared for.

Lingering about Covent Garden with Jean-Paul Mercier in the vicinity was less than wise, and she was glad to make her way to the comfortable town house of Gerald and Ivy Downing. Ivy even seemed genuinely pleased to see her as the butler showed her into the morning room.

"Kit!" she exclaimed, setting aside her pen and rising to pull her illusionary cousin into a warm embrace. "What a pleasant surprise!"

"Alex is in mee—"

"Meetings," Ivy finished with a grimace. "I know. Gerald, too." She shut the door and turned around to lean back against it. "That awful Frenchman's fault, no doubt." She gave a slight grin. "So. I am glad for your company this morning, my dear, but what truly brings you here today?"

"I only wanted to visit with y—"

"No, no," Ivy returned dryly, stepping forward to lead her guest over to the couch and taking a seat at one end, "when one is given the means to travel anywhere in London on a fine, sunny day, this is not where one goes."

It was, if that was the lie one had told. "But I like your company."

"I don't believe you, but you know, I'm glad you came to see me." She tilted her head to eye Kit speculatively. "We received an invitation yesterday, and it struck me as very interesting."

"What sort of invitation?" Kit asked, intrigued.

"The Thornhills are hosting a masquerade ball on Wednesday."

"I know," Kit answered. "Alex was invited . . ." All at once it occurred to her what Ivy must be suggesting, and she flushed. "Oh, no, I couldn't."

"Why ever not? Everyone will be in costumes and masks. It would be perfect, Kit. And the only chance you'll have to be a female in London."

It could be the only chance she would *ever* have to be a female. And for Alex to see her as one. "It's only a few days away," she protested weakly, her mind already running far ahead of her tongue. "I have nothing to wear."

"Of course, we'll have to get you a proper gown, and perhaps try a few lessons in female etiquette . . ."

"A thousand lessons," she returned nervously.

"I can see to that, if you wish. For of course, it must be up to you."

"Oh, lud," Kit breathed, finally beginning to see the merits of the word. "Yes, I would like to do it."

*   *   *

By the time she left the Downings, there were so many things spinning in her head that she didn't notice the familiar figure leaning against a lamppost in front of Cale House until after she stepped down from the hired hack and started up the drive.

"Kit."

She jumped and whipped around. "Jean-Paul!" she exclaimed with forced cheerfulness, and stepped forward to grip his hand. "What brings you to London?"

"I am here to assist your papa, of course," the comte answered, and gestured toward Cale House. "As are you, yes?"

"Yes." She nodded, watching him warily for anything that might reveal his true motive for being in England.

"I had hoped you would have news for me," Fouché prompted, his dark eyes searching hers with the same intensity that had made her uneasy the last few times they had encountered one another. "A name, perhaps."

She wrinkled her brow, pretending ignorance, though she knew exactly what he was asking. It would have been difficult enough to tell her father and beg his understanding in her wavering loyalties. Fouché, though, had little compassion that she had ever seen.

"We will all be ruined if the shipment is intercepted again," he pushed. "And your father already owes me and my associates ten thousand pounds. If you tell me who will move against us, I can make the next few days . . . difficult, to keep him from interfering."

Kit shook her head, wondering with a shudder what "difficulty" would keep Alex Cale from his duties. "I was only supposed to inform my father. He had something planned."

"Yes, I know. *I* was what he had planned." He regarded her, his dark eyes almost luminous in his lean, olive-complexioned face, and took a step closer. "I have kept secrets for you before, *belle chère*, perhaps without you even knowing."

He knew. Alex had been right. Fouché knew her secret. And that left her more uneasy than the Earl of Everton's knowing ever could. "I—"

"Give me a name, Kit." He glanced toward the mansion again. "Is it him?"

"Of course not," she stammered, abruptly deciding. She couldn't turn Alex over to this man. "I'm here only by coincidence."

He gave a slow smile. "Then give me a name. We French are a jealous breed, you know." Fouché reached out slowly toward her face and caressed her cheek. "I could keep you far safer and give you far more pleasure than a thin-blooded Englishman."

Kit swallowed, her skin crawling where he had touched her. "What has that to do with our task?" she countered, taking a step backward to put a little distance between them, trusting her supposed ally less than her known enemy. Alex could touch her like that, but no one else.

He moved forward to match her. "Give me a name, *m'amoureuse.*"

"I don't have one," she muttered, and took a quick breath when he scowled. "I thought I did," she continued quickly, "but just this morning I discovered that it could not be him. There are some other possibilities, but it will take me the rest of my time here to be certain." His frown didn't abate, and she pulled a grimace on her own face. "That is why my father set a fortnight for the task, after all. To make a mistake could be fatal for all of us."

Initially she didn't think he believed her, but after a moment Jean-Paul nodded. He took her chin between his thumb and forefinger. "I will be nearby."

With a nod and another deep breath, Kit excused herself from him and walked up the drive to Cale House. Her father didn't trust Fouché either, but he knew the comte was in London and hadn't bothered to inform her, which implied that they were working together. And so she had lied to both of them, to protect Alexander Cale. And she was growing so tired of lying.

*   *   *

Alex released the curtain and stepped back from the window of his study as Kit's acquaintance looked up toward the house again, and then with a slight smile turned and strolled down the street. The cut of his coat and the style of his hair were unmistakably French, and whoever he might be, Kit had bloody well let him paw at her enough to make him more than a casual acquaintance.

Wenton pulled the front door open, and Alex quickly returned across the hall to the library and dropped into the nearest chair. "How were my, er, our cousins?" he queried as she entered the room and curled into the seat opposite him.

"Ivy's splendid. Gerald was out," the chit answered easily, craning her neck to look at the book sitting beneath the stack of papers at his elbow. "Are you reading my Byron?" she demanded, a soft blush touching her cheeks.

"Your Byron?" he replied, raising an eyebrow.

"Well, you know what I mean," she said, looking as though she would like to snatch it off the table and abscond with it.

"You were gone for some time," he noted casually, running his finger slowly along the spine of the book to keep her attention there, rather than on what he was saying. "I was beginning to think you'd run across Reg or Francis and gone to the races."

"Oh, no. Ivy and I only chatted for longer than I realized."

"Becoming a regular gossip, aren't you?"

"I am not," she protested, clearly indignant.

He pursed his lips. It appeared that if he wished to know who the gentleman out on the street was, he was going to have to ask her directly. And he didn't wish to do that. If the aggravating chit had been a less proficient liar, she might have left him with some clue, but as it was, all he could do was withdraw and attack from a different direction. Slowly he lifted the stack of papers from the book and shuffled through them. "I received these today,'' he said, handing them to her. ''Care to explain?''

Kit looked down at them. And blanched.

''I see,'' he commented, taking them back, curiosity blazing through him. These, at least, he would have an answer about. He separated the top sheet and examined it. '' 'True verdant slippers, three shillings.' '' He glanced up to find her gaze on his hands. ''What sort of color is 'true verdant,' anyway?''

''Green.'' For once, the expression on her face was easy to interpret. Embarrassed and guilty about something, she curled smaller into the chair and made a face. ''Emerald, actually,'' she muttered.

He studied her face for another moment, then fished out another paper. '' 'Mrs. Beam's Beautifications, one day muslin, two pounds six; stockings, one pair, two shillings; hair clips, two shillings.' ''

''Alex,'' she finally implored, ''I—''

He grabbed her outstretched hand. ''How do they look on you?'' he asked softly, running his thumb across her fingers.

Slowly she met his gaze, trying to decipher his mood. ''You're not angry?''

''Of course not. How do they look?''

She sighed. ''Silly, actually,'' she admitted. ''The shoes are too small, and the gown is too large, and—''

''I should like to see them on you, anyway,'' he returned. ''To satisfy my considerable curiosity.''

She tilted her head at him, and gently tugged her fingers free. ''It's truly awful-looking,'' she insisted.

''Let me be the judge of that.''

Kit shrugged. ''All right,'' she acquiesced, and he thought she was not entirely displeased. ''But I'm damned well not wearing it down here.''

He raised an eyebrow. ''Shall I join you in your bedchamber, then?'' he suggested slyly.

Surprisingly, she sobered, rather than giving him the set-down he expected, but from her cautious expression he knew what must be running through her mind. The last time they had begun this sort of teasing he had practically rendered her naked, and then had broken off the seduction because he didn't trust her, or himself, if anything further should happen. And even with the boundaries he had made for himself, the desire to touch her, to kiss her and to hold her, was nearly overpowering.

"I have a better idea," she said after a moment, her manner hesitant, as though she was less than comfortable making the suggestion.

"You have my attention," he returned, sitting back and crossing his legs at the ankles.

Kit looked at him, then shook her head and stood. "Never mind."

He sat forward again, but forced himself to remain seated. "Indulge me, chit," he requested mildly, trying to avoid letting her know how very curious she made him.

She blew out her breath and stalked over to the window. "It's nothing, really. I just . . . well, the Thornhill ball."

"I'm aware of it," he commented when she stopped.

"Yes, well, I was thinking . . . That is, Ivy suggested . . ."

"Do spit it out, girl," he encouraged, a smile making his lips twitch. Kit at a loss was a rather unusual sight.

She turned around and took a deep breath. "I would like to attend."

He nodded. "You're welcome to, of course. Your last night in London and all."

"In a gown."

For a moment he was speechless. She continued to glare at him, her face reddening, while he stared back at her. Even after he regained control of his vocal cords, it took him two tries to get the words out. "You what?" he finally blurted, both brows soaring toward his hairline.

"No one will know it's me," she continued quickly, stepping up to him. "Everyone will be wearing masks."

"Are you completely mad?" he asked, standing and looking down at her.

"No. I just want to wear a gown," she said in a defiant voice that deflated and faltered at the end.

She truly wanted to, he realized. And she hadn't attempted to lie to him about it, or go behind his back, or make up some clever excuse why he must put her in skirts. Slowly he blew out his breath. "You know what a risk you'd be taking," he stated, holding her gaze.

Kit nodded. "I do."

Of course she did. She weighed every word and every action with a juggler's skill. Which made it even more out of character for her to decide upon such a rash exploit in the first place. "And this was Ivy's idea?"

"Don't be angry at her." Kit put one hand out to touch his sleeve. "Please, Everton? I can't do it without you."

He looked away, but could still feel her eyes on him. "It's damned dangerous, and I don't like it," he grumbled, glancing at her again and knowing full well that he couldn't refuse her. "And I'm only agreeing so I can keep an eye on you and prevent a worse disaster from befalling."

"*Merci*, Alex," she said softly, looking up at him from beneath her long lashes, and giving him that shy smile that made his breath quicken and his heart beat faster. "May I ask one more favor?"

With a snort, Alex threw his hands up and dropped back into the chair. "Please do," he chuckled. "I surrender."

Kit licked her lips and sat again as well. She reached out and touched the book at his elbow. "Will you read one for me?"

"Ah." As it was, he felt poorly balanced between gentlemanly and libertine behavior. Byron could easily tip the balance.

Fleeting loneliness and sadness touched her eyes. "I know. It's not wise." She sighed, and rose again. "Never mind."

There was more to this than a simple poem. And this time, what she wanted from him wasn't nearly as easy to decipher. He gave an exaggerated sigh and lifted the book. "Do you have a preference?" he asked, flipping through a few pages.

She settled back into the chair and grinned. "I'm certain you can find an appropriate stanza," she said, propping her elbow on the cushioned arm and leaning her chin on her hand.

Alex cleared his throat. "All right, here's a stanza for you, my dear." He lowered his eyes to the page, reluctant though he was to look away from her face. In a quiet voice he read,

> " '. . . He had no breath, no being, but in hers,
> She was his voice; he did not speak to her,
> But trembled on her words; she was his sight,
> For his eye followed hers, and saw with hers,
> Which colored all his objects—he had ceased
> To live within himself; she was his life,
> The ocean to the river of his thoughts . . . ' "

For a long moment there was nothing but silence, and then the dulcet sound of her sigh. "Oh, my," she whispered, clearly as loath to break the spell as he was. He raised his eyes to look at her. Her own eyes were closed, a slight smile on her sweet, sensuous lips. "What is it called?" she murmured.

" 'The Dream,' " he answered, and stood. "For you," he said, placing the book in her hands. Unable to resist, he gently touched his lips to hers. Before she could do more than open her eyes again, he turned and left the room.

In the morning Alex dropped Kit off at the Downings' and headed to Parliament. Upstairs in Ivy's bedchamber, Kit found herself going through a measuring session nearly identical to the one she had suffered through at the hands of Everton's tailor. Mrs. Adams, Ivy's dressmaker, was much more genial and full of compliments about her hair and her figure than Mr. Lewis had been, but then Kit would have handed Mr. Lewis his teeth if he had dared to tell her that she was perfectly proportioned.

When, in complete bewilderment, Kit gave over to Ivy the responsibility for all decisions regarding color, fabric, and style, the two ladies spent another hour eyeing her, having her turn this way and that, and holding what seemed like hundreds of fabric samples up to her neck, shoulders, and face. Finally they decided on a burgundy silk with black beading, a lace netting over the skirt, and frothing at the sleeves, which were apparently going to be off her shoulders.

"Are you certain?" she asked. "I don't wish to look like some sort of whore— um, light-skirt," she amended, as Mrs. Adams glanced in her direction, startled.

"Trust me in this, my dear." Ivy smiled, and launched into a list of petticoats, stockings, and shoes that Mrs. Adams was to bring with her on the morrow, when Kit would have her first fitting.

When the dressmaker finally bundled up her things and departed, Kit sighed and dropped into the nearest chair. "This is exhausting," she declared, and reached for a handful of the finger sandwiches a servant had delivered upstairs.

"Christine," Ivy murmured, gesturing with her chin at the sandwiches, "if you're to be a lady . . ."

"Oh, drat," Kit grumbled, and set all but one of the sandwiches back onto the platter. "Alex says I eat like a regiment, but he seems to like it."

A slight smile touched her companion's face. "Alexander is a rather unconventional man," Ivy agreed. "But in polite company, you must always consume as little as possible without seeming to dislike the fare."

"I don't think I can possibly learn everything," Kit returned, nibbling at the tiny morsel and grateful she had eaten that third biscuit at breakfast. "His lordship is anticipating complete disaster."

For a moment Ivy was silent, her cup of tea poised halfway to her lips. "You told Alex?" she finally said, looking at Kit.

"I didn't want to have to lie to him about it." She shrugged, making it as small a thing as she could. Lies upon lies upon lies, and when Alex had sat smiling at her yesterday, she had suddenly wished to tell him a truth. And so she had. The most innocent one she could think of.

"And he agreed to this?"

"Very reluctantly." Kit grimaced and started to lick her finger, stopping self-consciously when Ivy gave a small frown. "Do you think he's right, Ivy? Do you think it will be a disaster?"

Ivy actually gave her the compliment of thinking about her words before she answered. "No. I don't think so." She smiled. "I will do my best to see that it is not. And I welcome any opportunity to prove Alexander Cale wrong—he is right far too much of the time. Or he thinks he is." She narrowed her eyes. "Now. With the short amount of time we have, I believe we should concentrate only on what you will need to learn for the Thornhill ball. Walking, dancing, polite conversation . . ."

Kit blanched, wishing she had thought things through. Alex was right, after all. "I can't go," she groaned, crestfallen.

"Whyever not?"

"I can't dance."

"What?" Ivy chuckled incredulously. "Of course you can. I've seen you. I've waltzed with you. You dance beautifully."

Kit covered her eyes with her hands, the enormity of what she was contemplating finally crashing down on her. "Only when I lead," she mumbled.

It seemed she was able to stun her hostess rather easily, for again silence dragged on for several moments. Finally she raised her head, only to find that Ivy was doubled over, her shoulders trembling. It took another few miserable breaths before Kit realized that she was shaking with laughter.

"Well, I don't think it's at all funny," she said indignantly, folding her arms over her chest and sitting back.

"Oh, I'm sorry, Kit," Ivy chortled. "But you're right. You can't very well step out onto the floor and expect to lead when you're dressed as a female."

"But that's the way I learned."

Still chuckling, Ivy rose and stepped over to tug her to her feet. "Come downstairs. We shall see what we can do."

Gerald wasn't home from his meetings, so Fender, the butler, found himself recruited to play the pianoforte. Kit scowled, for they were letting more people in on her secret than she was comfortable with. But there were only three days left, and in this instance there seemed to be little choice.

"Remember," Ivy instructed as the music began, "it's what you were doing before, only backwards." She chuckled. "And put your hand on my shoulder, for goodness' sake. I am the man now."

Kit was unable to stifle a laugh of her own. "This is very confusing." Fender mumbled something unintelligible, and Kit grinned at him.

Doing everything backwards was more difficult than she had realized, and she stepped on her poor partner's toes at least as many times as her own were kicked. Ivy, apparently, was having her own difficulties. "Don't give up, Kit," she encouraged with a brave smile. "Once more. I believe we're both catching on."

At the sound of male laughter, they both stopped short. Gerald Downing, and to Kit's surprised embarrassment, the Earl of Everton, stood in the doorway watching their efforts. Alex's eyes were full of amusement as he pushed away from the frame.

"I'm gratified to see that there is at least one thing you have difficulty with," he chuckled, walking up to stand before her. "Perhaps you need a more practiced partner." He held out his hand to her. "Allow me, chit."

Dancing with Ivy was more comfortable, for they were both equally out of their element. As she accepted Everton's hand and he slid his other easily around her waist, she was again aware of feeling strangely vulnerable. Again he was the master, and she the awkward student. She took a quick breath and glanced away from his handsome face. "Well, I don't want everyone gawk-ing at me," she grumbled.

"Of course," Ivy agreed, and motioned Gerald to join her in the middle of the floor. "Fender? If you please."

With a sigh, the butler struck up the waltz again. Alex started to move, but Kit shook her head, her eyes on the other couple. "Let me study them for a moment," she protested.

He freed his hand from her waist long enough to touch her chin and lift her head so she had to look up at him. "You don't need to study anything," he mur-mured. "All you need to do is relax and follow my lead. If you trust me."

With that, he swept her into the dance. She'd seen him waltz before, and had wondered what it would be like to be in his arms. Kit tried to remember the steps, in reverse, and succeeded in keeping even with him for two complete circles. And then he smiled at her, and she lost count, kicked him in the shin, and stumbled against his chest. "Oh, drat," she muttered, stopping.

Alex shook his head and pulled her up against him again. "Relax," he whispered. "Don't try to unremem-ber anything. Just look at me. Just dance with me."

They began again, and she promptly stepped on his toe. "I'm sorry," Kit said miserably, slowing again.

He wouldn't let her stop. "You're a damned stubborn chit," he informed her, practically dragging her until she got her feet under herself again, "and you're so worried about not making a misstep that that is all you can do."

"That is not tr—" She tripped again, and again he pulled her closer against his chest until she untangled her legs and regained her balance. "Alex, let go," she demanded. "You were right. This is hope—"

He lowered his head and interrupted her protest with a kiss. "Do shut up," he suggested. "I want to dance with you."

She licked her lower lip with the tip of her tongue, and glanced quickly over at Gerald and Ivy. The Dow-nings were circling over by the window, eyes on one another and not paying any attention to their guests at all. She looked back up at Alex. His eyes were twinkling, and he touched his lips to hers again.

"I thought you were anticipating complete disaster," she commented, not minding that he seemed to be holding her closer than was strictly allowed.

"I am," he agreed, shifting his hand so that her fingers were twined with his, rather than being clasped by them.

"So why are you assisting?" *Kiss me again,* she entreated him silently, her senses soaring with Fender's well-played waltz. It was becoming fairly obvious that Alex was attempting to seduce her, and with all her heart she wished she knew whether it was out of curiosity and convenience, or because he felt remotely what she was beginning to feel toward him.

"I should have elaborated," he murmured as they circled the room. "I meant a complete disaster for *me.*" With a glance of his own at his cousins, he kissed her again, more roughly and more deeply than before.

"Alex!" Ivy chastised.

With a completely unrepentant grin, not even bothering to look over at his relations, Alex sighed and put the correct amount of distance between them. It was only then Kit realized that she had been waltzing with him for several minutes, swaying easily in his skillful, confident grip. "You distracted me," she accused without heat.

"Turnabout is fair play, my dear," he answered. "I declare you completely proficient at the waltz."

"As long as I waltz only with someone who kisses me when I crush his toes," she pointed out, and wondered fleetingly and wickedly what kicking him in the knee would gain her.

Surprisingly, a good portion of the humor left his eyes. "You'd best waltz only with me, then."

He was jealous. In her decision to dress as a female, she hadn't anticipated that. It felt quite wonderful, though, and she couldn't help smiling at him. The Earl of Everton was jealous, over her, a boy-thing in breeches, and without any suitors, real or imagined, to challenge him. "Then perhaps you'd best purchase stout boots."

Alex eyed her for a moment, and she was uncertain whether she'd said the wrong thing. Finally he chuckled. "I'm beginning to think I should simply wear a full suit of armor," he returned. "'Twould be safer, around you."

She lifted her chin. "Do you fear me then, Everton?" she queried, trying very hard to guess where this conversation was leading her this time, even as he led her in a wide, grand circle about the room.

He smiled a little, in a way that made her wish Fender and the Downings were not present. "You have no idea," he whispered.

They practiced the waltz, the quadrille, and two country dances before Alex put an end to the day. "My apologies, but if we continue, I will be maimed for life," he joked.

A reluctant laugh burst from Kit's lips. "I've only three more days until the ball, you know," she retorted, folding her arms and trying to disguise the sudden nervousness running through her.

It made Alex realize that he had done the right thing in agreeing to this masquerade within a masquerade. Dressing for one evening as a female was very important to Kit. And ill advised as it was, he would do whatever he could to see that the night, her last night, went as perfectly as possible for her.

"You're a quick study," he pointed out. "When is your gown to be ready?"

"In three days," she answered.

"Ah. Cutting it a bit close, aren't we?"

"It's the height of the Season. That's as quickly as my dressmaker can manage it," Ivy put in a bit defensively.

"You should have offered to pay her more," he said unsympathetically.

"Now, now," Gerald interrupted, "I'm certain we've

timed everything splendidly, as usual. No fighting *before* everything goes wrong.''

"Because it won't," Ivy added.

"As you say," Alex offered as graciously as he could, for it was fairly obvious that there were myriad things that could easily go awry. The Downings hardly knew the half of it. Nor could he tell them. "Come, chit."

"I'll see you tomorrow, Cousin Ivy." With a kiss on Ivy's cheek, Kit led the way out the door. "Take me to White's tonight, won't you?"

Alex frowned, little relishing the conversation that would follow. That was why he hadn't said anything until after he'd danced with her. She'd allowed him to hold her in his arms, and awkward as she'd been, it had been quite enjoyable. Too enjoyable, in all likelihood. "I've a previous engagement."

"With whom?"

Her lilting voice was cool enough, but he could hear the curiosity there. If he told her it was none of her business, she would turn it around on him later, as she had done before, and if he lied . . . "Barbara Sinclair."

She didn't even do him the favor of turning around to look at him. "I'd best go back inside and continue my female lessons, anyway. I've a great deal to learn."

Alex would have liked to dispute that, but neither did he wish to begin another shouting match in the Downings' drive. He put a hand on her shoulder, unwilling to explain that because of her secret, he was being forced to play pretty with his mistress. "Kit . . ."

She shrugged free. "Your stupidity is none of my affair, Everton."

"Stupidity?" he queried carefully, angry.

Kit faced him. "You're the one who turned away," she said. "Not me."

That much was true. And if he had possessed the ability to separate the wants of his body from the needs of his heart, he might very well have taken her as his mistress, Bonaparte's spy or not. But the web was already too tangled, the decisions that should have been clear and easy becoming murkier and more confusing by the moment. "Just honoring my father's debt to your father." He turned to climb into the phaeton. "And remember your promise to me, chit," he continued, looking down at her angry, frustrated expression. "You're not going anywhere until your father comes for you."

"I always keep my word," she spat, and turned on her heel.

He looked after her for a moment, then clucked to the team. "As do I, Miss Brantley," he muttered.

By the time he reached Cale House again, Alex had managed to convince himself that dancing about Barbara Sinclair, and letting Kit Brantley sneak about London with but three days left before her departure, was idiocy. Allowing Barbara to reveal her little secret shouldn't matter, because short of divine intervention, he would have to arrest Kit as a spy, anyway. It would make a sticky situation even worse, but he really didn't give a damn. The game should have been well over by now, and he was swiftly running out of any sort of reasonable excuse to prolong it. And the unreasonable excuses were all ones he wouldn't allow himself to examine too closely.

He turned in to the drive, then pulled Benvolio and Mercutio to an abrupt halt. A coach with a splendid crest emblazoned on the door stood at the foot of his front steps, a liveried groom in deep conversation with Conklin at the rear of the highly polished vehicle.

He should have realized it would happen sooner or later. His mind racing at nearly the same rate as his heart, he jumped to the ground as Conklin stepped forward to take the horses. Wenton was off for the day, and the front door was manned by one of the footmen, who looked flustered as he admitted his employer.

"My lord, he . . . the . . . His Grace . . ."

Alex nodded and pulled off his gloves. "Where is he?"

"In the drawing room, my lord. I didn't know—"

"No worries, Timothy," he said, nodding at his footman, and headed up the stairs.

The Duke of Furth stood in the middle of the drawing room gazing at the portrait above the mantel, much as his brother had done a little less than a fortnight ago. The older brother was taller than the younger, and more solidly built, but both possessed the same blond hair and sharp green eyes.

"Good afternoon, Your Grace," Alex greeted him, stepping into the room and shutting the door behind him.

Martin Brantley turned around. "Everton." He nodded, and folded his arms over his chest. "What in blazes are you up to?"

Alex pursed his lips, shrugged, and strolled over to open the brandy decanter. "That's a rare greeting," he returned. "What brings you to London?"

"Hanshaw's letter," the duke answered, following him over and accepting a snifter. With his other hand he pulled a missive from his pocket and dropped it onto the liquor table. "Care to explain?"

Alex kept his eyes on the brandy he was pouring himself. "Reg is a telltale who jumps to conclusions," he commented. "It will be handled. It always is."

"Weapons are missing, Alexander. And Napoleon is on the loose. You had no right to keep it from me."

"You shouldn't stay so far from London, then."

":Hm," Furth grunted, and took a swallow. "Putting me at the head of this commission was a mad king's decision. Not mine. And so was secrecy about the whole damned rigmarole—which is why I depend on you to keep me informed."

"And I do," Alex protested, cursing Hanshaw all over again. This deuced mess was complicated enough without Kit's uncle appearing and demanding answers he wasn't prepared yet to give. "When there's something to report."

"So you've learned nothing in the past two months?" Martin Brantley countered, lifting an eyebrow. "Rather lazy of you, Alexander."

"I've learned a few things," Alex admitted begrudgingly. "But I intend to be certain of my facts before I give over anything to you, Your Grace. With all due respect.''

"Whatever that means,'' the duke muttered. " 'Due respect.' A disguise for blatant disrespect, if you ask me.'' Furth looked at him closely, his eyes only a shade lighter than Kit's and his own daughter's, curious and intrigued. "You haven't much time left.''

Alex nodded and slowly replaced the stopper in the decanter. "I know. Just a few more days. I need to figure this out first.''

"A friend of yours, then?''

"Something like that.'' Alex motioned the duke to take a seat. When the older man refused, he leaned against the edge of the couch. "So what excuse do you give the masses for emerging from Furth?''

The duke gave a short smile. "Actually, you've provided me with that, as well.''

"Have I now? Do tell.''

"Yes. I believe your damned Irish cousin is courting my daughter,'' the duke said. "And I also believe I'm quite upset about it and need to warn him off, publicly if possible. Where is the rascal?''

Alex stopped breathing. "Kit? I don't know. Out somewhere.'' Thank God they'd fought and she hadn't returned home with him.

"Well, until I can encounter him somewhere more opportune, let him know that he is to stay away from Caroline.'' His expression briefly became more serious. "I don't know what his intentions are, and I don't care. Caroline is to marry a title. So unless this Christian of yours is secretly nobility, he is to stay away from her. Is that clear?''

For a moment Alex just looked at him. "I'll speak to him, yes,'' he finally replied.

Furth nodded, took a final swallow of brandy, and set the snifter aside. "Good. That'll do for now. As for the other, I can't give you much time. Prince George has been bellowing at me for weeks for someone to hang. I sympathize with your desire to be certain of your facts, but there is a great deal at stake here.''

"I am aware of that," Alex said stiffly. "You don't need to remind me of my duty."

"I know." With a sigh, the duke turned for the door. "I'd best make a show of being the concerned, protective parent for a few days. It might even be with good reason. I do believe Hanshaw might be after Caroline."

"Really?" Alex said absently, his mind on another tangle entirely. "I hadn't noticed."

The duke paused to look at him sideways. "Liar," he said smoothly, giving a slight, surprising smile that reminded Alex of Kit, and left the room.

Alex sank into the nearest chair and took a deep breath. If he had been doing his duty as he should, he would have informed Furth that his younger brother was their weapons smuggler. And that his niece was at the least a spy for her father, and perhaps even for Bonaparte. He ran a hand through his hair. Damnation, this was becoming more complicated by the moment.

Chapter 14

❦

"That is the most idiotic thing I have ever heard,'' Alex growled under his breath. His eyes were on his hostess, who was animatedly laughing with London's newest oddity, the Prussian baron Kurt Blanschauer. If Barbara was trying to make him jealous, she was sadly off target. The mule-faced buffoon was more likely to raise his bile than his ire.

Reg Hanshaw followed his gaze, then shrugged. "I got it straight from Wentworth," he returned in a low voice. "Half of London is sailing over to Belgium to watch the fun. He offered to put me up at the house he's taken there."

"Going over to watch the fun,'' Alex repeated cynically. "I wonder how much fun they would have standing a line and holding a musket while Boney's army marched down their throats." He shook his head. "They've whined about the bastard since before the Season began, and now they're off to watch the fun."

"I knew I shouldn't have told you about it,'' Lord Hanshaw grumbled. "Have you heard from Hanton or Hunt?"

"Hunt hasn't seen a thing, and there's no word yet from Hanton. The north country is my best guess, though. He won't want to make the same mistake twice."

" 'He'?" Reg repeated, pouncing on the word. "You have a name?"

Alex took a drink to stall giving an answer. There were so many tangles that he was starting to forget which thread he was pulling. "Nearly. Give me another few days and I will." He took another breath. "And, Reg, Kit doesn't know about any of this. I'd like to keep it that way." At least he could keep things from growing any worse.

"You don't trust him?"

"I don't want him to overhear something and go charging into battle."

Reg nodded. "Of course. I don't think it would take much encouragement, either. He's already pestered me to get him a commission. I sent him to bite your ankle."

So she knew about Reg, as well, damn her. "My thanks." He nodded.

The baron gave a slight smile. "Whatever it takes to stay on your good side. Especially as I need to ask your assistance."

"You have my attention." Alex nodded, pleased to be on a safer topic.

"Furth's in London. And yes, I know, it's my fault. But as long as I've roused the lion, I was going to ask you to speak to him on my behalf."

Alex nearly choked on his port. "You wish *me* to speak to Furth."

"Well, yes. He's always liked you. Just tell him what a noble, upright fellow I am, and how I have always upheld my position with dignity and respect."

"Lie, you mean." Alex grinned.

"Whatever it takes."

"I'd like to help, Reg," he said truthfully, "but considering Martin's professed reason for being in town is to warn my cousin away from his daughter, my interference on your behalf might be both rather awkward and somewhat suspicious."

The baron pursed his lips. "And poor Kit not knowing it's a ruse? Must have frightened the poor lad half to death." His expression became almost gleeful. "Though I can't say I'm all that upset to hear Furth's clearing out the competition."

"Just hope you're not next," Alex commented dryly.

"Especially with no one else to speak for me. You're my only titled crony with any sense in his skull."

"There's always Augustus," the earl offered stiffly.

Reg shook his head. "He's been completely unapproachable since the two of you had it out at the Society. Buried himself in his study with a case of brandy, and hasn't come out except to piss and send his footmen for cigars."

"Then you're on your own, Reg," Alex said, finding Hanshaw's information less than interesting. Augustus frequently pushed the borders of his tolerance, but the other evening he had gone too far. "As a rule, I hardly recommend marriage even to my enemies, anyway."

The baron was shaking his head again. "You only chose wrong. Caroline is . . ." He trailed off, his expression becoming disgustingly dreamy-eyed. "She's wonderful. Her looks, her voice, the sound of her laughter, the face she makes when she's trying not to smile, her delicate fingers, her—"

"Oh, good God," Everton growled. "Spare me. While you're standing here spewing out lovesick praises, Caroline is going about letting her parents know she's taken by my Kit." A moment later he realized he'd sounded rather possessive, but thankfully Reg didn't seem to have noticed.

Hanshaw frowned and shook his head. "She's only trying to keep my attention. Don't you see? It's all a carefully orchestrated plan. Compared to Kit, I'm very nearly the perfect choice."

"I see," Alex noted dryly, folding his arms. "Then what did you need me for, pray tell?"

"To make certain Furth sees." Reg chuckled and clapped him on the shoulder. "But never you mind. I'll find someone more in favor to do my bidding." He glanced across the room, and paused. "And speaking of being in favor, I believe it's your turn, Everton."

Alex turned. Barbara Sinclair was speaking to Lady Crasten, and smiling directly at him. Gritting his teeth, he smiled back. "Excuse me, Reg." He nodded, and strolled over to her. "Barbara," he murmured, leaning down to take her hand and bring it to his lips.

"Alex." She smiled back warmly. "I wanted to thank you for the lovely brooch you sent over this morning." She turned back to Jacqueline Crasten and leaned sideways into his chest. Gracefully, she flitted her fingers around the diamond-encrusted *B* pinned onto her chest. "It was far too generous of you."

"It's lovely, Everton," Jacqueline agreed. "Must have set you back a small fortune."

" 'Twas nothing," Alex returned, and wrapped his fingers around Lady Sinclair's arm. "Allow me to admire it on you in private for a moment, won't you, my dear?"

"On me, or off me?" Barbara answered so that Lady Crasten could hear and chuckle, then allowed herself to be led through the nearest door into the library. "Lovely, don't you think?" she said, looking down at her chest.

"Indeed. I assume I'll be getting the bill for it, then?"

"You did purchase it for me."

At her affirmation he leaned back against the bookcase and folded his arms. "How much did I spend on you, then?"

"Don't be a close-fist."

"You're the blackmailer," he pointed out. "I merely wish to know what today's price is."

"Nine hundred pounds."

"Good Lord, Barbara," he exclaimed in mock alarm, "at this rate I'll be penniless in a hundred years. Surely you can hurt me more than that."

"I don't wish to hurt you at all," she replied, stepping forward to run her hand down his chest, and then lower. "I'm only protecting what's mine. Everyone believes we're still lovers," she whispered, leaning into him and licking his chin. "We may as well be."

It was more difficult to resist than he expected. He had borne Barbara some affection, for she could be witty and charming, and she was certainly a willing lover. Sparring with Kit and being denied for nearly a fortnight had left him drawn so tight, he was practically vibrating with tension. Barbara's wandering hands were having more of an effect than he wished. He grasped her fingers to hold them away from him. "No."

"Are you afraid of upsetting that boy-thing you're keeping? Perhaps she'd enjoy an evening off."

"You do have a way with words, Barbara," he returned, "but I believe as I've already spent nine hundred pounds on you, you will have to be satisfied with your lovely brooch this evening."

"Oh, I'm certain you've spent at least that much on your toy. Don't pout."

As a matter of fact, Kit had apologized for spending ten pounds on female clothing. Nine hundred pounds for her would be an unbelievable fortune. "Once my cousin has left, Barbara," he said softly, "you will have nothing to bargain with. I suggest you keep that in mind." He reached out and touched the brooch. "I do like this— but the *B* doesn't stand for Barbara."

She stood glaring up at him until the door rattled and opened. Then, before he could react, she flung herself at him, twisted her arms behind his neck, and kissed him soundly. "Oh, Alex," she said, chuckling and leaning away from him, "what a marvelous idea."

He narrowed his eyes, wondering what devilment she was up to now, then looked up to see Viscount Mandilly shuffling his feet in the doorway. "Mandilly," he intoned, pulling Barbara away from his neck and turning for the door.

"Ev . . . Everton, apologies," Mandilly stuttered. "I . . . had no idea, of course."

"Of course you did," Alex responded, and returned to the drawing room.

He wandered about for another hour, exchanging greetings and mostly inane conversation with several of his cronies, and wondered whether Kit would have returned to Cale House yet, and whether she was still angry at him for being here. He was rather annoyed at himself, but appeasing Barbara seemed the least complicated way of delaying the explosion until Kit was safely away.

"Alex," Reg whispered from his elbow, and he blinked.

"Hanshaw," he acknowledged, turning to face his companion.

"What in God's name were you thinking?" the baron said.

He looked upset, and Alex furrowed his brow, wondering which of his secrets and lies had been uncovered. "Beg pardon?"

"You're marrying Barbara Sinclair?"

"*What?*"

"Since you returned from the library she's been going about whispering that the two of you have news, but nothing you can announce yet. Are you drunk?"

Fury coursed through him, fast and hot. "She has gone too far," he hissed, turning to find her. Her news that "couldn't be announced yet" would be all over London by midmorning. And the first thought that crossed his mind was that Christine would hear it, and she would have another excuse not to trust him. "I'll kill her."

Hanshaw grabbed his arm. "Not here," he muttered. "We'll have to drag her into a dark alley somewhere."

"That's not funny, Reg," he murmured darkly.

"I wasn't joking. I know something's been up between the two of you." He raised a hand when Alex opened his mouth. "I also know it's none of my bloody business. But you're going to have to put a stop to it now, or it'll be too late."

Reg's words gave him an unfortunate moment to consider what he was doing. Alex clenched his jaw. "I can't."

"What do you mean, you c—"

He drew a breath. Damn her, she'd likely been planning to trap him into marriage all along. That was the "more permanent arrangement" she'd mentioned when she'd first informed him that she knew about Kit. And unless he wished to let the entire house of cards fall down around him, including protecting Kit and stopping Stewart Brantley's smuggled weapons, he would have to let it go. For now. "Let her have her amusement," he continued slowly. "She can't very well force me into the chapel. It'll be all the worse for her, later."

"Alex, if you're not careful . . ."

"I know." She was a viscount's widow, and jilting her would not make him popular with his peers. Which she had also counted on, no doubt. "It's not as though she's some debutante I've led astray. At the least I'll weather the scandal better than she will."

"Good Lord, Everton. I don't understand why you're willing to risk—"

Alex clasped Reg on the shoulder. "I'll tell you some-day soon, my friend," he said solemnly. "I swear it." He glanced around the room to see Barbara basking in a flurry of poorly disguised congratulations in the corner. When she met his gaze he nodded to her and flicked her a fencing salute, then strolled for the door. It was time he returned home. He had to find a way to explain some-thing to a certain blond waif before she skewered him.

When Kit returned to Cale House from the Downings' it was quite late, and she expected Everton to be in bed. Instead, he was seated on the top step of the main stair-case, flipping restlessly through a farmer's almanac. As soon as she stepped into the hallway, he looked up and set the thing aside.

"Did you burn out the library?" she asked, starting up the stairs toward him.

"I didn't want to miss you," he replied, remaining seated as she stopped a few steps below, putting them at eye level. He looked very ill at ease about something, an unusual enough expression for him that it sent a shiver of uneasiness down her spine.

"What is it?" They'd arrested her father, she decided. And he was going to arrest her next.

"You're likely going to hear a rumor in the morning, and I wanted you to hear it from me first."

His words didn't calm her in the least. "What ru-mor?"

He cleared his throat and ran his fingers through his

hair, the gesture touchingly vulnerable. "That Barbara Sinclair and I are to be married."

Her heart stopped. Everything stopped, until she had a moment to understand what he had said. *"What?"* It was none of her affair, none at all, but it felt as though her very life depended on his words.

"That's exactly what I said when I heard it." Surprisingly, he gave a small, amused smile. That slight expression eased the tightness in her chest just a little.

With a frown she motioned him to move over, and sat down beside him. "It's late, Everton," she managed in a fairly normal tone, concentrating on breathing, "so would you mind explaining this in a bit more detail for me?"

He nodded, the smile touching his sensuous mouth again. It might have been relief she saw fleetingly on his lean face, but in the poor lighting it was difficult to be certain. "Barbara knows you're a female."

"She does?" Kit queried faintly.

"She does," he affirmed. "And she suggested that unless I . . . maintained the illusion of my relationship with her, she would start certain rumors about you and me."

"Is that why you spent the night at her house before?"

"Exactly why. Only tonight, she and I had a disagreement over this charade, and the next thing I knew, she'd outflanked me by announcing that the two of us had certain news."

"That bitch," Kit exclaimed.

A short laugh burst from Alex's lips. "My thoughts exactly, chit."

She looked at him, and his eyes met and held hers. "Why didn't you tell me?" she asked softly.

"Because Barbara Sinclair is a problem of my making." He reached out and gently touched her cheek with the back of his fingers. "So how was your evening? Did you woo Ivy away from stodgy old Gerald?"

She chuckled, treasuring the amusement in his eyes. It was impossible to imagine that in a little over two days he would be out of her life forever, that in all likelihood she would never see him again, never have him look at her as he was right now—as though he was trying to memorize her features. As she had already memorized his. "No, I'm still unattached," she whispered.

He hesitated again, then twisted, sliding down one step to turn and face her. "One more piece of news for you, my dear." Alex took her hands in his, his gaze still holding hers.

"Oh, lud." She sighed, wanting nothing more than to lean forward just a little and kiss him. He could never be her enemy. Never.

"Furth is in town."

Abruptly alarmed, she would have pulled free, but he tightened his grip. "Why? I thought he never came to London!"

"Almost never. Apparently he received word that his daughter was smitten with an untitled Irishman. He wished me to inform you to stay away from her."

Feeling rather faint, she did lean forward, tucking her forehead into his shoulder. Slowly he rubbed his cheek along her hair. The scent of Barbara Sinclair's expensive French perfume clung faintly to his collar, heavy and cloying, to mingle with the tantalizing mixture of shaving soap, leather, and Alex. It would be very easy to just turn her head a little to the side and kiss him, kiss the line of his jaw, and his ear, and his cheek. There was only a short time left, though, and then she would have to tell her father about the Earl of Everton and hope they could come up with something less deadly than involving Fouché. Unless she told Stewart Brantley nothing at all.

Surprised she would even think such a thing, she straightened and pulled away. Alex's gaze followed her, his expression curious and concerned. "Are you all right?"

She nodded, swallowing. "I . . . I don't want to see him."

The earl ran his index finger slowly along hers. "You

won't have to," he murmured. "I believe we can manage to avoid him for forty-eight hours."

"And then what?" she whispered.

He shrugged, then abruptly looked away from her and stood. "Were I a gypsy, I could tell you," he returned, and lowered a hand to pull her to her feet. "I'll see you in the morning, Christine."

"Good night, Alex," she murmured after him, as he disappeared into his bedchamber and softly shut the door.

The dress was completed on schedule, just as Mrs. Adams had promised.

After her fight two days before with Alex, Gerald had assisted her with dancing, and finally declared her a nonpareil at the waltz, the quadrille, and five different country dances. Ivy likewise seemed more than satisfied with her walk and her manner of speech, and only reminded her again not to say "deuced" or "blast" for the duration of the ball.

And so Christine Brantley spent the morning of the masquerade ball pacing. Alex had an afternoon session at the House of Lords, but promised to return in time to participate. She thought about taking the opportunity of his absence to track down Thadius Naring and interrogate him again, but she stopped that idea as soon as it was born. She was looking for excuses, trying to convince herself that she was wrong, that Alex couldn't possibly be who she knew him to be. And it was far too late for that, just as it was far too late for her to deny that she was in love with him.

The day, then, seemed to drag on forever. Fearing that if she continued pacing, her feet would swell and she wouldn't be able to fit into her new burgundy slippers, she finally sat herself down in the library and thumbed through Alex's copy of *A Comedy of Errors*. Though she'd never read it, the title, at least, felt appropriate.

The front door opened to the accompanying sound of Wenton greeting the earl, and Kit's eyes snapped up to the clock on the mantel. Only a few hours remained until the Thornhill ball, and her heart began beating with a nervous, excited rhythm which Alex's entrance into the library didn't help at all.

"All right." He smiled, tossing a few letters onto his desk and dropping into the chair opposite her. "What is the plan for the evening?"

She knew he still wasn't pleased with the whole idea, and was grateful that he was at least making an effort to be genial about it. "Well," she said, setting aside the play, "I don't think we should arrive together."

"That would be rather unwise, yes."

"So I believe you should go, and then I will take a hack to the Downings'. After my transformation"—she scowled at him when he chuckled—"I will make my way to the ball."

"With Gerald and Ivy."

She shook her head. "No. That won't do, either."

He sat forward and jabbed a finger at her, the humor swiftly fading from his eyes. "Proper chits do not go to balls unescorted," he said flatly.

"Alex, the whole idea is that I'll be wearing a mask. No one will know who I am, ever. So it won't matter if I go alone. It will only add to the mystery."

He was still frowning. "And afterward?" he queried skeptically.

"I'll return to the Downings', on my own, change, then take a hack back here."

"I don't like it."

Kit sighed heavily. "Alex . . ."

He tilted his head at her and sat back again. "I know, I know. Don't be a bore, Everton." His fingers beat a restless drum on the arm of his chair. "At least tell me what you'll be wearing, so I'll know which chit to flirt with."

With a relieved, delighted chuckle she shook her head. She hadn't been all that certain he would give in. "You have to guess."

Something touched his eyes for a moment, and he looked toward the window. "And tomorrow?"

"And tomorrow my father will be here. I've already

packed, so I won't need to worry about that." In fact, she was worried about something else entirely, for it had been nearly a week since she had last seen Stewart Brantley—a fact that had only belatedly begun to dawn on her. The time had flown so swiftly, she could scarcely believe it.

"Kit," he began, but she stood and turned for the door.

"Don't, Alex," she said. Hearing him ask her again to stay would break her heart. And so would having him say nothing of the kind. "Shouldn't you go bemask yourself?"

"Your wish is my command," he commented after a moment, and she heard him stand. "Just promise me you'll be careful. You'll be no headstrong young lad tonight."

He was genuinely concerned about her. Touched, she turned to grant him a smile. "Don't worry."

"It's far too late for that." The fleeting look he gave her as he moved past her made her blush, and very nearly made her lose her nerve about the evening.

Alex changed into his black evening suit, collected his black wolf's-head mask, and returned downstairs to retrieve his hat and greatcoat from Wenton. "Behave yourself, cousin," he said over his shoulder for effect, and then stepped outside.

As soon as the front door closed behind him, Kit took a deep breath and raced upstairs. From the window of his darkened study she watched him step into his coach. The vehicle trundled out of the drive and up the street while she counted to fifty as slowly as she could manage. Then with another breath she made her way back downstairs. "Wenton, I'm going out for a bit," she informed the butler.

"Very good, Mr. Riley," he returned, helping her into her own greatcoat.

With one last deep breath, Kit stepped out the door, down the front steps, and out to the street to hire a hack to take her to the Downings'.

*　　*　　*

The Earl of Everton lounged against one wall of the Thornhill ballroom and stifled a smile. Lady Wentworth glided by in a gilded mask that, given the white plume of feathers on the back of her head, was obviously meant to represent a swan. As the feathered neck atop her chapeau rather resembled a pachyderm's trunk, and her figure the rest of the beast, she looked a different animal entirely.

Kit would have been highly amused at some of the more elaborate masquerades of the evening, and he glanced toward the main entryway again. He'd been in attendance for over an hour, and was fretting like, well, like an idiot, waiting for the chit's arrival. He sighed behind his black wolf's-head mask and folded his arms.

"Everton."

Alex turned his head to view a rainbow peacock mask bobbing toward him. "Good Lord, Francis, you are resplendent," he said admiringly.

The peacock stopped beside him. "Dash it, Everton, how'd you know it was me?"

"You're still wearing your faux ruby ring."

"Can't get it off my demmed finger," Mr. Henning complained, lifting his hand to examine the offending bauble.

"How is your grandmother?" Alex asked amiably, grateful for the distraction.

"Oh, she's going like a racehorse," Francis grumbled. "Fawned over her for nearly a week, and she gives me fifty quid. 'You're a good boy, Francis,' she says, 'but you need to be more independent.' I told her if she'd give me a thousand pounds a year, I'd be as independent as a damned Virginian."

The earl chuckled. "And what did she say to that?"

"She said the colonies were far too unpleasant a place for her grandson, and gave me a shilling to go buy her some chocolates."

He'd have to remember that to repeat it to Kit, wherever in blazes she was. "Is Hanshaw here?"

The peacock plumage nodded. "He's over with Caroline and her parents. You know Furth's actually in town?''

Alex straightened and looked in the direction the ruby ring was indicating. Masked in plain black, Martin Brantley stood listening with apparent impassivity to what was likely one of Hanshaw's humorous tales of London life. His Grace didn't look particularly amused, and in fact, once the baron had expressed an interest in Caroline, Furth's sense of humor toward poor Reg had become noticeably absent. Alex admired the lad's fortitude. Caroline stood nearby, her eyes hidden behind a pretty blue veil of Indian design.

"Good Lord," Francis whispered heatedly from beside him, and he looked back at his friend in some concern, wondering if one of the peacock feathers had put Mr. Henning's eye out. Francis, though, was staring toward the ballroom's double doors.

Alex turned to look as well. And stopped breathing. "My God," he murmured.

She was . . . glorious. Christine Brantley, standing in the doorway waiting to be announced, was absolutely exquisite. There was no other way to describe her. Tall, with curling blond hair styled into a delicate, perfect tangle at the top of her head and wispy strands caressing her high, faintly blushing cheekbones, she politely conversed with the Marquis of Hague while at the same time coolly surveying the room through a black, glittering half mask. The mask picked up the beading that ran through the burgundy gown, which was daringly cut to set off porcelain shoulders and an exquisitely pale throat, and an equally perfect bosom and slender waist.

"Who is she?" Francis asked, lifting his mask onto his forehead in order to get a better look. "She come with Hague, you think?"

"Quiet," Alex murmured, as she stepped forward to hand over his invitation, the name carefully darkened, and to be introduced to the Thornhills.

"My lord and lady," the butler intoned, "may I present to you . . . Lady Masquerade? My lady, Lord and Lady Thornhill.''

"By God," Francis breathed. "Lady Masquerade."

Such presumption of address would have been tolerated nowhere but at a masquerade ball, and out of the corner of his eye Alex noted that her choice of title elicited chuckles and nods from several intrigued members of the *ton*. Christine stepped forward and smoothly accepted the proffered arm of the Marquis of Hague, and Alex realized that the nickname of Kit had somehow vanished from his mental description of her.

"Who in the world is she?" Mr. Henning queried with a baffled expression. "Not Peningfield's niece, do you think?"

Desdemona Peningfield couldn't hold a candle to Christine Brantley. "She's still in India with her brother," Alex said absently, watching as the vast majority of males in the room began to drift in her direction. He narrowed his eyes, fighting the urge to stride across the room, grab her, and remove her from their presence so he could have her for himself. A slow burn began to wind its way along every nerve in his body. Tonight was going to be absolute torture. And she was going to pay for it later, the tormenting chit.

"Damnation," Francis grunted, lowering his mask again. "They'll have every dance, the buzzards." He squared his shoulders and pushed into the crowd, his peacock feathers cutting a swath in the direction of Lady Masquerade.

For a long moment Alex simply watched her, watched the easy elegance with which she moved and talked and gestured. Francis finally reached her, and from the quick bob of the peacock feathers, Alex could tell he'd succeeded in securing a place on her dance card. The earl was trying to decide whether he was willing to give her the satisfaction of watching him clamoring for a dance with all the other fools when she looked up over Francis's shoulder, and her eyes behind the glitter of her black mask met his.

Electrified as he generally felt in her presence, it was . . . magnetic. He was halfway across the room before he had gathered his wits together enough to stop, and by then he had decided as long as he had come this far, he might as well ask for a waltz. As he reached the fringes of the crowd around her, though, the orchestra began a country dance, and that bastard Hague, taking unfair advantage of his temporary acquisition of her arm, led her out onto the floor. A slight, teasing smile curved Christine's painted ruby lips as her gaze held Alex's for another moment, then she turned to view her dance partner. She and the other participating females curtsied, and the dance began.

With another scowl Alex shook himself, and changed direction to head over to the laden refreshment table. The chit might be enjoying herself, but she was killing him. And he needed to warn her that Furth was present. A moment later it occurred to him that he should have been concerned with warning his mentor that one of their smugglers was present. Just as swiftly he quashed that thought. Not tonight. Tonight was Christine's.

Reg was fetching an armful of glasses of punch, his expression a comical mixture of hope and despair. "Alex." He nodded, glancing back in the direction of the Brantleys.

"How goes the battle?"

"I believe I'm being tolerated. He liked me at one time, I'm certain."

"You weren't trying to become a member of his household then."

The baron managed a chuckle. "True enough. Is Kit about? If he could manage a smile at Caroline, he might improve my odds of being accepted."

Alex barely refrained from giving in to his urge to glance at Christine. "Kit wasn't feeling quite the thing, and decided to stay in for the evening."

Reg nodded his chin in the direction of the dance floor. "So who is Lady Masquerade?"

With a slight, bracing breath, Alex turned to look at her again. "Don't have a clue. I was about to ask you the same question."

Kit gracefully turned about the room in time to the music, while sweat shone off of Hague's receded pate as he attempted to keep up with her. Served the buffoon right for stepping in where he wasn't needed, or wanted. She had better have saved him a waltz.

"By the by," Reg commented, his tone wary enough to snap Alex's attention back to him, "Augustus cornered Barbara for twenty minutes earlier, asking about your impending marriage."

Blast it, he'd nearly forgotten about that. "What did he want?"

"No idea. If you two were speaking, you could ask him yourself."

"Ah," the earl returned, annoyed, "but then I wouldn't need you." He sighed. "Do me a favor, will you?"

"I owe you enough of them. Speak and be obeyed."

"Keep Furth away from me tonight." As he intended on remaining as close as possible to Christine for the remainder of the evening, the request should also serve to keep the duke away from his niece.

"Aye, my lord, I'll do my best. And I don't blame you. He's not pleased that you won't give him a name." The baron frowned. "And neither am I, come to think of it. I know you're the devious mastermind, but you occasionally used to tell me what was going on."

"I know, and I will. But not tonight."

"We don't have much ti—"

"Go deliver your punch, boy," he ordered, only half joking.

"Not very subtle, but all right." Reg grinned, then strolled back toward the Brantleys.

Impatiently Alex turned to the dance floor again. He'd never heard a deuced country dance last so long as this one. As Christine turned she glanced at him again, and he felt as though sparks must be coming off his skin. The dance ended, and he headed toward her to claim the next round. Francis, though, was already standing before her, and with a regal nod and a smile she placed a hand on his shoulder as the orchestra struck up a waltz.

With a growl Alex spun on his heel and acquired a glass of punch from a rather startled footman. He downed it at one go, wishing heartily that it had been a brandy. Trying to ignore her, though he seemed to conjure her every step in his mind even with his back to her, he strolled about the fringes of the room, greeting various acquaintances and making an attempt to keep most of the room between Furth and himself. It had been bad enough before. Three hours ago he had thought he would go mad if he couldn't have her before she left. Now he was ready to murder Francis Henning for placing a gloved hand on her clothed waist. He tried not to watch her through four more dances, failing miserably to ignore her every move, her every gesture.

Finally he tracked down a glass of port and was making short work of it when a hand touched his shoulder. "My lord," a light, feminine voice said from close behind him, "I believe you are about to miss our waltz."

Without a word he returned the half-empty glass to a footman's tray, and turned around. Emerald eyes, lit with excitement and passion, caught his from behind the beaded half mask.

"Am I?" he replied. "How very uncouth of me." He held out his hand, and Christine slipped burgundy-gloved fingers into his and allowed him to lead her onto the floor as the orchestra struck up the waltz.

Her hand was shaking a little, and he reflected with some satisfaction that she must be suffering through the same reaction as he. Gerald's lessons in the waltz had paid off. She moved like liquid night in his arms. Perfectly together, perfectly in sync, it was as though they had waltzed in one another's embrace a thousand times before. Her skin smelled faintly of lavender, and he was pleased, if unsurprised. He hadn't expected her to select a heavy French perfume like the kind Barbara favored.

"Did you see Gerald and Ivy come in after me?" she murmured. "After I dressed, I think Gerald became a little less enthusiastic about the whole thing."

"I hadn't noticed them," he answered truthfully, though he could understand Gerald's sentiments. He hated these other men gawking at her. "You are astounding."

Her cheeks took on a soft flush deeper than her delicate rouge. "Thank you," she said softly. "Tonight I feel . . . beautiful."

Alex smiled down at her. "Only beautiful?" he teased, dazzled by the enchantress in his arms. "By God, I felt safer when you were in breeches."

"Safer?" she repeated, tilting her head to one side to contemplate him. "Are you still afraid of me, then, Sir Wolf's Head?"

"I am trembling, my Lady Masquerade," he murmured. And she was, as well. Her ruby lips gave him back a shy, sensuous smile, and it was with great effort that he kept from bending his head down and kissing her. He was holding her far closer than proper custom dictated, her burgundy skirt swirling about his black Hessian boots. He seemed aware of everything about her: her quickened breathing, her half-parted, smiling lips, how tightly she held his hand, the warmth of her other hand on his shoulder. Trembling he might be, but it was not with fear.

The waltz ended, and he brought her to a standstill. Reluctant to release her now that he had her, Alex kept hold of one hand and transferred it to his arm. "Who is next on your dance card, my lady?" he queried with forced lightness. Tonight was for her, after all, whatever he might wish.

Christine shook her head. "No one, my lord." She glanced about the room. "I do wonder," she continued, "if you would accompany me out to the balcony for a moment. I feel in need of a breath of fresh air."

All at once he did, as well. "Of course." He nodded, and with a swift look about the room, led her through the masked crowd to the doorway. Surprisingly enough for this late in the evening, the ivy-shrouded balcony was empty, and she freed her hand from his arm to lean over the railing and look out at the garden.

"I feel like a fairy princess," she said with a sigh.

"You are far more than that," he murmured in response, stepping up beside her.

She turned to face him, and lifted her gloved hands

to pull the mask from his face. She dropped it to the stone floor and ran her silken fingers lightly along the skin of his cheeks. Scarcely breathing, Alex leaned forward and tilted her chin up. Very slowly he lowered his mouth to hers. Her arms slid about his neck as she leaned into him, inviting him to kiss her more deeply. He complied, and her mouth opened to his teasing request.

When he finally lifted his head to draw a ragged breath, she pursued him, rising on her toes in her delicate slippers to kiss him again. "Don't stop, Alex," she whispered.

With a smile, he turned her toward the moonlit garden and carefully lifted her mask onto her hair. The small of his back against the railing, he slowly slid his hands down the sides of her face and down her neck, to pause along her bare, creamy white shoulders. The shoulders her damned prized lawn shirts had kept hidden from him for over a fortnight. On impulse he bent down and kissed them, then returned his mouth to hers.

"Everton—"

Christine jumped, pulling away, and Alex's eyes flew open to view the Duke of Furth coming to a stop in the shadows of the doorway. Before she could turn, he clamped his hands down hard on her shoulders, keeping her locked against him. "Your Grace." He nodded, the color draining from his face. He had hoped with every fiber of his being that it would not come to this, and at nearly the same moment realized that it had been heading in exactly this direction from the moment he had met Christine Brantley. And to his further dismay, he had already decided on which side he had landed.

"Sorry for the interrup—"

"No need to apologize, Your Grace," he cut in, lowering his eyes to find Christine's gaze locked on his. Her face was white, her expression alarmingly distressed. "Lady Masquerade and I were merely . . . becoming acquainted." Willing her not to bolt, he slowly slid his hands up her shoulders and carefully lowered the mask back over her eyes.

"Fine time and place for it," the duke grumbled, obviously out of countenance that one of his men could actually be enjoying himself when there was a spy to be caught. Thankfully, he knew to be subtle about the source of his irritation. Alex had no wish to see Christine leap from the balcony to make her escape.

"Anytime is a fine time for this," Alex murmured at her, and lowered his mouth to her ear. "I'll get him away. No need to worry."

She searched his face for a moment, clearly trying to decide whether or not she could trust him. Then, with a quick breath and an almost imperceptible nod, she slid along him until she gripped the railing with both hands, her stony face resolutely turned toward the garden and away from her uncle.

With a quick glance back at her, Alex bent and retrieved his own mask, then strolled over to take Furth around the arm and lead him back toward the bright, noisy ballroom. "Your Grace, have I ever complimented you on what an attractive young woman your Caroline has become?" he said amiably.

Furth ignored the bait, instead looking behind them toward the balcony. "Who is she?" he asked.

"No one you need be concerned about," Alex returned firmly, knowing full well he would be paying for whatever he said tomorrow, after she was gone. If he could let her leave.

The duke lifted an eyebrow, but continued toward Caroline and the duchess. "Defensive, aren't we?" he noted.

Alex forced a smile. "With your timing, you should be grateful I'm only being defensive." That part, at least, was true, for he was having a difficult time keeping his hands from shaking and his mind even remotely on the conversation.

"Hm. Odd thing for a betrothed gentleman to be saying in regard to another woman."

"That is another story entirely," Alex said swiftly, "and an entirely false one, which I will remedy in a few days."

"You've a great many things to accomplish in the next few days, then," Furth pointed out, making certain Alex knew exactly what he was implying.

"And I shall," he said, relinquishing his hold on Martin Brantley's arm. "Now, if you'll excuse me."

As quickly as he could manage without looking like he was hurrying, he turned back to stroll about the fringe of the crowd toward the balcony. He'd nearly reached the door when Barbara Sinclair, her eyes glinting through her gold sun-goddess mask, materialized before him.

"You have gone too far," she hissed, her fists clenched. "Flaunting her in front of everyone. I won't let it continue. I won't have them laughing at my expense."

"You're the one who went too far, Barbara," he returned calmly, keeping his voice low. "I'll discuss this with you later. Now smile and stand aside, or our betrothal will end before it's begun." He sketched her a jaunty bow, and watched the skin of her lips stretch into a false, unattractive smile. Apparently seeing an acquaintance she urgently needed to speak to, she waved at someone across the room and hurried away.

With a quick breath, he stepped through the double doors and back out to the cool balcony. It was deserted. "Damnation," he muttered, smacking his fist on the stone railing, not really surprised. He'd doubted she would stay at the ball with Furth in attendance. "Damn, damn, damn."

Chapter 15

❦

"**Y**ou could have stayed, you know, Ivy," Kit said, sitting at Mrs. Downing's dressing table and scouring makeup from her face. "You didn't have to follow me back here." She was in little mood for conversation or explanation, anyway; all she could think of was Alex kissing her, and Furth nearly finding her out. She was taking far too many chances.

"I know," Ivy returned, perching on the edge of the dressing table. "What did he say to you to upset you so?"

Kit eyed her pink-skinned reflection and set the cloth aside when it appeared that she had finally removed the last of the *faux* color from her cheeks and lips. "It wasn't Alex," she corrected, unable to explain further. She began on her hair, pulling at the clips and pins with which Ivy's maid had expertly put it up.

"Someone else did something to upset you, and Alex didn't kill him?" Ivy pressed, raising an eyebrow. "Now, that is a surprise."

At that Kit grinned. "A duel would have been exciting, wouldn't it?" She broke into laughter as she considered the possibility. "Can you imagine? The Earl of Everton and the Marquis of Hague, dueling over a female who until yesterday was a boy?"

Her companion eyed her. "I believe you had Francis Henning's attention, as well."

"Oh, Ivy," Kit returned, laughing harder, "Francis

proposed to me. He said I was Aphrodite come to visit
the mortals.'' She stood and offered an elaborate curtsy.
''Everyone said I was spectacular.''

''You were,'' Ivy agreed. ''You are.''

Suddenly feeling self-conscious in the face of the lav-
ish compliments she'd been given all evening, Kit sobered a little and looked over at Ivy. ''Do you think
so?''

''Oh, Kit, you can't have been displeased with your
transformation.''

''No,'' she replied slowly, smiling again. ''I wasn't.''
When her eyes had first met Alex's across the ballroom,
she had felt as if she were floating a foot above the floor.
He had said she was astounding, and had kissed her, and
hadn't turned away. ''I felt . . . beautiful.'' She sighed.
''I've had women tell me I was handsome, but who the
deuce could take that seriously? Tonight was the first
time I believed any of it.'' She stretched out her arms
and wrapped them around herself. ''And I liked it, Ivy.
I truly did. I liked the way they looked at me.'' Kit
closed her eyes for a moment, remembering. ''I liked
the way Alex looked at me.''

Ivy regarded her for a long moment, her gaze assessing. Finally a slow smile touched her lips. ''Do tell.''

Kit finished fastening the buttons of her waistcoat and
reached for her coat. ''I can't wait to hear Francis's version of events, tomorrow.''

Ivy's expression abruptly faltered, and Kit's own
smile faded. She was leaving London tomorrow. She
would never know what Francis thought of Lady Masquerade, or what the *ton* had thought of the mysterious
stranger at their masked ball.

''What would you like me to do with the gown?'' Ivy
inquired, gesturing at the garment draped across the bed.

''Whatever you like,'' Kit replied, stepping over and
regretfully fingering the soft silk skirt. It was the most
beautiful thing she'd ever owned. ''I'll never wear it
again.'' She reached down and picked up the black, glittering mask. ''I would like to keep this, though. Just to
remember.''

"You don't have to leave London, you know." Ivy's expression was earnest, her hands warm as they clutched Kit's.

"Yes, I do," she returned, pulling free and tugging on her coat. "Barbara Sinclair already knows about me. Sooner or later everyone else will. I doubt Alex would want the scandal." In an odd way, it made her grateful to Lady Sinclair. Whatever lay in her heart, Alex's mistress would undoubtedly make it impossible for her to remain. She had no choice but to carry out her father's wishes.

With a last look at the marvelous gown, she went downstairs and said her good-byes to the Downings, then climbed into the hack Gerald had hired for her. The Duke of Furth had very nearly seen her, and yet it seemed more important that Alex had not even hesitated to protect her from her uncle. More than anything else, she wanted him to look at her again as he had when they had kissed, as though he would shatter if he couldn't have her.

A few lights were still on at Cale House as she hopped down from the hack. Wenton pulled the door open as she topped the last step, and backed into the shadows of the entryway while she handed him her hat and gloves. She turned and he helped her off with her greatcoat, hanging it on its customary rack.

"Is Alex home yet?" she asked, though she wasn't certain her heart was steady enough to see him again.

The butler didn't answer, but instead ran his fingers under the collar of her coat and skimmed it off her shoulders.

"Wenton!" she exclaimed, shocked. As soon as her hands were free of the garment, she whipped around to let the butler know exactly what she thought of his behavior. "What do y—"

A hard, warm mouth clamped down over hers, smothering her protest. She knew the feel, the touch of the lips covering hers, and after a stunned moment returned the kiss with all the frustrated passion that had been gathering inside her. A hand reached up and tugged the

band free from her hair, letting the short, wavy locks fall
loose around her face. Alex forced her back until she
came up against the door. Only when he had her pinned
there did he lift his head.

"Alex—"

"Shh," he murmured roughly. "Shame on you for
leaving me there like that," he chastised. His eyes lowered, and his hands swiftly went to work on her waistcoat. "Drive a man mad, then vanish. Not this time,
chit." In a moment he had it open, and pulled it off her
shoulders, as well. "I'm only bloody human, after all."
It dropped to the floor beside her coat.

"I didn't mean—"

"Ruthless, you are," he muttered, continuing as
though she hadn't interrupted. His mouth claimed hers
again, teasing it open with his lips and his tongue. Kit's
fast, unsteady breath stopped in her throat as his long
fingers touched her cravat and began to untie it. His
mouth trailed along her cheekbone to her ear, and she
gasped as he took the sensitive lobe between his teeth.
Her heart beating raggedly, she pressed against his lean,
tall form, feeling the growing hardness through his
breeches, and the sudden warmth between her own legs.
As the cravat drifted to the floor, she gathered her wits
enough to glance about the darkened hallway.

"Where is Wenton?" she whispered, jumping a little
as his hands touched her waist and began pulling her
shirttail out of her leggings.

"Sent him to bed," he murmured in her ear.

"And everyone else?" she insisted, gasping as her
shirt came free and he began lifting it in his hands.

"Sweet Lucifer, chit. To bed, for heaven's sake," he
whispered.

She pulled her shirt down again, too accustomed to
caution to be able to give in even to him in such an
exposed place. "What if they hear something?"

"Christine," he murmured in exasperated protest, and
stepped away.

She thought with sudden, cold dismay that she had
ruined it again, and started toward him, ready to say, or

do, anything to convince him to continue. He held her off with one hand, then bent down and swiftly picked up her scattered things. With a swift tug he pulled her against him and kissed her, then easily swung her up into his arms.

"Where are we going?" she queried shakily, leaning up to kiss his ear in an awkward imitation of his own actions.

He swallowed. "Your bedchamber, my dear," he whispered, turning for the stairs.

"*Your* bedchamber," she corrected, with the last bit of rational thought left her. She wanted him, with a fierce, burning hunger, but she would not make it so easy for him. Whatever she might be, she was not Barbara Sinclair. She would not let him pass her off in his mind as a mistress to be bedded and forgotten—whether that's what she was or not.

He hesitated, then shifted her closer against him. "Mine," he agreed huskily, and headed up the stairs.

She half expected and more than half wanted to be dumped on the mattress and set upon, but Alex stopped beside the bed, set her on her feet, and dropped her clothes to the floor. He kicked the door shut in a satisfyingly impatient masculine manner, stopped for another lingering kiss, then strode over to the fireplace, tossed a few more logs onto the flames, and returned to stand in front of her.

"I believe this is where I am supposed to offer to take myself elsewhere and leave you in peace," he said softly, reaching out to caress her cheek. "I—"

Shaking with a sudden alarm that he might actually abandon her in this state, Christine closed the small distance between them and lifted her hands to pull his face down to hers. As she had been wanting to do for what seemed like forever, she ran her fingers through his wavy black hair. "Don't go," she whispered.

"I was about to say that I have no intention of doing any such thing," he continued. "Not tonight."

His hands skimmed down her back, and then tugged at her shirt again. For a moment she couldn't breathe.

He wanted her. Not Barbara Sinclair, or any other of his stupid mistresses. Alex wanted *her*. Trembling, she lifted her arms, and he pulled the garment off over her head. For a moment he paused, looking down at the tight wrap that bound her chest. Slowly he ran his finger along her skin just above the cloth, and she shivered again. He found the knot that she used to bind the thing, but abruptly embarrassed, she pushed his hand away.

"I want to see you," he said. "Let me see you." Alex smiled, and her heart skipped a beat. He was so handsome, with his disheveled hair, tousled by her fingers, and a hungry glint deep in his azure eyes. "You've kept yourself hidden from me for weeks," he continued, "and now tonight you let half of London see your splendid bosom. Don't torture me further, dear one."

Shakily she lowered her hand. He undid the knot, and slowly pulled the wrap from around her, making every soft tug of his fingers on the cloth a caress along her whole being. When the wrap finally slid to the floor, baring her breasts to his intense gaze, he stopped and took a quick, held breath.

"Finally," he murmured, lifting his hands to caress them. "And well worth the wait, I might add." Slowly he ran his thumbs over her nipples, bringing them to thrilled attention.

She gasped in response, and his gaze immediately returned to her face. She smiled shakily, and with a return smile he bent his head and kissed the base of her throat. His lips ran slowly along her shoulders and her collarbone, and down her sternum. His tongue traced a circle around her areola, and then he took her nipple into his mouth and sucked lightly. Unable to help herself, she moaned and arched against him, twining her fingers through his hair. Without his ever having touched her before, it amazed her that he could know so easily how to arouse her, how to set her trembling.

Alex trailed his lips over her left breast, then sat her down on the edge of the bed to pull off her boots. "You're wearing too damned many clothes," he grumbled with a half-annoyed grin, but she could see that his hands were shaking a little, and that he was not so composed as he apparently wished her to think.

"Well, take them off," she demanded breathlessly, and he chuckled.

Christine ran her fingers along his shoulders and arms restlessly, wishing he would hurry before he remembered how little business they had being together. Once she was in her bare feet he pulled her upright again, and went to work on the buttons of her breeches. He was looking at her face closely, gauging every expression, and with a swift, soft smile he leaned down and brushed his lips along her cheek. "My chit," he whispered, and the possessive tone made her tremble.

Her breeches followed the rest of her garments to the floor, and he spent a long moment gazing at her. "Sweet Lucifer," he finally murmured. "You are exquisite."

This time his kiss was hot and demanding, and she rose on tiptoe against him as his hands slid down her waist to her hips and buttocks, then pulled her closer still. Her bare skin beneath his touch seemed to burn in the night air, and the hardness pressing into her through his breeches was unbearably close, and unbearably far.

"Alex," she murmured, her hands tugging at his waist, "now you're wearing too many clothes."

He laughed, sending her floating again, then reluctantly loosed his arms from around her to shrug out of his coat. "Let's remedy that, shall we?" Her shaking fingers trailed and tripped over his as they both worked to remove his waistcoat, and she nearly choked him in her haste to pull off his cravat.

"I'm sorry." She grimaced, finally loosing the thing.

He smiled and bent down to kiss the nape of her neck. She tugged his shirt free, then pulled it off over his head. The warm, male scent of him sent another surge of moist heat between her legs. Alex removed his boots, and a moment later his breeches and stockings followed hers to the floor. As she looked down at his unfettered, aroused manhood, a twinge of uneasiness ran through her, but then he was kissing her again, and cupping her breasts in his experienced, long-fingered hands.

"Trust me," he breathed. "Just this once." Laying her down on the bed, he slid up beside her. His mouth teased at her breasts again, and she groaned, rising up against him. "You like that, don't you, chit?" he murmured, lifting his head to look at her, amusement and desire in his eyes. "You like me to touch you."

"Yes," she returned breathlessly.

His mouth trailed lower, his lips and tongue caressing her ribs and belly and tickling her navel, and then moved still lower, to the blond tangle below. "And do you like this?"

"Alex, stop teasing," she pleaded, wondering if he was driving her mad intentionally.

He lifted his face to look at her, while his hand brushed up along the inside of her thigh. "No tease this time," he said in a rather unsteady voice, and lowered his head again. As he reached the apex of her thighs she instinctively tried to close against him, but with his hands and his mouth he convinced her to relax again.

"Please," she whispered almost soundlessly, writhing beneath his expert ministrations. "Alex."

He slid up along her body to meet her eyes again, to kiss her deeply, probing her mouth demandingly with his tongue, while his hands continued to explore her. She had wanted this, wanted him, since she had set eyes on him. Her own hands began a hesitant exploration of his shoulders, his back, and his chest, and she tilted her head a little sideways to kiss his nipple. He made a small sound deep in his throat that turned the burning inside her to molten fire.

"Alex," she whispered again.

In response he moved over her, pushing her legs farther apart and settling his hips over hers, his hard shaft pressing against her, hot and throbbing. And he hesitated. "Are you certain?" he asked, his voice strained and his expression telling her that it would kill him if she said no.

But he had asked her, anyway. "Yes," she returned breathlessly, loving the feel of his hard weight on top of her. She raised her head to kiss him.

He kissed her back, his mouth teasing relentlessly at hers, while his hand stroked at the hot, secret, sensitive part of her so that she gasped again. She wanted more of him, she wanted everything, and when slowly, so slowly, he eased inside her, she gave a mingled cry of pain and wonder and desire.

Alex stopped. "I'm sorry, sweet one," he murmured tightly, holding very still. Gently he kissed her closed eyelids. "I know it hurts. But it means you're mine now. Mine only. It will stop hurting. I promise, waif." He began to move, slowly and carefully, and she gasped again, her eyes shooting open to look into his, but the pain had already begun to recede, as he had promised. "Better?" he whispered, shifting a little and brushing hair from her eyes.

She groaned, half shutting her eyes again as sensation flooded through her. "Yes." He raised up on his hands again, and kissed her once more. The movement of his hard staff inside her increased, his rhythm strong and steady and deep, and she began instinctively lifting her hips to meet him.

"Beautiful," he whispered, almost wonderingly, and lowered his dark head to lick her breast.

Her back arched, a deep, growing tension building through her, and she reached down to clasp his buttocks, pulling him deeper inside her, trying to make the two of them one with a compelling urgency that she understood without knowing. He felt it as well, for she could see it in the azure eyes that watched her every expression, could feel it in the rhythm of his body moving inside hers. Finally she shuddered as the tension exploded, in a pulsing pleasure unlike anything she had ever experienced in her life.

Feeling the change in her, Alex smiled. He slowed the rhythm of his hips and deepened his thrusts, and she groaned and gasped his name. With a quickening motion he shuddered, much as she had, then lowered his head to bury his face in her shoulder. Slowly and carefully he settled his weight back down on top of her.

Breathing hard, Kit ran her fingers over his sweat-

slicked back, wishing they could stay this way forever.
He slowly lifted his head, then raised himself up on one
elbow to look down at her. He stayed that way for a
long time, searching her face, while she dared not look
away. This man, this Englishman, this rakehell and interfering peer, couldn't be an enemy, because she loved
him. Only one question remained, the one that could
determine her path: she still had no idea what, other than
simple lust and desire, he felt for her.

With his free hand he gently curled a damp lock of
her hair behind her ear. "I believe I have failed your
father," he said dryly, slowly caressing her bare skin
with the palm of his hand.

"It's about time," she replied with more courage than
she felt. He left her feeling so . . . vulnerable, and yet so
strong, at the same time.

He gave a slow, lazy smile. "All that talk about a
dress that was too big, and shoes that were too small,
and then there you were at the Thornhills', Diana in all
her glory. Good God."

"That was a different dress," she reminded him with
a pleased grin, and kissed his chin.

That caused him to kiss her thoroughly for several
moments. "I know that," he finally returned, running
his finger along her lower lip, "but it does conjure a
certain image, you know."

Slowly he shifted off of her. She frowned as he removed himself, and he grinned at her. "Wanton," he
murmured, sitting to pull up the blankets, for the room
was still chilled even with the fire going. He tugged the
smooth sheets up around her shoulders and then settled
himself back down beside her.

"You need another pillow," she commented, turning
her head to face him. "Whatever do you and Barbara
Sinclair do with only one pillow?"

"This is not where Barbara and I spent our eve-
nings," he said.

Her deduction had been correct, after all. "Why not?"

"Why do you insist on discussing my former mistress

when I only wish to lie here and look at you?" he queried instead of answering.

He liked looking at her. "Your *former* mistress?" she
repeated. "Does that make me your current mistress?"

Alex frowned, his expression telling her he did not
wish to contemplate that at the moment. And neither did
she. Not when tonight was all they had. "I don't know
what it makes you, Christine Kit Riley Brantley. Other
than a great deal of trouble, of course."

The string of names served to remind her of the one
thing that had troubled her about the evening. "You are
acquainted with the Duke of Furth," she stated, daring
him to deny it.

"I am," he answered, only a slight shift in his body
alerting her that he was less easy with his answer than
he wanted her to think. "I never said I wasn't."

"No," she agreed reluctantly, "but you implied—"

He stopped her argument with a kiss. "Not tonight,
chit," he said softly. "Nothing to lie about later."

She looked at him closely, could read nothing in his
eyes but a reflection of the curiosity and desire in her
own. "Not tonight," she agreed.

He leaned over her and kissed her again, then slid his
hand around her waist to tug her against him. "Good."

Christine chuckled, delighted that he desired her again
already. "Now who is the wanton?" she asked slyly.

"We shall see. After I learn every inch of you, chit."

"Every inch?" she repeated, shivering in anticipation.

"Every inch? Inside and out."

"Oh, lud." She chuckled, then groaned as his mouth
closed again over hers.

Alex awoke before Christine. Her face was only a few
inches from his, as they had ended up sharing the single
pillow, after all. One of his arms was draped across her
shoulder, the other half-asleep under her side. Their legs
were such a tangle that without moving, he couldn't tell
where his ended and hers began.

For a long time he lay there watching her soft, slow
breathing. Rakehell though many called him, she was

only the second virgin he had ever taken. The first had been on his wedding night, and Mary's response had been as different from Kit's as ice was from fire. As for Christine Brantley, his hunch that first morning, when he had watched her devouring his breakfast, had been correct. As a female, she was dangerous.

Kit stirred in her sleep and tucked herself closer against him, trusting him in her dreams, at least. He shifted his arm so he could curl his fingers into the blond halo framing her face. Before her arrival, he had rarely spent a night alone, and had hated the mornings that followed—the expected coquettish banter and the rehearsed, unfelt excuses over how sorry he was to have to quit the bed, but he really did have things to do.

After Kit Brantley had exploded into his life, he'd spent every night alone, with his impractical single pillow, and the mornings had been the least lonely ones he had ever known. The extraordinary chit bursting into his bedchamber and wanting to learn how to shave, or insulting him in French, or devouring everything in sight, left him happier than he had been since before his parents had died and left him alone.

But she was still a traitor. He should never have let her get this close, even if he had never wanted something, someone, so badly in his life. His only excuse had been that she would be gone after today, but last night had tangled even that one definite into a mishmash he didn't care to delve into too deeply. He raised up onto his elbow and brushed his lips across her forehead. If he told nothing of what he knew, British soldiers could pay the price of his selfishness with their lives. If he did his duty, as the daughter of Stewart Brantley, she could face hanging, imprisonment, or at best, exile to Australia. Alex drew a quick breath. Unless she wasn't considered to be Stewart Brantley's daughter any longer. He closed his eyes, nervous tension running through him as he contemplated doing what he'd sworn never to do again.

"If you're pretending to be asleep, you shouldn't have your head propped up like that," Christine murmured, and he opened his eyes again.

"Thank you," he said. "Obviously I lack your skills at prevarication."

The easy amusement in her eyes changed to suspicion in an instant. "What's that supposed to mean?" she asked with her typical bold attack in the face of accusation.

He wasn't ready to confront her. "Only that you've been fooling the world about your gender for nearly fourteen years." He lifted an eyebrow. "What did you think I meant?"

She hesitated for a moment. "I didn't know. That's why I was angry."

Alex frowned, uncertain of exactly how he wished to proceed, especially in the face of her mercurial temperament. "I won't be able to ride to Canterbury until this afternoon," he said to himself, sitting up and running a hand through his hair.

Kit sat up beside him and kissed his shoulder. "Whatever are you going to Canterbury for?"

"For a special license, of course. Unraveling your tale will take some doing, but I think we can manage it."

She had become very still, but he kept his gaze locked on the bedpost. "What are you talking about?" she finally whispered.

"Our marriage, of course, goose," he returned brusquely. It was easier to say than he'd expected, especially as he had meant never to utter the word in connection with himself again.

He could feel her emerald stare burning into him. "We are not getting married," she stated.

"Of course we are." He took a breath. Soon, probably within the next day or so, he was going to have to confront her about her loyalties, but first he wanted her under the protection of his name. "You may be pregnant."

She swallowed, her eyes narrowing. "I am not."

"I didn't take any precautions, and I doubt you are skilled in methods of preventing conception." He forced himself to look straight at her. "Are you?"

Slowly she shook her head, her expression fleetingly uncertain.

"Well, it's settled, then. It'll take a few donations to the church, but we can be married by tomorrow evening."

"No."

He had expected her to balk, but had no intention of letting it stop him. "You have no choice, Kit. There's no—"

"I said no, Alex."

"Christine—"

"I did not do this to trap you into marriage, Everton. In a few days I'll be back in Paris, and you won't—"

"I will not have my by-blow wandering about Paris," he growled with what he hoped was the correct degree of anger, "and I would not leave you unmarried with a child."

She glared at him, as stubborn as he. "And I won't have you loathing me the way you did Mary because I can't be what you want in a w—"

That shook him. "You are not like Mary. And I—"

"I don't want to talk about it any longer." She shoved the sheets aside and rose, naked, to stalk over to the window. "You're already engaged, anyway."

"I am no such thing, damn it." Good Lord, she was lovely. And too blasted distracting. He shut his eyes and took a deep breath. "At least tell me when you last bled." Any other woman, he could browbeat into a marriage—wouldn't have to do more than suggest it, in fact. If that. But not this one. And stupid and absurd as it seemed, especially given his reason for proposing it, he wanted her to want to be wed to him.

She turned to look at him, splendid in the filtered sunlight. "A few days ago," she replied, clearly embarrassed.

"How many days ago?" he insisted, finding that her answer somewhat disappointed him. It might have been an excuse, but any reason to keep her there with him would do.

"Three or four."

"Not more than that?"

"No! *Bâtard*," she grumbled.

"All right," he acquiesced reluctantly, damning his sense of fair play. Truth where she was involved, though, seemed of the utmost importance now. "You are probably not pregnant."

"Why didn't you ask me that in the first place, then?" she demanded. "We could have avoided this entire stupid conversation."

Alex looked at her. She truly didn't wish to marry him. "Damned stubborn Irish chit," he muttered.

"And don't speak of it again," she ordered, jabbing a finger in his direction.

"I bloody well will speak—" The clock on the landing began chiming, and didn't stop until it reached ten. "Damnation!" He flung the remainder of the bedsheets aside and stormed to his feet, striding over to the dressing table.

"What now?" she demanded, her expression sliding from furious to concerned.

"I am late."

She put her hands on her hips, obviously still displeased with him. "Do you wish me to hide under the bed while Antoine assists you?"

He gave a reluctant chuckle. "If you can dress on your own, so can I." Alex burrowed into his wardrobe and pulled out a shirt, which he tossed back to her. "And put some clothes on before we end up back in bed."

"That's a splendid idea," she replied, catching the shirt. When he determinedly ignored her, she sighed and pulled the soft lawn over her disheveled head. "I'll shave you, then," she offered in what was obviously her version of an apology for their argument.

Alex remembered all too well what had nearly happened the last time she had interrupted him. "Absolutely not," he countered. "The gentleman I'm to meet would not be pleased if I kept him waiting." Neither would the other three gentlemen accompanying him, to whom he would have to lie one last time.

She scowled, then perched in the windowsill to watch him dress and shave. "You look quite . . . conservative this morning," she noted as he tied his cravat in a simple, rather severe knot. "Who are you meeting with?"

There was really no reason not to tell her. "Prince George."

She sat up straight. "Prinny? Really? If I hurry and dress, may I go?"

"No!" he returned sharply. For both the Regent's sake and her own, he wanted her nowhere near Buckingham Palace.

She pouted, her eyes cool. "Don't you trust me?"

He turned to look at her, searching her expression. "No, I do not." Alex took a breath. "But we'll discuss that when I return. Agreed?"

Christine swallowed, her eyes darting down to her clasped hands. Finally she met his gaze again. "Agreed."

"And, Kit, I want you to promise me something."

"What is it?" she asked slowly.

"That you won't disappear with your father until after I see you again."

Before she could answer, Wenton scratched at the door with the morning edition of the *London Times*. Alex retrieved the paper and then shut the door in the butler's face. Quickly he perused the front page, and its panicked suppositions that Napoleon would leave Paris for Calais, and from there would land in Dover with his army by the fifteenth.

"Anything interesting?"

"Not really." He set the paper aside and strolled up to stand in front of her. "Promise me," he repeated, reaching out to caress her cheek with his palm.

She leaned her face into his hand, her eyes holding his. "Alex—"

"I will tie you to this bed and put armed outriders all around the house if you say no," he warned her.

Evidently he was serious. "I won't leave until we've spoken again," she whispered, then forced a smile and a sigh. "Stubborn Englishman. May I meet you somewhere for luncheon, or should I go find Reg and Francis?"

Everton found that he was less than pleased with the idea of her spending time with any of his male friends. Just as he could no longer fool himself for a moment into thinking her an ill-mannered boy, neither did he relish the thought of her enjoying some other man's company, even in friendship. "The Navy at one, say?" He pulled on his boots. "We'll leave word for your father with Wenton, in case he should arrive before we return."

She nodded again. "All right."

Perhaps she disliked the half-truths and the lies and distrust as much as he did, Alex thought. There would be no more lies between them.

He walked to the door, opened it, then shut it again and strode back to her side. Putting an arm about her waist, he pulled her against him and leaned down to touch her lips with his. "Be good," he said, tugging on her hair and then turning away again. "I'll see you at one, chit."

Thankfully, Alex had thought to send all the servants downstairs so she could sneak into her own bedchamber without anyone spying her. She sat on the edge of her bed for a time, reluctant to remove his shirt from her skin. She pulled her hands back into the overlong sleeves and lifted the material to her face. It smelled like him, and unable to help herself, she lay back on the bed and laughed and kicked her bare legs in the air. Being female wasn't nearly as bad as she had supposed. At least not while she could be with Alexander Cale.

He'd said they would talk later, and she wondered how much she dared tell him. Nothing that would hurt her father, but she was tired of all the lies, and even more tired of lying to Alex.

Finally she dressed and made her way downstairs to eat. The beaded mask was still in her greatcoat pocket, and she retrieved it before Wenton or any of the other servants could notice it. There was room for it in the satchel she had packed for her return to Paris, so with a glance at the grandfather clock to check the time, she

returned upstairs and closed her door. She knelt and un-
buckled the two straps keeping the portmanteau closed.
Kit started to slip the mask in under one of her shirts,
then paused as her fingers touched something unfamiliar.

A slender leather pouch had been slipped deep into
the middle of the bag, and with a slight frown she pulled
it free and untied the knot holding it shut. And gasped.
It was filled with paper currency, both French and English, in varying denominations. Altogether it must have
been nearly two thousand pounds. A note was tucked
against one side, and with shaking fingers she pulled it
free. In Alex's familiar scrawl it read, ''Take care of
yourself, cousin. Fondly, Everton.'' The note was dated
two days earlier; he must have stowed it away while she
was at the Downings'.

Even considering that he enjoyed her company, it was
an astoundingly generous gift to give. Tears ran down
her cheeks. With this, she and her father could stop
smuggling, could move into Saint-Germain, or even out
of France altogether. And Alex had asked her to marry
him, even if it was out of some stupid, misguided sense
of duty and he really wanted no such entanglements.

Except that she did want to marry him, did want to
stay with him. But first she needed to know that she
could trust him, even after he knew exactly what she
was. And then she needed him to ask her again, not
because he was simply doing what was expected, but
because he loved her.

Chapter 16

The Earl of Everton kept his expression aloof and his eyes to the front as he forced himself to stroll calmly out of Buckingham Palace, when he truly wanted to call Prince George a fat oaf and put a vase through the lovely paned windows. Grateful that Furth at least had remained behind in conference, he avoided looking at his companions until the three of them were off the palace grounds and well onto the Mall. Only after he waved Waddle off and sent him home did he let out an explosive breath. "Arrogant, bloated buffoon," he snarled, slamming his fist into his thigh hard enough to bruise.

His companions shared an uneasy glance. "What did you expect, Alex?" Gerald Downing said in a voice obviously intended to calm his cousin down. "He wants someone to hang. Now."

"I can't give him what I don't have," Alex snapped, looking down the street.

"Well, forgive me if I'm being insensitive, but you've been on this little committee for what, six years? And before now, I've never known you to have contraband seized without being able to discover who's behind the shipment," Reg Hanshaw put in from his other side. "That was likely Prinny's, and His Grace's, line of thinking as well, I would ima—"

"I stopped the damned weapons, didn't I?"

"Yes, you did," the baron agreed. "The first load of

them, anyway. None of us has heard much about the sec—''

"He practically accused me of lying."

Gerald fiddled with his walking cane. "You were, weren't you?"

Alex snapped his gaze to his cousin's face. "Yes."

"But why?" Reg demanded. "Do you know how much trouble you may just have brought down on yourself?"

He knew quite well. "Just leave off, both of you," he growled. "I have my reasons." The major one being that he was trying to find a way to protect a spy before he turned her father's name over to the authorities.

Reg sighed and stopped to purchase a posy from a street vendor. He tucked the flower into his lapel, and shook his head. "Alex—"

A shot rang out across the street. In the same heartbeat, something burned past Alex's cheek, and Reg crashed backward into the Duchess of Devenbroke.

She promptly fainted, and in the ensuing hysteria of the most distinguished members of the *ton* flinging one another out of the way and diving for cover, Alex couldn't tell where the shot had come from, much less who had fired it. "Reg!" he bellowed, shoving through the crowd to his companion's side.

Gerald was already there, helping the baron to his feet. "I'm all right," Hanshaw said, fingering the graze across his temple. "Who the devil's shooting at me?"

"I don't know," Alex snarled, rubbing at his own singed cheek, his eyes darting across the rooftops and touching the alleys on the far side of the street. There were far too many places to hide, and too many avenues of escape. Behind him Lord Bandwyth and Lady Julia Penston were fanning the duchess's face, and she was already making promising groans. "You certain you're all right?" he queried, turning back to the baron.

Reg nodded and squinted one eye shut, obviously hurting. "Yes. You?"

"Splendid."

"I assume someone doesn't appreciate our meddling," Hanshaw continued. "Or Furth really doesn't like me at all anymore." He gave a weak grin and staggered sideways while Gerald kept hold of him.

"Gerald, get him tended to," Alex ordered. "And let Martin know what's happened."

His cousin nodded. "And you?"

Alex felt his jaw clench. "I have to follow up on a hunch."

"You be careful," Gerald suggested, looking at him closely and indicating his face. "We don't know who the target was."

"I intend to find that out," he returned, and strode up the street.

What he had done this morning, in denying knowledge of the identity of the weapons smuggler, had been treason. Prinny was angry at him, and whatever sort of buffoon he was reputed to be, Prince George was not a complete fool. Martin Brantley knew for a certainty that he was hiding something, and would not let it remain a secret for much longer. And he knew what Hanshaw and Gerald would say, that he was thinking with something other than his head. He had managed to let himself overlook the fact that Kit, in all likelihood, had partners. Partners who would have a stake in getting those weapons to France, and who, it seemed, were willing to kill over the issue.

The Navy came into sight up ahead, and he glanced down at his pocket watch. He was only a little early, and hopefully she would be there already. Unless she had pulled the trigger herself, and was elsewhere hiding the evidence. His mind would travel no further, though, on that road. It couldn't have been her. He wouldn't let it be her. In the cloakroom he was accosted by Francis on his way out.

"Everton," Francis greeted, accepting his gloves from a footman, "did you find out who she was?"

"Who who was?" Alex answered shortly, removing his hat and tossing it at a second startled servant.

"The girl, last night. Lady Masquerade. Whole town's

talking about her, you know. Gibson thinks she's a Russian princess.''

"Sounds plausible,'' the earl agreed, attempting to make his way into the parlor.

"Come, Alex, the two of you couldn't keep your hands off one another. Barbara was screeching like a barn owl in the powder room, Lady Putney said. So who is she, old boy?''

"She is Lady Masquerade." Alex gave a curt nod of dismissal, but Francis refused to release his sleeve. "Francis, I don't know," he continued impatiently. "She is as much a mystery to me as she is to you." That part, anyway, was true. "Now, if you don't mind, I'm in a bit of a hurry."

"Kit said you denied knowing anything about the chit as well, but I think he was merely trying to be rid of me, so he could go on babbling with that other fellow."

Alex's heart turned to ice. "What other fellow?"

"The one in the billiards room with him. They've been gabbing like old friends. Sounds more like French than Irish, but all babbling sounds fairly much the same to me. I say, are you going to Vauxhall with—''

Alex ignored the rest of Francis's yammering as he strode through the wide parlor, dodged Lord Ranley and an inquiry as to his feelings about the army's drain on the economy, and stepped into the billiards room. It couldn't be her father, he told himself as he glanced about. Stewart Brantley would never show his face in a club, not in the middle of Mayfair, and not when he was selling weapons to enemies of England. For a bare moment, though, Alex hesitated. If it was Brantley in there, he would have to arrest him. He would have to arrest both of them.

He didn't see her for a moment as he pushed past an eager Thadius Naring, scarcely noting the man and his bootlick greeting. When he finally found her, leaning over a table toward the back of the room, breath returned to him with a tight shudder. It wasn't Brantley beside her. The gentleman leaning at her elbow was the same handsome, dark-haired stranger who had stopped her outside Cale House, and Alex's eyes narrowed.

"Kit," he said, stepping forward and clenching his hands to keep from grabbing her, "apologies if I've kept you waiting."

She looked up, the surprise in her green eyes swiftly replaced by a warm, welcome look that did little to ease his disquiet. "No, you're early," she responded in her low lilt, and glanced over at her companion. "Alex, have you met Jean-Paul Mercier, the Comte de Fouché? Jean-Paul, my cousin Alexander Cale, the Earl of Everton."

"*Enchanté*," the comte said, studying him with hawk's eyes.

Kit had described Fouché's eyes as mysterious, but Alex would have termed the other's expression wary. This was the man whose nose she had bloodied, he recalled, yet Fouché appeared to have forgiven her. Forgiven her enough to seek her out in an exclusive London club and speak to her in the language of an enemy country.

"Good afternoon," the earl returned mildly, holding out his hand. "Kit mentioned that he had met you in Paris, I believe."

"Ah, I hope his words about me were kind," the comte said in a heavy French accent, gripping Alex's hand for a moment. There was no powder stain, and there was no cause to suspect him for reasons other than his presence and his association with Kit, but Alex continued to watch him warily.

"Of course, Jean-Paul," Kit said, her eyes returning to Alex. "What happened to you?" She reached up a finger to her own cheek, then motioned at his.

"Carriage kicked up a stone," he answered, searching her voice and eyes for any indication that she knew how he had acquired the wound.

Fouché set aside his billiards cue and nodded at Kit. "As I said, I only wanted to give you my farewell." The dark eyes glanced at Alex. "I am returning to France this evening," he explained.

Then he likely was involved, and was supposed to leave with Kit and her father. Quick panic touched Alex again at the thought of her going. "Ah," he commented, furrowing his brow with what he hoped was an expression of mild concern. "That seems a dangerous place to be, at the moment."

Fouché gave him a patient smile. "Not if one is careful. Which we always are, are we not, *mon ami*?"

"*Bien entendu*," Kit answered absently, her eyes on Alex. "Of course."

The comte sketched a quick, elegant bow. "A pleasure to meet you, Everton," he said. He gripped Kit's shoulder in a gesture that seemed altogether too friendly. "*Je te verrai encore bientôt.*"

"*Adieu*," Kit returned, nodding as he turned and strolled away from them.

"What did he say?" Alex asked quietly.

She shrugged. "Just to be careful," she replied.

Alex wanted to shake her, to inform her that *I'll see you soon* sounded nothing like *be careful* in any language, but instead he took the cue out of her hand and placed it on the table. "Come with me," he murmured.

After a close look at his face, she nodded and turned to follow him. He led her back to the coatroom and waited while they were given their things, then headed outside and had a footman hail them a coach.

"Where's Waddle?" Kit asked, pulling on her hat.

"Sent him home," he returned, concentrating on breathing calmly. A hack stopped beside them, and Alex motioned her to climb in. "Twelve Park Lane," he told the driver.

As soon as the door shut, the driver sent the team off. "Alex," Kit said from beside him, "what's wro—"

He grabbed her hands, yanked them up to his face, and breathed in deeply. They smelled of chalk, not gunpowder, and he relaxed a fraction. At least she hadn't been the assassin. He truly hadn't thought her capable of such a thing, but he wasn't thinking clearly where she was concerned.

"What are you doing?" she demanded, pulling her hands back to examine them when he released her.

"What were you and that damned Frenchman talking about?" he demanded.

"Jean-Paul?" she faltered. "Nothing really. Just—"

"Tell me, Christine!" he roared, beyond patience, beyond any sort of subtlety, beyond anything but a desperate, splintering need to be with her and to be able to trust her.

"He . . . he just told me that he'd spoken to my father. Papa had unexpected business in Calais, and was delayed another few days."

No doubt that business had something to do with an expected weapons shipment. Time was even shorter than he had realized. "How did you and your father make a living in Paris?" he continued, his hands tight around her upper arms.

"Alex, you're hurting me," she protested, struggling.

"And you're hurting me, damn it. Answer my bloody question, Christine."

She shrugged. "However we could."

He shook his head, yanking her closer beside him. "You will tell me the truth," he snarled. "No more lies."

"What's happened?" she asked, her expression growing alarmed.

"Someone shot Reg a few moments ago."

Christine went still, her face turning an alarming shade of white. "What?" she whispered, reaching out to touch his singed cheek. Her fingers jumped, and she sagged to cover her face with her hands. "No, no, no."

He pulled her hands away from her face, reminding himself that she was a superb actress, and that he couldn't trust her. "Did you have anything to do with it?"

"Is he . . ." she began, then took a quick breath, as though to steady herself. "Is he dead?"

"No. The ball grazed his skull. Luckily he has a hard head." He slid his hands on both sides of her face, compelling her to look him in the eye. "Did you have anything to do with it?"

"Yes," she answered almost soundlessly, a single tear

running down her cheek. "But I didn't—"

Alex shook her hard, trying to ignore the sensation of his world shredding around him. "You tell me exactly what I need to know. How did you and your father make your living in Paris?"

She took another shaky breath. "Papa gambled, and I did a little, as well. After Napoleon, and I suppose before, though I was too young to pay much attention, he smuggled."

"Smuggled what?"

"Whatever he could. Fresh fruit, vegetables, blankets, flour, silver, gold." Her words were coming more quickly, as though now that she had begun, she was anxious to tell the whole story. "Once the British set up their blockade, he couldn't do it on his own anymore. That's when he started working with Jean-Paul."

"The Comte de Fouché." So he was involved after all. And Alex had let him walk free as well, because of the woman beside him.

She nodded. "Yes. Over the last few months, Fouché found a new buyer. Papa kept saying it was some eccentric old lord, and whatever odd things he occasionally wanted, he paid well enough for us to get them for him. He kept pretending it was nothing, but . . . I knew it wasn't vegetables."

"And Reg?" Alex prompted quietly, hating every answer she was giving. "Why was he shot?"

She wrapped her hands around his, keeping him close to her. "Someone stopped the last shipment the old man wanted. Apparently he was furious, and threatened to . . . have Jean-Paul kill Papa if he failed again. So Papa and I came here. I was to help him find out who was behind all the trouble, so he could bribe whoever it was, give him a cut." Her green eyes held his steadily, while he searched her face for any sign she was lying. Another tear ran down her cheek. "Only it was you, wasn't it?"

"Yes."

"And you wouldn't be bribed."

"So why Reg? Or was it supposed to be me, after all?"

She shook her head tightly. "No, no," she whispered brokenly. "Oh, I don't know, I don't know. I never told anyone about you."

"You expect me to believe that?" he hissed. "After this?"

Kit blinked. "Papa hates the English. I always did, too . . . until I met you. I . . . I didn't want him to know I thought it was you."

"So you told him about Hanshaw, instead. Sweet—"

"No! I didn't! Please, Alex. I know all about you and Reg and Augustus. But I didn't say anything. I should have. But I couldn't."

The desire to believe her was almost overwhelming, but with the last of his willpower he shook her again and shoved her away from him. "Another lie!"

Kit flung herself back at him. "No! I know there's more to this than Papa will tell me, but I swear to you, Alex, I did not tell Fouché, or anyone else, what I know." Alex tried to shove her back again, but with a wrenching sob she grabbed on to his coat, pulling herself against him. "Please, Alex. I wouldn't let anyone hurt you."

"I want to believe you," he whispered raggedly, clutching at her arms. "God, I want to believe you."

"Then believe me," she returned, and closed her mouth fiercely over his.

If she truly didn't know what was being smuggled, and if she hadn't given their names to Fouché, there was still a chance. For her. For them. He slid his arms around her slim shoulders, pulling her tighter against him, and kissing her as desperately as she was kissing him. She lifted herself across his thighs, curling into him as though trying to get inside of him, to get as close to him as he wanted to be to her.

The ill-sprung coach lurched to a halt, and the coachman rapped on the door with his crop. "We're here, gov," he called.

Alex lifted Kit to her feet, though he didn't want to let go of her. Irrational though it was, he knew if he let go of her, he would lose her. He was certain of it. She held on to the lapel of his coat as she climbed down from the coach, him right behind her. He flipped a coin at the coachman and followed her up the steps. Wenton pulled the door open for them, but he might as well have been a stump for all the attention they paid him.

Kit, her hand still wrapped through his coat, pulled him toward the nearest door, the morning room. He balked at the doorway, but she wrapped an arm about his waist and leaned up to kiss him, and he stepped inside with her. He slammed the door shut with the palm of his hand, ignoring Wenton's stunned expression behind them, and locked it, while with his other hand he undid her breeches and tugged them off her legs.

Her mouth hungry against his, she backed with him toward the couch and pulled him down on top of her. Still without saying anything, Kit reached between them and freed him from his own leggings. Alex spread her legs apart with his knees, lowered himself down over her, and thrust forward. She gasped, lifting her hips to meet him, as he entered her hard and deep. Christine wrapped her long legs about his thighs, to pull him deeper inside, closer to her hot, tight center, closer to her soul. They took their release together, and for a moment, were one.

For a long time after they made love, Alex lay with his head upon her shoulder, and Christine softly stroked his hair. She had told him the truth, finally, and he hadn't turned her out, and he hadn't turned away. More than anything else, that was what she had been afraid of, that he would hate her.

Finally he lifted his head to look at her face. "I think we surprised Wenton," he murmured, laying his head down again.

She chuckled then, and a moment later his deep chuckle joined hers, resonating against her breastbone. "Good," she replied.

Alex was quiet again for a few moments, then shifted to raise up on one elbow beside her on the deep couch.

He reached out and tucked a straying strand of blond hair behind her ear. "You have to marry me now," he said, his beautiful eyes serious and worried.

Worried because of her. "No, I don't."

"Christine, do you have any idea how much trouble you're in? Smuggling during wartime?"

She held his gaze, looking for an answer in his eyes. "So you want to protect me."

"Of course I do."

"I can take care of myself, Alex. I told you before, I am not going to trap you into any—"

"Would you rather I arrested you? I could, you know."

"For smuggling vegetables and blankets?" she returned sharply, though she knew it wasn't about that. "Is that your idea of doing your duty to Prince George?"

He scowled. "You don't know everything that's going on."

"So tell me."

Alex shook his head. "No."

"You still don't trust me," she whispered. She could understand why, after all the lies she'd told, but it hurt, nevertheless.

"I want to, Kit. But if you don't know, it's safer for you, for everyone concerned." He ran the palm of his hand under her shirt, along her flat belly.

"So what happens now?" she asked slowly, studying his face.

Very softly he touched his lips to hers, again the gentle, controlled lover, as though the mad passion of a few minutes ago had been someone else entirely. "We keep you here. Safe."

"Will you tell Reg and Augustus about me?"

He frowned. "Hanshaw doesn't need to know right now. Eventually, maybe. Augustus can go to hell before I include him in any of this."

That sounded a bit odd, whatever their personal animosities. "Why not Aug—"

"He doesn't concern me, or this, Kit."

That made no sense. Of course, Augustus was a spy. She'd seen him. Perhaps not going off to meetings, but sneaking about at night, as though he didn't want even his friends to know what he was up to . . . "Alex," she whispered, her blood freezing. She hadn't told Fouché about Reg and Everton, but someone had. "I think you're wrong about Devlin."

"Why so obsessed with Devlin now?" he asked, heat coming into his expression again.

Looking at his distrustful, jealous gaze, she realized that he would hardly listen to her suspicions about his former brother-in-law. If their positions had been reversed, she would think him merely trying to distract her. "I'm not—"

Alex touched her lips with his fingers and took a slow breath. "Not now. I want you to promise me one last thing."

"What?" She would let Devlin go for the moment, but if he was helping Fouché, then Alex was still in danger.

"Promise me you won't go back to Paris with your father."

Kit looked at him. "You just don't want to lose track of him!" she snapped, trying to shove him away. "How dare—"

He shook his head, pinning her down with his shoulder and arms. "Don't turn the subject," he countered, grabbing her jaw so she had to look at him. "You know this has nothing to do with that. Just promise me that you'll stay. No obligations. Just stay."

He wasn't simply asking that to keep her safe, she sensed. He wanted her to stay in London with him. Only he couldn't ask it that way, because he was a man, and because he was likely worried that she would turn him down again. "All right," she whispered.

At two in the morning someone began pounding on the door downstairs.

"Sweet Lucifer," Alex snarled, while Kit sat bolt upright beside him. "Not again."

"It can't be Papa," she said, looking over at him. "I doubt he'd make such a ruckus."

That made sense, and it was something of a relief, as well. She might have agreed to stay, but Alex doubted she could stand by and see her father arrested. He wasn't certain he could put her through it. "It's not bill collectors," he ventured, sitting up beside her. "Unless you've been using my note of credit again." He slid his arm around her shoulders and pulled her back down beside him. "Let Wenton see to it."

"Alex!" Gerald Downing's voice came a moment later, and feet hammered on their way up the stairs.

"Good God," he grumbled, and grabbed for his nightshirt. "Stay here, chit."

Yanking the shirt on over his head, he strode for the door, pausing to retrieve his robe and pull it on. Gerald reached the door at the same time he did, but Alex managed to step out into the hallway and shut it before his cousin could see inside the bedchamber. "What in damnation is going on?"

James Samuels reached the top of the stairs behind Gerald. Alex glanced between the two of them, uneasiness tugging at him. There was news, and it wasn't good.

"Napoleon's less than a hundred leagues from Belgium," Gerald announced.

"And you were right, m'lord, about the crates going north," Samuels added. "Hanton spotted 'em two days ago."

"He's picking up supporters along the way," Gerald continued.

Two simultaneous conversations in the middle of the night was rather disconcerting, particularly when most of his thoughts were behind the closed door and in the warm bed behind him, but Alex found himself shocked into alertness. "He's trying to cut off Wellington, then."

Gerald nodded grimly. "If he can run Blücher and the Germans down, Wellington doesn't stand a chance."

"That would depend on how well armed Bonaparte's soldiers are," Alex mused darkly.

"Which would depend on how quickly we can snap up those damned weapons," his cousin snarled.

"Keep your voice down, if you please," Alex returned, glancing unconsciously toward his bedchamber door.

Gerald followed his gaze. "Kit?" He read the answer on his cousin's face. "Damnation, Alex! You know better than that."

"Leave off, Gerald," the earl warned.

"No, I won't," Gerald hissed, flushing. "I don't know much about her, but I do know she's no common bit, cousin. You will do right by her."

Apparently Kit had made yet another conquest. "I know," Alex muttered, "you're right. But it's more complicated than you realize."

"Enlighten me," Gerald demanded.

Alex took a breath. "Her father is our weapons smuggler."

Gerald opened his mouth and then slowly shut it again, myriad emotions, including sympathy, running across his face. "Is she aware of that?" he finally asked.

"I don't know," Alex said quietly, his heart beating a painful, hollow tattoo against his ribs. At least Gerald hadn't asked how deeply she was involved, because he was swiftly reaching the point where further lies would gain him enemies.

"Sweet . . . Damnation, Alex, are you trying to get yourself hanged?" his cousin pursued.

"Oh, they almost never do that to nobles any longer," Alex returned tiredly, rubbing at his temple.

"Well, what—"

"Listen to me," Alex interrupted, glancing at Samuels. "I'm going north with James to confiscate those bloody weapons before they reach the coast."

"No you're—"

"I'll send the lot I arrest, along with the guns, down to Prinny. That should keep him satisfied for a few days, until I can . . . settle this."

"And how do you plan to do that, pray tell?"

The earl looked down. "I have an idea."

"Unless you tell me exactly what you're up to, you're not going anywhere."

"Ah. And you can stop me, of course?"

"I don't wish to inherit Everton because you did something stupid," Gerald snapped back at him.

Alex paused to rub at his chin with his thumb and forefinger. "You were right about Kit not being common. Her father is Stewart Brantley. Furth's brother."

Gerald actually paled, quite a feat given the overheated flush of his cheeks. "Martin's brother? She's . . ." he said, pointing toward the closed door, "she's his niece?"

"Well, that would follow," Alex said dryly, reaching for what remained of his sense of humor. "And that does not go beyond us," he stated, his gaze taking in James and his cousin. When they both nodded, he took a breath. "So you see, this is a bit stickier than I'd originally anticipated."

"Furth needs to be told."

"I know."

"And—"

"And so I'll take care of it, Gerald. All you need do is tell Hanshaw and Furth that I'm going to retrieve those guns." As for the rest, although Christine continued to refuse his protection, he had no intention of seeing her hang. Furth's name would shield her, if Martin would agree to take her in. And if that was the only chance she had, Alex would see that she took it— whether she wanted to or not. However she might end up feeling about him, he didn't want her left with nowhere to turn.

"Oh, what a tangled web we weave," Gerald muttered, apparently reading his expression.

Alex glared at him. "Yes, we're a vipers' nest of deceit in this house," he growled. "James, have Tybalt saddled and get yourself a fresh mount."

"Aye, milord."

"Gerald, wait downstairs a moment."

Alex took a deep breath and pulled open his bedchamber door again. Kit sat on the edge of the bed, her slim body wrapped in the sheet, her expression as tense and serious as he had ever seen it. She was so beautiful.

"What's happened?" she asked quietly.

Alex wished with all his heart that he could tell her. She might very well be as enamored of him as he was of her, but she also had the makings of the perfect decoy. For all he knew, she might have been distracting and delaying him on purpose. "Nothing serious," he soothed. "I need to leave London for a few days."

"You're not going to Belgium to fight Napoleon," she stated, her face growing so pale that for a moment he was concerned she might faint.

"No. Of course not. But I need to leave immediately."

"Then I'm going with you," she said stubbornly, standing and running her hand down his arm to clasp his fingers.

Damnation, he couldn't resist her at all. Except in this one thing. He squeezed her hand, then released her. "No. You'll stay with Gerald and Ivy."

"You're going after my father, aren't you?" she whispered.

He shut his eyes for a moment. "I'm going after his shipment, yes," he answered slowly. Fast as he and James Samuels would be moving, she'd never be able to get word to Stewart Brantley first.

"They'll try to kill you," she said almost soundlessly, her eyes holding his with an intensity he'd never seen in her before.

Alex shook his head. "You've already told me your father's in Calais, and Fouché's back in France, as well."

"Please don't go," she said, stepping forward and wrapping her arms about his waist.

He enfolded her in his arms. "I have to," he murmured into her hair, surprised that she had accepted the news that he was going after her father's shipment so calmly. "Go get dressed. Gerald will take you home with him."

Alex felt her ragged intake of breath, and then her nod against his shoulder.

Afraid she would bolt, he sent Mrs. Hodges in with her while she changed. Then he hurriedly shaved and dressed. With typical efficiency, Antoine had packed Alex's saddlebags for him by the time he was ready to head downstairs. Kit was standing in the hallway there, Gerald beside her.

He took her hand and pulled her into the morning room. "I'll be back soon, chit," he said, "so behave yourself."

She pulled his face down to kiss him ferociously. "Be careful," she murmured, running a trembling finger down his chest and hooking it through the buttonhole of his waistcoat.

He touched his finger to the skin of her cheek. "I will," he said softly, studying her face and fearing that she would never look at him that way again. Once he spoke to Furth about her, it was entirely possible that the next time he set eyes on her, she would hate him. Finally he pulled free of her grip and turned for the door.

"Alex, *je t'aime,*" she whispered at his back. "You know what that means, don't you?"

He stopped short as the quiet words resounded through him like thunder, wrenching something hard and painful loose in his chest. "Yes," he said gruffly. She loved him. It was either a last effort to stop him from going, or she was telling the truth. If he turned around to look at Christine Brantley again, he would never be able to leave. Stiffly he made himself start walking again.

"Take care of her," he rasped at Gerald, who had enough sense to keep his mouth shut. Without waiting for an answer, he left Cale House for the stables, and a hard ride north.

Christine wondered when precisely it had happened. A handful of days ago she had hated all Englishmen, and one in particular, though she didn't yet know his identity. And suddenly she was ready to do anything to make certain that same English lord came through this safely. Her shift in loyalties made no sense. Her father would tell her she was a fool to risk her livelihood, and very likely her life, for someone like the Earl of Everton. He was everything she was supposed to detest; a blue-blooded rake who could ruin her, and worse, in a heart-beat.

With Alex storming off somewhere after her father, she should be hurt, and furious, and seeking revenge. Her mind was so muddled where they were concerned, though, that to keep from going mad she deliberately turned her attention elsewhere with the rather weak ex-cuse that eventually everything would sort itself out. If she knew anything about either of them, Alexander Cale and Stewart Brantley could take care of themselves. At least when they knew what they were facing. Fouché, Bonaparte, and one another.

What worried her, though, was that there was some-thing else. Something Alex apparently knew nothing about, and wanted to know nothing about. Someone had suggested that Fouché try to kill Reg Hanshaw, or per-haps even the Earl of Everton. And Augustus Devlin was meeting people in alleys in secret in the middle of the night.

The Downings kept a close eye on her all day, un-doubtedly having taken to heart Alex's suggestion—*hah*, threat—to keep a close eye on her. And so she made a show of moping about glumly until she'd worn them to a frazzle, then suggested that they might all attend Mercia Cralling's recital as a way to cheer them-selves up. The speed with which Everton's cousins agreed to the suggestion would have been amusing if she hadn't been so concerned with where in damnation Alex was, and whether Augustus and whomever the vis-count was in contact with knew he had gone.

Several times during Mercia's recital she heard people mention Lady Masquerade, and whether anyone had fig-ured out who she was. She could wonder that herself. It was becoming difficult even for her, remembering that she was supposed to be a boy and acting accordingly, so she could only imagine how Alex was coping with it. She wished he would tell her. She wished he would stop shutting her out from himself, and let her know how he truly felt about her, whether he felt anything close to what she felt for him.

And she was going to have to decide what, exactly, she was going to tell Stewart Brantley when he reappeared.

A relieved round of applause began around her, and Kit blinked and swiftly joined in. Mercia stood up at the pianoforte and curtsied, and her mother trundled forward to congratulate her while the guests stood to stretch cramped legs and head for the refreshment tables.

"May we go now?" Gerald queried in his wife's ear, and she elbowed him in the ribs.

"Not yet," she answered with good-humored exasperation. "Unless you'd rather wander about the house keeping an eye on our guest."

Kit stifled a guilty frown. They'd done nothing but show kindness and concern for her, and she was about to cause them a fair measure of trouble. She glanced about the room, hoping her quarry might be in attendance so she wouldn't have to search Mayfair for him in the dark.

Gerald sighed and looked about, then straightened with a grin. "There's Hanshaw. I'll be back in a moment."

"Please," Ivy agreed, waving him away. "Men," she muttered to Kit, who raised an eyebrow, attempting to play along.

"Beg pardon, cousin?" she asked innocently, tugging at her waistcoat.

"Oh, not you, of course, Kit," Ivy returned with a self-conscious smile.

Thankfully Deborah Glover waylaid Ivy, and Kit was able to make her excuses and head for the refreshment tables, with the intention of walking straight past and out the door to find Viscount Devlin. She glanced back at Ivy to see her looking in her direction, and with a silent curse at Alex for making such effective threats, she paused to sample one of the ham biscuits.

They were quite good, and she was helping herself to a second one when a gloved hand slid down her shoulder to her elbow, and curled around her arm. For a moment she thought it must be Mercia, and shrugged off her nervous impatience enough to turn and smile at the girl. The eyes that looked back at her, though, were far less innocent than Miss Cralling's, and rather than being a porcelain blue, were black as a raven's wing.

"Lady Sinclair." She grinned, trying not to choke on her biscuit, while her mind roiled to sort out a whole new set of complications she hadn't been prepared for. Not tonight. And not with Alexander Cale's mistress. Former mistress. "Ham biscuit, my lady?"

"Don't think you're fooling me," Barbara purred. "I know exactly what you are, you harlot."

As her father always said, when trapped, attack. "About deuced time you figured it out. What took you so long?" she mumbled around her mouthful, and lifted a glass of port from a nearby footman's tray.

For a moment Lady Sinclair just looked at her, her mouth open to make a response she could no longer use. "And what do you have to say?" she finally murmured.

Kit raised an eyebrow and swallowed the biscuit. "Seems the price of barley's going up this year," she suggested, smiling again.

Barbara kept her arm tightly gripped, which would make any escape attempt into a wrestling match. "I wouldn't be so smug if I were you. I could flat ruin you in two seconds."

"And I could set you on the floor in half that time," Kit responded promptly. "I'm a sterling boxer, you know."

Another hesitation followed, and Kit reflected that Barbara Sinclair was likely not used to being threatened with physical violence. "I don't care what you are," her ruby lips returned. "I only care that you leave London. Immediately."

Considering that was exactly what she should be doing, Christine found herself less than pleased at the suggestion. ''Or?'' she prompted.

''Or everyone will know you're Everton's whore,'' Barbara spat.

''Odd accusation for you to be making, Barbara,'' a male voice drawled from behind them. Augustus Devlin draped an arm over each of their shoulders and leaned forward between them. ''Pot calling the kettle black and all that rot, you know.''

''Get away from me, you sot,'' Lady Sinclair snapped.

''And you stay away from Everton,'' Kit warned in the same tone, then smiled. ''Remember, if everyone knows about me, there's no reason he should marry you.''

''And you're a greater fool than I, if you think he'll marry *you*,'' Barbara murmured. ''Where did he find you anyway, Covent Garden? Do you make him buy you things before you let him between your legs?'' She looked Christine up and down. ''Tall thing like you, what are you worth, a shilling a go?''

Augustus chuckled. ''More than what you'd earn humping knights and esquires on Regent Street, Barbara.'' He leaned closer to Lady Sinclair. ''Leave off the girl, witch, or I'll have to begin spreading tales about your fondness for the shepherd-and-the-lost-sheep game, shan't I, now.''

Barbara pulled free of his grip, her face white. ''You'll never have him,'' she whispered fiercely at Kit. ''I'll see you gone and his band on my finger by the end of the Season.''

Augustus smiled. ''Baa, baa.'' When Lady Sinclair turned her back on them and stormed from the room, he turned his gaze on Kit. ''Best watch her,'' he commented, reaching past her for a sweet tart. ''Not much for witty repartee, but some say she put a candlestick to the back of her late husband's skull, the night she found him playing lost sheep with the upstairs maid.''

Kit stood looking at him. He'd had the appearance of a specter before, but now his flesh had acquired an alabaster, paper-thin look to it, as if he might simply tear into small pieces and drift away in the next breeze. "I appreciate the warning," she returned, wondering whether Fouché had suggested the viscount keep an eye on her, or if the meeting had been a coincidence. It saved her the trouble of tracking him down, but neither was she ready to confront him about his loyalties at Mercia Cralling's recital.

"Not at all, Kit." He paused, lowering the tart. "What is your name, by the by?"

There had been little doubt that he knew, but it was still jarring to hear the question. "Christine," she said quietly.

He nodded. "You were stunning at the ball the other night."

"Thank you."

"I can see why Alex has kept you to himself."

He was far more dangerous than Barbara Sinclair, Kit sensed, because he had far less to lose. Augustus Devlin was dying, with no family, and no heirs to speak of. If it suited him to do so, he would bandy her tale throughout London. If he knew enough about her, he could effectively ruin Alex's reputation in the political arena, even get him arrested for harboring her under the noses of the *ton*. "It was necessary," she answered in a low voice.

"How much would you pay someone else to keep your secret, I wonder?" he continued, looking her slowly up and down. In the face of his sharp gaze, she realized that for once he was completely sober. "Or secrets, should I say? Would you lift your heels for me, Christine?"

"I'll tell Alex what you are, is what I'll do," she murmured, furious and uneasy.

"He'll never believe you." Slowly he shook his head, his eyes holding hers. "You have no proof of anything, my dear. And a ramshackle girl like yourself, lovely as you may be, would hardly be the one to convince anyone else."

"But why do you hate Alex?" she whispered. She'd

been the one raised to hate the English; he'd been raised as one of their elite.

"That's personal," he returned softly.

"I won't let you hurt him," she retorted fiercely.

"Such loyalty," he approved with a cynical smile. "But you'd be much wiser to simply stay out of it. And much safer." The gray specter's eyes held hers for another moment, then he slowly reached out and briefly touched her cheek with cool fingers. "Do tell Everton to make you come once, for me," Lord Devlin murmured. "If he has another chance."

"Go to hell," she said flatly, and turned on her heel, not wanting him to see that she was afraid for Alex.

For a long moment he stood looking after her, his expression unreadable, then gestured at the footman to bring him a brandy. A large one.

Chapter 17

Suffolk was cold and wet, and Alex was grateful for it. The poor weather and the bad roads kept his mind from wandering. Hanton McAndrews left word for them at several posts along the way, and from their brevity it was obvious that the Scot was moving fast to keep up with the smugglers. Yet neither the knowledge that time was short, nor that a very serious task lay ahead, was enough to keep Alex's thoughts from flying back to London—to Kit—every time he and Samuels stopped to rest the horses and ask for news.

Kit had accepted the fact that he was going after her father with a surprising degree of restraint. Undoubtedly she expected that Stewart Brantley would be able to elude him, as he had done in the past. Alex had no intention of turning his back so completely on his duty, however, whatever he might secretly wish. And when he did catch their smuggler, he would lose Kit. And that was what haunted him.

A day later and three miles from the sea, Alex and Samuels caught up to Hanton and the crates of weapons he was trailing. Despite his best efforts, Alex still had no idea whether Stewart Brantley had returned from Calais to personally escort the muskets.

"Ye ready, m'lord?" Hanton inquired, crouching down with him among the gray, weather-worn rocks where they'd been waiting for the past three hours to finally move against their quarry.

Alex rested his chin on his arm and looked down at the smugglers in the cove below. The boat had put in a little over an hour ago, but the men appeared to be in no hurry to load the crates. It made sense. There was still some time before the tide turned, and heavy, dark clouds were rumbling in from the northeast. In all likelihood they would wait for the first tide of the morning before they crossed the length of the Channel to Calais.

"May as well," he muttered, sliding back away from the crest of the hill.

"Ye sound like you're plannin' a funeral, m'lord," Hanton commented in his thick Scots brogue, his breath clouding in the cold air.

"It feels like it," Alex admitted darkly, climbing to his feet and brushing at his breeches.

"Ye used t'enjoy this part, as I recall," Hanton continued, following him back down the hill toward James Samuels and their waiting horses. "Ye'd be riding down on 'em like Lucifer himself, firing your pistols and bellowin'."

"Yes, well, I'm much older and wiser now," the earl retorted, grabbing his reins and swinging up into the saddle.

"Your da used t'hate those damned meetings, too, ye know," Hanton said, mounting beside him. "Used t'say how much he envied that ye could go out and do something 'sides sit on yer arse and talk. Like ye have to do now, I mean."

"You still play the bagpipes, Hanton?" Alex returned, kneeing Tybalt into a canter.

"Aye, m'lord. Why d'ye ask?"

"You have the wind for it. That's for damned certain."

On his other side Samuels gave a short laugh. "He's got wind enough to play one under each arm."

"Shut up, ye damned English," Hanton retorted. "Should never've let me one daughter marry ye."

The earl smiled at the exchange. It had been a year since he had last seen Hanton McAndrews, and better than three since he had last ridden with the Scot. Back then, the French had been raiding the coast and "confiscating" British goods, under Napoleon's so-called Decree of Fontainebleau. Prince George had assigned Furth, Hanshaw, and the Cales to put a stop to it. After his father's death, Alex had listened to Gerald and had stayed in London, to keep his precious Cale blood from being spilled in something as mundane as service to his country. Despite his frustration at not being able to take direct action, he had played politics, become bored, and played at being a rakehell again. It had taken Christine Brantley to drive him back out into the cold wet. And as he kicked Tybalt into a gallop to charge down into the cove, he was loving every minute of it.

Almost as much as he loved the spy waiting for him back in London. Alex took a ragged breath, surprised he had let himself admit to it, and surprised he had lasted for as long as he had without doing so.

A shot cracked sharply in the rocks around them as the smugglers spotted them, and Hanton shouldered his gelding into Alex's black. "Keep your bloody head down, yer lordship!" he bellowed, firing a return round.

Alex shook himself, and motioned for Samuels and the two men pounding behind him to take the lead. While Hanton and his crew rode around the back of the cove to flank any escape attempt to the west or north, Alex and his men turned sharply east along the water to cut the smugglers off from the boat and the Channel as they bolted toward the sea.

"Stop right there!" he bellowed, pulling Tybalt up so short that they both nearly went down. He yanked his pistol free of his belt and pointed it at the head of the nearest man, while his associates moved to flank him on either side. At the sight of the weapons, the smugglers stopped and dropped their own arms.

"Got 'em, m'lord!" Hanton's brogue came from the direction of the wagons. "Thirty crates, at least!"

Alex gave a short, relieved grin. They'd been in time. English soldiers weren't going to die because he'd been a fool. "All right," he said, urging Tybalt forward a few steps, "whom do these wagons belong to?"

No one stepped forward, though in truth he hadn't expected anyone to do so. Hanton McAndrews made his way over beside him to hold Tybalt's head while Alex dismounted. "No volunteers, eh?" the Scotsman scoffed.

"Doesn't appear that way," he replied. "I suppose they'd rather talk to the jailers in Old Bailey." He pursed his lips for show, though real anger coursed through him at the thought of what would have happened if Hanton had been slower in tracking down the muskets. "Or better yet, Mr. Samuels, why don't you bring us some rope?"

That produced an unsettled grumbling. A moment later, a gray-haired man with a round gut and bad teeth, whom he'd already pegged as the group's leader, spat onto the rocks at his feet and slouched forward sullenly. "Will Debner," he grunted in a thick Yorkshire accent. "They ain't my wagons."

Alex nodded. "Good afternoon, Mr. Debner. Let's have a little chat, shall we?"

With Samuels watching the others and Hanton trailing a few steps behind them, they clambered over the rough rocks around the point. Once they were out of sight and earshot, Alex turned around again. "Tell me how you came to acquire those weapons," he said, grateful for his caped greatcoat. Out of the protection of the cove, the storm winds gusted hard and wet from the north.

Debner spat again and folded his arms. "And what do I get, then?"

"How about we don't string ye up right here, ye bloody traitor?" Hanton snarled.

The earl raised a hand, and the Scotsman subsided. "I can put in a word to keep you from hanging."

"For pulling some damned crates about?" the smuggler returned, his deep-set eyes shifting warily between Alex and the Scot.

"For smuggling weapons to the enemy during wartime," Alex corrected succinctly. "That's treason. Punishable by death." He stepped forward and shoved Debner hard into a boulder, wondering if he was going to have to say those same words to Kit. "Where did you get the muskets?"

The smuggler rubbed at his chest. "You'll keep me alive, yer lordship?"

"I'll not let them hang you," Alex corrected, wondering if the man understood the distinction. Even with a handful of supposedly more humane ordinances in place, there was still a wide variety of ways to put a criminal to death.

Debner scowled, narrowed his eyes, and shifted his feet on the stones. "I know a gentleman, in France. An ex-English blue blood, he is."

"His name?" Alex insisted, hoping the smuggler couldn't read his expression.

"Brantley, he calls himself. Stewart Brantley. He sent word that I was to go to York, and those wagons would be waiting for me in an old barn. And they were. And here I am. Hardly worth a hangin' at all, wouldn't you say?"

Alex ignored the appeal. "Once you loaded them on the boat, where were the crates to go?"

He felt rather than saw Hanton holding his breath. This was the critical question. Because they'd seized the crates before they left English soil, no real crime but theft had been committed. Unless they got an admission of one.

"Brantley was t'meet us in Calais 'n a few days. We started for the coast early because of the damned foul weather."

The earl glanced at Hanton, who nodded. He started forward to lead the smuggler back to the others, but Alex put an arm across his barrel chest and stopped him.

"You've worked with this Brantley before, I assume?" Alex continued, every part of him wishing not to. But he had to know.

"Aye," Debner admitted, squinting his good eye. "But I ain't confessing to nothing you don't already know about."

"Quite right." Alex nodded, keeping his frustration hidden behind a neutral expression and clenched fists.

"I was wondering, though, if you've had dealings with any other English, ah, blue bloods."

The smuggler spat again. "And what'll this get me?"

"The best I can manage for you," Alex snarled, what remained of his patience seeping away in cold and agonizing uncertainty. Hanton was alert beside him, obviously curious at the questions. "Which is a great deal. Answer the damned question."

"Aye. Skinny, light-haired fellow. Sharp, 'e was, and pretty in that blue-blood way o' yours. Ain't seen 'im for maybe a year, though."

Alex's mouth was so dry, he had to swallow before he could speak. "I'll do what I can for you."

With a slow breath, he turned around to face the sea. Without a word Hanton marched past him and shoved Will Debner back in the direction of the cove. Alex heard them leave, but didn't turn. For a long time he stood looking out at the rough, wind-scalloped waters of the Channel. France was there, out of sight behind a wall of clouds to the south, Belgium and Wellington slightly farther east. And Napoleon Bonaparte was somewhere between the two.

He felt somewhere between the two himself. He'd known already that Kit had been involved with her father's small-coin smuggling, and he didn't really care much about that. Napoleon had been on Elba then, and hungry people would be fed, one way or another. It was the guns that concerned him. Debner's not seeing the skinny, pretty blond boy for a year didn't mean that she hadn't been involved. Or it might. Alex grimaced and ran a hand through his windblown hair. Enough was enough. He'd played the game against too many opponents who were supposed to be his allies, and it was time he let at least one of them in on what was happening.

"It'll be dark soon, m'lord," Hanton said from behind him, and Alex nodded.

"Everyone ready to go?" he asked without turning around.

"Aye. Everybody wrapped up nice and tight for 'Is

Majesty.'' The Scot stood silently on the rocks for a moment. ''This skinny boy. Ye know him,'' he stated finally.

''I do.'' He sighed and turned around. ''You'd best get the crates and horses to shelter before the storm breaks, and then head south in the morning.''

''And you, Master Alex?''

''I'm headed back to London tonight.''

Christine squatted down in the bushes along the main path at Vauxhall Gardens and waited. The ground was damp and cold, and with the fog having rolled in, the leaves and twigs pricking into her arms were already picking up a share of nightly dew. Ivy and Gerald would be furious if they discovered her absence, but then if they wanted to keep her inside, they shouldn't have given her a room with a window and a convenient rose trellis outside. In fact, she had planned to return before now, in case Gerald decided to try to cheer her up with a game of billiards as he had done last evening. And she *would* have been back at Downing House already if Reg Hanshaw had bothered to be home when she went calling. But he hadn't been, and this was the direction his stuffy butler had given, and so she waited.

Prowling about Vauxhall might have been more productive, except that her loathsome uncle was still in London, and Reg was just as likely to be in the company of the entire damned Brantley clan as to be alone with Caroline. In truth, hating Caroline was somewhat more difficult than she had expected. Resolving her feelings toward her cousin, however, was not her reason for hiding in the bushes. She wasn't exactly certain why she was there, for presumably if Augustus Devlin was working with Fouché and she was working with Stewart Brantley, they were on the same side. Except that Fouché would kill the Earl of Everton if he could arrange it, and she would do anything, *anything*, to keep that from happening.

Finally, while strolling about the fountains in the

company of Lord Bandwyth and after nearly having her
hand stepped on by Lady Julia Penston, she spied Reg
over by the gazebo. Caroline was with him, but so were
Mercia Cralling, Celeste Montgomery, Francis Henning,
and Lord Andrew Grambush. Kit took a moment to
wonder when Mercia had begun seeing Grambush behind her back, then shook herself, rose, brushed off her
coat, and strolled over to greet them.

"Kit." Reg grinned, stepping forward as he spied her
approaching. "Thought you'd be back in Ireland by
now." He put out his hand, and Kit shook it.

He was genuinely pleased to see her. Alex then really
had told him nothing about her. "Father was delayed.
I'll be going in a day or two."

"I do wish you could persuade him to let you stay
the remainder of the Season, Mr. Riley," Caroline cajoled with an enchanting smile.

Kit smiled back at her a bit absently, and returned her
attention to Reg. "Might I have a word with you?" she
requested, trying to make the query meaningful to him,
but innocent to everyone else in the party.

The baron looked at her speculatively for a moment,
then nodded. "Grambush, do buy the ladies some ices,"
he suggested. "Kit and I will be along in a bit."

Grambush offered an arm each to Mercia and Caroline, while Francis and Miss Montgomery fell in behind.
"Take your time, gentlemen."

When the rest of the party had made their way down
the path, Reg turned to look at her. "If you're wondering
where Everton's gone, I can't—"

"No, no," she cut him off, shaking her head. "I know
it's secret state's business and all that rot. What I want
to know is, does Augustus know where he's gone?"

The baron frowned. "Augustus? Why would he—"

"Does he know, Reg?" she repeated firmly, wondering just how much she was willing to divulge. She was
balancing on a very thin rail, and the wind was gusting.
Falling on one side would kill Alex, and landing on the
other would get her father, and likely herself, hanged.

"No. I never told him, at any rate. And Alex still isn't

speaking to him. So no. I don't see how he could."

Kit gave a small sigh of relief and nodded. "Thank you."

Before she could turn away, Reg grabbed her arm. "Why are you worried over Augustus?"

Looking into the serious blue eyes below his rakishly bandaged forehead, Kit realized that he had been playing a game all along, as well. Whimsical and a bit silly, perhaps, but only on the outside. On the inside, he was likely as formidable an opponent as she knew Alex to be. He was also the only one in London right now whom she could trust. If she dared. "I . . . saw him, the other day, talking to a Frenchman."

Reg relaxed a fraction and released his hold on her sleeve. "There are some living in London," he noted.

She swallowed. "He was in an alley at the time."

The frown returned. "In an al—"

"At midnight."

The frown remained on his face while he held her gaze, though his attention wasn't on her. He was running calculations, possibilities, through his mind, she knew, trying to weigh what she'd said against what he knew about Augustus and the French smugglers they were after. Finally he blinked and shook his head. "No. I know you want to help, and that things have been a bit . . . exciting," he offered, fingering his bandage, "but Augustus is not only our friend, he's practically Everton's family. This is important business, Kit. Don't repeat what you've told me to anyone else, or you might get yourself, and Alex, into difficulties."

He had no idea what she was risking, so of course, there was no real reason to believe a foolish young Irishman who'd been begging after an exciting royal appointment. "Reg, don't be so stupid," she said urgently. "Devlin knows what's going on, and he hates Alex."

"He does not hate Alex. He merely . . . says things when he's cast away. They'll be bosom cronies again in a week. It's happened before." Reg clapped her on the shoulder. "Don't worry. Everton'll be home tomorrow. Day after, at the latest. You can let him in on your suspicions, and he'll tell you the same thing."

Kit shrugged free of his grip. "He already has."

"Well, come and join us, then. We're on our way to see the fireworks."

"Thank you, no. I've got to get back." She turned around, then bit her lower lip and faced the baron again. "Reg, don't tell Devlin I said that about him."

He looked at her oddly for a brief moment, then shook himself. "Don't worry, Kit. I won't."

Hopefully that would keep Hanshaw safe until she could convince Alex—or, if she was left no other choice, take care of Devlin herself. "Good," she muttered, hurrying back into the shadows.

Reg looked after her for a moment, then shook his head and turned to rejoin his party. "Couldn't be," he muttered. "Impossible."

Bone-tired and cold, Alex climbed the shallow granite steps of Brantley House and struck the knocker against the door panel. A moment later Royce pulled open the door, and with a polite greeting and a distasteful look at his muddy boots, ushered him up to the drawing room. It had been over a year since Alex had last set foot inside these walls. Though he had known Martin Brantley for years, he found himself viewing the place with new eyes. The rooms all had the formal, stiff feel of unused furniture, which made sense considering the small amount of time the Brantleys, and particularly Martin, spent in London. Not until Caroline's coming-out this Season had any of the family stayed more than a few days in town at one time.

He took a turn about the drawing room while Royce went to inform His Grace that he had a caller. Two walls of the room were lined with family portraits, including, surprisingly enough, one of a younger Martin Brantley and his brother astride a pair of bay hunters. Perhaps the anger between the brothers only ran in one direction.

There were several portraits of Caroline at varying ages, and he glanced over them with mild curiosity. He'd known her since she was twelve, likely the reason he hadn't become infatuated with the young beauty as Hanshaw and some of the other *ton* bucks had. One of the paintings close to the corner of the room caught his attention, and he stopped to examine it more closely. The girl, perhaps five years old and dressed in a high-waisted pink muslin, smiled as she dragged her bonnet along behind her while she strolled in front of a bed of daisies. Whoever the artist was, he had captured with stunning perfection the mischievous glint in the green eyes, and the grin that lighted her face. He smiled back and reached out to touch the child's cheek gently with the back of one finger. "Kit," he whispered.

"I trust you were successful?" Martin Brantley's deep voice inquired from the hallway.

Alex lowered his hand and turned to face the duke. "We've stopped the weapons."

"Thank God," Furth said, letting out a breath as he stepped into the room and shut the door. "You had me damned worried, Alexander."

"Myself, as well." It was time for him to tell Furth what he knew, and to ask for his help in protecting Kit from the scandal and accusations that would follow. Still, he hesitated, for if what he had done so far hadn't made an enemy of Christine, what he was about to do would ensure it. "I . . . have news, Your Grace. News you will not like hearing."

The duke narrowed his eyes for a moment, then nodded and gestured. "Proceed."

"I have the name of the smuggler we've been seeking."

"You've had the name for some time, I believe," Furth said dryly. "Or am I mistaken?"

Alex sighed, feeling rather like a student being censured by his headmaster. "You are not mistaken." Furth waited. "As you know, this is the second time I've intercepted weapons meant for Napoleon. This is also the second time one of the smugglers named . . . Stewart Brantley as his contact in France."

For a moment Martin Brantley's expression froze. "Stewart Brantley," he repeated almost soundlessly.

"Stewart . . ." He shut his eyes for a moment, then looked again at Alex. "You're certain of this?" he demanded.

"Well, y—"

"No, no, of course you are, blast it, or you would never have said it in the first place. Damn, damn, damn!" Furth paced toward the window, then to the fireplace, then back to the window, and came to a stop. It was the most agitated Alex had ever seen him, and it didn't bode well for the duke's reception to the news yet to come.

"I would have said something sooner," Alex offered, "but I wanted to be certain."

Furth turned on him. "Afraid I would do something to stop you?" he accused.

Alex steadily held his gaze. "No."

For a long moment Martin Brantley glared at him. Abruptly then, the duke seemed to deflate, and with a groan he dropped into a chair. "It's my own bloody fault, I suppose," he muttered, gazing down at his hands. "He hates me, and so he takes it out on the entire country." He glanced up again. "You've already given the information to Prince George, then?"

Everton shook his head. "I rode straight here from Suffolk." He gestured at his dust-covered clothes. "As you can see."

"So I'm to be the one to deliver the delightful news." Furth stood and walked over to survey the portraits, much as Alex had. "I knew he was doing some smuggling, actually, but it never seemed enough to warrant the scandal it would cause if I, or anyone else, were to expose him." He sighed, then reached out to straighten the painting of Kit. "Though I would have preferred that scandal to the one this will bring down on my house."

Alex took a quick breath, and resisted the urge to clench his hands together to keep them from trembling. "There was another reason I came here first," he said slowly. "Your brother's child is—"

The duke whipped around to face him. "Christine?"

he snapped, paling. "What have you heard about Christine?"

He hadn't expected the anxiety he heard clearly in Furth's voice, and it stopped him for a moment. "She . . . has apparently been living with him in Paris. I believe she has been assisting her father in his smuggling, though I'm not cert—"

"Never," Furth snarled, turning back to look at the portrait of the sunlit child. "She would never."

"With all due respect, Martin," Alex said carefully, "you haven't seen her since she was six."

Furth slowly turned around. "And how do you know that?" he murmured, his green eyes on Alex's face.

"I have met her," Alex returned. "She told me."

The duke went white. "You have arrested her?"

Alex shook his head. "No."

"Thank God," Furth whispered. "Did she happen to . . . mention me at all?"

Though the Duke of Furth was often aggravating and evasive, he always radiated a certain confidence, a sense that he knew exactly where he was headed, even though no one else had yet figured it out. This time, though, he was clearly stumbling, and Alex had to wonder why. The man was obviously fond of his niece, but it had been nearly fourteen years since he had last set eyes on her. Then again, Alex thought, glancing toward her portrait, once those green eyes smiled, they were difficult to forget. He was missing her himself, with a keen yearning that made it seem like weeks, rather than days, since they'd parted. "She didn't wish to speak of you," he answered, reaching for whatever truths were left him, "except to say that you had something to do with her mother's death."

"I didn't," Martin rasped, and sat heavily in the deep windowsill. "I didn't." He shut his eyes and took several deep breaths, looking old and used up. "Anne was a remarkable woman. I had, and still have, great admiration for her. I bear no grudge against Stewart, and certainly none against Christine." Finally he glanced up at Alex. "You know where she is, don't you?"

It was the hardest sentence he would ever utter. "Yes, I do."

The duke rose and strode quickly in Alex's direction. "Tell me."

"Your Grace, I . . . Under the circumstances, I can do little to protect her," he began, declining to mention that he had proposed marriage twice and been turned down both times. "But I thought your name would do what mine cannot."

For a fleeting moment, hope entered the duke's eyes. "Yes," he whispered. "Yes, of course. I will offer her the greatest protection my name affords. I could not do otherwise."

The words Furth spoke seemed to echo in Alex's chest with the same longing and concern he felt for her himself. "She won't like what I've done here," he admitted reluctantly.

"Is she in London?"

"Yes."

The duke pounced on the word hungrily. "Where? Where is she? Everton, I demand to see her at once."

"Friends though we may be, Martin," Alex said stiffly, "I place her wishes far above your demands." It was what he had come for, but now that it was time, he was reluctant to relinquish his secret, or her.

The duke looked considerably intrigued, but he was wise enough not to pry. "Alexander—Alex, please tell me."

He hadn't expected Furth to beg. "All right." It would have to be someplace public, where she would be concerned enough about keeping her disguise intact that she could be induced to sit still long enough to listen to reason. In private she would likely shoot the two of them and be done with it. "I'll need to speak to her first. I'll meet you at the Traveller's at eight tonight. I can't promise anything further than that, Martin."

Slowly the Duke of Furth nodded. "Thank you," he said quietly. "Now let's go see Prinny."

Chapter 18

❦

"**I**vy," Kit said firmly, "I do not wish to learn how to embroider."

Fond as she had become of the Downings over the past few weeks, Kit was nearing the end of her patience, and her sanity. They had no inkling that she'd slipped out to meet Reg last evening, but for some reason Ivy had gotten it into her head that their houseguest would sink into an unsurvivable depression if she wasn't entertained for every solid moment of the day. Their concern was touching, but the constant surveillance made it impossible for her to hunt down Augustus Devlin and at least determine whether he was still in London. What she would do after that, she hadn't yet decided.

Part of her still liked the viscount, and all things taken, Devlin wasn't all that different from her. Whatever their individual motivations, they'd both chosen to side against the English in the war against Bonaparte. Except that she'd changed her mind, and Augustus hadn't. In fact, if Alex's safety hadn't factored into the equation, she would have had no qualms about leaving him be. Business, her father always said, was business. Until someone she loved happened to be involved.

"All proper young ladies learn to embroider," Ivy commented with a slightly strained smile.

At least she seemed to be suffering from the prolonged captivity, as well. "I'm not proper," Kit pointed out, edging away in some horror from the embroidery hoop on the couch beside her. Gerald had made his escape from the morning room half an hour ago, and skinning him again at billiards, though hardly a challenge, was seeming more attractive by the moment.

"Yes, well, Alex will be required to address that problem when he returns." Ivy scowled. "For heaven's sake. Mauling you out on the balcony at the Thornhills' as though you were a . . ." She blushed. "Well, you know."

"Whore?" Kit suggested. "And he was not mauling me."

"He was, according to the Duke of Furth."

Just barely, she resisted the temptation to give her own description of Martin Brantley. It would have been very colorful, but circumspect as Ivy generally was, it would no doubt shock her. "No one knew it was me."

"I knew. And his behavior will be suitably answered for."

It was fairly easy to decipher to what her hostess was referring, and Kit frowned. Saving the reputation of a breeches-wearing smuggler was hardly a sound reason for a marriage, nor would it make it any less a trap and an obligation for Alex. She'd already turned him down in the face of a better excuse than her reputation. And part of her did wish she might be bearing his child. Then she would have part of him, a precious part of him, with her when this was done with. "Ivy, I'm not so certain pressing him on that would be a wise—"

"Kit?" a familiar voice came from the direction of the entryway.

Christine shot to her feet, her breath catching. "Alex!" She ran for the doorway.

He reached it just as she did. He looked down at her for the space of a dozen heartbeats, then grabbed her arm and glanced at Ivy in the room behind her. "Excuse us for a moment," he said, and yanked her around the corner.

His kiss was hard and ferocious, and his hands pulled her to him hungrily. She threw her arms around his

waist, surprised at her own abrupt desire to cry in relief
that he was back, safe, with her.

"I'm pleased to see you haven't sold the house out
from under my cousin." He smiled, holding her close,
and she wondered at the tired, troubled expression hiding behind his eyes.

He was dirty, splattered with mud and covered with
a thin layer of dirt and dust from the road. "The market's terrible," she answered. "And you're ruining my
waistcoat, Everton."

"I'll buy you another," he responded, kissing her
again.

"Speaking of being ruined," Ivy said from the doorway, "I think we need to have a little chat, Alexander."

The earl furrowed his brow. "All right," he returned,
reluctantly freeing Kit from his embrace.

"No, no, no," Kit argued, shoving at him to head
him toward the stairs. "It's no worry."

Alex planted his feet, his tall strength surprising as he
turned and caught her hands in his own. "What's no
worry, brat?"

"I'll tell you later," she stated, glaring at Ivy. His
return had just rattled her out of one disaster, and she
wanted more than the space of a breath before they were
tumbled into another. And she wanted to ask him about
her father, and whether he'd finally come to the same
conclusion as she about Devlin. "Alex," she pleaded.

"You'll tell me now," he ordered, his expression becoming steadily less amused as she continued to try to
nudge him from the doorway. "And stop shoving at me,
chit."

Kit took a step back and folded her arms. "*Cochon,*"
she muttered, wrinkling her nose at him.

Surprisingly enough, that brought a slight smile to his
face. He looked at her, obviously trying to decipher what
was going on, then turned to Ivy. "Well?"

"I should like to know what you intend to do about
Christine," Ivy enunciated, tapping her fingers along her
thigh.

Alex raised an eyebrow. "I haven't the faintest," he replied dryly, glancing at Kit before he returned his attention to his cousin-in-law. "Though I presume that you have a suggestion, as you brought it up."

"You did ruin her, you know."

"Ah," the earl murmured, his expression cooling further. "Innocent in assisting the whole thing along, then, are you?"

"That's enough, Alex," Gerald said from the landing.

"Yes, stop arguing," Kit seconded, grateful to hear another reasonable voice.

Gerald stepped down to stand beside his wife. "What's done is done. But Ivy's correct. You've broken the rules." His gaze at Alex was angry and concerned at the same time. "In more ways than one. It becomes a question of who will pay the price."

"If there's a price, Gerald," Alex returned shortly, "I'll pay it. Happily. Leave be."

The cousins spent a moment glaring at one another, but Kit wasn't surprised when Gerald was the first to glance away. "Damnation, Alex," he muttered. "Someday all this will catch up to you."

"Sooner than you think," he replied flatly. "Come, chit." He held out his hand, and she wrapped her fingers around his.

"Absolutely not," Ivy stated, the energetic tapping of her fingers increasing. "The two of you may be content, but it can't continue like this. Someone will be hurt." Her gaze settled on Alex. "And I doubt you'll suffer the more. Barbara Sinclair won't—"

"Damn Barbara Sinclair," Alex retorted. "I'll see her in Jericho before I let her hurt Christine."

"It would only take one sentence," Ivy insisted. "And the damage would be more than even you could undo."

Kit frowned. Ivy was correct, but there seemed to be little to be done about it. As long as Kit remained in England, Barbara could name her price. Lady Sinclair might not know the particulars of Kit's visit, but she knew that Alex wished to protect her secret. And that would be enough to keep him at Barbara's heel indefinitely.

"I think we should shoot her," Kit announced.

Alex turned to look down at her, one eyebrow raised. "You are a bloodthirsty chit after all, aren't you?"

"Just practical," she replied.

Slowly he smiled, then shook his head. "I told you, I won't let Barbara hurt—"

"I'm not worried about me, Everton."

He squeezed her fingers. "So gallant. But we can't go about murdering people—bad form, don't you know. Do give me a little credit in this, my dear. And trust me, just a little."

Kit searched his expression, seeing uncertainty in his eyes again, but she nodded. "I'll get my things."

"No, you won't," Ivy and Gerald said in unison.

"If you return to Cale House, there will be no salvaging anything, Kit," Ivy continued. "You deserve more than that."

They were worried about all the wrong things. "I already said that I—"

Furtively Alex shook his head at her.

"—appreciate what you've done for me," she finished, stifling her curious glance at the earl. "I can stay here until we figure something out."

Gerald nodded. "Very good." He cleared his throat and looked over at his cousin. "Care to stay for a brandy and tell me your news?"

Alex sighed. "Thank you, no." His gaze flicked for a bare moment in Kit's direction. "I can tell you that the news is good, for all concerned."

Her father had escaped him, then. And Alex considered that news good. He'd been after Stewart Brantley for months, she well knew. It seemed that her own loyalties weren't the only ones being tested. But the Earl of Everton had considerably more to risk than she did.

"Splendid," Gerald said, relaxing into a faint smile. "Thank God."

"Well, I'd best be off. I need to change, I believe."
He looked at Kit. "You know what they say; travelers
need to be in by eight, or they shut the gate."

"They say no such thing," Gerald returned, furrowing his brow.

"They don't?" Alex responded absently. "Well, they
should." His eyes still on Kit, he stepped forward and
took her hand again, bringing it slowly to his lips. It was
an unexpected, sensual gesture, and she felt herself flush.
"I'll come see you in the morning, chit," he murmured.

She nodded and gave a knowing smile. "Once they
open the gate."

He grinned in return. "Thought you'd heard of that
saying," he approved. With a wink at her and nod for
his cousins, he turned for the door.

"I think he may have received a blow to the head,"
Gerald offered, strolling for the gaming room.

"I hope I wasn't too hard on him," Ivy said after a
moment, "but sometimes he's so stubborn, I simply
want to bloody his nose."

Kit chuckled and followed Gerald. If she behaved for
the remainder of the afternoon, it wouldn't be all that
difficult to claim a headache and slip out the back way
in time to meet Alex at the Traveller's by eight. Before
they shut the gate, as he'd said. "Gerald, how about a
game?"

"Haven't I suffered enough at your hands?" he answered with a good-humored scowl.

"No." She grinned.

It took only three games until he was more than happy
to stop for an early dinner. Ivy had apparently given up
on teaching her embroidery for the evening, and when
Kit made a show of selecting a book from the library,
the Downings allowed her to escape upstairs. Ten
minutes later, she was in a hack on her way to the club.

It was odd that he'd wanted to meet her there, she
decided as she flipped the driver a coin, then strolled
into the club's dimly lit parlor. Cale House would have
been a much more pleasantly private place to meet with

Alex after three days apart. She had missed his touch, his laugh, his knowing azure eyes, with a keen longing she'd never felt before. It was almost frightening, the way she could so intensely crave his nearness.

He was sitting at a table in the back, where he could observe everyone else's comings and goings. He spied her immediately, and with a look she couldn't quite read, he leaned forward and poured her a brandy. "Gerald and Ivy tied up in the cellar, I presume?" he murmured.

"Nonsense," she returned, watching him carefully for any sign of what he might be thinking. "So my father . . ."

"Is God knows where, making life more difficult for the rest of us," he finished, taking a heavy swallow of brandy and glancing over her shoulder toward the door.

She followed his gaze, but only the club regulars seemed to be about this early in the evening. "Is something wrong?" she asked quietly, wanting to run her fingers along his cheek.

"Well, not entirely," he admitted, fiddling with the snifter and avoiding her gaze. "I did something that you may not—damnation, won't like, but I want you to know that it is only because I want what's best for you."

She tilted her head at him. "What the deuce are you talking about?" she demanded, an uneasy chill running through her.

Alex glanced toward the door again, then shut his eyes for a moment and took a breath. "I have to ask you a question."

She leaned forward. "Not that silly marital obligation mess, I hope," she said under her breath. "This is hardly the place for it."

He shook his head, his expression easing into humorous exasperation. "You truly play hell with a man's ego, chit," he muttered.

She gave a brief smile. "Why don't we go back to Cale House, and I'll make it up to you?" she suggested slyly.

"Wanton," he whispered. "Don't tempt me." He sat

forward, further closing the distance between them. "Do you know exactly what your father has been smuggling?"

She went still. "What did you find out?"

He reached out and gripped her fingers, which caused the gaggle of bucks at the neighboring table to begin nudging one another and chuckling. Either Alex didn't notice, or he didn't care. "Tell me the truth. Just for one damned time. Whatever your answer is, I swear I won't let anything happen to you."

She pulled her hand free. "I don't know what you're talking about," she said. "And I've already told you, over and over again, that I can take care of myself."

"This isn't about that," he retorted. "Please. Tell me."

"Ask me straight out, anything, and I'll tell you," she responded, his serious expression frightening her a little. "I won't play at fishing."

"All right." He took a shallow breath, obviously reluctant to continue. "Are you aware that your father is smuggling weapons to Bonaparte?"

Kit could only stare at him. Gold, she'd thought all along, and hadn't let herself dwell on what Napoleon might be purchasing with it. Not weapons. Her father wouldn't do that. "Liar," she spat, recoiling as he reached for her hand again.

"I am not lying." Alex's face was drawn and pale, no trace of amusement in his eyes. "Do you think I enjoyed knowing about this?"

"You are lying. My father would never—*never*—go that far." She slammed her fist on the table.

"He has, Kit. I have witnesses. And some of them say you're involved, as well."

"You bastard," she whispered. "I hate you."

He leaned forward quickly, surprised dismay crossing his features before the proud, angry mask settled over his face. "I'm trying to help you, Christine," he murmured roughly. "Don't you understand what this means? Your father is wanted by the government of England for treason. I, *I*, had to give Prince George his name this morning. And I did not give him yours. Nothing will happen to you.'' He held her gaze. ''But I need to know, just between us, if you knew about this. If you knew about the weapons.''

''You're mad,'' she snarled, shoving to her feet. ''How could you think—'' She stopped herself, unable to continue the accusation. Of course he could think such a thing. From looking at the facts of her presence here, from the spying she'd been doing, there was no reason he should not. Unless he truly knew her, knew that she could never help kill anyone. Even British soldiers. But he didn't know her. Not at all. ''I'm leaving,'' she whispered, wanting to flee before he said anything even more terrible. She turned around quickly, and slammed into someone. ''Apologies,'' she managed, backing up.

''My God,'' a faintly familiar, faintly remembered voice said from directly in front of her. ''It was you all along.''

She looked up, and froze. The Duke of Furth stood staring at her. There was gray in his hair now, and wrinkles at the corners of his eyes, and his face was a little less angular. But she'd heard his voice only days ago, and it could be no other. ''You . . .'' she began, stepping back and turning away from his gaze.

''Kit,'' Alex's voice came from behind her, more controlled now. ''I'm sorry. I hadn't expected it to happen this way. I meant to tell you first. I—''

She whipped around to face him. ''You are the traitor here!'' she shouted, unmindful of the astounded stir she was causing throughout the club. ''And I will have nothing further to do with you!'' She turned on her heel. ''With any of you!''

Alex slammed to his feet as, with a look of furious contempt, Christine turned her back on him and strode from the room. ''Kit!'' he roared, as if volume would somehow make her turn around and come back to listen to reason. She disappeared from sight, and he rounded the table to go after her. Something had gone terribly wrong, and he had more than an inkling that he had made a grave error in judgment. He hoped with all his heart that he had. But she damned well wasn't leaving until he was certain.

"Everton," the Duke of Furth snarled from beside him.

Alex had forgotten his presence, and he spared the duke a quick glance. "Later," he growled.

"Now," Furth returned, and drove his fist full into Alex's jaw.

Taken completely by surprise, the earl sat down hard on Kit's chair, which thankfully she had left standing, or he would have ended up sprawled on the floor. His first impulse was to snap back to his feet and level Martin Brantley. Instead, he sat where he was and lifted a hand to rub at his jaw. "I assume you have a damned good explanation for that," he growled.

"You knew all along that Kit Riley was my niece," Furth hissed, sitting opposite him, his face white with fury. "And I have no doubt from what I witnessed at that bloody masquerade ball, and just now, that you have ruined her. By God, Alexander, I should kill you!"

Alex leaned forward, his own temper pushed as far as it could go without exploding. "She blames you for the death of her mother, and the very mention of your name makes her ill. You—"

"That is not—"

"You," Alex hammered over the duke's protest, "are here only because after we arrest your dear brother, I didn't want her to leave my protection and have nowhere to turn." He stood, still holding Furth's angry gaze steadily. "At the moment, I don't give a damn about your concerns. I am going to find Kit." He turned for the door.

"I'm going with you," came from behind him.

Alex spared a glance over his shoulder, though he didn't slow down. "You can go to hell, Your Grace."

Kit had, of course, absconded with Waddle and the coach, which he counted as a good sign. If she was stealing his things, perhaps she could still be reasoned with. As one of the club's footmen flagged down a hack for him, he checked his pocket watch, and was rather amazed to realize that the entire argument and following debacle had only lasted twelve minutes. He ordered the coach to Cale House, reasoning that she would head where she felt most comfortable.

Wenton appeared surprised to see the master of the house returning in a hired hack, but claimed not to have seen Kit.

"Are you certain, blast it?" Alex growled, angry that he had guessed wrong. He'd been doing far too much of that this evening.

"Yes, my lord. I haven't seen . . . him for several days."

"Damnation," he said, then jabbed a finger at the butler. "If Kit appears, keep her here. I don't care if you have to knock her out and tie her up to do it. Is that clear?"

"Yes, my lord," Wenton answered, a rather anticipatory gleam entering his eyes. "Quite clear."

He sent the hack away and had Conklin saddle Tybalt, who was none too pleased at the short rest. Alex wasn't, either. Weariness and tension tightened his shoulders as he pounded through Mayfair in the dark. If she wasn't at the Downings', he was going to wring her neck.

She was at the Downings'. He knew it as soon as he rode into the drive and saw Waddle sitting on his perch looking bewildered. Gerald was halfway onto his gray gelding, his expression frighteningly sober. "Alex, thank God," he said, removing his foot from the stirrup and striding forward to grab Tybalt's bridle.

"Where is she?"

"I was just riding to find you. What in God's name did you say to that girl?" his cousin asked hotly.

Everyone in London appeared to be angry at him tonight, but only one woman's feelings concerned him in the slightest. "None of your damned affair. Where is she?"

"Alex?" Ivy's voice came from the doorway.

The worried, uneasy feeling that had been building inside him since Christine had run out of the Traveller's edged into full-fledged panic. He jumped out of the saddle and made his way around the Downings and into the house. "Kit!" he bellowed, shoving past Fender and making for the stairs. "Kit, I'm sorry! Let me explain!"

"Alex!" Gerald's sharp voice came from behind him.

"What?" he snarled, taking the steps two at a time.

"She's not here."

He froze. One hand gripping the railing, he shut his eyes. "Where did she go?"

"She came running in," Ivy's voice took up, "though how she got out, I don't know. She never—"

"Where did she go?" Alex repeated harshly, opening his eyes and turning to look down at his cousin.

"She said she was going to join her father."

Alex slowly sat down on the stairs. It felt as though the air had been knocked out of his lungs, and it took him a moment before he could even say the words aloud. "She's gone back to France," he whispered.

"We tried to stop her," Gerald offered, "but she was quite angry."

The earl lurched to his feet again. "She's a damned female, Gerald," he rasped, vaulting back down the stairs. "You could have stopped her."

He made his way outside again, the Downings trailing behind him, both wearing deeply wounded expressions. "Alex, I'm sorry," Gerald repeated.

"Don't be," he said shortly, swinging up onto Tybalt again. "She's not going anywhere. Not until I get a chance to straighten this out."

"She took my best hunter," his cousin pointed out.

"Over half an hour ago," Ivy added.

"I'll catch her in Dover," Alex insisted, trying not to listen.

"I know you're fond of her," Ivy commented, obviously trying to soothe him. "Gerald and I are, too. Quite fond. But she couldn't stay here any longer, anyway.

You know that. Perhaps she'll be better off in Paris, after—''

''No!'' Tybalt skittered beneath him at the outburst, and Alex yanked him back around.

''Alex, you—''

''No! She's not leaving me this easily. Not without one bloody hell of a fight.'' He kicked the stallion and rode out into the dark.

Chapter 19

❧

A lex paced angrily at the end of Dover pier, while Gerald engaged in a lengthy and cumbersome interrogation of an increasingly suspicious ferryman. After what felt like hours, but must have been no more than a few minutes, his cousin handed the man a few shillings and tipped his hat. With a last look at him, the ferryman strolled off, whistling, to his shanty.

"Is he certain it was she?" Alex asked impatiently, stalking over to where Gerald stood looking out over the water.

"He nearly wouldn't talk to me at all, with you standing there glowering like a gargoyle," his cousin grumbled.

"Was she on the ship?" Alex insisted, not interested in his cousin's commentary.

"Tall, well-featured, yellow-haired boy with a portmanteau, tipped well, and wouldn't talk to anyone," Gerald returned, ticking off each point on his fingers.

"Except for the not talking, it sounds like her," Alex admitted reluctantly, alarm over her safety tearing through him with each pulse of the waters carrying her away. "And of course, she just made the tide, which puts her another twelve hours ahead of me, at the least." He slapped his hand against the pilings. "Bloody chit has the luck of the Irish, that's for damned certain."

"Precisely what do you mean, 'ahead of you'?" Gerald asked slowly.

"She's not escaping that easily," Alex stated, glancing at his pocket watch for the fiftieth time since they'd left London.

His cousin began shaking his head. "No. You are *not* going to France, Alexander."

"Yes, I am."

"There's a war on, damn it!"

"I know that. And Christine Brantley's going to be right in the middle of it. And it's my fault." That was what troubled him most. Whatever she felt about him, he wanted her to be safe.

"What exactly is it that you did, to make her flee the country?"

Alex glared at his cousin for a moment. "I had Furth meet us at the Traveller's," he admitted reluctantly.

Gerald looked at him. "Why, pray tell?" he queried faintly.

"I wanted him to protect her. I'd thought to cushion the blow first, but being my usual ham-fisted self, I managed to start an argument with her over her father, instead."

"Even so, cousin, she's the one who decided to leave."

"She said she wouldn't," Alex insisted, knowing he was being stubborn and unreasonable and irrational.

"Don't you think you're being rather, how shall I say . . . obsessive?" Gerald asked carefully.

Alex looked out over the dark waters of the Channel, and at the lights of Calais glowing faintly through the mist just under the horizon. Somewhere between here and there was Christine. Weariness, frustration, anger, and loneliness hit him in succession, as they had when Ivy first announced that Kit had left him. "I love her, Gerald," he murmured.

For a long moment Gerald just looked at him. "I'll go with you," he said finally.

Alex shook his head. "If something happens to me, you are the end of the Cale-Downing bloodline. Besides that, Ivy would murder me if I let you go. You stay here."

"You are not going alone," Gerald protested, though he appeared somewhat relieved to be excluded. Alex didn't blame him. For anyone but Christine, he wouldn't for a moment consider making the journey himself. A captured Englishman, especially one in the employ of His Majesty, would be a dead Englishman.

"I'll be fine," he returned, turning back to the head of the pier for Tybalt and the hunter Kit had left behind. With almost twelve hours before the tide changed again, he would just have time to ride back to London, gather some essentials, and return to Dover to take the next ship to Calais.

"If I may pose a question?" Gerald asked, falling in behind him.

"What?"

"How will you find her once you get to France?"

Alex stopped. By the time he put in at Calais, she would have twelve hours on him. All he knew of her whereabouts in Paris was that she and her father lived in Saint-Marcel, if that wasn't another lie. Beyond that it would be hunches and guesswork, which under the circumstances would be neither the fastest nor the safest route to follow. Not that it mattered, for he would do whatever was necessary to find her. He started to answer that he would manage somehow, when it abruptly occurred to him that he might have an easier time of it than he'd imagined. "She'll come to me."

"And how will you manage that feat, when she's already crossed the Channel to get away from you?" Gerald asked skeptically.

"I told you, it was a misunderstanding," Alex growled.

"The size of Yorkshire," his cousin added.

"Shut up, Gerald." Alex swung into the saddle.

"Angry as you may be, cousin," Gerald persisted, "you're not leaving England without telling me what you're planning."

"Stewart Brantley is expecting a shipment of weapons to arrive in Calais any time now," he returned impatiently as his cousin mounted up beside him. "He'll be waiting there for them. And he'll take me to her, or I'll kill him.''

"Saints bless us, Alexander," his cousin said resignedly as they started back on the road to London. "You're going to get us all in one hell of a lot of trouble.''

Alex gave a brief grin, grateful to have something to do besides worry. "I already have. But you're right. I'm certain it will get worse."

The Duke of Furth paced in his study, unmindful that it was several hours past midnight, and that his wife and daughter had retired to their respective bedchambers some time ago. Despite Everton's plainly voiced wishes, he had followed the earl to Gerald Downing's town house. While he had been unable to overhear the conversation, from the speed at which Everton, followed by his cousin, had departed, they were in pursuit of someone, and it took little deductive reasoning to guess who it might be. It had taken even less effort to return to Brantley House and dispatch one of his more trustworthy footmen to Cale House to watch for Alex Cale, and another to Dover.

He would not let events slip away from him again. And as Everton seemed to have the best idea of what was going on, keeping an eye on the earl seemed the wisest decision. And so Martin Brantley was still pacing an hour later when the man he had dispatched to Dover returned, tired and breathless. "Out with it," he snapped, seating himself behind his desk.

"The Earl of Everton and Mr. Downing went to Dover, all right, but they weren't there for long."

"They set sail?" he asked sharply, leaning forward.

"No, Your Grace. The tide had turned. They stood about talking for a few minutes, then rode back to town like the devil was after them. I came straight back here to tell you."

"So she's gone back to Stewart," Furth muttered darkly. "Damn Alexander for not telling her I would be there." He was a little surprised that Alex had returned to London; it seemed he'd misinterpreted several things concerning Everton and Christine. Odd, that.

"Your Grace?"

"Nothing, Edmund. Go get some rest."

The footman bowed. "Thank you, Your Grace."

It made sense that the earl would return to Cale House, and Furth was less than surprised when half an hour later his second footman appeared to give his report. "An old man came to the house, and then a few minutes later he and his lordship left again. His lordship was wearing old clothes, like a commoner."

Martin Brantley watched his footman out the door and then sat back in his chair. "So he's going to Calais after all," he murmured. "And with a war on yet." The Earl of Everton had been behaving in a rather uncharacteristically haphazard manner for the past few weeks, in fact, a circumstance that coincided with Christine's arrival in London. Apparently he had been correct in his interpretation of Everton's state of mind, after all. Displeased by events and yet at the same time slightly reassured, he stood and went to wake his butler. He had some preparations of his own to make.

Calais was in a worse state than it had been when Christine had departed France a little less than a month ago. Confident as she was in her ability to navigate the streets, the heavy portmanteau she carried, and the nearly two thousand pounds inside it, made her acutely conscious of the beggars and thieves and army deserters wandering the streets in profusion. She should have left the blunt behind, but it was dearer than lifeblood to her right now. Aside from her clothes, it was all of him that she had taken, and such a sum meant less than nothing to someone as wealthy as Alexander Cale.

Besides, Everton had brought in the Duke of Furth, knowing full well how much she detested her uncle. Damn Alex anyway, for deciding he needed to take care of her, as if she were some sort of weak-minded miss. She could fend for herself. She didn't need him. And she didn't miss him. And she didn't care that Viscount

Devlin wanted him dead, and that Everton hadn't a clue.

Her father wasn't at the tiny room they kept a short distance from the waterfront, but he obviously was living there, and she heaved a relieved sigh. At least Fouché hadn't been lying about Stewart's whereabouts or his well-being. She removed the money from the portmanteau, and then stuffed the bag under her cot. They'd been burglarized before, in Paris, and she would feel safer if the blunt stayed with her.

Relieved as she was at having caught up to her father, she hesitated a time before going out to seek him. He would be furious at her for returning on her own, and for the ruckus she had no doubt made in London upon her departure. She opened the small cupboard by the one and only door the shabby room boasted, and grimaced. As usual, there was nothing to eat. It startled her a little to realize that she had eaten nothing since dining with the Downings the night before, nearly twenty-four hours earlier. With another sigh, she made her way down in the gathering dark to one of the local taverns to get a meal.

The first person she encountered in the doorway of L'Ange Déchu was a large, drunk blacksmith, and as she elbowed him out of the way and stepped inside, she reflected with a slight grin that Francis Henning would be appalled at the company she was keeping.

"Kit!" Bertrand called from his usual spot behind the bar, and lifted a pair of mugs in her direction. "Welcome back, boy!"

Kit gave him a mock salute and dropped into a chair by the fire. "Thank you, Bertrand," she returned in French, and requested a bowl of gravy and biscuits. After a month of thinking and speaking in English, except for a few choice insults to Alex, switching back to French felt odd. And in times such as these, making a slip would be dangerous. She would have to be careful.

"Kit!" Stewart Brantley's jovial voice came from the doorway, and she looked up as he stepped into the tavern. "Welcome to Calais, my son."

As Kit smiled and rose to receive a kiss on either

cheek, she studied her father's countenance, looking both for some sign that he was angry at her, and any indication that what Alex had told her about him was true. She saw nothing other than pleased welcome in his eyes, but that was no surprise. She'd played games of chance against him often enough to know how proficient he was at disguising his thoughts. She stepped back from her father, motioning him to take a seat, and called for a bottle of ale.

"So, dear one," Stewart murmured, sliding onto the bench opposite her. "Why have you left London and your cousin?"

"I was worried about you," she replied in the same tone, reluctant to tell him the entire tale. "I expected you to collect me before you vanished."

"You should know by now, child, that I can take care of myself quite adequately, and that I would come for you when I was ready for you to return." He leaned forward, a displeased look crossing his features for the first time.

Kit nodded, angrier than she expected at his cool assumption that she would simply follow his lead, even not knowing where in God's name he'd gotten to. "Forgive me for being concerned about you, then."

He raised an eyebrow. "Angry, child? I thought you would be pleased to stay with your cousin another few days."

There was the possibility, she realized, that he had known all along that Alexander Cale was his English spy. As she eyed him, though, it was impossible to tell whether he knew anything of Everton's involvement. And if he didn't know, she didn't wish to tell him. He would ask too many questions, and it would hurt too much. She didn't dare question her own silence beyond that. "Why would I want to spend more time with that arrogant bastard than I have to?"

Stewart Brantley motioned Bertrand for a plate of stew. "No reason."

"By the by," she added, "Fouché shot Lord Hanshaw before I could give him the name." She leaned forward. "Which raises the question, if the comte had his own informant, what the deuce did you need me in London for?"

He looked at her for a moment, then lifted his mug and drank. "I refuse to put my monetary and physical well-being in the hands of the Comte de Fouché." Stewart Brantley pursed his lips, brief humor lighting his characteristically hard features. "But neither do I care to put all of my proverbial eggs in one basket."

So she was simply part of his plot. That wasn't so unusual, though in the past he had at least told her the circumstances. Christine found that she didn't like the idea of being one of his pawns. "Fouché knows . . . about me," she commented, watching again for his reaction.

Stewart nodded, his cool, assessing gaze on her. "It doesn't matter. We'll be leaving France in another few days." He took another swallow. "Whichever way this commotion ends, there's more profit to be found elsewhere."

Christine stirred at her gravy with one finger. Anywhere away from London, away from *him*, seemed both terrible and a tremendous relief. She wanted to be nowhere she might ever see him again, even by accident. "Good," she muttered at her dinner.

There was silence for a moment. "So may I assume that Everton has satisfied his debt of honor to me?" her father murmured finally, looking into his mug.

"As much as such a man cares for honor," she returned, the words difficult to force out through her tightening throat. "When do we leave?"

"Ah," he breathed, sipping at his ale. "I see. He bedded you, and—"

Kit blanched. "Papa," she hissed, glancing about.

"—you suddenly became offended at the transgression and ran home," he finished. The look he gave her was both annoyed and disappointed. "Or do I err?"

It wasn't remotely what she had thought to hear. He'd expected it, perhaps even anticipated it, and had probably thought to use her connection with Everton to further

his own plans. "I didn't run because of him," she muttered between clenched jaws, abruptly very tired of being used. "He introduced me to someone last night."

Stewart's expression flicked into puzzlement for a
bare moment. "Who?"

"It seems he was concerned enough about your failure to reappear for me in London that—"

"Oh, he was, was he?" her father murmured.

"He was concerned enough about my being without
family that he introduced me to the Duke of Furth."

It wasn't strictly the truth, for she had a hunch that
Alex had been motivated more by his continuing absurd
desire to protect her from harm than by concern for her
loneliness, but it had the intended effect. Her father's
face went white. He slammed to his feet, the bench over-
turning behind him. "You spoke to that . . . bastard?"

Kit delayed answering for a moment. He kept his eyes
on her face, and she could feel his deep annoyance at
her. Angry as she was, though, she'd never refused to
answer him before, and she couldn't do it now. He was
her father, her only family. "Just long enough to take
my leave and get out."

Stewart held her gaze for another heartbeat, then let
out his breath and turned to right the bench again. "Feel
better now?" he queried.

"Not really. I've always trusted you. I don't know
why you won't trust me. I'm not a wee babe anymore."

"I know that. And so does Everton, I presume." The
tavern was filling as the night grew darker, and through
the rising sounds around them, his low voice was barely
audible. "You've become quite a dancer, Kit," her father continued. "But never dance with me. Or, for your
own sake, with Fouché." He grimaced. "At least he's
still kicking his heels in London."

"No, he's not."

Stewart blinked. "Damnation," he hissed, in English.
"You're certain?" When she nodded, her father finished
off his ale and stood. "In that case, I've something to
attend to. I'll see you in the morning."

"Why? Where are you going?" she asked, tossing a

few coins on the table and rising to follow him outside.

Though it was summer and the evening fairly warm, a few bonfires were scattered about the street corners, the citizens standing in their yellow light, laughing and passing bottles of cheap wine around. The groups were smaller than they had been before she'd left for London, and she could feel a faint line of tension in the air. Napoleon would have arrived in Belgium by now. The Duke of Wellington and the British army were there as well, and France was waiting, its breath held, to see what would happen next.

"There's a shipment waiting here for me to collect," her father was saying. "I'd thought to keep my distance for another few days, in case . . . you and Fouché were unsuccessful. But if Fouché's here, he'll be howling at my door for them."

"For what?" she asked coolly. She would have her answer now. There would be no more secrets, no more lies, and no more pawns. She would know, or they would be through.

He stopped and turned to face her. "So, what do you think you know, daughter?" he queried, folding his arms over his chest, skepticism running across his features in the near darkness.

"I think you're supplying weapons to Napoleon," she answered slowly. "And I want to know why."

"Because he'll lose, and leave me wealthy," her father replied easily. "And we won't have to live in bloody, filthy Saint-Marcel any longer."

"So you kill English soldiers to butter your bread," she snapped. "With the profit for goods, I could understand your selling supplies to Bonaparte. But weapons? Against your own countrymen?"

"They are not my damned countrymen," he snarled. "The entire island can sink into the cold North Sea, for all I care."

Kit licked her lips, and self-consciously touched her coat above the pouch of currency she carried. "What if we didn't have to sell weapons to be wealthy?"

"What's your scheme then, girl?"

She hesitated, and lowered her hand. Eventually she would tell him about the blunt, but for tonight it would remain her secret. Hers and Alex Cale's. "None. But what if it wasn't necess—"

He grabbed her arm and shook it hard enough to jar her neck. "I do not have room or time for dreaming, Kit! And it is not your place to question me, or my motives, just because you've spent a few weeks in a grand mansion in London and got yourself bedded by an earl. You weren't his first, and you won't be his last." He released her, taking a few stiff steps away and then turning back again. "*I* make the decisions for this family. Is that clear?"

Kit looked at him. Because he'd lied to her, she'd run away from the only chance, slim though it might have been, to have a happy life. She'd run away from someone she loved more dearly than she had ever thought or hoped to. But Stewart Brantley's lies and schemes were what had kept them alive for thirteen years and through a handful of wars. And, quite simply, there was nowhere else she could go. "Yes, Papa." She nodded slowly.

"Good girl. I'll see you in a few hours."

She shook her head, refusing to be left in the blind any longer. "I'm going with you."

"Ah, a child after my own heart," he cooed, and motioned for her to precede him up the stairs.

"I'm not a child any longer," she said almost soundlessly, wiping at the tears gathering in her eyes. The Earl of Everton thought her a traitor. She might as well become one.

Chapter 20

"**C**alm down now, Master Alex," Hanton McAndrews soothed. The Scotsman squatted and tugged at the ropes keeping the smuggler Will Debner in their company. Satisfied that the bindings remained tight, he faced the earl again. "Ye'll have the local constabulary down on us, ye keep bellowing like that."

"I'm not bellowing," Alex retorted, rising and stalking over to the nearest window. Like the half dozen others in the old warehouse, it was shuttered, but the wood was half-rotted from age and damp, and splintered twilight scattered over the dirt at his feet. With no air circulating, it was warm and close inside, but they didn't dare open a window for ventilation. Not with the French, growing more agitated by the moment, all around them. Even now, the faint sounds of a street rally reverberated down the narrow alleyway the warehouse backed up to. The *citoyens* were working themselves into a fine lather as battle loomed between Napoleon and the British, and Alex had no wish to be at the receiving end of their hostility. "I'm merely concerned." He scowled. "Extremely concerned."

"Our boys'll make a go of it yet, m'lord. Ye'll see," Hanton returned confidently. "They stopped him before, and they'll do it again."

"But you heard the news before we sailed, the same as I did," the earl argued hotly, frustrated and worried

323

about a certain chit who could very easily be half a hundred miles away on the road to Paris, even as he kicked his heels, waiting for her father's arrival. "Bonaparte's running Blücher down. As soon as he does, he'll cut off Wellington and—"

"It'll never happen," McAndrews interrupted, folding his arms and leaning back against the wall.

"I admire your optimism. But it looks like a rout to me." Alex returned to the stacks of crates piled against the far wall, and sank down on the nearest one. "And Prinny thanks me for stopping a few bloody crates of muskets."

"Ye have other obligations. And ye've done more than most."

Alex looked over at him. "I'm not looking for sympathy, old man."

Hanton gave him a crooked grin. "I know. I just remember how little your father wanted ye involved in any o' this. But he'd be bloody proud of ye, Master Alex."

The earl sighed and chased a dust ball about the floor with the toe of one boot. "He'd think I'm behaving like an idiot."

"Aye," the Scot agreed easily. "And I've a wish to meet this girl, could send ye marching into France in the middle of a war."

Alex grunted noncommittally, in no mood to explain himself to McAndrews—especially when he wasn't certain how, exactly, Christine Brantley had become so precious to him that he was willing to risk his life for a chance to apologize to her. It wouldn't stop there, though, if he had any say at all. He wanted her back, wanted her with an ache that hurt too much to even dwell on.

Gerald had tried to convince him that it was simply because he'd never been turned down before, and that the rejection had bruised his ego. His cousin, though, had failed to remember that Mary had done a fair job of rejecting him, and that given the circumstances, it had been unfortunate and unpleasant and regrettable, but nothing he hadn't been able to recover from. What he felt toward Kit was a raging hurricane, to the stiff breeze of Mary Devlin Cale. There was no one like Kit anywhere in his experience, and the intensity of what he felt had left him with no option but to follow her and to find her. Wherever she was. And however long it took.

He stepped on the dust ball and turned to face their captive. "You're certain Brantley will come to take the shipment himself?" Alex patted the crate he was seated upon.

Carting the crates to the ship, offloading them at the Calais harbor, taking them by wagon to the warehouse Debner had indicated, and then unloading them a final time had been annoyingly dirty and tiring work, and more than a little dangerous. But it was the best and only bait they had. He only hoped that the Duke of Furth and Prince George never discovered the details of exactly what he was up to, though he had a fair hunch His Grace would come calling to demand an explanation.

"Aye," Debner answered. "When he'll do that, though, I ain't certain. Particular fellow, Stewart Brantley."

Alex had decided against gagging their prisoner; the French would be as happy to hang Debner for setting foot in Calais as they would himself and Hanton. The smuggler apparently realized this as well, for though he groused about the ropes and the heat, he kept his silence whenever anyone came too near the old structure. At this point Alex could only hope that Prince George would be willing to overlook the fact that he had borrowed Debner from his cell in Old Bailey without receiving permission to do so. He supposed, though, that the degree of the Prince's generosity and forgiveness would depend more on Wellington's successes than on his own.

"Well, I hope Brantley comes soon," Hanton grumbled, "because win or lose, I don't want to be about when the Frenchies hear the news. They're agitated enough, not knowing. And either way, they're likely to skewer us for amusement."

"I told you to leave when the ship did," Alex reminded him darkly.

"I couldnae abandon ye, lad," the Scotsman said. "Damn me if I ever did."

Alex cleared his throat, moved despite himself. "Thank you, Hanton. But I want you to know, if Stewart Brantley doesn't appear in the next twenty-four hours, I'm heading for Paris to look for her."

Finally McAndrews looked annoyed. "Beggin' yer pardon, m'lord, but are ye completely mad?"

"As a March hare," Alex agreed mildly.

"I ain't going to Paris," Debner grumbled.

The earl ignored him. He'd known from the moment he'd decided to go after Christine that he couldn't, wouldn't, stop his search until he found her. Not until he'd fallen in love with Kit had he realized what the word meant, how much it meant. And he was absolutely certain he would never feel this way again. She was the one. If he couldn't make her forgive him . . . He shook his head. He *would* make her listen. There was nothing else he could contemplate.

The Scot sighed. "Then I suppose I'll be going with ye, lad."

As it turned out, they didn't need to travel to Paris. It had been dark for a few hours, and already two separate crowds of marchers had stormed past, shouting slogans and damning the English as they went. It would only get worse, Alex knew, and he sent up a quick prayer that Kit was somewhere safe. At half past ten, Hanton, gazing outside from between the warped shutter slats, straightened and gestured at him. "Wagon stopped outside," the Scot murmured at him as he approached. "Two men, heading this way. One of 'em has a pistol."

He stepped aside as, heart hammering against his ribs, Alex took his place at the window. Through the gaps in the shutters he could see only parts, but he had memorized all of her, and it was enough to know. The side of her face with her high cheekbones, her left hand and

slender, graceful fingers, her thigh in the blue breeches
he'd had made for her. "Thank God," he whispered.

"That them?" Hanton muttered at his shoulder.

"Yes."

"We'd best get you hidden then, m'lord."

Reluctantly Everton turned away from the window.
McAndrews was already across the room, kneeling in
front of Will Debner and slitting the ropes that bound
his legs. "You remember our agreement," Alex warned,
stopping before the smuggler. "You assist us, and we'll
lose you somewhere on the road back to London."

Debner groaned and climbed to his feet. "Aye, my
lord."

With another glance at the door, Alex made his way
across the uneven floor to the stack of crates. Swiftly he
clambered up the boxes and edged out onto one of the
wide beams supporting the roof. Debner and Hanton
could pass for smugglers, but both Brantleys knew him.
He would have to wait, and watch. A pistol rested in his
greatcoat pocket, but he had no intention of shooting
either of them, and he left it where it was.

Only secondarily was he concerned over her reasons
for being there, and the realization surprised him. It was
as if his heart had somehow grasped how desperately
unhappy and lonely he would be in a lifetime without
her. If she was a spy and a traitor to England, they
wouldn't return there. He owned a small estate in Spain,
thanks to his grandmother, and the crown could never
touch either of them there.

Hanton returned to the door, while Debner moved
over to the crates and Everton settled himself carefully
along one of the dusty beams. A fist rapped softly at the
door, and Alex fanned a cobweb from his face and
forced himself to take a slow breath.

With a glance up at him, Hanton nodded and pulled
open the door. Alex found himself holding the breath he
had taken as Stewart Brantley and his daughter greeted
Debner and, more cautiously, Hanton, and strolled into
the warehouse. Christine glanced about, her eyes tired

and uninterested as they took in the dirty surroundings. It seemed a lifetime longer than a day since he had last beheld her, and the defeated resignation in her eyes was heartbreaking.

"Apologies for the delay, Mr. Debner," Stewart Brantley said, as he walked over to nudge one of the crates with the toe of his boot, "but I'll make it worth your time."

The smuggler nodded. "Not as though there was anywhere I could go with them, anyway."

"Oh, there's always somewhere one can go," Brantley returned with a cynical half smile, obviously pleased with himself. He toed the crates again. "Well, let's open one and check my wares, and then get them loaded. They'll be starting for Belgium tonight."

Hanton and Debner dragged the crate off the stack and onto the floor. Kit stood behind the men, her expression altering a little as she looked at the mound of crates. She shut her eyes for a moment, then stepped over beside her father.

"Papa," she said quietly, so that Alex had to strain to hear the familiar low lilt, "please don't do this. We can hide them until after the war, and then sell them to whomever we wish."

A brief look of impatience crossed Stewart's face. "For half the profit."

"What if I had the means to support us for a time?" she offered.

"Do you have ten thousand pounds?" he queried, lifting an eyebrow. "Because that is what we owe the Comte de Fouché."

"But you're killing men," Kit insisted. "It's blood money you'll be making."

"Not our blood," he returned shortly, and stepped away from her.

She'd been telling the truth, then, about the weapons. She hadn't known. A smuggler, she might be, but not a traitor. Just barely, Alex resisted the urge to jump down from the rafters and pull her into his arms. He dared not, though, until he found time and a quiet place to convince her that he was merely an idiot, and that he loved her. She'd trusted him, far more than he'd allowed himself to trust her, and that was a great deal to make amends for.

They pried the lid off the crate. Brantley leaned forward and pushed the top layer of straw aside—and cursed, the gaze he shot toward Debner hard as winter. "What the devil is this?"

A faint, pungent odor drifted up toward the rafters. Kit stepped forward to peer over her father's shoulder. A stunned expression crossed her sensitive features, suspicion swiftly following. Her expressive lips twitched, and she sent a glance in her father's direction. "Onions, smells like." She took a step backward and looked about the warehouse again, her gaze lingering this time on Hanton McAndrews, who was busily looking puzzled.

You're not the only one who can play games, Alex said to himself, resting his chin on one hand as he gazed down at Stewart Brantley's infuriated expression. Let's see how much you like being played for a fool.

Her father spun around to glare at her. "Did you know about this?"

She frowned and returned her attention to him. "How could I have?"

"You knew I was shipping weapons! How?"

She hesitated. "He told me."

"Who, Furth?" he demanded.

"Everton."

"Ev . . . Sweet Lucifer," her father murmured, looking at her intently. "It was him all along."

She folded her arms, defiant and uncertain. "Yes, it was. And I knew he was after you, but I didn't know he'd found your shipment." Kit drew a breath. "But if this was his doing, I'm glad of it."

"So now, after everything I've done for you, you turn on me?" Brantley asked cynically. "What a shame, then, that you left your lover in London." He leaned forward, taking her chin in his fingers. "And you're in France, with a shipment of onions and a debt of ten thousand pounds to the Comte de Fouché. It seems, my dear, that the Earl of Everton has saved some English soldiers and gotten both of us killed."

"A shame indeed," a third voice said in French, and Jean-Paul Mercier stepped through the doorway. "Especially considering that the muskets were meant for French reinforcements even now gathering at the Belgian border." The comte's jaw clenched. "And someone *will* pay, believe me." Two other men stepped in behind him, both armed. Fouché moved sideways and pulled a brace of pistols from his belt.

From up above, Alex tried to attract Hanton's attention, but it was already too late. The Scot grabbed the crate lid and swung it into the stomach of the nearest of Fouché's men. The wood split with a loud crack, and the gunman dropped to the ground without so much as a grunt. The comte and the other man both turned on McAndrews. With a quick curse, Alex drew himself up onto his haunches and leaped. He hit Fouché in the chest, his momentum knocking both of them to the floor.

A pistol went off, close enough that stinging powder burned the side of his face. He rolled sideways and came to his feet to find himself looking straight into Christine's beautiful, astounded gaze. "Hello, my love," he said jauntily.

Her eyes flicked sideways, and he threw himself in the opposite direction as Fouché's man came at him, swinging the spent pistol like a club. Alex ducked and threw a quick, hard jab. With a windless curse, the smuggler hit the floor on his backside.

Hanton was doing a fine job of keeping his own opponent leveled. Fouché remained crumpled against the wall. Everton turned to find Kit again. A fist flew at his face, catching him flush on the jaw before he could dodge.

"Damnation!" he swore, staggering. "Stop hitting me, chit!"

She stood glaring at him with her feet apart and her arms flexed, obviously ready to level him if he took another step toward her. Her green eyes snapped with anger, and he couldn't help the relieved, appreciative smile that touched his lips at the sight of her.

"Don't you look at me that way," she snarled. "I told you I never wanted to see you again, Everton. I don't know what the deuce you're doing here, but—"

"Alexander!"

At Hanton's bellow, the earl instinctively flung himself forward, throwing both Kit and himself to the floor as another shot thundered behind him. He wrapped her lithe body in his arms and rolled sideways with her. There were far too many pistols going off in the immediate vicinity, and he wanted her as far as possible from them. He stopped with her pinned beneath him, looked up to see Will Debner going after the third Frenchman, and returned his attention to Kit.

Her hat had come off, and wavy blond hair spilled over his arm. A scratch reddened a line across one cheek, and her lips were parted as she prepared to hand him another insult. He lowered his mouth over hers and kissed her warm, pliant lips. "You left before I could apologize," he murmured, looking down at her.

"Get off me, you big lout," she snapped hotly, slamming her fist into his shoulder. "I hate you! Don't you even try to tell me you came all this way to apologize to me. You only want to arrest my father."

He shook his head, wishing that something as simple as shaking her would convince her he was telling the truth. "Finding him was the only way I could think of to find you." Behind them, Hanton was cursing, but when he glanced over his shoulder the Scot was grinning as he waded back into the fight, and Alex returned his attention to Kit.

"Some spy, then," she hissed back at him. "You don't even speak French, and you came here for *me* in the middle of a war?"

"I do speak French," he murmured.

She narrowed her eyes to emerald slits. "No, you don't."

"*Je suis un bâtard, un boeuf stupide, un bravache, et un fou,*" he offered softly.

She shook her head. "You're only repeating all the insults I handed you."

"*Non. Ce n'est pas—*"

The muzzle of a pistol pressed against his right temple. He froze, noting her startled glance up over his shoulder.

"Get off my daughter, Everton," Stewart Brantley said softly.

Kit's eyes caught and held his as he slowly raised himself up on his hands and knees. Unless he was mistaken, she was worried. About him, he hoped, and not about whether she would get bloodstains on her coat.

"Don't shoot him, Papa," she growled, scrambling out from under him as he carefully climbed to his feet. "I'll take care of it."

"No, allow me," Fouché snarled from behind her.

If she hadn't been standing there, halfway between them, Alex would have dodged. As it was, he took the ball high in the left shoulder. The impact spun him halfway around and knocked him to the floor.

With an animal shriek, Christine threw herself at the comte. Fouché cuffed her sideways with the back of his hand, and she staggered hard into the wall and sank to the floor. "You bastard!" she hissed, turning on him again.

"Christine!" her father bellowed, and she stopped her advance. "Come away!"

Instead, pulled by fear and yearning, she scrambled forward to kneel beside Alex, who lay on his back with his eyes closed. A dark stain of blood spread from his left shoulder, soaking into the dirty peasant's clothes he was wearing. "Alex," she whispered, reaching out a shaking hand to touch his face. His eyes opened. Deepest azure looked up at her, and she swallowed. She had thought never to look into those eyes again.

He gave a slight smile. *"Dites moi ques vous ne me déteste pas,"* he said softly.

Even his accent was perfect, if his timing left something to be desired. "I do hate you," she whispered. "You've lied to me about everything. More than I ever lied to you."

"That's not so."

"Ye all right, m'lord?" the Scotsman called from across the room.

His voice sounded strained, and Kit glanced up. Beloche had a pistol leveled at the old man. Both were bloody and bruised, and if not for the weapon, Kit would have given the fight to the big Scot.

"I'll live, Hanton," the earl returned, and with a wincing groan, struggled to sit upright.

"No, you will not," Fouché countered coolly. "Where are my muskets?"

"Ask my corpse," Alex stated, and Kit looked at him in some alarm. Fouché was a killer; she'd seen evidence of it herself. Taunting him was idiocy.

"So you think to make a fool of me, eh?" Jean-Paul replied. "There are other lives you risk here."

Alex's back stiffened beneath her supporting hand. "They're in London," he ground out, his jaw clenched.

"You will get them for me."

"I will do no such—"

Fouché grabbed Kit's arm, dragging her away from Everton. "You will return to London and bring them to me." His pistol aimed at Alex's head, the comte yanked Kit to her feet. His lip was cut and bleeding from his collision with the earl, and Christine had seen the look of contempt and anger in his eyes before, when he had killed Fâlo the innkeeper over a bottle of watered-down whiskey.

"Alex," she began, trying to warn him, but the comte grabbed her chin and pulled her face toward his. His handsome lips lowered over hers, crushing his mouth against hers in a brutal, foul kiss.

"Damn you!" Kit fought to free her arm and brought her hand up to hit him across the jaw.

In response, Fouché slapped her hard enough to make her ears ring. While she reeled, he shoved her down and grabbed her by the hair before she could scramble away. "You see, Everton," he said leering, "I will attempt to keep myself occupied here while you fetch me my weapons. I can use her just as well as you have. Better, perhaps."

Kit saw that Alex's face was white, his lips compressed into a thin line of pain and fury. Even her father seemed to sense that he would be wise to stay clear of this particular argument, because for once he kept his mouth shut and only stood, watching intently, looking for an opportunity.

The earl shoved himself to his feet with his good arm. "Up until two minutes ago, Comte," he said in a dark, cold voice she'd never heard him use before, "I would have been willing to let you live."

"Lad," Hanton warned from behind him, his pale eyes shifting warily between Beloche, Guillaume, Fouché, and the earl. "Don't do anything rash, now."

The comte gave a short, humorless grin and tugged hard at Kit's hair again. "Empty threats do not impress me, English. You go bring me those muskets. If they arrive in the next forty-eight hours, I'll let you have what's left of her. If she still wants you, after she's had me."

"Please do as he says, Alex," Kit whimpered, then gave a defeated sob and sagged. Alex's eyes flicked down to hers, and she held them.

He couldn't possibly know what she was up to, but he abruptly winced and doubled over, holding his wounded shoulder. Hoping he was faking, Kit reached down to her boot, yanked free her knife, and jabbed it into Jean-Paul Mercier's thigh.

Warm wetness gushed over her hand, and Fouché yelped and staggered backward. Before he could regain his balance, Everton hit him, and they both went down into the dirt. After a heartbeat of surprise, both Hanton and old Debner turned on an equally startled Beloche and Guillaume, but Christine's attention was on the fight before her.

The comte regained his footing first. He yanked her knife free from his leg, and with a snarl slashed at Alex's face. "You are dead," he snarled. *"Tu étes mort, bâtard."*

Alex ducked under the blow and slammed Fouché against the stack of crates. The top one teetered and crashed to the floor, breaking open to a pungent tumble of onions.

Outside, church bells began ringing, the sound spreading across Calais from north to south. Something exploded in the distance, coming from the direction of the sea. All afternoon she and her father had seen small groups of soldiers heading south, but he'd said they were likely deserters. Unless Napoleon was for some reason heading back to France.

Onions rolled beneath Everton's foot, and he slipped, going down on one knee. The comte darted forward and slashed. A thin red line opened across Alex's cheek, and Kit flinched. "No," she whispered. She couldn't let this go any further. Not if what he had told her was true. Not if he had come all this way for her.

She strode forward, then stopped abruptly as a hand clamped down on her shoulder.

"No, Kit," her father muttered in her ear. "They're distracted now. Let's go."

"You go," she returned, pulling free. "I'm staying."

Her father flung his arm out toward Alex. "With him? You're a fool. We'll find someone else for you."

"I don't want someone else, Papa," she retorted, backing away as he stepped forward.

"An hour ago you never wanted to hear his name spoken again," he reminded her, but stopped his advance. "He gave you a night of pleasure, and you're ready to forget all your loyalties. You're ready to forget how much I've done for you."

"You raised me to do whatever was necessary to get what I wanted. I want him."

"Bah," he spat. "You're fickle and selfish, just like your mother. I should have known better than to waste my time on you."

Gunfire sounded close outside, and she jumped.

"Don't lose your heart, Christine," her father said, the anger gone from his face as though it had never existed. "It's your mind that will win you the game, every time."

"I don't want to play the game anymore, Papa," she whispered. Fouché gave a loud curse, and she whipped around. The comte slashed out at Alex, and the earl stepped back, blood streaming from his wounded shoulder. He tripped over the shattered crate, and went down backward.

"You're dead!" Fouché snarled, and leaped, sweeping the knife down toward Alex's chest.

Kit screamed in protest and launched herself forward, even though she knew it would be too late. Frantically Everton dug for his pocket. A thunderous report echoed through the warehouse, and the comte lurched backward. He sagged onto his knees, and then toppled over, boneless as a broken marionette, and stopped moving.

For a moment Christine stood staring at Fouché, then turned to see the smoking hole opened in the pocket of Alex's coat. He looked at her, his face gray and exhausted, then laid his head back on the floor and shut his eyes.

Kit took a ragged, relieved breath. "I can't stay with you, Papa." Hopes and dreams and hard, dark reality all collided with one another in her throbbing skull. "I hope you can forgive me." She turned to him.

"You're a fool, Kit," Stewart said again. He gave her a brief, unexpected hug, pulling her close, then sighed and glanced at Alex. For a moment his expression softened. "He was a wild boy, that one. Smartest thing I ever did, saving his life. You tell him we're even." He shrugged and eyed her for a moment. "Tell Martin the same thing."

More gunfire, followed by angry shouting, sounded

from close by, and she looked toward the nearest shuttered window. "I'll tell him, Papa," she agreed, "if you're certain you want me to speak to . . ." She turned back to face him, but he was gone. "Papa," she whispered, unsurprised, and stepped over to where Hanton and Debner were dragging Alex free from the tangle of the crate. *"Au revoir."*

•

Chapter 21

"Damnation, old man," the earl rasped. "That hurts."

"Then ye shouldnae have gotten yourself shot," the Scotsman replied, as he pulled Alex's shirt away from the bloody wound.

Kit watched the two of them for a moment, then edged closer as Alex winced again. His face was still gray, and despite his half-joking words, she knew he must be in a great deal of pain.

"You should have dodged," she stated, the last of her anger at him draining away.

Everton and the Scot both looked up at her, deepest azure and cloudy gray. Alex's eyes, as they always did, drew her in, stole her breath, made her heart beat faster. "I'll remember that next time," he returned.

"Lass," the Scotsman commented, glancing between them, "if ye'd care to help me bind his lordship's shoulder, I'd be obliged to ye."

She nodded and sat on the crate beside Alex. Her thigh brushed against his, and he stirred a little, turning his head to look at her. The Scot handed her a strip of folded cloth, and carefully she pressed it over the wound. Alex hissed, but said nothing as she leaned across him. His skin felt warm under her fingers, and she wondered if he felt the same electric jolt that ran through her.

"Christine," he murmured finally into her hair, and

lifted his hand to cup her elbow. She shivered.

"Stop it," she said. "Sit still or you'll bleed to death."

"Aye," Hanton concurred. "Listen to the lass, at least."

"Apologies," Everton grunted, wincing again as they began binding the cloth around his shoulder and arm. He tightened his grip on her elbow, and leaned his tousled dark head against her shoulder. "Kit, my . . . associate, Hanton McAndrews," he muttered in a pained voice. "Hanton, Miss Christine Brantley. The woman who won't marry me."

His comment startled her. She hadn't expected him to say anything more about it. And certainly not here, and not in front of anyone else, as though he meant it.

"Where's your father?" he asked after a moment, lifting his head to look at her.

"He's gone," she returned succinctly, trying to hide her discomfiture in a last attempt at anger. "I'm sorry, but you won't be able to arrest him, after all."

He shook his head, something light and jubilant crossing his features for a moment before he sobered again. "I told you that wasn't why I came here." He shifted his good arm, leaning forward a little to brace himself upright and effectively catching her in the circle of his body at the same time. "You stayed," he said simply.

"Someone had to look after you," she said, avoiding his gaze.

"That's the only reason?" he pursued softly, sliding his cheek slowly across her hair.

A cascade of shivers ran down her spine. "You . . . truly came for me?" she demanded. "After everything that's happened?"

"Of course I did," he murmured. "How could I not?"

"But you don't have anyone to arrest now," she persisted.

More gunfire and shouting sounded up the street. Debner stood looking out the broken window slats, his expression grim.

"I imagine Prinny'll be taking care of arresting someone when we land in Dover," Hanton commented, his eyes on Alex.

"What did you do, Everton?" Kit asked, looking from one to the other and wondering again how, exactly, the earl had come to be in Calais.

"Leave off, Hanton," Alex growled, slowly removing his arm from around her as they helped him on with his shirt again. "I've merely bent a few rules. Nothing serious."

He stood, and swayed dizzily. Kit reached for his arm and hauled it over her shoulder, letting him lean on her. "I don't believe you," she said.

Alex smiled and pulled her closer into the hard line of his body. "I've ruined your cravat," he noted. "I'll have to buy you another."

"What do you want from me, Everton?" she asked slowly.

"Only the rest of your life, Christine."

"But I'm—"

"Shh. We'll argue about it when we get you safely back to Dover." The warm, wanting grip became iron and fire. "And you are coming, so don't even think about running off again," he said fiercely.

"I have nowhere else to go at the moment," she returned, wondering if he could read the thrill that went through her at his words. He wanted her, still.

An explosion from very close by rocked the warehouse, and involuntarily Kit ducked as dirt rained down around their heads.

"Getting us safely to Dover may be more of a task than we thought," Hanton grumbled.

"Can you hear what they're saying?" Everton asked Debner, taking a step toward the door.

"*Napoleon il se bat, la défaite, la défaite,*" the smuggler repeated dourly.

"Napoleon is beaten, defeat, defeat," she and the earl

translated at the same time. As she looked up at him,
surprised, he closed his eyes.

"Thank God," he whispered.

"You *do* speak French," she stated, not certain
whether to be embarrassed or angry at the realization.

"I never actually said that I didn't," he pointed out
with a hint of his old humor.

"I'd thank God more heartily if he'd let us get out of
France first," Hanton grumbled.

"And how were you planning on getting out of
France?" Kit queried, gripping Alex about the waist as
tightly as she dared.

"We've hired an old fishing boat, anchored out in the
harbor," he answered. "And we'd best go find it."

They stepped out into the street, and she paused again.
It was like walking into a scene from Dante's *Inferno*.
Buildings were on fire, black smoke churning up into
the dark, overcast sky. Torch-carrying mobs chanted
threats and obscenities at the absent British, and vented
their anger and frustration on one another when there
was nowhere else to turn it. Hanton, a few steps ahead
of them, gestured. Alex shoved her into the shadows,
stepping into the dark with her as a platoon of French
regulars hurried south and east through the streets.

"They're retreating back to Paris, no doubt," he murmured, watching them with alert, wary eyes.

Hanton emerged from an alleyway. "Debner'n I'll go
see to getting the boat ready. Don't want ye waiting
about on the docks wounded like that."

Kit could tell from the tight line of Alex's jaw that
he didn't like the idea of them splitting up, but the Scot
was right, and after a moment he nodded. "Be careful."

"Always am," McAndrews replied, and with a quick
grin led Debner back into the alley and out the other
side.

"You'd be safer with them," Alex said, glancing at
her.

She shook her head, far more concerned over his
safety than her own. "You saved my father ten thousand
pounds by killing Fouché. I'll attempt to repay—"

He straightened and pulled away from her, his eyes almost black in the heavy shadows. "No," he growled. "I'm tired of playing games, Christine. I love you, and I want to be with you. But not because of some obligation, or some lie. Is that clear?"

"You love me?" she repeated, whispering the words to keep their magic.

"Have ever since I set eyes on you, chit," he said gruffly, sagging against the wall. "And I know you love me, or at least you did, because you told me so."

"In French," she pointed out. "I didn't think you would understand it."

"Yes, you did. Lies and hiding on both sides, Kit. But it's over. We're even all around, I'd say." His eyes shut hard, and a small, strangled groan escaped lips compressed to a white, pained line.

"Alex?" she whispered.

He took a breath and opened his eyes again. "I'd thought to be enjoying this more," he muttered. Everton slid his arm back over her shoulders, his touch warm and possessive. They left the shelter of the shadows, and made their way as swiftly as they dared. More people were pouring out onto the streets as news of Napoleon's defeat spread. From the orange glow in the sky to the west, at least one of the waterfront buildings was ablaze, and they turned north in an attempt to avoid the worst of the mobs. In front of them a rabble of young men charged the front of a clothier's shop, and hurled rocks and torches in through the windows. Almost instantly the building erupted into flames, lighting the sky and the street around them for half a block.

"Hellfire," Alex murmured, trying to duck them back into the shadows. It was too late.

"*Vive Napoleon!*" one of them shouted, the cry taken up by the others as they swarmed toward Christine and Everton.

"*Vive Napoleon,*" she returned, fighting the well-honed survival instinct that told her to turn and run.

"*Qui est que c'est?*" one of them asked, jabbing a finger into Alex's shoulder.

The earl winced, but made no sound other than to take a quick, pained breath.

"He is my brother," Kit said in rapid French. "The damned English shot him two days ago, and now you fools have burned down our house."

"How do we know you're telling the truth?" another asked.

"Do you want to see the hole in my shoulder?" Everton offered in perfect Parisian-accented French. "And you touch me again, boy, I'll break your arm."

"Where do you go, then?" another asked, apparently at least somewhat convinced by Alex's show of affronted anger.

"To our uncle's," the earl supplied, "if you can avoid setting his home on fire tonight, as well."

He sagged further, and as Kit braced her knees against his weight, she couldn't tell whether it was an act or he was actually about to lose consciousness in the middle of the street. She'd never be able to drag him to the harbor on her own. "Let us pass," she demanded somewhat frantically, trying to turn the tone to indignation. "Save your anger for the English, not those who have already bled for you."

Apparently they believed her, for after shouting a few more patriotic and obscene slogans into the smoke-filled air, they ran off to the east, in the direction of the warehouse.

"Let's hope they don't find Fouché," Alex muttered, straightening a little. "I've no doubt his men would be happy to identify us."

There had been a few moments of debate over Guillaume and Beloche, but they could neither take the Frenchmen back to England with them nor kill them in cold blood. Ropes and gags would hopefully suffice until they were back out into the Channel, though with the way their luck had been running, Kit tended to doubt it. "You're a good liar," she complimented, leading him west toward the harbor again.

"*Merci, ma chère,*" he returned with a slight smile.

"What will happen to me in London?" she queried.

Unconsciously she reached up to cover the pouch of blunt he'd given her, the only escape she had left. It was gone. That explained her father's unexpected embrace. He would need it to escape Fouché's followers, anyway. "What will they do to me, after what I've done?"

"Nothing," he answered flatly.

"You can't know that," she worried, a yearning to be away from France and a greater fear of what lay before her in London leaving her cold with dread. "Perhaps . . . perhaps I should wait in Dover for a ship to take me to Italy, or Spain."

He shook his head. "We're going to London."

It was said with so much certainty that it would have been easy simply to give in and let him take care of everything. Except that she'd never been able to rely on anyone but herself. "I can't go back," she returned. "Not after what I did."

Alex stopped so suddenly, she lost her grip on him. Before she could regain it, he had turned on his heel and begun walking back the way they had come. "Then I'm not leaving, either," he stated.

She chased after him and dragged him to a stop by one arm. "Don't be a fool, Everton. You'll be killed."

"I'm not letting you go again, Kit. I'm not."

"Alex," she protested. An old beggar woman hobbled by on the far side of the street and paused to eye them suspiciously. With a stifled curse, Kit turned the earl back toward the sea and shoved him forward. "Please don't say such things. You'll make me believe them."

"I want you to believe them," he murmured, allowing himself to be pushed toward the harbor. "Because they're all true."

She did want to believe him, with all her heart. "But my father is a traitor," she insisted, still afraid to trust what she was hearing. He was delirious. That must be it; he was completely out of his head. "I'm the same, if not wor—"

"I told you I wouldn't let anything happen to you."

"You can't protect me from everything," she protested. "And Hanton said you're in trouble now, as well."

"Hanton's a stubborn old goat, and it doesn't matter anyway," he insisted.

She would have continued arguing, but he stumbled hard on the slick cobblestones, and would have fallen if she hadn't been holding on to him. "Do you want to rest?"

He shook his head, blinking hard. "We've dawdled too long as it is."

They turned down a narrow alleyway, up another street past a mob burning a makeshift Union Jack, then finally cleared the last row of shops and stepped out onto the dock. Alex came to an abrupt halt, his angry eyes turned toward the water. She followed his gaze toward the row of fishing boats on the south side of the harbor. All of them were on fire. As she watched, the nearest of them slowly canted sideways and slid into the water, to the accompanying hiss of drowned flames and white steam and smoke.

"Our boat, I presume?" she murmured.

"Yes, devil it all," he replied vehemently. In addition to the boats, half the dock was on fire, the heat blistering even from halfway across the waterfront. "Do you see Hanton?" he asked, leaning more heavily on her shoulder.

"No," she answered, trying to look for the Scot amid the clutter of the abandoned dock. "Perhaps he's looking for other transportation."

Alex nodded and shut his eyes. "I think I'd best sit down for a moment."

His legs gave way just as they reached a small cluster of empty crates and fish barrels. She half dragged him into their slight shelter, then crouched down beside him.

"This is a biasted nuisance," he grumbled, leaning back and narrowing his eyes to look across the orange-flecked water.

She reached across him to check his wound, but he grabbed her hand and held it away from himself. "Don't be so deuced stubborn," she scolded. "Let me look."

"It's still bleeding and it hurts," he returned. "Don't worry yourself."

Her lips pursed between humor and exasperation, she reached again. Again he blocked her. "Don't make me flatten you, Everton," she warned.

"That would make me feel completely recovered, I'm certain. Leave off, chit."

The next time she reached out, she grabbed his good hand and knelt on it, then swung her other leg across his hips, straddling him. It took her a bare moment to realize what an exposed and erotic position she had placed herself in, and the expression in his eyes as he looked up at her went from weary to surprised to amused in a heartbeat.

"Well, if you're that determined," he murmured. "But do get off my hand." She complied, and he tilted his head back against the barrel, surrendering.

It was the most intimate she'd been with him in close to a week, and it was a blasted pity they were in the middle of packs of rioters on a burning pier. She took a breath, then carefully peeled back the collar of his shirt to look at the wound beneath. Blood had soaked through the folded layers of cloth, oozing sluggishly from the ragged hole in his shoulder. "I'm so sorry," she whispered.

"You didn't do it," he said quietly.

"It's my fault you're here."

He opened his eyes to look into hers. "I'd have gone through far worse to find you, chit."

She sat across his hips, gazing at his exhausted, handsome face, then leaned down and very gently touched her lips to his. "I love you, Alex," she whispered.

"Then stop being so damned stubborn and say you'll go back to London with me," he insisted.

She nodded, not speaking, not wanting to be forced into promising more than that. Not when she didn't know what might happen. She would return with him, but she wouldn't tell him she would stay. Because she would never lie to him again.

He reached up his good hand to gently twist one of

the straying strands of her hair around his fingers. Another building exploded into flames just to the south of them, and she jumped.

"We're in a shocking lot of trouble, I think," she stated.

He nodded, his eyes glinting in the reflected firelight, and pulled her face down to kiss her roughly. Careful of his wounded shoulder, she reached up to grasp the lip of the barrel on either side of his head and leaned into him. All of the loneliness and hurt and longing of the past weeks melted out of her bones, out of her soul, as she kissed him over and over again, hungry for his mouth, for his touch. Nothing, nothing, mattered so much as being with him.

After an eternity of moments, shouting slowly penetrated her hearing over the crackle of burning timber. She broke their kiss and sat back a little. Alex leaned forward, pursuing her, and captured her lips again. "Alex . . . Alex," she managed breathlessly, pulling back reluctantly. "Listen!"

He turned his gaze from her face to look up along the waterfront.

"*Trouvez l'Anglais! Tuez l'Anglais!*" rose from behind the nearest of the warehouse buildings. *Find the English. Kill the English.*

"Stubble it," he grunted as she scrambled off his legs.

"Fouché's men," Kit suggested grimly. "I told you we should have shot them."

"We may still have the chance."

She helped pull him to his feet, but he immediately doubled over, and would have fallen if not for her arms about his waist. "Everton?" she murmured, holding him tightly.

"I'm all right," he said after a moment. "Just dizzy." He turned north toward the shops that covered the end of the waterfront, tugging her after him. "Let's get you hidden." He pulled out his pistol and carefully reloaded it, his left hand clumsy.

"Let's get *you* hidden," she countered, glancing at

his grim face in some alarm. "You're in no condition to be a damned decoy. Papa and I have a room just to the north."

"Someone has to watch for Hanton," he insisted stubbornly.

"I'll watch."

The shouting abruptly became very clear, and she looked south. Beloche and Guillaume came out onto the waterfront, a mob of Frenchmen streaming behind them. They immediately spied her and the earl, and the yelling took on a bloodthirsty timbre that sent a chill down her spine.

"Tuez l'Anglais!"

"Get behind me!" Alex growled, and yanked her closer. "Into the alley!"

A musket ball tore into the barrel right beside her, and she involuntarily shrank against him. In all her escapades, she'd never actually been shot at before.

"Go, Christine!"

"I won't leave you!" she returned, grabbing on to his sleeve as he tried to shove her toward the alleyway.

"Kit, don't be a f—"

"Everton!"

The voice wasn't Hanton's. Kit whipped around toward the north end of the dock.

"Reg!" Alex called back, exhausted relief edging his voice.

He pushed her toward Hanshaw. A pair of men pounded behind the baron, Hanton and one other, as he charged forward to meet them.

Reg fired past her, and someone behind them screamed. She and Everton dodged past barrels and crates and burning debris, making their way north. Hanton gave a Scots battle yell and discharged his musket.

The third man fired off a shot from a pistol. She'd thought him Will Debner, but as the groups neared one another it became obvious that he was not. Christine balked. Alex slammed into her from behind, cursing as he wrenched his shoulder.

"Go!" he ordered, turning to fire his own pistol.

"It's Furth," she returned, pushing back against him.

"I don't care if it's the devil himself!" he said. "They're the ones who aren't shooting at us. Go!"

The mob was close behind them, and they weren't slowing even with the return fire eating into their ranks. She hauled Alex's arm over her shoulder, clasped his waist with her other hand, and began running.

"Can you shoot?" the Duke of Furth bellowed at her above the din as she and Alex reached them.

"Yes!"

He finished reloading a pistol and tossed it to her. She winced at the spent heat of the barrel, flipped it around, aimed at Beloche, and fired. The smuggler went down on his face, heels over head, and stopped moving. The rest of the mob didn't. Hanton pulled Alex away from her, and they started out along the narrow, northernmost pier. A private yacht was tied at the end of it, she realized, a fourth figure waving them on from beside it.

Reg gestured with his pistol for her to precede him, then dumped a substantial pouchful of powder onto the center of the pier. Kit turned and ran. The explosion behind her made her stumble, and she glanced back to see a good twelve feet of pier vanished. Hanshaw and Furth pounded behind her.

Hanton was helping Alex up the wildly swinging rope ladder when she reached them. A pistol discharged directly in front of her, and she flinched, surprised. The ball that passed through the Scotsman's hand and flung him backward onto the slick pier also grazed her temple, and she slammed into one of the pilings. Fire erupted in her skull, and she staggered to one knee.

"Kit!" Alex roared, dropping back down to the pier. *"Don't bloody move!"*

Alex skidded to a halt as Augustus Devlin stepped away from the shelter of the hull. Silently he pulled a second pistol from his belt, and leveled it at the earl's back.

"Christine," Alex murmured, his expression unnervingly grim, his eyes on the blood trickling down one side of her face.

"I'm . . . I'm all right," she gasped, holding on to the piling to keep from pitching into the water.

"Turn around, Everton."

"Devlin, put that away," Furth ordered from behind her. "We've no time for this. Have you gone mad?" To add an exclamation to his sentence, a pair of musket balls tore into the stern of the yacht with a hollow thunk.

"Completely," Augustus agreed calmly, his gray eyes burning. "Turn around, Alexander."

With a last look at her, Alex did as he said. Christine hauled herself upright, her head throbbing. Hanton knelt opposite her, cradling his left hand in his right, his eyes narrowed points of fury directed at Viscount Devlin. Reg and Furth stood behind her, and beyond them the mob continued to shout obscenities and fire in their direction.

"Augustus," Alex said, his voice tight, "put it down. Now."

"You should have listened to Kit," Devlin returned evenly. "She knew." His eyes flicked in Kit's direction, and the madness there stilled her heart. "You killed my sister, you bastard," he continued. "My only family. And now you go on, find yourself another little bit to rut with, and leave me dying. I'll have my vengeance, Everton, cold and bloody."

Kit released her hold on the piling and slid one foot carefully forward. Devlin's eyes remained locked with Alex's. She dared not protest; if she spoke and Everton broke his gaze, Devlin would fire. She was certain of it. And it would be her fault, and she couldn't live with that.

"I did not kill her, Augustus," Alex said. "I'll not lie. I didn't love her, but I did not want her dead."

Augustus shook his head slightly. "And I say I'll not go to hell alone. I want you there first, Alex, to guide my way." His hand jerked, his fingers tightening on the trigger.

Kit took a swift breath, shut her eyes, and stepped in front of Alex. The pistol thundered, followed in echo by another. A hot rush of wind lifted her hair at her neck, and then Alex slammed into her from behind, throwing them both to the hard wood. Something fell heavily into the water before her. She twisted her head to see Hanshaw lowering a smoking pistol, his face white. Augustus was gone.

Alex pulled her to him and wrapped his arms around her tightly. "Christine," he rasped, his voice nearly a sob.

"I'm all right," she returned shakily, grabbing on to his coat and pulling him closer with frantic fingers. "I'm all right." Tears spilled from her eyes as she folded herself up against him. He was alive. He was alive and Augustus was dead.

"By God, lass," Hanton muttered. "Sweet Jasus."

"We have to go," Furth's deep voice came, subdued and tense. "Tide's nearly out, and they've almost got the pier planked."

Reg helped them both to their feet. His expression was hard and grim, his eyes on hers. "He said he wanted to help," he said tightly. "You were right. I should have listened to you."

Everton grabbed her shoulder and jerked her around to face him. "Never," he hissed, his face whiter than Hanshaw's, "never do that again."

"In a heartbeat," she said, her voice breaking, covering his hand with hers. Never had she felt that way before, that she would die to protect another's life. It was frightening and comforting at the same time, to know deep inside her that he felt the same.

"Let's go," Furth ordered again, hauling Hanton to his feet and helping him up the ladder. The rest of them climbed onto the deck. Hanshaw and the duke released the guide ropes, and the yacht drifted out into the harbor. Devlin had locked Debner and the crew below, and the baron freed them. Once safely out of musket range, they unfurled the sails, and the wind and tide pushed them north and west toward Dover.

Kit found herself crowded into the main cabin with Everton, Reg, and the Duke of Furth. Alex sat her down on a bench and pressed a cloth against her temple, his expression so worried that she had to smile. "Let go," she complained, trying to take the compress from him. "I can hold it, thank you very much."

"I will hold it," he stated, refusing to relinquish his grip.

"You're wounded more badly than I am," she retorted.

"Despite every effort on your part," he added darkly. "That was worse than foolish, chit."

"Next time perhaps you'll listen to me when I tell you one of your cronies is a spy," she sputtered. She could feel Furth's eyes on her from across the cabin, but refused to look in his direction.

Everton's expression became still. "I never knew he hated me so much," he murmured, so that only she could hear.

"Oh, Alex," she whispered.

The Duke of Furth stirred, hesitated, and then took a step forward. "Can I offer anyone a brandy?" he queried.

Alex kept his eyes on Kit for a moment, then handed her the cloth and turned to the duke. "I owe you a debt of thanks, Your Grace," he said. "You have impeccable timing."

"It was half blind luck," Reg offered. "His Grace figured out where you'd gone, and Gerald found me, but we foundered about the harbor all evening before I spied Hanton trying to steal a boat." He paused. "We weren't certain you'd even be here. It was suggested you might have gone on to Paris."

Alex gave a quick glance at Kit. "We nearly did."

Furth cleared his throat. "Any word about my brother?" he asked slowly, his gaze flicking between her and the earl.

"He's gone," she said brusquely when Alex chose to remain silent.

"He left you?" the duke asked more sharply.

"I wouldn't go with him," she corrected, and Alex stirred beside her.

"Christine," Martin Brantley said, taking a breath, hesitant and unsure. It was so different from anything her father had ever exhibited that it caught her attention. "I . . . know you believe some awful things about me. I may not be able to change your mind, but I'd like, very much, the opportunity to tell you my side of the story."

Kit didn't want to listen to him. It must have shown on her face, for Everton leaned sideways. "Hear him out, at least," he said quietly. "I've known him to be a fair and honest man. But you never need to see him again after tonight, if you don't wish it."

Furth didn't like that; she could see it in the tight set of his jaw. Apparently, though, he considered it wiser to be silent and let her make up her own mind. That silence, the willingness to wait, was what decided her. "I'll listen to you," she conceded. "And that's all."

Reg stood. "I should go check . . . on something. On Hanton," he offered, and stepped quickly from the room, shutting the cabin door behind him.

"Do you wish me to leave?" Alex asked her.

She shot him an annoyed look, for this reunion was all his fault, after all. "Don't you dare," she growled.

He gave her a brief smile. "I'll take that as a no, then."

Furth looked between the two of them for a moment, then took a seat opposite. Rubbing his hands together, his gaze directed downward, he inhaled deeply. "I don't know how to begin this," he said, lifting his head to look at her again.

"Do whatever you please," Kit replied sharply, trying to hide her nervousness in her temper.

"Very well." He cleared his throat again. "Your mother, Anne, died of pneumonia. I did not harm her in any way. I couldn't have. I was . . . very fond of her." Christine squirmed, wanting to protest that she had heard all of this before, but the look in his eyes stopped her. Whatever it was he had to say, it was something that had been eating at him, perhaps as much as it had eaten at her father, and at her. "My first years of marriage to Constance were difficult," he continued. "It was arranged by my father, and I knew little more about her than her name and the size of her dowry. When I met your mother, she was betrothed to Stewart. And I was dumbstruck.''

''You go too far,'' she burst out, standing. Alex climbed stiffly to his feet beside her, evidently to leave with her if she chose to do so.

''Christine,'' the Duke of Furth pressed, ''I do not mean to hurt you. But you need to know this. And I need to tell you. Finally. Stewart left England after Anne died because she finally at the last moment told him— confessed to him—that you were not his daughter.'' He bowed his head. ''You are mine.''

A rush of ice swept through Kit, freezing her down to the marrow of her bones. ''No,'' she whispered.

''Good God, Martin,'' Alex growled angrily, ''you might have done that with a little more finesse.''

''You knew?'' she demanded, whipping around to face him. If he had lied about this, it was one lie too many.

He shook his head wearily. ''I suspected that part of the tale was missing. I had no idea what, though.''

''You believe me, then,'' Martin cut in, clenching his hands together, but making no move to close the distance between them.

''I don't know why I should,'' she stated, abruptly tired and hurt and wanting to go somewhere very quiet and think.

''Stewart was furious . . . understandably so, at the news. He thought, I suppose, that I had taken the last thing he had of Anne away from him. So he took you away from me.'' Finally he took a step forward. ''I looked for you for quite a long time. I tracked the two of you to Spain, then lost you somewhere in Italy. I would hear rumors and set out after you again, only to find no trace. And Caroline was growing into a spirited young lady, and I had other duties . . .'' He looked down, then met her eyes squarely with his light green ones. ''But I never gave up hope of finding you.''

''I—'' Kit began, then stopped. It made sense. The different places they'd lived, her father's hatred of everything English, and especially his brother, his plan of dressing her as a boy to keep her safe. She looked up at Alex, to find him gazing at her, sympathy and compassion in his eyes. "I don't know what to do," she confessed.

"I'll give you time, of course, to consider what I've said," Furth offered, unexpectedly understanding. "I know it's not an easy thing." With a last hesitant look in her direction, he turned and left the cabin.

Christine stared after him for a long time. "Not an easy thing," she muttered. "Not an easy thing."

"Bit of an understatement, under the circumstances," Alex commented, echoing her thoughts.

She turned to face him. "What am I going to do?" she asked, reaching a hand out. He took it in his own. "This is too much. It's too much."

"It's piffle, compared to what you've been through," he said flatly. "You'll manage."

"But he'll want me about now, dutiful whatever it is I am to him, and I don't want to live with him."

"That's simple," he murmured, and touched her cheek with his fingers. "Live with me."

"As Kit Riley? I don't think—"

"As the Countess of Everton, Christine," he interrupted.

"I can't marry you," she returned, wishing for nothing more than to be able to say yes. A storybook maiden would have been able to say yes, but she would never have a smuggler for a father—an uncle—and she would not be illegitimate or a spy.

"Why in God's name not?" he snapped, obviously beyond exasperation.

She reached for an excuse, her mind and her heart tearing her in two directions. "You don't mean it."

"Haven't I given you enough bloody proof that I mean it?" he countered. "If I haven't, then by God, please tell me how I can prove to you how much I love you." He brushed a strand of hair from her face. "You made me see how very lonely I was before you came into my life. I don't ever want to be that way again. I don't ever want to be without you. *Je t'aime, ma chère,*" he murmured. "I love you. Say you'll marry me."

Christine was having difficulty breathing. "It almost sounds as though you mean it," she whispered.

"I do mean it. Marry me."

She took a step backward, and he followed her. "But I'm completely absurd," she protested. "I don't know how to do anything female, and—"

"Yes, you do," he pointed out, wicked amusement touching his gaze.

She blushed. "Not anything proper," she countered. "And I'll never fit into society, Alex, you know I won't."

"Marry me," he insisted, pursuing her as she continued to retreat. "The Countess of Everton may be as eccentric as she pleases."

"But why do you want *me*," she insisted desperately, "when you could have anyone? Barbara Sinclair would give a limb to wed you."

He tilted his head at her. "Because I will die without you," he said simply.

She stopped her retreat. Her heart was pounding so hard, she wondered that it didn't burst through her chest. "No, you—"

"I want to see you in gowns and curls, and in those damned uncomfortable pointy-toed shoes," he said. "I want to see you at Everton. I want you to teach me how you cheat at hazard. I want you to insult me in French. I want to see your smile and your eyes in my children's faces." His expression became more serious. "And I don't ever want you to leave me again."

"Alex," she whispered.

He wouldn't stop his assault. "I love you, Christine Brantley. Marry me. Please. *Mariez moi, s'il vous plait.*"

She shut her eyes, trying to shut out the images he was conjuring, but that only made them more vivid. He gently kissed her eyelids, and tears fell from beneath them. He kissed them, as well.

"Please say you'll marry me, Kit, because you're breaking my heart."

She opened her eyes. "I can't imagine myself anywhere but with you," she said. "I will marry you, Alexander Lawrence Bennett Cale."

He smiled at her, his eyes lighting with relief and elation. "Thank God."

Chapter 22

The Earl of Everton was exhausted. He was also sore, battered, and bruised, had a hole in one shoulder, and atop everything else, he was afraid to fall asleep. It was not that demons haunted his nightmares, or that he worried his wounds were so severe he would expire in the night. Actually, he was terrified that when he awoke in the morning, he would discover that everything that had transpired over the last twenty-four hours had been a dream.

And so he lay awake, counting the chimes of the grandfather clock on the landing, and trying to decide whether it would be worth the effort to go fetch himself a glass of brandy, or whether he should actually be outside Gerald and Ivy's, watching to make certain that Kit didn't change her mind during the night about marrying him and attempt to flee again.

Martin had wanted her at Brantley House, but she had adamantly refused. With the speed at which her world was changing, Alex wasn't surprised. The duke had apparently understood as well, for other than making her swear that she would still be in London in the morning—not all that safe an oath given that she would then consider being anywhere within the environs of the city to be keeping her word—he hadn't pushed her over her choice of residence. Alex hadn't either, though it had been supremely difficult to watch her climb into the

Downings' carriage and disappear once more into the night.

The clock chimed four, and he sighed irritably. It didn't help his ease that Prince George had left a missive indicating that he was expected to appear for an audience immediately upon his return to London. Fouché's death would certainly help put him back in favor, but there was still the theft of Will Debner, the betrayal and death of Augustus Devlin, and his own outright lies to explain.

The handle of his chamber door turned. Alex tensed and narrowed his eyes as the door swung slowly open and a figure in coat and breeches slipped into the room. A short tail of blond hair, silver-blue in the fading moonlight, caught his gaze, and he relaxed. "How did you get in here?" he asked quietly.

Christine jumped, then shut the door and turned around. "Damnation, Everton, you nearly scared me witless. I thought you asleep." She stepped forward, stopping beside the bed. "I climbed in through the library window. You'll need to fix the latch."

"I don't think I will," he returned, looking up at her. "Not until we're married, at least. Not every man has his wife-to-be breaking into his home to speak to him in the middle of the night."

With her fleeting grin, she climbed up onto the bed and swung her leg across his hips, straddling him. "Who said I was here to speak to you?" she queried boldly.

He chuckled, delighted. "I'm wounded, chit," he said in mock protest.

Immediately she shifted off him. "Then I won't disturb you, *monsieur le châtelain. Bon soir.*"

Alex reached up and grabbed her arm, yanking her back down over him. "You're not going anywhere," he informed her.

Christine leaned down and kissed him, slowly and possessively. "That's better," she murmured, straightening again.

She rocked back and forth across his hips, obviously experimenting. The familiar slow fire he always felt in her presence began burning hotter, and he grinned, half closing his eyes. *"Baisez moi encore,"* he demanded softly. "Kiss me again."

Kit kissed him again, running her tongue along his lips and his teeth, teasing him as he had teased her. Then she lifted her hands to her cravat and slowly untied it. With a slither of silk she pulled it free and cast it aside, letting it drift to the floor beside the bed. She raised herself up onto her knees so he could free his nightshirt, and she helped him pull it from his wounded shoulder and off over his head. He would have sat up, but she firmly pushed him back down flat. While he watched her, she settled down on him again, only her leggings and the thin blanket about his hips between them.

"Do you believe in fate?" she asked, tracing the outline of his bandages with her fingers.

He reached up and pulled the band from her hair, letting the wavy blond cascade flow loose through his fingers. "I didn't used to."

"And now?" Christine leaned down and touched the tip of her tongue to his flat nipple, then trailed across his chest to repeat the action with its twin.

Alex drew in a breath through his teeth, more than burning now. "If I hadn't been trying to catch that frog," he began slowly, watching as her coat, carefully folded first, followed the cravat to the floor, "and if I hadn't fallen into that river at just the moment Stewart Brantley came by on his morning ride," he continued as her waistcoat dropped off the side of the bed, "and if he hadn't known how to swim and jumped in after me," he added as the fine lawn shirt came off over her head, "then twenty years later, he would have had no excuse to bring you to me when you needed a place from which to spy on English lords."

"And so?" she whispered, drawing the wrap from around her breasts and letting it slide to the floor.

"And so yes, I do believe in fate," he told her.

She leaned over him, her hair falling in a curtain around her face, and covered his lips with her own. This time her exploration of his mouth was hungry and demanding, and he reveled in the fact that she wanted him as badly as he wanted her. He slid his hands up to caress her full breasts, rolling her tender nipples between his thumb and forefinger, feeling them tighten in response, feeling her quick intake of breath and the way she arched toward him.

Christine lifted onto her knees again, letting him undo the fastenings of her breeches and help her pull them down her long legs. This time when she settled back on him, he moaned, and she smiled. "I believe in fate, as well," she whispered.

"Before we get along any further," Alex said, doing his damndest to keep from throwing her over and having at her, "I should like to mention that you've missed my surprise."

She rocked back and forth across him again, rendering him painfully hard, and obviously loving the torture she was inflicting. "I don't believe I've missed anything at all," she countered with a sly grin, her face flushed and her breathing fast and shallow. "But what is your surprise, *mon amant*?"

"Look," he gasped, gesturing behind his head. "Two pillows."

Christine looked down at him, then threw back her head and gave a full-throated laugh. "So you do listen to me occasionally, after all, then," she chuckled, and raised up just long enough to yank the blanket down past his knees.

"As long as you persuade me in this manner, I'll always listen to you," he promised.

"I like your surprise," she continued, as she reached down to grasp his full, hard, manhood, positioned herself over him, and then slowly, excruciatingly slowly, sank down to sheathe him in her tight, hot flesh.

"And I love yours," he groaned.

She laughed again, breathlessly, and placed her hands flat on his chest to begin lifting her hips up and down, faster and faster, again and again. "A shame we won't be needing the pillows." She moaned, flinging her head forward as he gripped her buttocks in his hands, holding her against him, thrusting upward with his hips to match her rhythm. She cried out as she began to pulse, pulling him in deeper, and with a groan, he sped his own release to join her.

"I don't like this," Kit muttered to Everton as he lounged beside her in an anteroom outside the packed Brantley House ballroom, munching on a biscuit and looking as though he hadn't a care in the world.

"I do," he replied unsympathetically, and glanced up as a footman cracked open the door.

"It'll be just a moment, my lord," he said. At Alex's nod, he shut the door again.

Another flock of bats took flight in Kit's insides, banging about so energetically, it took an effort not to become ill. Actually, that wasn't such a bad idea. It would get her out of what was coming, at any rate. "I'm going to be sick," she announced.

Everton straightened and tossed his biscuit into the branches of a potted plant. "You are not, chit," he stated. "And if you are, I'll carry you out there anyway."

"You're an evil man," she retorted. "You don't even care that I don't want to be here."

"Of course I care. It's best for you, though, and you know it."

"I know what's best for me, and it's not wearing this gown and going out there in front of everyone, and telling them I've been lying to them all about who I am."

"It's a lovely gown, my dear," he soothed. "The same emerald as your eyes." He chuckled, then sobered when she glared at him. "I'm certain your father is spinning a wonderful tale. And even if he isn't, once you're presented as the Duke of Furth's daughter, no one will dare gainsay you."

She'd been against the plot from the moment Furth and Everton had cooked it up, but for once Alex had absolutely refused to listen to any of her objections, protests, and arguments. On the surface, of course, it did seem rather clever. Furth had called a grand ball to announce the return of his long-lost daughter, with the idea that he would spend the evening confidentially informing a select group of his fellows that Christine had come to London in the guise of a youth in order to stop her uncle's purported smuggling activities. In the course of looking for assistance she had found the Earl of Everton, and the two of them had fallen in love. Then, after Furth's trusted friends had been given enough time to bandy the tale about the entire assemblage, she and Alex would appear, fashionably late, to be announced.

The tale did make her sound rather noble, and it kept Alex's activities secret, but nothing could disguise the fact that she'd been lying to most of the London nobility since her arrival. She was more than uncomfortable with facing them about it. They might not know her true purpose for being there, but they knew they'd been made fools of. And if she'd learned one thing, it was that the *ton* didn't like to look foolish.

"You should at least have let me wear my breeches," she grumbled, tugging at her bodice and wishing it didn't fit quite so snugly. "I feel so . . . exposed this way."

"No more lies, Christine," he said quietly. "We agreed on that."

"I know, I know. But that was between you and me. They"—she gestured toward the ballroom—"don't count."

"Well, not entirely. But to preserve the reputation of Everton, past, present, and future, I want it to be known that I'm marrying a female, and not an ill-mannered boy."

Kit was so nervous, her hands were shaking. "Alex—"

He stepped forward and put his hands on her bare shoulders, his touch warm and solid against her chilled skin. "You won't be alone, Kit. I know you're strong, and I know you can take care of yourself. But you *may* rely on me." He very gently touched his lips to hers. "Just for once, let me take care of you." He kissed her again. "Trust me."

Kit followed his lips as he retreated, seeking Alex's

mouth, and he chuckled as she kissed him back. "Are you certain there isn't something else you'd rather do than engineer my public unveiling?" she suggested slyly, pushing him backward against the couch and fingering the buttons of his waistcoat.

"What a hoyden you are," he murmured, encircling her waist with his arms.

The door opened again and Furth's butler appeared. "His Grace believes it is time for your arrival," Royce informed them, then stood aside to hold open the door.

Alex sighed and rested his forehead against Kit's. "Be brave, my love," he whispered. "Since you were ready to take a ball in the heart for me, this should be easy for you." His eyes held hers for another moment, saying more than words could.

Kit sighed, then took his proffered arm. They entered the hallway and, preceded by Royce, walked up to the ballroom door. Everton squeezed her fingers encouragingly, then nodded at the butler.

Royce threw open the door, stepped through ahead of them, and came to attention at one side of the doorway. "My lords and ladies," he intoned in a carrying voice, "the Earl of Everton and Lady Christine Brantley."

Everyone turned to look. The rumble of voices and music faltered. No doubt most of them expected something out of the ordinary—a skinny boy in a gown, perhaps. From the cacophony of noise that erupted as she and Alex entered the room, though, they hadn't been expecting *her*. Being recognized and appreciated as a female was still a very new sensation for her, and nervous though she was, it was rewarding.

"By God, she's Lady Masquerade," Philip Dunsmore uttered. He turned to guffaw at the Marquis of Hague, who looked as though he wanted to sink through the floor. "You were dancing with a boy, Hague!"

"She's a blasted female. Anyone can see that," Hague mumbled, grabbing frantically for a brandy.

Kit glanced at the assembled faces all looking back at her. Alex stood calmly at her side, obviously not caring a fig what anyone might think. Her gaze paused on Mercia Cralling, who stood staring, white-faced. Celeste Montgomery beside her giggled and whispered something to another friend. Abruptly Mercia shrieked, dropped her glass of punch, and fell to the floor in a dead faint.

"Oops," Alex murmured unruffled. "You do have a certain effect on people, dear one."

He touched her hand again, and they strolled across the floor toward the refreshment table to give the rest of the guests a chance to look her over. Kit's legs felt wooden, but Everton's arm was strong and unwavering, and she simply kept moving and held on for dear life.

"How dare she," Lady Crasten muttered to a companion as they neared. "Pretending to be a boy to snare Everton out from under—"

"Lady Crasten." Reg's voice came from Kit's other side, though she hadn't heard him approach. "I know you've met, but I should like to formally introduce you to Lady Christine."

Lady Crasten swirled about with a rustle of skirts, a beatific smile on her thin face. "Of course. Lady Christine," she gushed, taking Kit's free hand in both of her own, "I'm so pleased you're safe." She leaned closer as though speaking in confidence, though she didn't bother lowering her voice. "I hope you're not alarmed to know that I did suspect you, my dear." Her smile widened. "I told Lisette that you were far too lovely for a boy, you know."

"Thank you, Lady Crasten," Kit managed, torn between annoyance and amusement, and retrieved her hand. Thankfully the countess beat a swift retreat, and Kit turned to greet Reg with a smile. "And thank you, Reg," she said, relieved to see a friendly face. "I've not seen you for a few days. I thought you might be angry."

He sketched a bow. "My pleasure. I admit to being a bit startled in Calais, but I've had time to recover my wits. I did think a few things about you didn't quite add up, especially that night at Vauxhall, but . . ." Reg trailed off and gestured at her, grinning. "I am humbled."

"Well, I am baffled," Francis Henning added from behind Reg. "Just when did you become a female, Kit?"

Christine stifled a smile. "I've always been one, Francis."

"But you drank me under the table and took me for twenty quid at hazard," he complained. Then he blanched. "And I asked you to marry me, didn't I?" He turned to Everton. "Didn't mean it, Alex. I thought she was a boy—I mean, not then, of course, but I didn't know—"

Alex raised a hand and chuckled. "No worries, Francis. I find it all rather confusing myself at times."

"Well, thank God," Francis sighed. "I thought it was just me."

The Duke of Furth appeared, the crowd parting before him, and with a wink Reg dragged Francis into the background. With a warm smile, hesitation only in his eyes, the duke kissed Kit on the cheek and shook Alex's hand.

Taking two glasses of champagne from a footman's tray, he gave them to Kit and Alex, then took another for himself. "My lords and ladies," he said, turning to the assembly, "I should like to take this opportunity in front of you, my friends, to make two announcements. The first is that my daughter Christine"—he took her hand—"has been returned to me after years of separation." Their audience applauded, and he nodded graciously. "The second is that yesterday Alexander Cale, the Earl of Everton, asked my permission to wed Christine. I have given my consent."

That was a lie, for Alex had never actually asked anyone's permission but her own. A second round of applause began, interrupted by a flurry of movement to Kit's left as her cousin—no, her half sister—Caroline hurried up exactly on cue and hugged her, making a great show of being surprised. She, of course, had learned the news several days ago, and had been more than willing to participate in the charade. "You should have told me who you were," she had said with a delighted smile when Furth had first dragged Kit, nervous and unwilling and firmly in the company of Everton and the Downings, to Brantley House. "I would never have given you away, you know."

The next minutes were a blur of congratulations and toasts and *sotto voce* speculations as to the exact nature and circumstance of her parentage. Alex fielded most of the more direct inquiries, cool and amusing, yet aloof enough that no one asked too many sticky questions.

As another familiar face approached, the muscles of Alex's arm tightened, but he gave no other sign that he was the least bit ruffled. "Barbara," he intoned, inclining his head.

"Allow me to tender my congratulations to the happy couple." Lady Sinclair smiled, showing her teeth.

"Thank you," he answered, with a return smile that left his eyes cool. "And I do appreciate the care you took in keeping Lady Christine's secret safe."

"Of course," Barbara answered, spearing a glance at Kit.

Christine found herself feeling more sturdy than she had a moment ago. Direct hostility was easier to deal with than the toad-eating and bootlicking she and Everton had been subjected to since they entered the room. "And I am sorry," she offered with some relish, "for any misunderstanding that might have arisen regarding Alex's . . . intentions toward you."

"Oh, not to worry," Barbara returned warmly. "My relationship with Everton has nothing to do with his intentions toward *you*, I'm certain."

So she thought to continue as Alex's mistress after their marriage! Kit coiled her fist and longingly imagined pulling out a handful or two of Barbara's lovely black hair. "I suggest," she bit out, "that you go ply your wares elsewhere, Lady Sinclair."

"So naive, my dear," Barbara chided. "You may know how to be a boy, but I would imagine that as a woman, you are lacking—"

"Barbara," Alex interrupted, all humor gone from his voice. "Be reminded that Lady Christine is to be my wife, and that to insult her is to insult me." He narrowed his eyes and lowered his voice. "And I don't think you wish to insult me."

Lady Sinclair took a quick breath and rethought whatever it was she had been about to say. "Very well," she conceded disdainfully. "Enjoy your little boy-thing. When you tire of her, I will be here, waiting."

Alex shook his head and, surprisingly, chuckled. "You'll still be waiting in your grave."

With that he tugged on Kit's hand and led her toward the dance floor, where the orchestra had just struck up a waltz.

"You should have let me punch her," Christine grumbled.

"Much as I would have enjoyed seeing it," he said, "I'd prefer to dance with you." He stopped and turned her to face him. "And I apologize for not taking care of her earlier. You had enough to go through this evening without facing unpleasantries from my past as well."

"I'd rather face your unpleasant past than mine, any time," she said feelingly.

Alex smiled, and her heart thudded at just the sight of him. " 'She walks in beauty, like the night Of cloudless climes and starry skies, And—' "

She blushed. "Alex, Byron? Here?"

" 'And all that's best of dark and bright Meets in her aspect and her eyes,' " he finished slowly, his azure gaze filled with a hundred secrets and passions, just for her.

For a long moment she just looked at him. "I love you, Alex," she whispered. "And I want to marry you. I don't want anyone to be able to take you away from me."

He smiled, then leaned down and very gently kissed her, ignoring the startled exclamations of the nearest onlookers. "And I love you, Christine. Forever."

Christine was glad that they had decided to wed at Everton. Martin Brantley had naturally pressed for Furth, and the duchess for stuffy Westminster Abbey, but surprisingly, Alex had been the one to disagree, in terms that delighted Kit—they would wed at Everton, or they would elope to Scotland. She wasn't certain if he was serious, but the duke had evidently believed the threat, and had acquiesced with great speed.

She glanced over at Martin Brantley, standing between the duchess and Caroline in Everton's vast rose and wildflower gardens. He had been patient and gracious with her skittishness, and that, more than anything else, induced her to begin to trust him a little. Even so, it would be some time before she would be able to bring herself to call him "father." The duke, though, seemed to understand.

She stood in the garden, as well, Alex close beside her, as they accepted an endless stream of congratulations from the jovial, well-dressed assemblage who had witnessed the morning's event. The substantial orchestra, set out on the lawn between twin fountains, seemed to be playing a scandalous number of waltzes, but Alex had already informed her that since it was their own deuced wedding, they could dance together as many times as they liked.

Kit looked over at him, to find his twinkling eyes on her. They had said their vows an hour ago, and despite her worries that he would come to his senses and make a run for it, he had pledged his heart to her without hesitation, as she had done for him. She touched the gold band around her finger, still marveling that they had been allowed to wed without any more disasters or entanglements. Napoleon was a prisoner once more, and thanks to the Duke of Furth's influence, Prince George had agreed that certain other matters need not be delved into any more deeply. As for Stewart Brantley, she hadn't heard any word of him at all since they had parted company in France. Undoubtedly he had escaped Calais, and with the blunt he had lifted from her, he could be anywhere in the world by now.

Kit was happy to be just where she was. Huge Everton manor rose white and gray just to the south of the gardens, a lake beyond it. The town of Cheltenham lay to the east, and the farmlands belonging to Everton spread for miles in every direction. She hadn't seen such a vast estate, or such an impressive display of wealth and power, since she had last been to Furth. Even so, Everton felt like home, as no other place ever had. She loved Everton, both the place and the man—loved the wildness and the spirit and strength underlying both of them.

The orchestra began yet another waltz, and with a put-upon smile, Alex excused himself from Lady Cralling and reached for Kit's hand. "I believe this is my dance, my lady." He grinned.

"Has Mercia forgiven me yet?" Kit asked, glancing at the departing Lady Cralling as she trundled across the grass to the overflowing refreshment tables.

"I believe so," he said, leading her in the direction of the other dancers. "Eunice made it clear that your unconventional behavior was quite shocking, and she informed me that after her upset at Brantley House, Mercia was bedridden for three days."

Kit pursed her lips. "Considering that she was allowing Grambush to court her at the same time she was encouraging me, I can't think she was that devastated."

Alex laughed. "So hard-hearted, chit."

"How long before we can escape?" she asked with a sly smile for her husband, so handsome in his black and gray formal attire.

"As this entire event is for our benefit, I believe we should remain in attendance for another few hours," Alex answered patiently. He squeezed her hand and smiled. "So you'll just have to suffer."

"I'm not suffering," she returned quickly, trying to make it clear by her own smile that today was by far the happiest day of her life. "It's only that I want you to myself."

"We'll have that for the rest of our lives, love. And thank you for not handing the archbishop a flusher."

Kit made a face. "I didn't like all of that 'obey this and that' nonsense."

"I told him to leave it out."

"You did?" Kit's brief annoyance faded as she looked into his dancing eyes, and she grinned back at him. "That was sterling of you, Alex."

He inclined his head, his expression briefly growing more serious. "Anything to keep you, Kit." With his fingers he caressed her cheek, and she leaned into his embrace.

Christine sighed happily and glanced about the garden. It would be weeks before the hordes of guests departed, but Everton was vast enough that she and Alex would have a fair share of privacy. Before they reached the area set aside for dancing, Lord Sumpton waylaid Alex to offer his Spanish villa for their honeymoon, although they'd already decided to stay at Everton. Since Lord Sumpton was rather stuffy and long-winded, Kit turned to head for Gerald and Ivy.

At the far edge of the rose beds a flash of reflected light caught her eye, and she paused to look. A very familiar man stood there, a horse waiting a short distance behind him. As she watched, he lowered a mirror, then bent and set a small package down at his feet. He hesitated, then blew her a kiss before turning to swing up into the saddle. A moment later he headed out through the bordering hedges, and down the rise.

Her heart beating rapidly, Christine glanced back at Alex, but he was still occupied with Sumpton. With a quick look around, she gathered her skirts in one hand and swiftly made her way over to where the package waited in the short grass. Kit slowly picked it up. It was small and brown and rectangular, held closed with twine. Her fingers shaking a little, she untied it and lifted the lid. Gleaming white pearls, strung in four interwined strands clasped by gold, lay nestled inside.

"Another gift?" Alex walked slowly up between the rows of roses toward her.

"Alex," she whispered, lifting the necklace in her fingers. "I remember these. They were my mother's."

He nodded, stopping before her. "They're exquisite." Alex glanced in the direction the rider had vanished, and she realized that he had seen everything. "It seems

Stewart Brantley wishes you well, my love.''

"What are you going to do?" Despite what had happened between them, she bore her "father" no ill will. And he had come all the way to Cotswold Hills in Gloucestershire just to tell her good-bye, and to bring her the one thing he had kept of her mother.

"Me?" Alex responded with a tender, loving smile, his eyes holding hers as he reached out and took her hand. "I'm going to dance with my wife."

NEW YORK TIMES BESTSELLING AUTHOR

Suzanne Enoch

"One of my very favorite authors." —Julia Quinn

Something Sinful

From author Suzanne Enoch comes this exciting and exotic tale of intrigue and seduction, featuring the popular Griffin family.

ON SALE: AUGUST 29, 2006

ISBN: 0-06-084255-5 • $6.99/$9.99 Can.

"Suzanne Enoch's sparkling talent makes each book witty, romantic, and always an eagerly anticipated pleasure."
—Christina Dodd

◆ Avon Books   An Imprint of HarperCollinsPublishers   www.harpercollins.com

Visit www.AuthorTracker.com for exclusive
information on your favorite HarperCollins authors.

Available wherever books are sold or please call 1-800-331-3761 to order

SINA 0806

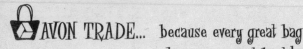